I0831542

This volume introduces the oral literature of Native American peoples in Puget Salish–speaking areas of western Washington. Seven stories told by Lushootseed elders are transcribed and translated into English, accompanied by information on narrative design and cultural background. Upper Skagit elder and cotranslator Vi Hilbert, a 1994 recipient of the NEH National Heritage Fellowship in Folk Arts, includes a cultural welcome and offers childhood reminiscences of the storytellers. Cotranslator Thomas M. Hess, associate professor of linguistics at the University of Victoria, parses the beginning lines of a text to show the grammatical structures; he also includes his recollections of working with the storytellers in the 1960s as a graduate student. Editor and cotranslator Crisca Bierwert, assistant professor of anthropology at the University of Michigan, provides information on the processes of language translation and of rendering oral traditions into written form. Annotator T. C. S. Langen, who holds a Ph.D. in English literature and is a curriculum developer for the Tulalip tribe, provides analyses of Lushootseed poetics.

STUDIES
IN THE ANTHROPOLOGY OF
NORTH AMERICAN INDIANS

Editors
Raymond J. DeMallie
Douglas R. Parks

# LUSHOOTSEED TEXTS

## An Introduction to Puget Salish Narrative Aesthetics

Narrated by Emma Conrad, Martha Lamont,
Edward (Hagen) Sam
Translated by Crisca Bierwert, Vi Hilbert,
Thomas M. Hess
Edited by Crisca Bierwert
With annotations by T. C. S. Langen

Published by the University of Nebraska Press
Lincoln and London

In cooperation with the American Indian Studies Research
Institute, Indiana University, Bloomington

Transcribed and Compiled by: Vi Hilbert, Thomas M. Hess, Dawn Bates
Design of Transcriptions and Translations: Crisca Bierwert
Editorial Production: Dawn Bates, Crisca Bierwert, Bridget Hayden


Manufactured in the United States of America

⊗The paper in this book meets the minimum requirements of American National Standard for Information Sciences—Permanence of Paper for Printed Library Materials, ANSI Z39.48-1984.
Library of Congress Cataloging-in-Publication Data
Lushootseed texts: an introduction to Puget Salish narrative aesthetics/ narrated by Emma Conrad, Martha Lamont, Edward (Hagen) Sam; translated by Crisca Bierwert, Vi Hilbert, Thomas M. Hess; edited by Crisca Bierwert p. cm.—(Studies in the anthropology of North American Indians) Includes bibliographical references and index.
ISBN 0-8032-1262-3 (cloth: alk. paper)
1. Puget Sound Salish languages—Texts. 2. Puget Sound Salish Indians—Folklore. 3. Tales—Washington (State) I. Bierwert, Crisca.
II. Indiana University. American Indian Studies Research Institute.
III. Series. PM2264.A2L87 1996 497'.9—dc20
95-37060 CIP

Tape recordings of the Lushootseed texts are available.
To receive the set of three cassettes, send a check for $15, which includes shipping and handling, to the following address:

The Language Learning Center
Denny 108
University of Washington
Box 353140
Seattle, Washington 98198-3140

Checks should be made out to The Language Learning Center–UW.
Please include a note stating that you want the *Lushootseed Texts* tape cassettes and include your return address. Allow 3-4 weeks for delivery.

for

*tsiʔ dkʷúyaʔ*

CONTENTS

# ACKNOWLEDGMENTS

I am grateful for the tireless dedication of the many people who made this volume possible. Lushootseed elders and young people who know the value of their traditions and history and who have confidence in the future continually inspire the work; Vi Hilbert and her great family are foremost in my mind. Her cousin, the late Isadore Tom, and his family are also constantly working to ensure that the traditional cultures benefit Native peoples. Thomas M. Hess, Dale Kinkade, Barry Carlson, and Tony Mattina are among scholars whose commitment to work with Salish people has kept me going, even when I had only a glimmer of the nature of their work. Dell Hymes provided a thorough and valuable critical review of the manuscript. The Coqualeetza Elders Group in Sardis, B.C., and the staffs of the cultural and tribal centers there have all been tremendously supportive of me and have helped teach me how to exercise editorial respect and power.

In addition to the named contributors, several people have worked long hours on this project. All have generously contributed not only creative energy and companionship but the commitment needed for marathon sessions that knew no difference between day and night. Tom Ridgeway (Humanities and Arts Computer Center, University of Washington) created software solutions whenever called on, solving enormous problems with the forceful patience and delightful inventiveness that characterize his wit, words, and good company. Bridget Hayden undertook the burdens of learning TeX and related programming, beyond what others thought possible; her determination, reliability and good humor have kept this project moving. She also translated the "Hand" sign of Salish basketry into TeX and created the nested boxes of the annotated text. At early stages of this project, Tim Montler resolved countless computer questions. Pamela Cahn was both our engine and our glue in the beginning, mediating the skills of all, and contributing software programming, resourcefulness, drive, and a steady concern.

For patience when mine was spent, for the constant presence of their love and humor when mine were crushed under pressure, and for enjoying macaroni and cheese when time was short, I give my enduring thanks to Robin Russell, Lars Russell, and Morgan Russell.

This work has been supported by grants from the National Endowment for the Humanities, an independent federal agency. A grant from the University of Michigan assisted in preparing final copy.

Crisca Bierwert
Ann Arbor

Edward [Hagen] Sam and Ethel Kitsap Sam
Courtesy of William Edward (*sʔádacut*) Sam.
The date of the photo is not known.

Martha Lamont
Courtesy of T. C. S. Langen.
Photo by Leon Metcalf taken at Tulalip in 1954.

Because no photograph is available,
this page stands in remembrance of Emma Conrad

# EDITOR'S INTRODUCTION

Crisca Bierwert

The seven stories comprising this volume, told by Martha Lamont, Edward (Hagen) Sam, and Emma Conrad, exemplify the diversity of Lushootseed oral literature and of Lushootseed storytellers. Some are humorous; some are intensely serious; most of the narratives move among moments that can be taken lightly and others that are laden with significance. The styles of artistry vary as well. Some of the stories are embellished; some are laconic; each is distinctive. All have figures of speech and ways of presenting intricate knowledge that are conspicuously different from Western traditions. Some are stories of the transformation of the world, some are emblematic of more personal transformation, one is a personal recollection of great power.

Taken together, these seven texts provide a sampling of a much larger corpus of Lushootseed oral literature that was recorded in the past. Today, young people grow up speaking English, not Lushootseed, and fluent native speakers of the language are passing on. Yet these texts do not canonize a tradition that is gone. Some storytellers, still fluent in the language, carry on the versions of these texts that they remember. Others recollect stories in English, and some even revive traditional tellings from archival sources. Thus, the styles of Lushootseed oral traditions are changing dramatically. We who have worked to publish these texts see this volume as a way of enhancing the diversity and richness of the traditions, drawing critical and appreciative attention to Lushootseed imagination and thought.

## On Writing the Oral Traditions

Recorded traditions are valuable as part of the living cultures of Lushootseed people, and they become more broadly accessible through publication. But accessibility is problematic, especially because we intend for the volume to reach many different kinds of audiences. Can the same words reach many different people? How do we cross the borders of translation and writing simultaneously, and for the first time in print, without diminishing the texts in the effort to make them accessible? In keeping the translations lucid, do we dilute academic interest? In following Lushootseed patterns in our English translations, do we create a language barrier? In providing technical commentary, do we remove the stories from "the people?" To answer these questions for ourselves, we had to look more closely at the apparent contradictions on which they are based. Reaching different and changing audiences is a part of what gives Lushootseed traditions vitality. We resolved the contradictions in the questions that beset us by seeing them as related, not conflicting, demands, demands to keep alive the qualities of traditional stories that are intended to connect with people, and to protect the interpretive richness of the stories by offering multiple perspectives on them. Thus, this volume presents texts with directness and diversity. The introductions explain our choices and intents, describing the multiple efforts that have shaped this book.

In writing oral tradition, we lose the immediacy of telling, but we have sought to keep some of its beauty by making the patterns of the translation those of the original and by translating aural patterns into visually apparent ones. The page layouts graphically illustrate different kinds of textures located in the Lushootseed stories and replicated in the English texts, so that they can be better seen. The liveliness of these forms is not the same as that of English poetry or prose; rather, it derives from the storytellers' patternings, and we thank the press for supporting our use of white space to introduce this approach to text translation. We have given the Lushootseed texts priority by locating the Lushootseed version on the right-hand side, the side of the page that we privilege as English speakers. In this way, we hope to encourage readers to look at the Lushootseed language as the original—as a resource, rather than as a relic—that which lies alongside the translation. In reproducing and publishing the arts of others, we see ourselves as exercising the care we would use to retell the wisdom of friends. For those of us who have worked with them for years, the stories are—like our elders—venerated, yet still fresh with insight.

### Introductions to the Volume

Like Lushootseed texts, the introductions to this volume vary markedly in their style and intent. They are an assemblage that reveals our diverse perspectives on the texts and storytellers. They also reveal something of ourselves. And they provide sketches of the social and intellectual histories that stand behind this book, important dimensions of any literary effort.

Upper Skagit elder Vi Hilbert offers in her introduction, *sʔabałx̌əč ʔə taqʷšəblu*, a guide to thinking about the texts. Her heartfelt words, in English, remind us all that she has been the motivating spirit behind this publication. And for her, Lushootseed has a power that has directed her efforts to this end.

"The Documentation of Lushootseed Language and Literature," written by linguist Thomas M. Hess, locates this volume and his own research within academic tradition. Creating a written record of an oral tradition is an immense task involving endless detail. Hess's essay and my short sequel ("Notes on Producing This Volume") provide a chronology of the documentary, analytical, pedagogical, and technical work behind this publication. A brief note by Browner comments on the songs of the first three stories; her transcriptions appear after the notes to each of these texts.

"Remembering the Storytellers" provides more personal glimpses of Hilbert, Hess, and the tellers themselves. In interviews, Hess and Hilbert reminisced with humor and affection. Hilbert provides some childhood recollections; Hess gives us his recollections of fieldwork relationships.

The "Translator's Introduction" details the principles I used to organize the Lushootseed texts in print and then to translate them, building on more literal translations by Hess and Hilbert. "Writing and Reading Lushootseed" includes notes on transcription and an explication of the Lushootseed orthography.

The annotated text stands here in lieu of a grammatical description. Hess parses grammatical structures as they appear in the first text, which starts with a few simple and basic structures, and he moves quickly through fundamental grammatical elaborations. His morpheme-by-morpheme analysis explicates word formation as well. (See Hess and Hilbert forthcoming for a grammatical description.) An unusual feature of this annotation is the mapping of affixes, roots, and suffixes in concentric boxes to show the enfolding pattern of Lushootseed polysynthesis. (The current source for lexical data is the new ***Lushootseed Dictionary***, Bates, Hess, and Hilbert 1994.)

The annotator's introduction, by T. C. S. Langen, provides a summary of the literary principles found in Lushootseed oral literature. Langen's introductions for each text provide more detailed commentary on the narratives as literature, the cultural background, and suggested additional reading. Notes identify literary figures in the texts, and give some explanatory data. Because our space was limited and complete documentation of literary figuring could not be provided on every text, I asked the annotator to provide different kinds of commentary on different texts. Langen's commentaries are cumulative; each assumes familiarity with the notes for the previous texts. In addition, outlines of narrative structures precede texts 5 and 7 as a shorthand guide to the figuring of those texts. Additional literary analysis of Lushootseed literature supplements this volume; the reader is referred to other materials published by Langen, which are included in the Bibliography.

Vi Hilbert has often said, "Lushootseed takes care of itself." It is with gratitude for the teachings of Lushootseed storytellers, and with great respect, that we contributors pass the texts in this written form into the future.

# INTRODUCTION

*sʔabałx̌əč ʔə taqʷšəblu*

Vi Hilbert

It gives me great satisfaction to see this collection of my people's oral treasures presented to an audience extending far beyond our several river valleys along Puget Sound. Now my people can share with many others at least a small part of the rich and multifaceted literature that has both guided and amused us for thousands of years. We hope that these seven texts with their translations and commentary will convey something of the meaning and beauty of our former way of life. There will be those in this vaster audience who will also come to appreciate the beautiful cadences of traditional Lushootseed narrative preserved here on the available tape cassettes. That too pleases us.

In some traditional families, including my own, no one presumes to explain the meanings of the old stories. The most one might do is present a few oblique references analogous to the way my father used to travel on the Skagit River. He did not try to go straight across to his destination. He poled his canoe along the shallow bank as far as he estimated he would need to go before heading into the current. That current then carried the canoe right where he had planned to go. Only a few pushes with his paddle ended the journey.

We listen and learn as our experience and maturity enable us. With every telling, continually deeper insights are revealed.

However, for those beyond our valleys, more direct discussion of the narratives is essential, because our way of life, which long ago gave rise to these texts, differs in many, many respects from the world of most English speakers in the 20th century. For our stories to be understood by others, we have had to present some background about ourselves.

More troublesome than the presumption implied in giving background explanation however, is the personal struggle I have had with the question of taboo topics. What my people do not discuss openly, our literature delights in poking fun at. We do not talk freely about someone's class status or certain facets of our religion, but the protagonists of our old stories do so with abandon. If I were to explain fully some incidents, I would disgrace myself. On those points, therefore, I have, in the traditional manner, given only an indirect clarification and trust the intelligence of our audience to perceive the full significance of the event.

It is my fervent wish and that of my colleagues in Lushootseed Research that this collection will make known to a wide audience both for today and tomorrow, something of my people's way of life, our wisdom, our sense of humor.

# THE DOCUMENTATION OF LUSHOOTSEED LANGUAGE AND LITERATURE

Thomas M. Hess

Lushootseed is an indigenous American language spoken by people of the land between the Cascade Mountains and Puget Sound in western Washington state. The name "Lushootseed" derives from the native word for the language, *dəxʷləšucid*, which means approximately, "language (of the) people." This language belongs to a family of twenty-three members spoken over much of what is now British Columbia and Washington as well as parts of Oregon, Idaho, and Montana. In the 20th century, four Salish languages have become extinct and many others have only ten or so speakers left.

The very first published study of any Lushootseed dialect was the glossary compiled by a medical doctor, George Gibbs; his *Dictionary of Niskwalli* appeared in 1877. From the late 1920s until 1950 another serious collector, Arthur C. Ballard, wrote several articles about the Muckleshoot and Puyallup culture, in which various Southern Lushootseed words appear. Ballard also published two collections of short texts in Southern Lushootseed, using approximate transcriptions of the language sounds (Ballard 1927, 1929). Articles by anthropologists writing on various cultural topics usually included numerous Lushootseed lexical items. These begin with the studies by T. T. Waterman in the second decade of this century and include publications and manuscripts by H. Haeberlin, E. Gunther, M. Smith, W. Suttles, S. Snyder, and J. Collins.

It was not until 1945 that a purely grammatical description of any sort concerning Lushootseed appeared. This was an article by Jay Ellis Ransom entitled "Notes on Duwamish Phonology and Morphology," published in the *International Journal of American Linguistics*. Duwamish is a variety of Southern Lushootseed. Five years later Colin E. Tweddell had published a short grammar of Duwamish and Snoqualmie called "The Snoqualmie-Duwamish Dialects of Puget Sound Coast Salish." Snoqualmie is also a variety of Southern Lushootseed. The first successful ordering of Lushootseed material is the grammar of Warren A. Snyder, *Southern Puget Sound Salish: Phonology and Morphology*, published in 1968 and followed in the same year by a text collection, glossary and place name map. Although the title designates all Southern Lushootseed, the data are drawn from the Suquamish, a dialect virtually identical with Duwamish and Snoqualmie. The authors of these three grammatical descriptions were anthropologists, and none continued his linguistic research beyond these initial publications.

Linguistic study of Northern Lushootseed did not begin until the autumn of 1961, when Professor Laurence C. Thompson, then of the University of Washington, conducted a field methods class with the help of Mrs. Louise *cisxʷisaɬ* George, a Skagit–speaking Nooksack. (The ancestral language of the Nooksack people, a related Salish language, had become moribund by Mrs. George's time. Most of her generation grew up speaking Lushootseed, the language immediately to the south of Nooksack, or Halkomelem, the Salish language immediately to the north (or both), as well as English. Mrs. George spoke the Upriver Skagit dialect of Lushootseed.) The study and teaching of all Salish languages, which have flourished in the subsequent 30 years, owes a great debt to the far-sighted encouragement of Dr. Thompson and the impetus and training he has provided from the start.

I was a student in that first field methods class, and I continued to investigate the grammar of Skagit after the term ended the following June. Gradually I began to study other Lushootseed dialects, especially Snohomish. This research was supported by the Survey of Northwest Indian Languages sponsored by the National Science Foundation and the University of Washington Graduate School Research Committee.

One method I used to gather data was the tape recording of "old stories" and occasional other commentary. The original tapes were all recorded at $3\frac{3}{4}$ ips on .65mil tensilized polyester. The recorder was a very small and light Grundig, which accommodated only three–inch reels. These small reels required that the raconteur pause—often several times in a single story—while I turned over or changed the reel. These interruptions are particularly noticeable and annoying in text 6 of this volume. Different from the first six texts, the seventh was taped on a seven-inch reel using a Wollensack recorder.

At the time, my only motivation for tape recording was my concern with the grammar and the vocabulary. For me the texts provided examples of natural flowing Lushootseed free of the distortions that result from speaking at dictation pace and that arise from responding to grammatical questions framed in English. It was only after the language began to become clear to me that the literary and cultural value of the stories slowly dawned.

I made most of the recordings in 1963–1964 with Mrs. Martha Lamont, Mr. Edward (Hagen) Sam (both Snohomish), and Mrs. Emma Conrad, a speaker from the Sauk-Suiattle region. A few other speakers also contributed. [See "Remembering the Storytellers."—Ed.] All recordings were made in the speakers' homes, which precluded ideal acoustic conditions and which accounts for various backgound noises from crying children to closing doors and the pinging of an iron stove as the fire within caused it to expand. The Lamonts shared their house with eleven pet dogs, which created their share of disturbances during some recordings also.

Twenty-five years ago I did not consider these background noises to be a problem, because of my focus on the grammatical and lexical information the recordings contained. So long as the tapes provided those data, I had no further concern. Certainly, this volume was not then conceived; and even if it had been, the two raconteuses were too feeble to make the trip to a Seattle recording studio, although Mr. Sam could have. Nevertheless, we believe that the tape quality is good enough to merit making tapes available to supplement the printed texts. Certainly students in the Lushootseed language classes at the University of Washington and the University of Victoria have found that listening to the tapes greatly enhanced their pleasure in studying this literature.

I transcribed and translated most of the tapes immediately with the active participation of the raconteur, except in the case of Mrs. Conrad. I played Mr. Sam's stories back to him a few seconds at a time so that they could be repeated exactly as originally worded but at a rate that I could hear and write. During this process Mr. Sam also provided translations, and answered questions about grammar.

I used the same basic procedure to write out the stories of Mrs. Lamont. However, her husband, Mr. Levi *dxʷsdiɬiliyus* Lamont, repeated his wife's words from the tape, provided translations, and answered grammatical and lexical questions instead of Mrs. Lamont herself. He spoke for his wife because Mrs. Lamont's English was not equal to the task. She was able to follow some of the discussions between Mr. Lamont and me, and she occasionally offered comments in Snohomish, which Mr. Lamont passed along in English.

Mrs. Conrad died shortly after our one and only storytelling session. (Fortunately, that session was a very long and enjoyable one.) Mrs. Conrad's good friend, Mrs. George, provided the slow repetitions and translations for me.

Later, in preparation for this volume, Vi *taqʷšəblu* Hilbert who is herself Skagit, listened to all the tapes of the texts included here and went over the transcriptions very carefully.

From 1964 to date, I have continued to study Lushootseed grammar and have gradually developed an appreciation for Lushootseed oral traditions. With a grant from the University of Kansas awarded to Dr. M. Dale Kinkade I received some funds to begin the study of Southern Lushootseed in the first five months of 1968. At first I investigated the Puyallup and Suquamish dialects. Later I also studied Muckleshoot and Sahewamish.

It was in 1967 that Mrs. Hilbert and I were introduced through Mrs. George, who had the ability to see that her younger Skagit relative could work with me beautifully. I began to teach Mrs. Hilbert a technique for writing Lushootseed. In the spring of 1972, I was asked to present a Lushootseed language class for American Indian Studies at the University of Washington. The class was continued the next autumn with the help of Mrs. Hilbert. She eventually took over all teaching of the language and continued to teach first and second year courses every year thereafter until 1987. Mrs. Hilbert also organized and taught a class on Lushootseed literature in English translation for the last eight of those years.

My teaching the language at the University of Washington plus my preparation of teaching materials for the Muckleshoot Tribe in Southern Lushootseed and the Swinomish Tribe in Northern Lushootseed led me to develop a standardized, pan-Lushootseed orthography. [See "Writing and Reading Lushootseed"—Ed.] This writing system spread beyond the tribal and university classrooms. Many Lushootseed–speaking elders have delighted in seeing their language written. A number of them used their grandchildren's language books to teach themselves to read and write Lushootseed. Others asked for specific instruction in writing from Mrs. Hilbert and me.

Over the years, I published several articles on Lushootseed grammar, dialectology, language, and culture. Yet, after taking a position at the University of Victoria, I had began to work almost exclusively with language of Vancouver Island people. In 1985, I returned to work with Mrs. Hilbert again on the lexicon that Dr. Dawn Bates has completed (Bates 1994), on the texts included in this volume, and with additional texts.

# NOTES ON PRODUCING THIS VOLUME

Crisca Bierwert

Vi Hilbert, Thomas M. Hess, Dawn Bates, and I began to work together in 1985 in order to refine transcriptions of selected Lushootseed texts, create a concordance of this corpus of the literature, compile a new Lushootseed dictionary, and publish texts with translations that reflected the poetics of the originals.

Our decision to make tape recordings available with this volume reinforced the need for accuracy in transcription. Hilbert, Hess, and Bates spent thousands of hours going over the tapes, marking roots and stress and also noting the asides, which are not usually provided in transcriptions. Texts were entered in computer files for the first time; countless revisions were made. Rob Hagawara, then an undergraduate student in linguistics, helped in data entry at various stages of this project. Bates created a computer-assisted concordance when transcriptions were refined, and that material is part of the *Lushootseed Dictionary* she has prepared, along with Hess and Hilbert (Bates, Hess, and Hilbert 1994).

I was responsible for representing the texts, both determining the graphic layout and completing the English translation after Hess and Hilbert's more literal translation. I was committed to developing a translation worked out at the level of the entire text, while the literal translation was worked out on a sentence-by-sentence basis. Further, I wanted to render the translation in a style that revealed Lushootseed poetic structures in English, a contrast to the more culturally interpreted translations Hilbert had then recently published after working in collaboration with Jay Miller (Hilbert 1985).

The decision to leave cultural explanations out of the text narrative meant that notes were required. As all of our hands were already full at the time, the team drew T. C. S. Langen into the project at that point to prepare the necessary commentary. Langen, a literary scholar who had studied with Hilbert, prepared annotations that included both cultural information and a discussion of the texts as literature (see "Annotator's Introduction").

As the Lushootseed transcriptions for each text neared completion, I reorganized the lines to make Lushootseed word patterning stand out on the printed page. Then, I worked out both translations and their layout on the page, using the Lushootseed word patterning as a guiding principle. [See "Translator's Introduction."] I reviewed the results with Hilbert and Hess and provided copies to Langen, who in turn provided me with copies of her emergent analyses.

In order to reproduce the orthography in the highest quality then available, I turned to Tom Ridgeway of the Humanities and Arts Computing Center, University of Washington. He developed a Lushootseed font for us to use, and he also adapted existing TeX software—which was compatible with the font—for the text layouts that I wanted. Over the years of preparation, Ridgeway provided modifications in the software to suit our needs. He also helped us produce a special edition of the texts in extra-large type, which Vi Hilbert distributed to elders around Puget Sound. The version of software we used (which is by now archaic) required that every placement on the page be marked, and Bridget Hayden, a graduate student at the University of Michigan, learned the programming necessary to produce our publication and marked every page of the text. As the manuscript went through the review process, revisions required technical and editorial work. As the book drew to completion, Vi Hilbert and T. C. S. Langen supplied photographs, and Tara Browner and Richard Crawford provided transcriptions and commentary on the songs. Brian Mooney helped me produce the final camera-ready copy.

## NOTES ON THE SONGS IN TEXTS 1, 2, AND 3

Tara Browner

One of the features of Martha Lamont's music that is impossible to transcribe is the sense that she was clearly enjoying herself when she recorded these songs. Her voice is vigorous, her sense of pitch is steady, and her tempo is unwavering, even at the ends of phrases when she is running out of breath. Salish singing has been described as tight, with strong vocal pulsations (Herzog 1949). Yet this quality is not apparent in these songs.

Melodically, all of the songs have characteristics that Herzog identified as differentiating Salish music from other Native North American styles (Herzog 1949). They all have a fairly limited tonal range, from a sixth in Crow's song from "The Marriage of Crow" to only a minor third in Raven's song in "Crow Is Sick." Crow's song in "Martha Lamont's Changer Story" follows the descending terraced contour found in many Native American melodies. The other three songs feature level or undulating melodic movement.

Transcriptions of the songs are found on pages 102, 131, 144, and 145.

[**Editor's Note:** Vi Hilbert and Thomas M. Hess came to know the storytellers of this volume under very diffferent circumstances. As a young girl in the 1920s, the only child of Upper Skagits Charles and Louise Anderson, Vi visited with a wide range of relatives and close friends among Lushootseed people. In the 1960s, as a fledgling graduate student, Thom met Lushootseed elders as he was introduced to those who were still most fluent in their language. Thus, the two circles of familiarity overlapped.

Having heard some of their stories as we worked together, I asked Vi and Thom if I could interview them and transcribe the tapes to include in this volume. I wanted to add a more personal dimension to the book, and I also wanted to include more glimpses into my elder collaborators while keeping the focus of the book on the Lushootseed storytellers. Rather than asking Vi and Thom to write more formal narratives, I asked them to provide a storytelling commentary. Both agreed, and we were all delighted with what came out. We did the interviews in separate sessions, to maintain the differences in immediacy of their recollections. Vi and Thom have distinctive styles of remembering and ways of evoking the scenes they recall. Vi includes some vivid recollections of her own life growing up, and Thom's account reveals both the anxiety and discovery of field research. The contrasts between their different perspectives are cross-cut by the contrasts in the historical moments I asked them to focus on: between the 1920s and the 1960s the language diminished in use, the principals aged, and their cultural influences expanded; some of these changes are evident in the accounts. I have edited the transcripts but preserved most of the ordering and almost all the content of what Vi and Thom recorded. I deleted many of my responses and questions, except to include a slim interview frame and to connect what might appear disjunctive on the printed page.]

## Vi Hilbert

### Levi Lamont

*We're discussing the storytellers whose work you have transcribed and translated. Where would you like to start?*

I didn't know Martha Lamont intimately. I saw her many times as I was growing up, but mainly I knew her husband Levi Lamont. Levi was not her first husband. And Levi was previously married to my dad's niece, Lily; he had two children with Lily. I grew up with those two cousins. We were at each other's homes many times because I went to the Tulalip* boarding school. Levi and Lily lived in Tulalip way up in the woods from the boarding school, and every Friday they would come

* Tulalip is the site of a reservation forty miles north of Seattle.

and get me and take me home from Tulalip. They would take me and their two children. I always looked forward to these visits because it was fun to play with my cousins off in the woods where they lived. Levi and Lily made things fun for kids, especially if you're me.

Levi was a good marksman with his gun, and as we would be driving up to their home in the woods, he would spot either pheasants or quail or grouse, stop the car quickly, get out and shoot these birds for our meal over the weekend. He never failed to shoot just the head off so he didn't ruin the meat.

Lily played the violin, and she played the mandolin. She was musically inclined in this way. And so she would encourage the children to dance together as she played her musical instruments. She wanted to teach her son how to dance with a girl, so he would dance first with his sister, then with me. We learned to do all the different steps that she knew how to teach: the one-step, the two-step, the waltz, the schottische, all of these things. So we had a well-rounded education playing together.

In the summertime my parents would be with Levi and his family or they would be with us, with my mother and dad. I recall being with Levi, Lily, and the children at *sbibədaʔ*.* This was Barney Guss's cabin down at Tulalip; it was right on the beach. We stayed there all summer long. Levi had a rowboat, and every morning he would load us into the rowboat and we would go out with our little hand lines and fish. We caught many, many kinds of fish to eat while we were living there. They weren't salmon; there were sole, flounder, perch.... When we would come in from fishing, Bobby and Leona and I would play on the beach and find snags and interesting logs to use for our playgrounds. So this was the way we spent our summers....

Levi looked like a *pə́stəd* [white person]. His mother looked like a *pə́stəd*, but she spoke Snohomish Lushootseed. Levi knew Snohomish Lushootseed, but strangely, all the time we were together, I don't recall that he spoke the language to me. When my parents spoke to each other, he would converse with them in the language. I don't recall that Levi tended to speak Lushootseed; he understood and would answer.

He was a very intense man. He had a curt way of speaking, and he was very strict with his children and a taskmaster for everyone around him. His voice was always raised. But for me his voice would change and he would speak to me in soft tones and always with tenderness. I never ever perceived him as an angry man. I admired all the things that he could do as far as understanding the land we lived on and enjoyed. He seemed to know all the ways that Indian people know to benefit from

* A beach now part of the Tulalip reservation.

the land around them. I thought he knew almost as much as my dad, and they appreciated each other....

Levi came to work with my dad in logging camps. Sometimes this was in the Skagit area. Wherever there was a logging camp in operation and my dad needed a partner, he could call on Levi because they worked well together and appreciated each other.

After Levi and his wife separated it was many, many years later that I saw and heard about Levi being married to *Mata*, which is what people called Martha Lamont. Some made fun of the fact that he was married to that old lady "...and they have a house full of dogs." But Levi was very, very happy with Martha. He appreciated her native intelligence, he appreciated her skills and her conversation, and he appreciated the fact that she was a good Shaker even though he himself did not belong to the Shaker church. He valued the strength that she had in that area. He also was not a member of the longhouse, but he knew that he had access to that part of our culture. He felt that he had been given the song that was his own....

Vi Hilbert

**Emma Conrad**

Emma Conrad was one of the most interesting personalities in my childhood, I think. I think that I perceived her this way because I thought of her as independent. I didn't see how she could do what she did: live all by herself with her children in an isolated place by a river. I don't know exactly which tributary this was. It was up in the Sauk-Suiattle area I think, Upper Skagit somewhere.

My parents were very fond of her, because they were related to her of course. They would say, "Let's go visit Emma." So we would drive down to her place by a river and they would honk the horn. Emma would come out of her house, get in her canoe, and pole it across. The water, the river, was not so deep that she had to do more than pole as I recall. Then she would put all of us in her canoe and take us across to her house. Her house was just a small cabin and she lived there all alone, as I say, with her two children.

*Were they your age?*

Yes, they were. They were my age. There was a girl and a boy. I asked Emma's brother [Jim Enick] if that was really so. It's been so long ago that I thought I could have been mistaken, maybe there were two other children that I was playing with. But he said, no, she had two children. So it wasn't just a dream that I had.

Emma would always start building a fire as soon as we got there. She would put something on to cook so that we could share a meal together. It might be just a potato soup or a bowl of potatoes and some dried salmon that she had. But she always set the table when we came to visit; that was just part of Emma's way.

She was so soft-spoken and so gentle, with such a musical voice, I loved listening to her, and listening to the conversations that she and my parents had together. I had a very warm gentle feeling about this woman who lived all by herself. I didn't know why her husband wasn't there, that's not something that is in my memory, or how long she lived there, or had lived there.

Her parents must have been very closely related to mine, because I recall living in the old Enick homestead in Darrington. And the Enick ancestor must have been a farmer, because he had a barn as well as a house. These things were very old, but they were the remnants of someone who had been a farmer. And this again was a very isolated place east of Darrington, the little town of Darrington.

I went to school in this area. It was one of the very first schools that I went to, I think ... because I started in Concrete, Washington. I think I spent part of a year in Concrete and then went to Darrington, where we lived in the old Enick "estate." (I used to think of it as that because it was wonderful.) It was great to have both a house and a barn, although I believe the barn was pretty ramshackle. But this was a beautiful, beautiful country. And there was a stream not too far from the area. And my cousins from back in British Columbia were there with their father and mother. They'd come to live with us so that the father, Gus Cambell, could work out in the logging camp with my dad. So again I was happy because there were lots of children for me to play with.

None of the Enicks were living there. I don't know where they were. But I think it was at this time that we went to visit Emma, by the river, while we were living on the Enick estate. It all gets kind of foggy. I walked to school from the Enick place up in the woods. It seemed like a long, long way, but I had my cousins to walk with. But in the middle of winter, it was indeed a long way. And my mother would bundle me up so that I could get to school without getting too cold. She would always get up very early in the morning to put potatoes in the oven to bake, so that I would have hot potatoes to have in my coat pockets. Then she'd put her heavy hand-spun wool socks over my shoes so that my feet would stay warm. And the socks would have inches of snow adhering to them by the time I got to school....

*When you were at Emma's, did she speak Lushootseed to you?*

She and my folks spoke both English and Lushootseed, but I think that I remember them speaking mostly Lushootseed.... [And] I remember the way I appreciated how she talked to her children because it was always in a gentle way....

Thomas M. Hess

### Starting Fieldwork

*Please give me your rendition of the first meeting with people ... and then something about the setting of the fieldwork relationships.*

I started working with Mrs. Elizabeth Krise in November 1961. I had simply gone out to Tulalip and walked into the head office and explained to them that I wanted to study the languages. Sabastian Williams was tribal chairman at the time. First he questioned me: Did I know anything about the language? I was in a field methods class, working with Mrs. [Louise] George. So I mentioned her name and said that I was doing work with Skagit. He thought then that maybe I did know what I was talking about, and it would be all right. He suggested that I try Mrs. Krise, whom I later learned was his aunt. He gave me directions and sent me to her house.

Ah, it was raining cats and dogs. I went to the door and knocked on the door, but she didn't open it. She just shouted through the door, "Who is it?" I told her what I wanted, that I was from the University, and so on. I don't remember all of the conversation, but I recall she was unwilling yet curious.

There were no eaves (I guess they call them gutters out here) along the roof. So the rain was coming off the roof, going right down my neck, as I stood there talking to this door.

I remember one thing she said quite exactly: "Well, where would we work?"

I said, "Well, here, if it's all right with you."

"You mean you'd come into an Indian house?"

I said, "Well, if you don't mind."

And then, the door opened just a crack, and she talked a little bit more, but that was about it. We arranged that I would return, I think, on a Thursday. Yes, it was always on a Thursday to start with. And in those days we were paying only two dollars an hour.

I worked with her for a two–hour session once a week, all through that academic year. And then in the summer I continued to drive out from Seattle. I worked with her for over a year before I ever worked with anyone else.

*What kind of elicitation did you start with?*

We started in a typical manner. I would make out a list of words and short sentences that I wanted and proceed from there. I kept asking her for stories, but she felt she didn't know any. That may well be true. She did give me the one episode about *dúkʷibəɬ* and deer in which *dúkʷibəɬ* inserted deer's prongs, and she told me the one famous around here now—Lady Louse.*

I kept asking about stories, thinking, "Well, she must know them," not realizing I myself couldn't tell one tale from my own culture if my life depended on it....

Mrs. Krise also brought her sister in one time, and they talked together in conversation. And, my goodness, her sister could talk. I have that on tape. At one point they are reminiscing about an incident that isn't clear to me at all. And there's much there that I'm sure was alluded to only. She was an older sister and perhaps less acculturated than Mrs. Krise. Or maybe Mrs. Krise put on her European culture, her American ways, when I showed up. But when they were together, the older sister struck me as being more in the old way. There's that old intonation, the language spoken without influence of English. The accent is, I'm sure, the old way of talking.

Mrs. Krise kept suggesting that I stop to see Hagen Sam, and it was in 1963 that I stopped to see him. It was also that same summer Mrs. Krise arranged for me to meet Harriet Dover, who, in a sense, called in backup: she had Martha Lamont and Levi come down to her house. So we had quite a session there. Martha told a story and a bit of history. Levi had driven her in, so he was there, and Harriet Dover and Mrs. Krise.... The first words Levi used were in English, I remember that. But then they started in Snohomish. On one of the tapes you can hear Harriet Dover and Elizabeth Krise talking in the language in the background, when Levi is dealing with me.

Thomas M. Hess

**Edward (Hagen) Sam**

When I first stopped to see Hagen Sam, I recall that I did use a little bit of the language. It was in the spring, and in the evening. There was a lot of daylight, and the children were out playing. His wife was there too. He was more reluctant to serve as language consultant than Mrs. Krise had been, but, as he told me later, he was in a good mood that day and finally agreed.

I've forgotten what [Lushootseed] phrase I used with him, but it startled him slightly. And he corrected my pronunciation. I said that I was studying the language, that I wanted to ask him some questions, and that I would like some stories to help work on sentence arrangement, something like that. He said, well, he could teach me a few words,

* Mrs. Krise's ten-line story is famous because Vi Hilbert has used it for many years both in family settings and in public storytellings to prompt listeners into actively interpreting the stories as she tells them. -Ed.

maybe. We made arrangements that I would come back in a couple of days.

Well, it happened that in one of the first stories he told me, a reduplicated pattern came out that I hadn't encountered before and I was fascinated by it. Furthermore, he sang the song in that story with a very good voice. I was quite enthralled with the music. And then there was this *$d^{z}$alal$d^{z}$alcut.* I had never seen that pattern, and I got kind of excited about it. Well, he responded to my enthusiasm very favorably, in fact; he liked that. And also, as he told me a little later, he liked that I wasn't "looking all around the house to see how I lived," as he said.

We continued to work all that summer. I saw him twice a week. His wife was always around; she would usually be in the kitchen, or in another room. He was just sitting in a rocking chair in the living room. The children were out playing and we were working in the house. I don't remember that it ever rained. It always seemed to be beautiful weather every time that summer. Maybe it was a particularly dry one....

*Did you have a feeling that he was prepared for your sessions?*

He just answered the questions.... I got the impression that he enjoyed it immensely....

*Would he just start off then, talking to you, or—?*

I always had a question. One thing it is important to record, though, is that, when it came to telling stories, Hagen never told them directly in the language. He always recited them in English first, at dictation pace. I would write them rapidly, which means a long way from legibly. Then he would ask for what I had written. I would hand him the sheet, and he was always very careful. (You would rarely hear the sound of paper on the tape.) He'd read the sentences; he'd read English and speak Snohomish. It was my impression he did this simply to be sure that he got it right. I have felt that was perhaps a little suspect, particularly because it seemed to me that there was a different style. Now I realize that his style was slightly different, but then everybody has their idiosyncracies. And it is all well within the bounds of good, normal, everyday Snohomish. (By the way, Hagen had a tendency to use Southern Lushootseed a bit from his wife. I think, like all the people, he liked to use other peoples' words. In fact, once in a while she would interject, "That's my word; yours is—.")

The only time he didn't dictate was the time he wanted to give me a speech, which I've since learned was somewhat modeled after a speech given at the original [1855] treaty. That he did prepare for and was very proud of. I had the impression that it was somewhat original of him. I recognized it a long time later, when I saw some of the Ruth Shelton recollections of the treaty as told to her by her father-in-law, who had been there.

*Do you think his style of dictating may have reflected past work with outside researchers?*

There may have been anthropology students out there. But I **think** I was the first linguist.

At this time we [linguists] didn't know anything about the language, [about] all those neat paradigms that you're [familiar with]. We didn't even know whether Skagit and Snohomish were the same language or not. We knew nothing....

*Did his oratorical style derive from church sources at all?*

He was a preacher—and a country and western singer....

*Was he analytical about the language?*

Yes. Levi [Lamont] was even better at it.

My experience in working with both men and women on this language is kind of interesting. From it, I now advise students who plan to work in this area, when you're getting the phonology, work with the women. They will articulate more clearly, more slowly, and more patiently. But when it comes to morphological and syntactic analysis, and especially to the semantics, work with men. The men seem to delight in playing around with the nuances and women grow impatient: "That's what it means." And I found that true everywhere from Skagit to Muckleshoot.

Thomas M. Hess

**Emma Conrad**

*What about Emma Conrad?*

Mrs. George introduced me to her. She and Emma had been very good friends apparently for years and years and years.... We went up twice, as I recall. Dr. Thompson was with us the first time.

*Did you drive to the river bank and call over?*

By this time, she was staying in Burlington [near Darrington, Wash.] in a little house behind some people in her church. I went back at one point, hoping to transcribe some of the stories she had told. This was about a week later, and she didn't remember me. And she clearly wasn't feeling well, so I didn't stay. Shortly after that, Mrs. George told me she was in the hospital, here in Seattle. I took Mrs. George over there one time. So that, other than telling me stories in two sessions, that was all....

*She had obviously had experience telling her stories to other people.*

I'm sure she did. In fact, Mrs. George had made the comment, with "The All-Year-Around Story," "If you tell that, it snows." I heard it one time, and sure enough, it snowed the next day.

*Was there any sense of their speaking the language together?*

On the tape, remember, you can hear where Mrs.George provides the Skagit word when Emma couldn't remember it and was using the English word, "ball." ...And also they were just chattering one night, and I heard. I turned on the tape recorder one night early to start telling the stories, and you could still hear them. They enjoyed that.

Thomas M. Hess

**Martha and Levi Lamont**

When I met the Lamonts at the Dovers', I said that I would like to to stop by their place, and they said fine. But they were older people, and of course I was just one white face out of many. They had forgotten me completely when I turned up at the door, some few days later. Levi thought that I had come to have my laundry done. (Apparently Martha took in laundry.) I said no, explained my name and whatever, and asked would Martha be willing to tell a story. I had the tape recorder in my hand, a big old Wollensack. I think by this time we were paying two dollars fifty cents an hour. (The amount of money for consultants was determined in the grant, from which I was getting the money, a grant that Dr. Laurence C. Thompson had from NSF.) That was entirely acceptable to her, so he just opened the door and welcomed me in and then closed the door.... Later he told me that he admitted me so readily because none of the eleven dogs barked at me. **That** was unusual. In fact, they never did bark at me, but they certainly did at all else....

Some years earlier, Leon Metcalf [an amateur but effective collector of data on the old cultures] had been in the habit of dropping in, and Martha had told him stories. He would just drop in when he was in the area or something of that sort, I'm not quite sure. Levi remarked that I came at a particular time, and that I always said when I was coming....

Their cabin was divided into two rooms. There was the kitchen in the one and then the sleeping/general living area in the other. And that was where we met, where we would have our sessions. In the summertime the door would be open. They had eleven dogs, and the dogs would wander in and out at will, so there were a variety of insects flying in the air. I learned never to eat dessert before going there because there was a hornet's nest or something nearby, and just the sweetness on my breath from, say, pie would attract them. It was very distracting.

When I arrived, Martha was almost always lying down. When I arrived in the early days Levi would get a large wooden crate, not as big as one of the old orange crates, and set it up on end. Then Martha could sit on the edge of the bed and her feet then would not be dangling. It was a foot rest for her. Most of the time when she was telling us stories she would sit up. In fact one time when she sang the Snohomish song, she grabbed her knitting needles and beat rhythm on the iron edge of the bed. She was quite enthusiastic about things that day....

*What about other gestures?*

Martha did have some gestures. I recall when she was talking about flounder, she reached behind her back. She did have gestures. I did not watch her closely, though. I was more concerned about running out of tape, the dog knocking the tape recorder over. Some of the dogs were big, some were small, and that kept my eye on their tails swishing over the turning spools, making sure that the microphone was picking up the sound—all that sort of stuff. And I failed to observe the other things that I should have been observing. She did sometimes tend to sort of rock with the rhythm of her speaking.

*What would you call her usual pose, then?*

Clearly, I would say she was a classic lady.... She was always dignified yet humble. She was wise.

I would sit on a chair, and Levi would sit halfway across the room in his usual chair. It was a little far for me to hear as well as I would have liked; I should have been much closer, but that was the arrangement and that was the way it stayed .... And everything came through clearly on the microphone. We put the big, awkward recorder on the floor (among the dogs) because there was no table big enough for it in that room....

*What was the setting for translation with Levi?*

It was the same. Martha would be there listening, and every now and then she would interject. Not very often but every now and then, she would interject a comment or offer a gloss. I remember one time she came up with the word "scrubs," which was just **exactly** the right word. Levi—I can still see his face—was astonished.

*Was there a sense of them deferring to one another in terms of knowledge?*

Martha was the storyteller, and Levi deferred to her in the stories. I **know** that he could have told me stories, but he didn't and that was that. And furthermore, he was more Victorian in viewpoint than she was. Whatever she said on tape he would translate, however. Well, there were two terms that he did **not** translate, and I still don't know what they mean.

*And Mrs. George didn't?*

I didn't even consider asking her. I figured there was so much else that I needed to find out anyway, why make them uncomfortable by pressing the point? Although now I would like to know.

Levi used to enjoy the sessions. But he made me very, very ill at ease, very nervous. He was obviously very bright, and I felt as if he were going to explode if I didn't get it down better. I felt, I'm just not up to his expectations and hopes for preserving the language. I thought, he's got all this that he could give me. Furthermore, quite unfortunately, I was devoting all my time to grammar, figuring out paradigms and things like that. And he was a wealth of information; the two of them were, together. And all that just didn't get recorded. I'm sick about it every time I think about it. They were getting older. He was already not well, but I didn't know it.

*Do you think they were discussing the sessions between your visits?*

No. They were quite willing to tell me about the language and the stories, because it was nice to have someone who visited enough regularly. And we did do other things. I took him in to Everett. He didn't like to drive further away than Marysville, so when he had to get his driver's license I drove him in and he got his driver's license there. And one time his car wouldn't start, so I gave him a push and a pull and got it going enough to get it to the local service station....

*Was anyone else visiting them when you were there?*

I met one of Martha's grandsons. He was chatting with them, and when I came, he shook hands and left. I have yet to meet Levi's daughter; his son had already died. His daughter lives in Tacoma; I've talked with her on the phone. And Martha had grandchildren and, I think, great-grandchildren at that time.

*Did you know if they had communicated what they knew to the children?*

They made it very clear that the young people weren't interested anymore. So did Mrs. Krise. It was sort of a repeated theme. This was a decade before the red power period.

*Where did Martha learn the stories?*

Martha was right there from Tulalip. She was not from Snohomish as Mrs. Krise's family was. Mrs. Krise had given me a Snohomish word that came up at another point, and Levi said it a little bit differently. I said, "ohh—Mrs. Krise said it was ..." And he said, not sarcastically, "oh well she would know, because her people are from there." As it turns out, it was a question of /gw/ versus /kw/ pronunciation, that sort of alternation.

I don't think Martha had traveled far, but she did have a good sense of geography. One day she started giving place names, and she left the reservation, went up the coast, over to Vancouver Island, and up the west coast talking about peoples. That was the first time I heard a pharyngeal. I was flabbergasted. I didn't know where she was at this point, as I had lost track completely. Later I was surprised that she knew that, and the fact that she was using a completely foreign sound.

There was a pharyngeal, and of course I didn't have the tape recorder running. My only excuse was that **that** was my first experience, and that we were discouraged from using tape recorders. We needed to use them, but we were also told, "The more you get on tape, the less you're going to get in notebooks. Whatever you tape, be sure to transcribe it." Well, of course, you can tape much faster than you can transcribe. And it just wasn't in our field methods at the time to have someone transcribe who was literate in the language.

At that point then, I started working with all of them. I would see Hagen, usually in the evenings. I would work with Mrs. Krise and Harriet Dover when she was able. I'd often get to her house and there would be a note on the door: she'd had to go to a meeting of Democrats in Olympia or something like that. But when I could, I worked with her. And I worked with the Lamonts. Martha was most willing to tell stories, and I collected a lot of them through her. I collected more than were ever transcribed, although I started transcribing right away. Levi was quite patient, although I could tell that sometimes his patience was stretched a bit thin. Often I would work on the stories first with Mrs. George, whose patience was infinite, get them roughed out fairly well, and then go to Levi....

*Is there anything else you wanted to add?*

My last visit to the Lamont's was after I had come back from Hawaii when I had taught over there. My first impression was how awful Levi looked. The tuberculosis was well on its way, but I didn't understand that. He didn't look well at all.

Levi had already sung some power songs for me, but he told me to turn on the tape recorder, and then he sang three songs. His voice cracking, he was having an awful time doing it, but he did. They also offered me some baskets that Martha had. They wanted to give them to me, and I said "No, your grandchildren will want these." I've kicked myself since. They were well aware that the children and grandchildren weren't interested in them. The baskets were gathering dust on a high shelf.

Levi knew what I was trying to do. He knew about a Ph.D. He knew about dissertations. One thing he asked me to bring him was a dictionary. And his English vocabulary was probably as good as mine, in general, sophisticated. He understood my efforts. He appreciated the tenacity with which I would grapple with a grammatical point. That appealed to him; he liked that a lot.

Anyway I had this strong sense. They knew that I was going up to Victoria, and he knew that he wouldn't be around when I came back. Martha wanted me to go to the Shaker church there in Tulalip. She herself apparently wasn't able to go anymore or wasn't going. I'm not sure. I didn't go; I should have.

But there was something else there. They had considerable insight into me, insight to the point that some days I felt uncomfortable. And the only similar experience I've had was once or twice with a priest in a confessional where that priest knew exactly what you're saying and what you're not saying, and what's behind your words. They took more of an interest in me than I really wanted to have anybody do. Very definitely did, and I was much too young or immature to appreciate that. But I was at least smart enough to appreciate them.

# TRANSLATOR'S INTRODUCTION

Crisca Bierwert

And there are other words in other languages. Always in movement.
—Joy Harjo

For the contemporary reader, Lushootseed stories and their English translations here may seem startlingly avant-garde in the spare and vivid use of words, the outlining of characters rich with emotional motivation yet thin as archetypes, the shifting between prose and poetic rhythms, and the variable patterning of sound and plot.

Traditional Lushootseed storytellers are dramatists. In minimizing description, they emphasize enactment, making their stories immediate to their audience. The artistry of Native American oral literature has been obscured for many generations of English translation by non-Native and Native people alike. Translators have replaced the rhetorical and poetic devices of Native languages with English and American rhetorical equivalents of the time. (Native American speakers have conventionally been known for oratory, not poetry.) But it is now well known that the patterns in the original languages are not only artful; they make commentary on the text and on language itself. (See D. Hymes's references to metacommentary in 1981:303–308, Tedlock's position of "reading over the shoulder" in 1983:312–320, and Mattina's affirmation of publishing a translation in un-"versified" Red English in 1987:137–143 for three views.)

The English translations in this volume follow a Lushootseed word patterning, even though the word order and morphology I use are conventional American English. The translations are neither strictly literal, nor are they free; they are literary in the sense that the principles of ordering serve to heighten their imaginative impact. My translation work is probably most similar to that of Nora and Richard Dauenhauer who have translated Tlingit texts with structures and diction conforming to the originals (1987, 1990). On the following pages, I detail the features of the English texts, and I explicate the principles I used in working out the translations.

**Performance**

Performance features are not marked in the written text, in general. The tapes provide this aural information. In the Lushootseed texts 1, 6, and 7, pauses are marked. Where there is no pause at the end of the printed line, or where a space appears for reasons of alignment (see "Organization of the Texts on the Page," below), → appears to indicate that the storyteller continues without a pause. Otherwise, the end of a line or a space in a line signals a pause. "A pause" is an audible silence (we did not use scientific instruments to measure this) or an audible intake of breath. No marking of silences is provided in the other texts. The storytellers' paces did vary, and sometimes they used particular voices and cadences. In text 3, boldface type indicates a special voice that Martha Lamont sometimes used for Crow and for the seagulls' words. This typeface variation only hints at the variations of voicing in her text; however, the annotator's notes and introductions provide general information on the delivery of the texts. Lines are sometimes units of delivery; sometimes they are not. Hagen Sam (text 4) and Emma Conrad (texts 5 and 6) generally spoke in sentences that are marked here as lines. Martha Lamont (texts 1–3, 7) spoke continuously past lines and sentences, often pausing *after* conjunctions. Emma Conrad usually used conjunctions after a pause.

There are some performance features in the Lushootseed texts that are entirely untranslated in the English. These are what we have called "false starts," the partial words and utterances that are not part of a narrative line, the storyteller's version of "um"s and "ah"s and rephrasing. (See "Conventions Used in Transcription" in "Writing and Reading Lushootseed.") Only a continuous narrative line is translated, so that when a storyteller goes back over a previous syllable, only the revised statement is translated. I varied this practice in the last lines of text 2, taking unusual liberty to translate a repeated deictic "false start" by repeating "that's it" in the last line.

### Text Divisions: The Basket Motif Called "Hand" or "Fingers"

In the texts, a Salish basketry motif (printed above) marks changes in scene, shifts in the focus of the narrative, or narrative repetitions—depending on the story. There are other breaks as well: a blank line that signals a lesser change. These smaller breaks occur as attention or speech shifts from one character to another or from a character to a narrator's comment. The breaks are not intended to mark hierarchically ordered segments; they are included to alert the reader that a change has occurred. Changes in focus are often not obvious in the text because the Lushootseed verbs need no pronoun in the third person. Action or speech may change subject without any marking. Even with the marking of focus change, the subjects of sentences may be unclear for a few lines. In text 1, for example, lines 9–12 read

9 And this old man was asleep.
10 And then
this guy came, this certain Mink.

11 Then he ate the salmon himself
that someone else was roasting.
12 And then, his food was gone.

We have to follow the story to know who "he" is. Even more dependent on context are the third person subjects in lines 89–99:

89 Then he spoke.
90 He spoke
91 as soon as that certain one drank.
92 His throat was dry.
93 so he drank.
94 He drank with his face in the water.
95 Changer drank.
96 He really wanted water.

To follow the text, we have to know that it was Changer who was thirsting here, prey to Mink's ploy.

In general, analysis of these texts emphasizes circular and interweaving narrative techniques, rather than marking and segmentation. (See the "Annotator's Introduction" and the introductions to texts.) Text 6 alone includes the word "scene" separating major episodes of the narrative. For texts 5 and 7, Langen includes a schematic analysis of the text structure after the introductory essay.

### Line Numbers

The line numbers in all the texts are those assigned by Thomas M. Hess in his original transcription and translation work, with a few modifications. Hess's units of analysis were clauses. As a phonologist who was assembling, based on these texts and others, the grammatical principles of the Snohomish language, minimal syntactic units gave him the data he needed. Furthermore, conjunctions seemed, even from the start, to open sentences rather than to link them. Presenting the texts as literature opened up the possibility of translating them more freely and looking at larger units of analysis. However, we decided early on to preserve the line numbers as they were, because the translations are part of a larger project including a dictionary with examples drawn from the text. The line numbers referred to in the dictionary (Bates, Hess, and Hilbert 1994) are the same as those published here. That is, line 112 in text 2 is referred to there as 2.112; line 20 in episode two of text 1 is referred to as 1b.20. (Only text 1 has episode markings.)

### Conjunctions

The conjunctions *g<sup>w</sup>əl*, *huy*, *g<sup>w</sup>əl huy*, and *huy g<sup>w</sup>əl* ("and," "then," and "and then" for the last two forms) are all markers of narrative framing, and they stand out in the text (see "Organization of the Texts on the Page," below). Very occasionally, I varied the gloss of a conjunction to "so" or "for" or "thus"; otherwise they are glossed as stated. These markers and others invite further analyses.

Dell Hymes changed the field of Native American narrative studies with his analysis of patterned markings in Chinookan and Kalapuyan storytelling (cf. D. Hymes 1981). Dale Kinkade has published a comparable analysis of Chehalis Salish (Kinkade 1987). Dell Hymes's analysis orders the text in nested units in three levels: verses, stanzas, and scenes. These units are patterned in groups of three and five, pattern numbers for the culture. Rather than presenting the texts in nested hierarchies, I marked the conjunctions at the margins of the text and added focus on the patterning that is interior to sentences.

### Syntax

The syntactic complexity of Lushootseed is paralleled in most of the translations: the English generally follows the Lushootseed in using a simpler or more complex syntax. Like Tedlock (1972), I use ordinary English word order where the storyteller uses ordinary Lushootseed word order, and I invert or elaborate it where she or he does. Single-word predicates are sometimes translated by single English words, but more often a subject or verb (as the case requires) is added in English to produce the grammatical completeness that is carried by a single Lushootseed word. Narrative context also influenced the syntax of my translation. Where the Lushootseed text is more formal, the closer the parallel between English and Lushootseed structure. On the other hand, where a character speaks, translation of diction carries more weight than translation of syntax.

I almost always use subordinate clauses to translate subordinate clauses. For example in the next to the last line of text 1, I use the phrase "when it was sometime later," rather than the simpler and adequate "later" to translate Martha Lamont's mention of when Changer transformed Deer. (See "Word Choice," below.) (For another perspective see the discussion of lines 7 and 11 in the annotated text, where Hess uses the possessive and adjectival forms "the old man's roasting/roasted salmon." My choice is "the salmon that the old man was roasting." Hess's translation compresses the phrase, making it comparable to the Lushootseed form in its density. My translation leaves the phrase in the form of a subordinated clause to maintain a different accuracy: stress on the verb form. I have generally kept verb-centered constructions explicit in the English because in my understanding the language's reliance on and development of verb-centered morphology is a distinctive feature of Lushootseed as well as of other Salishan and North American languages.

A problematic example that illustrates translation choices occurs in the first line of text 3. "They are dwelling where they are" is a slight elaboration of the conventional opening "They are dwelling" (see discussion of *ʔəsɬaɬlil*, "dwell," below). The complement phrase "where they are" translates *ʔal tiʔiɬ dəx*$^{w}$*-ʔá-s*, which means "at that place-being-it." "At that place" expresses the Lushootseed phrase structurally and echoes the phrase rhythmically but condenses a verb-centered construction into an English noun. "Where they are" then follows the Lushootseed in being a three-part phrase that subordinates a predicate. This phrase expresses the tautology or circularity of *dəx*$^{w}$*ʔás* and some of the directionality of the deictic *tiʔiɬ* "that" (in "where"). My intent has been to stay away from laborious constructions, leave some Lushootseed intricacy, and sound good in English but not necessarily sound like ordinary English.

When dəx$^{w}$ʔás occurs again in the story, in line 29, it is in a larger construction: *ʔa ʔal tiʔəʔ dəx*$^{w}$*ʔás ə́lg*$^{w}$*ə*, which I translate "there, right where they are." Here the locative/being *ʔa* is iterated in Lushootseed emphatically; thus I use "there," emphatically (not "there it is," more literally). To parallel the echoing of Lushootseed *ʔa* and *ʔás*, my translation echoes "there" and "where." "They," *ə́lg*$^{w}$*ə*, is explicit in this instance. It could operate in English as the possessive, "at their place." But the phrase "where they are" works well too, in a context quite different from that of the opening line.

Semantic patterning of the original text was my principal guide for translation. That is, I generally mapped word repetition and variation according to the Lushootseed. The opening passage of the first text, for example, uses dense repetition with changes in word order. Note the formal correspondence between Lushootseed and English, and see "Sound," below, for a discussion of a different gloss.

1 ʔácəc tiʔíɬ bə́ščəb.
2 bə́ščəb t[ə ʔ]a; <tul...,>
3 tuləʔíbəš.
4 ʔi·, tuləʔíbəš tiʔíɬ bə́ščəb. →
5 ləʔíbəš tíʔəʔ bə́ščəb.

1 There was Mink.
2 Mink was there.
3 He was walking.
4 Yes, Mink was walking.
5 Mink was walking.

### Word Choice

English glosses are generally simple, everyday language, reflecting the everyday diction that prevails in these particular stories. More restricted Lushootseed diction occurs at times in all the texts, and I chose English glosses accordingly. Although root forms are short, Lushootseed is a polysynthetic language (see the annotated text), which means that most words have prefixes and suffixes that change the meaning, nuance, or grammatical role of the word. Unpacking this meaning may be unwieldy in English. Since complex words are the norm in Lushootseed, this density poses a problem for translating diction. To avoid words that sound inflated, short word glosses are called for, but glossing with short words (in which the complexities of polysynthesis are dissolved) creates an effect of simple syntactical construction. This was another reason for my translating subordinate clauses as such, even where a simpler English gloss could have sufficed (see "Syntax," above, and see the annotated text for another view).

Lushootseed words are retained in the English translation where no English word is suitable to carry the cultural meaning. Most frequent is the word *siʔab*, which is variously glossed in anthropological literature as "noble," "high-class," "honorable" (cf. Suttles 1958). Langen's notes to text 2 provide necessary cultural perspective on the status *siʔab*. For the sake of the stories and the word, I avoided establishing an English gloss, preferring that a sense of meaning emerge as much as possible from the texts themselves.

Compound words in Lushootseed that are idiomatic are generally translated by a simple English word. A useful contrast in text 6 is *sd*$^z$*ix*$^w$*qs* (line 5) and *six*$^w$*siʔabs* (line 6). *s-d*$^z$*ix*$^w$*-qs*, translated morpheme by morpheme, means "nominalized-first-nose"; as a whole it means "leader" and is translated thus. *six*$^w$*-siʔab-s* means "one who stands in the capacity of/for someone-*siʔab*-3rd person possessive." This word is less idiomatic than the former and is translated by the English idiom "head man." I felt somewhat freer to introduce the English metaphor because these two terms have the same referent and are close to one another in the text. I decided that I was relocating the body-imagery idiom in "head man" that I had displaced from *sd*$^z$*ix*$^w$*qs*. Risking questions and comments about the shift from "nose" to "head," I was satisfied to settle on a translation that retains the kind of idiomatic imagery that was already in the text.

### Articles

Within reasonably comfortable English, I tried to translate the deictic *tiʔił* as "this" or (rarely) "that," to distinguish it consistently from *tiʔə* (or rarely *təʔ*), which I translated as "the." In truth, the deictic contrast in meaning is much less significant in Lushootseed than it is in English, but I chose to copy the sound contrast. The reader should interpret the English accordingly. I took unusual liberty with one phrase, *tiʔił cədił*, which means "this particular...." The phrase is an emphatic marker that adds a rhythmic pulse to the person it refers to. Martha Lamont uses it strategically in text 1: it adds a note of familiarity and notoriety after the characters' first appearance, and then it tails off by the end of the episode. Thus, the text is not whole without it. I avoided using "this here" as a gloss, since the rest of the diction I use, although informal, is not so rustic. I used "this certain..." or "that certain..." and later on in the text I changed to "this old [Mink]," to add the tone of reprise that inheres in the original.

**Aspect**

The problem with translating aspect is that Lushootseed categories are quite different from those in English. Thus, the one-syllable prefixes that mark Lushootseed aspect require additional words, sometimes several words, to adequately translate. Moreover, they are often strung together, compounding their unwieldy expansion in English. Where parataxis or word repetition occurs in Lushootseed, I have chosen economical translations to reflect the rhythm or sound patterning, or both, and glossed over most of the differences in Lushootseed aspect. I translated texts 2 and 3 with a prevailing English present tense because they open with the Lushootseed *ʔəs-*, the stative (state of being) aspect marker, and most of the verbs are unmarked (which leaves the aspect open). The concluding lines of both of these stories include the absolute completive *tu-* (also used to refer to people who have died); thus, I conclude the translations in the past tense. Text 4 opens with the *tu-* marking the Lushootseed for "remember" and continues the story about Hagen Sam's late grandparents with the absolute completive. I translated the first sentence in the English present, as it makes more sense to us, and continued with the past tense. The other texts open with completive aspect markings, and I have translated these others with a prevailing English past tense. An exception is text 1. There, I used "on" or "again" to mark the repetitive *bə-*, the past participle for the continuative *lə-*, and "would be" for the habitual-repetitive *ƛ̓u-*. The first occurrence of *bə-* (in line 7) is translated not merely as a repetitive aspect but as a habitual or even typical: "as usual." This translation is an exception to the rule of glossing aspect with the smallest number of syllables possible. "As usual he stole the salmon" reflects Vi Hilbert's and Levi Lamont's interpretation that this line signals Mink's thieving nature.

**Consistent Glossing**

As a rule, each Lushootseed word is translated with the same English gloss throughout a text, even though different contexts suggest different English terms. The purpose of this consistency is to ensure that Lushootseed repetitions are evident in the translations. In formally patterned passages, the iterations in English are most obviously important, but I have chosen to retain constant glosses even in unpatterned passages, with the idea that the recurrences of words here provide minor landmarks in the text. My intent is that configurations of sound and shape due to such repetitions are preserved in translation. (This choice was the subject of some debate among us. I was more willing to sacrifice semantic range, in order to replicate surface patterning.)

In order for the translations to work best, the reader must think of the glosses not in conventional English but as English words that are open to different senses in their different contexts. A commonplace word must resonate with metaphorical possibility to work in the English text as the Lushootseed words work in the literature. For example, in text 1, rather than using different glosses to translate the semantic range of *ʔibəš*, "walk" must express the senses of "travel," "roam," "go on," which the Lushootseed *ʔibəš* has in context. What is gained is that "walk" (like *ʔibəš*) recurs throughout the Lushootseed story, moving and marking the narrative flow.

In other words, faced with the choice of having multiple glosses radiating, if you will, from Lushootseed words with expansive range, or pushing English words into contexts where they carried more than their usual load, I chose the latter. I was concerned that a bias toward translating the Lushootseed words more richly (i.e. with more variety) would cause the richness of those words to be lost in the translation. Since most readers would be paying most attention to the English, I reasoned, it was important to stretch the English in Lushootseed dimensions. My argument is summed up well in the position of Benjamin that a good translation "may be achieved above all by a literal rendering of the syntax which proves words rather than sentences to be the primary element of the translator. For if the sentence is the wall before the language of the original, literalness is the arcade"(Benjamin 1968:79). To create a *Lushootseed* arcade in English, I felt I had to use the same distribution of glosses more than glosses that changed to reflect the "same" signification as the Lushootseed originals.

While I am convinced by and committed to the pattern of glossing I followed, I must acknowledge what my strategy precludes at times: choosing context-specific glosses to heighten dramatic accuracy. Lines 21–23 of text 2 provide an example where *ʔibəš*, again translated "walk" or "walks" throughout the text, could be glossed with a more vivid

English verb. The context of these lines is the laying of a ceremonial blanket under the feet of Crow. A more precise gloss for *ʔibəš* would add to the dramatic effect of the passage:

21 ... they made a woven path,
a place for Crow to walk
in order to get into the canoe.
22 It is spread out all the way to the canoe.
23 There must be a covering where she walks, that Crow.

Consider a change in line 23:

There must be a covering where she *steps*, that Crow.
or: There must be a covering where she *parades*, that Crow.

The image of Crow's "stepping" is charged with some delicacy and the image of Crow's "parade" carries some swagger that her "walk" does not convey. The dramatic terms could heft irony or parody in a more precise translation, where Crow is more conclusively defined as a character, and thus where a gloss can communicate her attributes unambiguously. But the sense of the passage is conveyed even without more precisely glossing *ʔibəš*. In this instance, the carpeting is sufficient to signal that Crow's walk is processional. In the reader's mind she will walk with (Crow-like) dignity even if the word "steps" does not cue that meaning. Martha Lamont left Crow's physical attitude ambiguous in the word *ʔibəš*; so does the translation. What might have been a loss becomes a gain: that of a more open text. If future translators choose to prioritize dramatic action, they may make different choices, but at least they will know what they start with here in English.

Although Lushootseed words are consistently translated within texts, some are translated differently in different texts. The most important of these is the verb *ʔəsƛ̕aƛ̕lil*, which refers to residing and is translated as "live" most often, but "dwell" in text 3 and "settle" in text 6. Since the word is often used to establish people's presence in the opening line or lines of a story, the variation is conspicuous. Hess argued against "live," since the verb does not refer to "aliveness," and for "dwell." I resisted the anachronistic tone I heard in "dwell." The variation is an honest by-product of changing minds and different minds working together.

### Sound

The sound of Lushootseed is so different from that of English that one could argue that the translation should not include even a partial modeling on Lushootseed sound patterns. In fact, consistent glossing throughout the text conflicts with translating sound patterns. Sounds pattern by clustering "locally," that is to say in proximity—not in distribution through the text. For example, in the five short lines that begin text 1 (quoted in "Syntax," above), there are 29 syllables altogether. Fourteen of those syllables comprise words that contain the syllable *bəš*; *bəš* occurs 7 times in as many words: 4 times in *bəščəb* ("Mink") and 3 times in *ʔibəš* ("walk"). (Twelve of the remaining 15 syllables are one- or two-syllable lexemes starting with the sound /t/.) The English sentences echo the Lushootseed parallelisms fairly well, but cannot approach the sound repetitions. To repeat the pattern would have required a different word choice, perhaps the following:

1 There was Mink.
2 Mink was there.
3 He was slinking.
4 Yes, Mink was slinking.
5 Mink was slinking.

While this pattern adds something both to the character of Mink and to the opening that is amusing in a way that I think is good and true to the story, the word "slink" just doesn't carry the ambiguity (or the power or respect) that a simple "walk" can. Moreover, of 18 syllables, "-ink" or "-ing" appears 10 times, which rather overdoes the density of "-ink." In my translation, "wa-" appears in 8 of 18 syllables, which may be a closer fit with the original, but fails to connect—through sound—the character with the action.

In rare cases, I selected a gloss to fit a sound correspondence. For example, in lines 26–28 of text 1, the verb stems in Lushootseed each begin with /q̓ʷ/ or /qʷ/ and end in /dəxʷ/ or /bəxʷ/.

26 huy → qʷíbidəxʷ. →
27 huy, → q̓ʷəldáxʷ.
28 q̓ʷəlbáxʷ tíʔəʔ cədíɬ bə́ščəb ʔal tíʔəʔ <dəxʷ. . . ,>
x̌əɬ ti ɬudəxʷq̓ə́lbs.

26 Then he readied it.
27 Then he roasted it.
28 This certain Mink roasted where he was making a sort of camp.

In English I chose "readied" rather than "prepared," which is a more usual, broadly applicable gloss for *qʷib*. Thus the translation carries a bit of the local sound repetition and parataxis of the original.

I chose to use a single gloss for each story, in almost every case, despite polysemy, then, and despite most opportunities to echo other sound patterning. The purpose was to emphasize a certain kind of sound patterning, that occasioned by the repetition of words in the text (see "Organization of the Texts on the Page," below).

### Organization of the Texts on the Page

While texts 4 and 5 are organized in paragraph format, the others are laid out in lines. For these texts, lines were rearranged to reveal formal structures of the storytelling that are most apparent when displayed graphically. (The shorter lines and the structure of this organization also make the Lushootseed tapes easier to follow.)

The amount of space on the page is no indication of silences (see "Performance," above). For example, Martha Lamont's stories (texts 1–3 and 7) are all in line format and leave lots of white space, but they were all rapidly told. Aurally, her stories are as dense with language as the texts are dense with structure. Hagen Sam's curing story (text 4), by contrast, is slower-paced, although the paragraph format gives an impression of packed space.

The texts organized by lines reveal the regularity of Lushootseed syntax. Conjunctions are always at the beginning of the sentence. When they are aligned separately from the rest of the text in a section, they appear clearly as framing devices, and other patterns in the text become clearer. The verb usually follows in the sentence, next the object of action, and next the subject of the predicate if it is stated. The nominals may also be reversed without a change in signification. The object of the predicate may be a subordinate clause even if it takes the form of a single word (cf. the annotated text, sec. 7). A series of lines may contain verbs that either vary or repeat prefixes and suffixes. The pattern of affixes in a series of verbs can create a rhythmic repetition (parataxis). Occurrences of rhythmic repetition are aligned in the Lushootseed text, so they fall one above the other. The English translation is matched, where possible, so that the rhythmic repetition occurs in English as well (although it is often not so noticeable there). (See the example of lines 1.26–28 in "Sound," above.)

Repetitions of words in the Lushootseed text are echoed in English as much as possible (see "Word Choice," above). Regularity of glossing contributes to visual marking of repetition patterns. In text 2, for example, several words and phrases are repeated (see also Langen's introduction to text 2).

2 gʷəl ʔəsx̌əɬ́ tsiʔəʔ k̓áʔk̓aʔ.
3 hágʷəxʷ tux̌əɬ́ tsiʔíɬ k̓áʔk̓aʔ.
4 xʷíʔəxʷ [gʷə] shaʔɬs.

5 gʷəl (h)uy ƛ̕ub.

6 (ʔu) x̌ʷáx̌ʷaq̓ʷbitəbəxʷ ʔə tiʔəʔ ʔalš[s], kaw̓qs.
7a x̌ʷáx̌ʷaq̓ʷbidəxʷ tsiʔəʔ ʔalšs
dxʷʔal kʷi gʷədəxʷ(h)əlíʔils

7b ʔux̌ə́ł.
8 xʷi·ʔ kʷi suƛ̕úbils.
9 huy gʷəl, x̌ʷáx̌ʷaq̓ʷəxʷ tíʔəʔ kaw̓qs.

2 Then Crow is sick.
3 Crow is sick for a long time.
4 She is not well.

5 But she [will] be all right.

6 He is worried about his sister, Raven is.
7a He is worried about his sister
for a way to cure her.
7b She was sick.
8 She was not getting well.
9 And so Raven is worried.

Aligning "is/was sick" and "is worried" makes the patterning of the section graphically clear for the English reader. This technique is intended to direct the reader's attention to the Lushootseed, which is aligned as well. The repetition of *x̌ʷáx̌ʷaq̓ʷ*, for example, stands out more in the aligned format; these shapes get lost for the reader in a paragraph of Lushootseed orthography that is still strange to the eye. Note that lines 4 and 8 provide a negative parallel for lines 2, 3, and 7b, and they are all aligned together.

Text 3 is full of examples of word patterning that is founded on repetition. Lines 90–91 provide an example of showing this pattern through a somewhat forced repetition of the gloss "paint." What the English translation misses, but alignment in Lushootseed displays, is that the root for Raccoon, *x̌álus*, is the word for "marked face" and is glossed as "paint-up face" (notes to the text fill in such information).

90 cədił dᶻəł cəxʷəʔúx̌ʷ ʔəxʷ x̌álus(s),
ʔəxʷ x̌áʔx̌alusəd."
91 bəqx̌átəb tíʔəʔ ʔušəbábdxʷx̌áʔx̌alus.

90 Am I going for somebody painted up like that,
little paint-up face?"
91 She insults poor Raccoon again.

Word repetitions cluster as Martha Lamont describes Drake Bufflehead in lines 104–111 from the same text. Aligning repeated words creates vertical series, which weave across the horizontal lines. The graphic pattern mimics a memory pattern that the spoken text creates as it is heard. What is displayed here is not a *libretto*, as Tedlock provides for Zuni texts (1972), but a diagram of the webs of connections.

104 put haʔɬ <stəb. . . >.
105 ʔuləlíʔcut.
106 ʔuləlíʔcut tíʔəʔ sx̌əy̓úss
x̌əɬ ti səshúys sq̓ədᶻúʔs
gʷəsq̓ədᶻúʔsəs.

104 He is very fine.
105 He kept changing.
106 His head kept changing.
There is something about how his hair is,
something about his hair.

107 put haʔɬ
ʔuləlíʔcut.
108 bək̓ʷ ʔəsʔəx̌ídəb:
109 x̌ʷiq̓ʷíx̌ʷ,
x̌əɬ ti ʔəxʷčíligʷəd,
x̌əɬ ti *pink* kʷədíʔ
səshúy ʔə tíʔəʔ.
110 <x̌əɬ ti ʔəs. . . ,> stab <gʷəs. . . ,> gʷəscút(t)əbs,
x̌əɬ ti x̌ʷiq̓ʷác.
111 ha·ʔɬ tiʔíɬ
suləlíʔcut ʔə tíʔəʔ sx̌əy̓ús <ʔə tíʔəʔ. . . ,>
ʔə tíʔəʔ cədíɬ sʔušəbábdxʷ.

107 He is very fine.
He kept changing.
108 It is every color:
109 blue,
sort of red inside,
sort of pink.
That's how it is.
110 sort of what? what would you say?
sort of yellowish-green.
111 That is fine.
His head kept changing,
that poor man.

In English, we see clearly the repetition of *ʔuləlalíʔcut*, "He kept changing/ His head kept changing" in the vignette. The sheen changes colors (or color terms) in the Lushootseed, and references to its many colors are connected through the recurrence of the *x̌əł ti*, "sort of," phrase.

The paragraphs of texts 4 and 5 were formed by arranging lines continuously, with paragraph breaks where focus shifts occur. The translations never simulate English prose narrative style by adding descriptions and explanations. The difference between these texts and those rendered in lines is not drastic; both fall within a fairly narrow range of fidelity to the Lushootseed. I used the same basic strategies for translating these two texts as I did for the others. Putting the resultant English text in prose format simply gives the reader a different feel for the patterning.

We chose to represent text 4 in paragraph form largely because it is a more straightforward narration, compared to Martha Lamont's stories. Langen notes the rhetorical figures and framing devices in her introductions. The point of rendering text 5 in paragraph form is to include diversity in our presentations of texts. Langen lists this text's episodes and the narrative structures at the close of her introductions.

Variations from the original Lushootseed lines do occur. Sometimes lines have been translated into English prose, compounding two Lushootseed lines into a single English sentence. In text 6, lines 545–610 are uniquely arranged. In this scene, a man who is invisible drinks coffee from a woman's cup. The text is arranged in two columns, with lines about her world on the left and lines about him to the right.

### Words Added

In text 2, additional Lushootseed words and their English translations were provided by Levi Lamont during Hess's fieldwork. (See notes to text 2.) In text 7, explanatory words and phrases occur frequently in brackets (as they did in all the texts at earlier stages of translation). Many referents in this text are implied, and the notes would have been burdened by the amount of information to fill in. The other texts were pared down to include only those words that translate what the teller actually said.

### Interpretation of the Whole

In sum, my English translations are selective replications, mimetic versions of the Lushootseed texts; they are a language of re-creation that no one, in fact, speaks. Walter Benjamin suggested this technique in his essay "The Task of the Translator." In it, he drew on the exhortation of Rudolf Pannwitz that the purpose of translation was not to put the language of origin into the language of translation. " 'The basic error of the translator is that he preserves the state in which his own language happens to be instead of allowing his language to be powerfully affected by the foreign tongue' " (Benjamin 1968:81). Of course, the task—for both the translator and the reader—is much greater when the differences between the languages are as great as the differences between Lushootseed and English. The benefit of this approach is that the resulting translations carry their reader farther into the organization of the thought and the art of the Lushootseed language and storytellers.

Some of these patternings that I recreate are found in the English that Lushootseed people speak. Ceremonial oratory includes much circular structuring, and the repetition of words and of statements in different word orders also marks formal speech. The late Martin Sampson, a cousin to Vi Hilbert whom she tape recorded while discussing translations, sometimes spoke in English patterned according to an old Lushootseed storytelling style. (See my analysis of a discourse he gave on poetics in Bierwert 1993). And Vi Hilbert's reminiscences in this volume reflect a similar patterning, though a more relaxed one. Thus, when I characterize the language of my translations as a re-creation, I mean to emphasize that it is like a tracing of Lushootseed into English, an English form of the Lushootseed language, and in the general sense it echoes the old language in a way that formal speakers do, although they do it with more flexibility.

The details of my task as a translator, set forth in this introduction, may read as the work of an artisan rather than that of a poet. If so, it is because I have tried to be like the carver in "The Story of the Seal Hunters," who works and reworks a cedar log until it has the shape of a seal, can move as a seal does, and finally sounds like a seal. He worked to copy something already in existence, not to convey his own idea of it. Similarly, I have worked to keep my interpretations from controlling these texts, attempting to give the original transcriptions an upper hand. In terms of a theory and practice of translation, this effort is more ambitious than it is self-effacing. My English translations of Lushootseed patterns may sound awkward at times in their effort to display the inner workings of a very foreign language, but they are intended to do much more than trace the structures of the original language. My hope is that they allow the reader to hear unfamiliar kinds of beauty in the storytellings.

In trying to keep from imposing my interpretations, have I introduced ambiguities where the original text had definite ideas? In light of Vi Hilbert's metaphor of poling across a river, my intention as translator has been to refrain from adding cross-currents and debris to the waterway. I trust the Lushootseed texts to generate possible meanings. This means risking misinterpretation, but it also keeps the field more open for other interpretations. These texts have not been published before; they are just beginning a historic travel. Our intent all along has been for future readers to create interpretations, and for the stories and their ideas to live on in this way.

To the extent that my translations map the poetics and the narrative power of the originals, they may direct the reader's attention to the Lushootseed texts, where the greater beauty lies. To the extent that they carry some power in themselves, I am grateful to the Lushootseed speakers for showing the way.

# WRITING AND READING LUSHOOTSEED

Crisca Bierwert

## Conventions Used in Transcription

The Lushootseed orthography uses the standard Americanist symbols with x̌ and x̌ʷ in lieu of x̣ and x̣ʷ. Primary and secondary stress are marked according to performance (e.g., á and à, respectively).

Lexicals that are part of grammatical construction but not pronounced by the speaker have been inserted by Hess, Hilbert, or Bates in brackets. For example, in text 1, lines 7, 8, and 11, Martha Lamont omits subordinating lexicals that slower speech would reveal and that she includes in the almost identical line 46. Without the grammatical additions, a student of the language would have difficulty making the connections between clauses here. The annotated text, below, which is our guide to Lushootseed grammar, discusses these three lines as if they were grammatically "standard." Such additions are not, of course, indisputable.

Articulations by the storyteller that we call "false starts" are included between < > marks. These include syllables or rarely word strings that were interrupted by the speaker. The end of the false start is marked by the discontinued syntax; the beginning is marked by the place where the syllable following picks up the text. At least four types of configurations exist, as is illustrated in the following examples from text 1a.

1. Repeating and carrying on: <tul...> tuləʔibəš 2–3
2. Rephrasing: <bələ...> huy ləsčáladəxʷ 119
3. Elaborating: <dəxʷ...> x̌əɬ ti ɬudəxʷq̓ə́lbs 28
4. Throwing a word in the gap: <stəb...> qəlʼqəládi 131
   stəb means "what."

These "false starts" are not translated. They are valuable performance markers, however. These words were omitted from Hess's original transcriptions (not being significant to that work) and had to be added for our present work. Including these syllables makes the tapes easier to follow. More importantly, there are some places where a "false start" string operates not to distract from the text's architecture but adds to or triggers parataxis or other formalisms. And on the whole, the pause and overlap of language that we have called a "false start" may in fact be part of narrative rhythm. These junctures may signal not only interstices but jolts and bursts that interlace the tracery of thought. Mapping their distribution may illustrate not only structures but driving powers of language, growth points of the storytelling.

### Reading Lushootseed Orthography

Native speakers can read Lushootseed orthography without special training in the symbols used. Some speakers have also used the orthography for writing the language. (Vi Hilbert has uniquely developed expertise as a transcriber, as well as a translator.) For all others, practicing the individual sounds, the consonant clusters, and the inflections is a difficult task. The sounds of Lushootseed are quite different from those of English. Archaic forms of the language have been recorded, telling us that the language of today is different from what it has been in the past. Hess remarks on the different quality of pronunciation that he has heard from speakers whose mouths have never shaped the English language. Lushootseed language today, like all aspects of the culture, has transformed over time and through cultural exchange. The orthographic symbols mark the future use of the language as much as they are legacies from the past. None of these symbols should be understood to have absolute values. Moreover, the Lushootseed orthography is morphophonemic: the spelling of words is constant, rather than expressing the sounds made exactly by each speaker in each instance.

### Sound Values of the Symbols

The following descriptions of sound values are taken largely from the descriptions in the *Lushootseed Dictionary* (Bates, Hess, and Hilbert 1994).

**ʔ** a stop representing the catch in the throat in the English exclamation *Uh-oh.* [glottal stop]

**ʼ** combines with other stops to signal a closure of the throat as the sound is made. This glottalization generally causes a small amount of popping sound as the stop is released. The glottal markings are called "glottalized *b*," "glottalized *c*," etc.).

**a** is pronounced like the *a* in *father*. When unstressed, *a* is pronounced ə. [low back unrounded vowel]

**b** is pronounced like English *b* in *baby*. [voiced bilabial stop]

**c** sounds like the *ts* in English *cats*. [voiceless alveolar affricate]

**c̓** combines the Lushootseed *c* with a glottal stop. [voiceless ejective alveolar affricate]

**č** sounds like the English *ch* in *church*. [voiceless palatal affricate] (called "c-wedge")

**č̓** combines the Lushootseed *č* with a glottal stop. [voiceless ejective palatal affricate]

**d** is pronounced like the English *d*. [voiced alveolar stop]

**d$^z$** sounds like the English *ds* in *kids*. [voiced alveolar affricate] (called "d-raised-z")

**ə** sounds like the vowel sound in English *but* and *of* and the first sound of *around*. [mid central vowel] (called "schwa")

**(ə)** is used in the texts to represent a contraction of *ə* so swiftly passed by in speech that it is not heard; it then represents a movement between two other sounds and is included to help a reader by keeping the spelling of words more constant.

**g** is pronounced like the English *g* in *good* or *guess* never as in *giant*. [voiced velar stop]

**gʷ** is pronounced like the English *g* with the lips pursed, like the *gw* in *Gwen*. [voiced labialized velar stop] (called "g-raised-w")

**h** sounds like the English *h* in *happy*. [voiceless glottal glide]

**i** is pronounced in the range of the English vowels from *beet* to *bait*, depending on the sounds around it. [nonlow front unrounded vowel]

**ǰ** is pronounced like the first sound in the English *giant* or *jay*. [voiced palatal affricate] (called "j-wedge")

**k** sounds like the English *k* starting and ending *kick*. [voiceless velar stop]

**k̓** combines the Lushootseed *k* with a glottal stop. [voiceless ejective velar stop]

**kʷ** sounds like the English *qu* in *quick*, a Lushootseed *k* with the lips pursed. [voiceless labialized velar stop] (called "k-raised-w")

**k̓ʷ** combines the Lushootseed *kʷ* with a glottal stop. [voiceless labialized ejective velar stop]

**l** is pronounced like the English *l* in *live*, *not* in *feel*. [lateral alveolar liquid] (note contrast in position with other laterals.)

**l̓** sounds similar to the English *l* in *feel*, with the glottalization here causing a roughness in sound. [laryngealized lateral alveolar liquid]

**ł** sounds similar to a whispered English *l* or a lisp; air flows down one or both sides of the tongue. If the initial sounds of the English word *clay* are drawn out, and the speaker gently blows air out the sides of the mouth, *ł* is heard between the *c-* and *-lay*. [voiceless lateral alveolar fricative] (called "barred-l")

**ƛ̓** combines the Lushootseed *t* and *l* simultaneously with a glottal stop. The sound is similar to a clicking sound some English speakers use to call horses, except that the English sound brings air into the mouth, while the Lushootseed *ƛ̓* moves trapped air out of the mouth along the side of the tongue. [voiceless ejective lateral alveolar affricate] (called "glottalized barred-lambda")

**m** is pronounced like the English *m* in *mother*. [bilabial nasal]

**m̓** combines the Lushootseed *m* with throat tension like that in the Lushootseed *l̓*. [laryngealized bilabial nasal] (called "strictured *m*")

**n** is pronounced like the English *n* in *night*. [alveolar nasal]

**n̓** combines the Lushootseed *n* with throat tension like that in the Lushootseed *l̓*. [laryngealized alveolar nasal] (called "strictured *n*")

**p** is pronounced like the English *p* in *pop*. [voiceless bilabial stop]

**p̓** combines the Lushootseed *p* with a glottal stop. [voiceless ejective bilabial stop]

**q** is made farther back in the mouth than the English *k*. [voiceless uvular stop] (sometimes called an "Indian k," it occurs frequently in comparison to the Lushootseed *k*)

**q̓** combines the Lushootseed *q* with a glottal stop. [voiceless ejective uvular stop]

**qʷ** is pronounced like the Lushootseed *q* with lips pursed. [voiceless labialized uvular stop] (called "q-raised-w")

**q̓ʷ** combines the Lushootseed *qʷ* and *q̓*. [voiceless ejective labialized uvular stop]

**s** is pronounced like the English *s*. [voiceless alveolar fricative]

**š** is pronounced like the English *sh* in *ship*. [voiceless palatal fricative] (called "s-wedge")

**t** is pronounced like the English *t* in *tote*. [voiceless alveolar stop]

**t'** combines the Lushootseed *t* with a glottal stop. [voiceless ejective alveolar stop]

**u** is pronounced in the range of the English vowels from *boot* to *boat*, depending on the sounds around it. [rounded nonlow back vowel]

**w** sounds like the English *w* in *work*. [high back rounded glide]

**w̓** combines the Lushootseed *w* with throat tension like that in the Lushootseed *l̕*. [laryngealized high back rounded glide] (called "strictured w")

**xʷ** sounds similar to someone blowing out a candle. The tongue is in the same position as that for making *k*, as the air blows forward, and the lips are pursed. The sound is also similar to the *wh* in *which* when it is pronounced with a breathy initial sound. [voiceless labialized velar fricative] (called "x-w")

**x̌** sounds like a raspy *h*. The tongue is in approximately the same position used for making the Lushootseed *q* and the lips are rather open. The sound is sometimes written elsewhere with a dot below the "x." [voiceless uvular fricative] (called "x-wedge")

**x̌ʷ** is pronounced like the *x̌*, but the lips are pursed. [voiceless labialized uvular fricative] (called "rounded x-wedge")

**y** sounds like the English *y* in *yellow* and *yes*. [high front unrounded glide]

**y̓** combines the Lushootseed *y* with throat tension like that in the Lushootseed *l̕*. [laryngealized high front unrounded glide] (called "strictured y")

## Typographical Information

Fonts used in this text were customized for Lushootseed by Thomas Ridgeway, University of Washington.

# LUSHOOTSEED GRAMMAR IN AN ANNOTATED TEXT

Thomas M. Hess

**[Editor's Note:** The following grammatical analysis provides the reader with models of Lushootseed syntax drawn from the first sixteen lines of text 1. These lines progress from simpler to complex construction and comprise the basic grammatical rules of Lushootseed. For a descriptive outline of Lushootseed grammar see Hess (1995). Numbers in parentheses indicate the corresponding line numbers in the first episode of "Martha Lamont's Changer Story." The translations here are literal and thus do not correspond to the English translations facing the Lushootseed text in this volume.]

(1) ʔacəc tiʔił bəščəb — Mink was there

ʔacəc

Predicate having just one constituent, the predicate head. It is a locative meaning "be there/exist." Compare *ʔa* in (16).

tiʔił bəščəb

Direct complement.

tiʔił

Demonstrative "that."

bəščəb

Complement head, the noun "Mink," one of the three tricksters in Lushootseed mythology.

(2) bəščəb t[ə ʔ]a — It was Mink there

bəščəb

Predicate with just one constituent, the predicate head, which here is a noun.

tə ʔa

Locative augment meaning "there."

(3) tuləʔibəš — He was traveling

In this predication there is only one word, the predicate head. It comprises three morphemes.

ʔibəš

Radical stem meaning "walk/travel over land" (as opposed to journeying by water).

lə-

Aspectual prefix meaning approximately "progressive."

tu-

General prefix designating "past time." Normally, it would be pronounced as *tə-* when occurring before another prefix that is consonant initial. See *tə-* in (11). However, in these introductory lines, the raconteuse is articulating very precisely.

(4) ʔi, tuləʔibəš tiʔił bəščəb — Yes, Mink was traveling

ʔi

Affirmative particle meaning "yes, indeed." This particle is independent of the following predication. It might be thought of as a predication in its own right.

tuləʔibəš

See (3).

tiʔił bəščəb

See (1).

(5) ləʔibəš tiʔəʔ bəščəb — Mink was traveling

The structure of this predication is the same as the preceding except for the absence of *ʔi.*

Time is not an obligatory category, and here, as often, the raconteuse has elected to omit *tu-* from the predicate. See *tu-* in (3).

tiʔəʔ

Demonstrative "this." Compare *tiʔił* in (1). The demonstratives *tiʔəʔ* "this" and *tiʔił* "that" often lack much deictic force in the old stories where time and place are either unknown or unimportant. Consequently, they are often used more or less interchangeably.

(6) gʷəl huy, łčisəxʷ — And then he came upon him

gʷəl huy

Sentential particles meaning approximately "and then." They are outside the predication. (The /h/ of *huy* "then" is seldom articulated following *gʷəl* "and.") Compare *gʷəl hay* in (12).

łčisəxʷ

Predicate serving as the sole member of the predication; the patient is not expressed. This predicate has two constituents: a predicate head, the verb *łčis*, and the enclitic *-əxʷ*.

łčis

A transitive verb consisting of the stem *łčił* "arrive" and the transitive suffix *-s*. The stem suffix *-il* is pronounced /-i/ before the transitive suffix *-s* (but remains /-il/ before the sound /s/ representing other suffixes or parts of suffixes. That is, the change from /-il/ to /-i-/ is morphologically—not phonologically—conditioned.

-əxʷ

Enclitic meaning that a new act or condition is now in effect at the time in focus. Often translated as "now."

(7) bəqadadidəxʷ [ʔə] tiʔəʔ [s]əsq̓ʷəlb [ʔə ti] luX̌
ʔə tiʔəʔ sʔuladxʷ, tiʔił bəščəb

Again he stole an old man's roasting salmon, Mink (did)

This predication has two principal constituents plus a tail. The principal parts are the predicate, *bəqadadidəxʷ*, and the oblique complement, *ʔə ti luX̌ ʔə tiʔəʔ sʔuladxʷ*. The tail, an afterthought to the predication, is *tiʔił bəščəb*, which here expresses the agent. A direct complement of the secondary stem *qadadi-d* designates the one who suffers from the stealing and NOT the item stolen. The object(s) taken are conveyed by an oblique complement. In this particular line, however (and the one following), the storyteller has elected to omit the direct complement. (The would-be referent comes to light in the long oblique complement anyway.)

bəqadadidəxʷ

A predicate having only one member, the predicate head, which has the following structure:

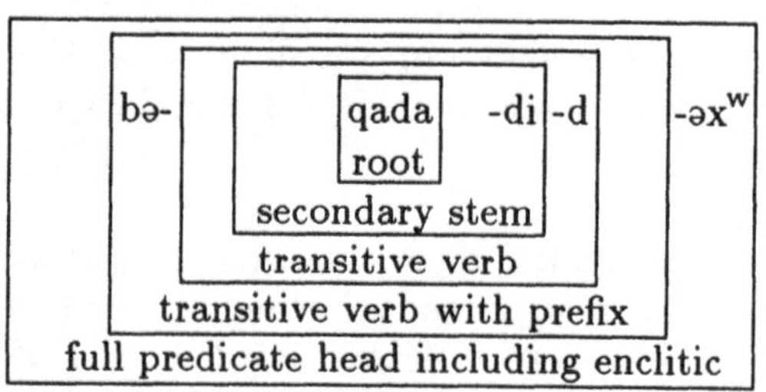


It means, approximately, "now he stole from someone again." Compare *ləkʷyidəxʷ* in (11).

qada-di-

Secondary stem built on the root *qada(ʔ)* "steal" with the secondary suffix *-di-*.

-d

The transitive suffix *-d* built on *qadadi-*.

bə-

General prefix meaning "again/anew."

-əxʷ

See *-əxʷ* in (6).

<u>ʔə tiʔəʔ səsq̓ʷəlb ʔə ti luƛ̓ ʔə tiʔəʔ sʔuladxʷ</u>

Oblique complement naming the item stolen.

<u>ʔə</u>

Preposition introducing a variety of oblique or satellite notions. In this case it provides for explicit mention of the item taken—which is not in direct focus with *qadadid*.

<u>tiʔəʔ səsq̓ʷəlb ʔə ti luƛ̓ ʔə tiʔəʔ sʔuladxʷ</u>

Complement of the preposition *ʔə*, perhaps best rendered in English as "an old man's roasting salmon." This complement has two immediate constituents: the demonstrative *tiʔəʔ* (See *tiʔəʔ* in [5]) and the rest, which fills the role of complement head but is itself an embedded predication.

<u>səsq̓ʷəlb ʔə ti luƛ̓ ʔə tiʔəʔ sʔuladxʷ</u>

Embedded predication with the predicate inflected for embedding in oblique complements by means of the complement prefix *s-*. Often predicates bearing a complement prefix are marked for person with complement person affixes. In the case of third person, this affix is the suffix *-s*. Here in lieu of a suffix marking person, the oblique construction *ʔə* (+ dem.) + noun renders explicit that the third person is involved. Compare *ʔə tiʔəʔ səsq̓ʷəlbs ʔə tiʔił sʔuladxʷ* in (8).

<u>ʔəsq̓ʷəlb ti luƛ̓ ʔə tiʔəʔ sʔuladxʷ</u>

The embedded predication above as it would be stated in an independent sentence. It means, "The old man roasted a salmon." There are three principle constituents: the predicate, *ʔəsq̓ʷəlb*, the direct complement expressing agent, *ti luƛ̓*, and the oblique complement giving patient, *ʔə tiʔəʔ sʔuladxʷ*.

<u>ʔəsq̓ʷəlb</u>

A predicate having only one member, the predicate head, which means, roughly, "be roasted/ roasting." It consists of a medio-passive stem and an aspectual prefix *as-*, which is pronounced /ʔəs-/ when initial.

<u>ʔəs-</u>

The stative prefix *as-*.

q̓ʷəlb

A medio-passive stem comprising the root *q̓ʷəl*, "cook/hot/ripe," and the middle voice suffix *-b*.

ti luƛ̓

Direct complement expressing agent, meaning "the old man."

ti

Demonstrative.

luƛ̓

The complement head is luƛ̓ "old/old person/elder."

ʔə tiʔəʔ sʔuladxʷ

Oblique complement expressing patient of non-transitive predicate. Its immediate constituents are the preposition *ʔə* and *tiʔəʔ sʔuladxʷ*.

ʔə

See *ʔə* above. In this case it provides for the specific mention of the patient with a predicate that is not transitive.

tiʔəʔ sʔuladxʷ

Complement of the preposition *ʔə* meaning "this salmon/a salmon." The complement of a preposition is structurally identical to direct complements. Thus, *tiʔəʔ sʔuladxʷ* is grammatically similar to *tiʔił bəščəb* in (1) and *ti luƛ̓* just above.

tiʔił bəščəb

Tail of predication meaning "Mink" (literally, "that Mink"). It is an afterthought expressing the agent. Third person agents are usually not included with transitive predicates and ordinarily can be only by means of *-b* following the transitive suffix. The tail is not an integral part of the predication. In structure, this one is a direct complement.

(8) qadadid [ʔə] tiʔəʔ [s]əsq̓ʷəlb[s] ʔə tiʔił sʔuladxʷ ʔal tiʔəʔ huds
He stole the salmon which [the old man] was roasting on his fire

This predication has three principal constituents: the predicate, *qadadid*, the oblique complement, *ʔə tiʔəʔ səsq̓ʷəlbs ʔə tiʔił sʔuladxʷ*, and a second oblique complement giving location, *ʔal tiʔəʔ huds*.

qadadid

See *qada-di* and *-d* in (7).

ʔə tiʔəʔ səsq̓ʷəlbs ʔə tiʔəʔ sʔuladxʷ

Oblique complement with embedded predication. It is identical to the oblique complement in (7) except that the agent of the embedded predicate is conveyed by the third person complement suffix *-s* rather than explicitly by an oblique complement.

ʔal tiʔəʔ huds

Oblique complement expressing the source of the stolen item, "on his fire." The structure is identical to *ʔə tiʔəʔ sʔuladxʷ* in (7).

ʔal

Preposition meaning "on."

huds

Head of the oblique complement consisting of the root *hud* "fire/burn/(fire)wood" and the third person complement suffix *-s*, here meaning "his."

(9) gʷəl tuʔitutəxʷ tiʔəʔ lux̌ — For this old man had fallen asleep

gʷəl

Sentential particle meaning "and/but/or/because/of" and similar narrative sentential concepts.

tuʔitutəxʷ

Sole member of predicate meaning "(he) had fallen asleep." The root is *ʔitut* "sleep." See *tu-* in (3) and *-əxʷ* in (6).

tiʔəʔ lux̌

Direct complement of the predicate.

(10) gʷəl huy łčiləxʷ tiʔəʔ gət, tiʔəʔ cədił bəščəb — And then this guy, Mink, arrived

gʷəl huy

See *gʷəl huy* in (6).

łčiləxʷ tiʔəʔ gət, tiʔəʔ cədił bəščəb

This predication is equivalent to the one in line (6), but here the predicate is not transitive and the agent is stated explicitly twice—the second mention being in apposition to the first.

łčiləxʷ

Intransitve verb meaning "arrive," serving as head and sole member of the predicate. Compare *łčisəxʷ* ff. in (6).

tiʔəʔ gət

Direct complement expressing agent. Compare (5) above.

gət

Head of direct complement meaning "guy/fellow." It is mildly disrespectful of or indifferent to the referent.

tiʔəʔ cədił bəščəb

Direct complement in apposition to *tiʔəʔ gət.* Complements are sometimes expanded with one deictic word (very rarely two) in addition to the demonstrative. These deictic words can be from several different, very small classes. In this complement, *cədił* is an example.

cədił

Modifier of complement head that imparts a mild focusing to that head, "this very mink/this same mink/this particular mink." With some speakers, however, including this raconteuse, *cədił* is usually little more than a rhythmic filler, not unlike "here" in some English dialects in phrases like "this here book." Compare the similar use of *diʔəʔ* in texts 5 and 6.

(11) huy, lək̓ʷyidəxʷ [ʔə] tiʔəʔ cədił tə[s]əsq̓ʷəlb[s] ʔə tiʔił sʔuladxʷ

Then he (Mink) instead of him (the old man) ate that roasted salmon

This predication has two principal constituents, the predicate *lək̓ʷyidəxʷ* and the oblique complement *ʔə tiʔəʔ cədił təsəsq̓ʷəlbs ʔə tiʔił sʔuladxʷ*.

huy

See *gʷəl huy* in (6).

lək̓ʷyidəxʷ

Head and sole member of the predicate having the following structure:

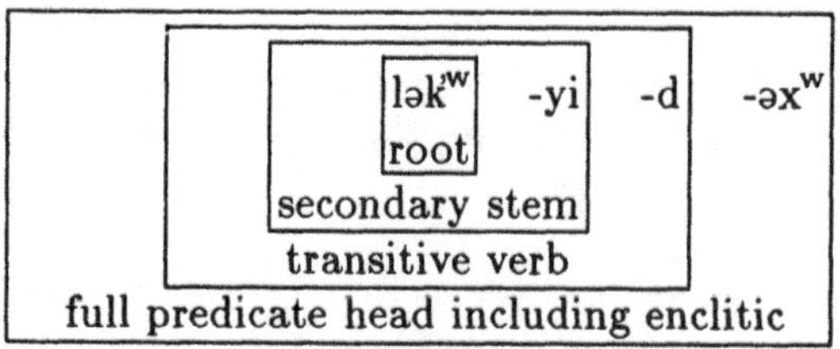


(Compare *bəqadadidəxʷ* in [7].) It means approximately, "Now someone other than the expected or normal agent ate something." A free and colloquial English rendering might be "he ate it out from under him" or "he ate it from under his very nose."

ləḱʷ-yi-

Secondary stem built on the root *ləḱʷ* "put in mouth/ eat" with the secondary suffix *-yi*, which means that the agent is different from the customary or anticipated one.

-d-

The transitive suffix *-d* built on *ləḱʷyi-*.

-əxʷ

See *-əxʷ* in (6).

ʔə tiʔəʔ cədił təsəsq̓ʷəlbs ʔə tiʔił sʔuladxʷ

Oblique complement required of *-yi-* predicates to express time transferred. With the exception of three very superficial differences, it is the same as the oblique complement in (8). These differences are the addition of *cədił*, the addition of *tə-* (from *tu-*) to the embedded prefix, and the change from *tiʔəʔ* to *tiʔił*.

cədił

See *cədił* in (10).

təsəsq̓ʷəlbs

Head of embedded predicate. It has the following structure:

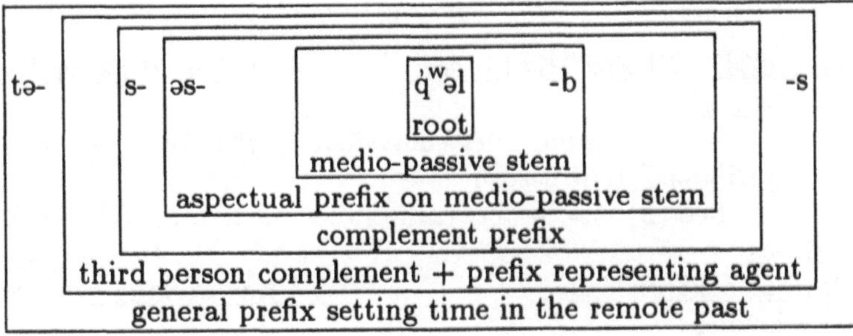


tə-

General prefix designating past time. It has the form of *tə-* instead of *tu-* when preceding inflectional prefixes that are consonant initial. Compare *tu-* in (3).

(12) gʷəl hay, huy tiʔəʔ sʔəłəds — And next he finished (off) his food

gʷəl hay

Sentential particles meaning approximately "and next." They are outside the predication. (The /h/ of *hay* "next" is seldom articulated following *gʷəl* "and.") Compare *gʷəl huy* in (6).

huy tiʔəʔ sʔəɬəds

Predication with two principal constituents. The predicate *huy* and direct complement *tiʔəʔ sʔəɬəds.*

huy

Predicate head and sole member of the predicate. It consists of a single morpheme, the root, meaning "make, do; finish." This last gloss is usually the appropriate one when, as here, the root lacks derivational and inflectional suffixes. (This morpheme is different from *huy* "then" discussed in [6] and [11].)

tiʔəʔ sʔəɬəds

Direct complement meaning "his food."

sʔəɬəds

Complement head made up of the root *ʔəɬəd* "eat" and the complement prefix *s-* to which the third person complement suffix *-s* is added.

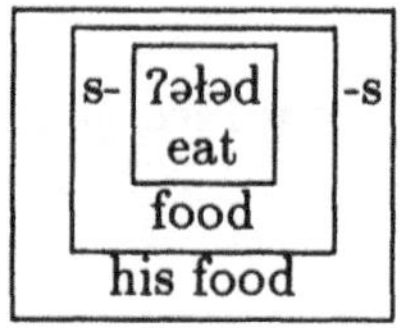


(13) huy gʷəl bəʔibəšəxʷ tiʔiɬ bəščəb — And then Mink walked on

huy gʷəl

Sentential particles equivalent to *gʷəl huy.* (See [6].)

bəʔibəšəxʷ tiʔiɬ bəščəb

See (3), *bə-* in (7), *-əxʷ* in (6) and *tiʔiɬ bəščəb* in (1).

(14) ləʔibəš — He was walking

(15) ləʔibəš bək̓ʷ dxʷčad — He was walking everywhere

ləʔibəš

See (5).

bək̓ʷ dxʷčad

Locative augment meaning "to(ward) everywhere." This constituent has two components, the head *dxʷčad* and the modifier *bək̓ʷ*.

dxʷčad

Head of the locative augment having two morphemes, *dxʷ-* and *čad.*

dxʷ-

Derivational prefix meaning "toward/to."

čad

Locative and interrogative root meaning "where."

bəkʷ

"all/every" This root occurs in a variety of syntactic roles, e.g. head of predicate, head of complement, modifier of complement head, adverb, and, as here, modifier of the head of a locative augment.

(16) xʷuʔələʔ ʔa kʷi səʔibəšs ʔal tiʔəʔ liɬʔilgʷiɬ ʔə tə x̌ʷəlč

I guess he was there walking along the shore of the sea

xʷuʔələʔ

Modal particle expressing indefiniteness and meaning approximately "I guess" or "maybe." It occurs as a component of predicates, of complements, and as here, it can modify an entire predication.

ʔa

Predicate having just one constituent, the predicate head. It is a locative meaning "be there." Compare *ʔacəc* in (1).

kʷi səʔibəšs ʔal tiʔəʔ liɬʔilgʷiɬ ʔə tə x̌ʷəlč

Direct complement consisting of an embedded sentence *ləʔibəš ʔal tiʔəʔ liɬʔilgʷiɬ ʔə tə x̌ʷəlč* "he was walking along the shore of the sea," wherein *ləʔibəš* is the predicate followed by an oblique complement, which is further expanded by another oblique complement.

kʷi

Demonstrative introducing direct complement. It differs from all previous demonstratives in this text by adding to the complement an idea of the hypothetical or the vague and remote.

səʔibəšs

Predicate head and sole member of the predicate of the embedded sentence serving as the complement to *ʔa* "he was there." It is inflected for the progressive aspect by the prefix *(l)ə-*. This formation bears the complement prefix *s-*, which, with the third person agents, requires *-s*, the complement affix of third person reference.

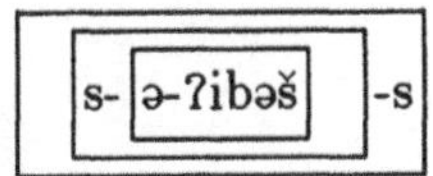


ə-

Allomorph of *lə-* "progressive" (see [3]), which occurs following the complement prefixes *s-* and *dəxʷ-*.

ʔal tiʔəʔ lił̣ʔilgʷił ʔə tə x̌ʷəlč

Sequence of two oblique complements, the first of which is expanded by the second.

ʔal tiʔəʔ lił̣ʔilgʷił

Oblique complement expressing location, "along the shore."

ʔal

Preposition that typically introduces locative and temporal phrases.

tiʔəʔ

See *tiʔəʔ* in (4).

lił̣ʔilgʷił

The head of complement meaning "along (the) shore." The stem, *ʔilgʷił*, means "shore."

lił-

Derivational prefix meaning "by way of/along/by means of."

ʔə tə x̌ʷəlč

Oblique complement expressing a genitive relationship. It means "of the sea."

ʔə

Same preposition as in (7), but here conveying a genitive relation.

tə x̌ʷəlč

Complement of the preposition *ʔə*. Compare *tiʔəʔ sʔuladxʷ* in (7).

tə

Demonstrative.

x̌ʷəlč

Complement head meaning "sea/ocean."

# ANNOTATOR'S INTRODUCTION

T. C. S. Langen

## i

The endnotes and introductions to individual texts in this volume are the result of the following process: Hess, Hilbert, Bates, and Bierwert went through the texts, writing down on note cards items for which they thought the general reader might be glad of some explanation. Many of the items noted were ethnographic, but there were also notes on translations and transcriptions, on the Lushootseed canon and lexicon, and on transmission and collection history. The cards were passed along to the annotator with the request that they be used as the basis for endnotes and a short introduction to each text. Ethnographic background for the general reader was treated in the introductions; more specific details were dealt with in the endnotes.

As it was first conceived, this volume was to provide an annotated discussion of the "literary" qualities of each story. Considerations of space, however, have constrained the editor to limit this discussion to part ii of this introduction and the commentary for text 1, which alone appears with the kind of annotation originally envisioned for all of the stories. Detailed analyses of text 2 may be found in Bierwert (1991), and in Langen (1989b, forthcoming). Essays on texts 5–7 are in preparation.

## ii

This introduction to Lushootseed narrative practice makes use of the following terms: "circular figure," "concentric figure," "hysteron-proteron," "parallelism," "interlocking repetition," and "pattern story."

The elements of a circular figure are arranged in the order **A1**, **B**, **A2**, with **A1** and **A2** constituting the circumference of the figure and **B** its core. **A1** and **A2** are usually single statements that echo each other, while the core of a figure may be several statements long:

**A1** gʷəl (h)uy, łčísəxʷ.
**B** bəqádadidəxʷ [ʔə] tíʔəʔ [s]əsq̓ʷə́lb [ʔə ti] luƛ̓ ʔə tíʔəʔ sʔuládxʷ, tiʔíł bə́ščəb.
**B** qádadid [ʔə] tíʔəʔ [s]əsq̓ʷə́lb[s] ʔə tiʔíł sʔuládxʷ ʔal tíʔəʔ huds.
**B** gʷəl tuʔítutəxʷ < ti...,> tíʔəʔ luƛ̓.
**A2** gʷəl (h)uy łčíləxʷ tíʔəʔ gət, tíʔəʔ cədíł bə́ščəb.

And then he came upon someone.
As usual he stole the salmon that the old man was roasting, that Mink.
He stole that salmon that he was roasting on his fire.
And this old man was asleep,

And then this guy came, this certain Mink.

(text 1a, lines 6–10)

[The mirror-image arrangements here were developed by Bridget Hayden. –Ed.]

**A1** and **A2** are usually repetitions or parallel versions of each other. When they repeat the same ideas couched in different words or in a different syntactical form, then the passage is referred to as circular in organization, not as a circular figure. A passage that is circular in organization but incorporates extraneous material into the circumference or has a discursive core is referred to as circular narration.

When the core of a circular figure is restated after **A2**, the figure is said to be capped. Here is the cap to the circular figure quoted above:

huy ləǩʷyídəxʷ [ʔə] tiʔə́ʔ cədíɬ tə[s]əsq̓ʷə́lb[s] ʔə tiʔíɬ sʔuládxʷ.
gʷəl (h)ay, huy tíʔəʔ sʔə́ɬəds.

Then he ate the salmon himself that someone else was roasting.
And then, his food was gone.

(text 1a, lines 11–12)

When the subject matter of the core is taken up at some length or further developed after the circular figure, the figure is said to have a pendant. (An example of a figure with a pendant, too long to quote here, may be found in text 2: lines 164–168 constitute the circular figure, and the pendant is in lines 169–176.)

A circular figure is said to be weighted when the information in the core makes **A2**—though it may on its surface be no more than a repetition of **A1**—more or differently meaningful from **A1**. In the following example, *ʔəs(h)áydxʷ* in **A2** is understood to be supernatural knowledge, whereas in **A1**, it might have been taken to be only hearsay:

**A1** ʔəs(h)áydub ʔə tiʔíɬ cədíɬ bə́ščəb.
**B** huy, x̌əɬ ti bədxʷqáhigʷəd tiʔíɬ bəščəb.
**B** x̌əɬ ti b(ə)asdúkʷil.
**A2** ʔəs(h)áydxʷ tiʔíɬ ƛ̕əsəʔíbəš ʔə tiʔíɬ dúkʷibəɬ.

That old Mink knew.
Because, Mink was sort of clever.
He was sort of supernatural.
He knew that Changer would be walking about.

(text 1a, lines 61–64)

Circular figures, as well as passages of circular organization or circular narration, may be juxtaposed, (**A1 core A2**, **C1 core C2**), overlapping (when the **A1** of the second is the **A2** of the first: **A1 core A2**

(= **C1**) **core C2**) and even interlocking (when the second is begun before the first has been closed: **A1 core C1 A2 core C2**).

When overlapped or interlocking circular figures contain interstitial material to the extent that the circular feel of the narration is diminished to a sense of simple recurrence, then we may speak of interlace. A structure [**A1 C1 core** (interstitial material) **A2 core C2**], then, may be considered either as interlocking circular narration or as interlace, depending on the way it works where it occurs. Interlace is the alternating of elements in rhythmic succession over a stretch of narrative, with or without interstitial material. The term is used to refer to the alternation of plot elements; the alternation of motifs or concepts is referred to as rhythm.

Some circular figures may be seen as simple framing devices. This is especially true of figures in which the circumference encircles a speech: he said—"speech"—this is what he said. We refer to this device as "speech-framing." In general, when a circular figure has as its core a set piece complete in itself, the circular figure is considered a frame.

There is an elaborated form of the circular figure, the concentric figure, in which one circle is found inside another. The elements of the concentric figure are in the order **A1**, **B1** ... X ... **B2**, **A2**. The core, X, may be any length, but the A and B elements are usually one statement long. (The ellipsis points indicate that concentric figures may have varying numbers of rings, not just two, although Lushootseed examples most frequently have only two rings.) Here is an example of a concentric figure from text 2:

| | | |
|---|---|---|
| **A1** | hay gʷəl ʔúlułəxʷ tsíʔəʔ k̓áʔk̓aʔ. | So then Crow travels on the water. |
| **B1** | cick̓ʷ haʔł sləx̌íl. | The day is very bright. |
| **X** | ʔəsháʔləb. | It is calm. |
| **B2** | pu·t (h)aʔł sləx̌íl. | The day is intensely bright. |
| **A2** | huy ʔúlułəxʷ. | Thus she travels. |
| | (text 2, lines 9–13) | |

Concentric figures may be weighted or overlapping like circular figures, and they may have caps or pendants. If interstitial material (IM) occurs between the rings of a figure (**A1 B1 X B2 IM A2**), the passage is termed "concentric narration" (see text 1, lines 89–97). If the rings are conceptually, but not verbally, parallel, the passage is considered to be concentrically organized, rather than strictly figured (See text 1b, lines 29–44). Concentric figures have been much discussed by critics working with a variety of literatures, and a variety of terms have been employed, among them "ring composition," "annular structure" and "enveloping" (see, e.g., Thalmann 1984, Dunn 1988).

The hysteron-proteron figure (its name means "last first") is composed of two elements: **A B** and **B A**:

**AB** qʷiqʷqʷistáy̓bixʷ mám̓ad ʔáciłtalbixʷ.
**BA** mám̓ad ʔácʔaciłtalbixʷ tiʔił qʷiqʷqʷistáy̓bixʷ.

The little people are dwarfs.
The dwarfs are a lot of little people.

(text 7, lines 427 and 429)

For obvious reasons, the figure is rarely more than two statements in length. (The example quoted here uses the elements of the hysteron-proteron themselves to form a circular figure around line 428: "*tux̌ʷ (h)uy lúƛ̓luƛ̓.*" ["But they are adults"].) We may see in the hysteron-proteron something very similar to a simple circular figure with a reduplicated core (**A B**, **B A** thought of as **A1 BB A2**), and in fact some of the figures analyzed here as circular are also analyzable as hysteron-proteron. The criterion used in the present analysis has been that if a figure were static or rhetorical only, it was called hysteron-proteron; if it were reiterative in the service of the development of characterization, plot, or point of view, it was called circular.

Parallelism is the part-variable repetition of elements in a passage when that passage does not constitute an entire episode. I use the term "parallelism" as it is used in the study of folklore, to refer not only to verbal echo but also to scenes and content, and not as it is used in the study of biblical parallelism, to refer only to the relationship between pairs of lines (cf. Berlin 1985). I use the term "augmenting repetition" to refer to repetition in which the element is repeated with the addition of new information: gʷəl (h)uy, łčísəxʷ . . . gʷəl (h)uy łčíləxʷ tíʔəʔ gət, tíʔəʔ cədíł bə́ščəb (text 1, lines 6 and 10). Parallelism may also involve the incremental addition of elements, as found in lines from two proximate passages of text 1a, below. [The numbers in parentheses at the ends of lines indicate the comparable lines in the variant passage -Ed.]

| | |
|---|---|
| 73 huy, ʔúx̌ʷəxʷ lił t̓áq̓t. | 82 huy gʷəl ʔux̌ʷ dxʷt̓áq̓t, lił t̓aq̓t. |
| 74 gʷəl ləʔúx̌ʷ. | 83 gʷəl ʔu·x̌ʷ. |
| | 84 ləbíʔbəlx̌ʷəd. |
| 75 gʷəl → ləhúyud tíʔəʔ qʷuʔ. | 85 huy <k̓ʷəł> húyudəxʷ tiʔəʔ qʷuʔ. |
| 76 húyud tíʔəʔ qʷuʔ. | |
| 77 ʔuk̓ʷə́ł dxʷčáʔkʷ. | 86 k̓ʷłáxʷ tiʔəʔ qʷuʔ dxʷčaʔkʷ. |
| | 87 x̌əł ti p̓áƛ̓aƛ̓. |
| | 88 ƛ̓uk̓ʷə́ł dxʷčaʔkʷ. |

. . .

| | |
|---|---|
| 73 Then he went up along the bluff. | 82 And then he went upland up along the bluff. |
| 74 And he was going. | 83 And he went. |
| | 84 He went a little past him. |
| 75 And he was making water. | 85 Then, he made water. |
| 76 He made water. | |
| 77 It spilled down toward the sea. | 86 This water spilled down to the sea. |
| | 87 It wasn't much, just a "little water." |
| | 88 It would spill down to the sea. |

(text 1a, lines 73–77 and 82–88)

Interlocking repetition, a specialized form of parallelism, involves a series of pairs of repeated items in which the last element of the former pair becomes the first element of the next pair [(**A**) **A B**, **B C**, **C D**, etc.: jumped up; jumped up and ran out; ran out and began calling, etc.]. Interlocking repetition is a subcategory of a device called incremental repetition, which uses the technique not only with individual words, but also with plot elements (see the example given to illustrate parallelism above).

When a passage constituting an entire episode is repeated with elements varied, it is called a pattern-story. In text 2, Crow goes in search of a husband. As she makes her way along the coast, various suitors come down to the shore, only to be rejected. Each suitor's episode is told according to the same pattern; and in each, some of the same statements are repeated. The variations occur in the identities of the suitors, the reasons for rejection, and the abbreviation or elaboration of personal descriptions and speeches.

In the notes to the first text in this volume, all of the formal features discussed above have been identified as they occur and (space permitting) portions of them quoted so as to help the reader to locate them. The discussion of formal features in the first set of texts has been kept at the descriptive level; readers interested in a more analytical approach are referred to the appropriate publications, when such exist, in the suggestions for further reading appended to the introduction to each text. Notes to later stories refer to narrative figures, but the reader is left to identify them more precisely. For texts 5 and 7 formal features are located in the schematic analyses preceding the texts.

Most of the texts in this volume have been divided into lines for the purposes of grammatical analysis, and it has been convenient to refer to the line numbers in the course of discussing formal features of the narratives. But the line divisions do not always correspond to the pauses and other formal devices used by the narrators, and so from time to time the discussion in the notes will concern itself with a narrative shape that is not reflected in the formatting of the text.

## iii

One aspect of the formal analysis of the stories undertaken in this volume is an attempt to see Lushootseed literature in the context of the world's literary heritage. Readers may find it interesting to turn to works that deal with the qualities of oral narrative as they appear in other literatures.

A short introductory discussion of structured repetition, both circular and linear, is to be found in the first chapter of William Thalmann's *Conventions of Form and Thought in Early Greek Epic Poetry* (1984). Robert Alter in *The Art of Biblical Narrative* (1981) discusses, among others, these topics that will interest readers of Lushootseed stories: characterization and reticence, the alternation of scene and summary, the use of direct speech, and the type-scene. There are numerous parallels in narrative practice between Tlingit literature and Lushootseed, as readers of Haa Shuka's *Our Ancestors: Tlingit Oral Narratives*, edited by Nora Marks Dauenhauer and Richard Dauenhauer (1987) will discover. Critical essays that attempt to consider Native American oral literature in comparison to other literary traditions are hard to find, but Karl Kroeber has written two: "Poem, Dream and the Consuming of Culture" (1978) and "Deconstructionist Criticism and American Indian Literature" (1979).

Like all literatures, that of the Lushootseed people rewards many different critical approaches. Perhaps the best-known analyst of Native American transcribed literature is Dell Hymes, whose method is to divide stories into acts, scenes, and verses and to arrange these elements on the page in a fashion designed to show their relationships within an organizational hierarchy. More than any other scholar, Hymes has insisted on the duty of the literary critic to approach the text in its original language; and his method of text formatting makes it possible for a critic (or any reader) who does not know the language in question nonetheless to see structural and rhetorical features of the original. An essential collection of Hymes's essays is *"In Vain I Tried to Tell You": Essays in Native American Ethnopoetics* (D. Hymes 1981). A good short introduction to the Hymesian method, showing how it can work along with a consideration of more purely literary values, is Virginia Hymes's "Warm Springs Sahaptin Narrative Analysis (V. Hymes 1987).

Another influential analyst of Native American literature is Dennis Tedlock, whose primary goal has been to reflect on the printed page the sound of the story as it is spoken, so that readers who have never heard the story they are looking at can nonetheless read it aloud and replicate some features of the spoken original. A collection of Tedlock's essays is *The Spoken Word and the Work of Interpretation* (1983).

Two recent attempts to deal with the concerns of both Hymes and Tedlock together are to be found in Anthony Woodbury's analysis of a Central Alaskan Yupik story, in which a Hymesian analysis is annotated to show the acoustic features of the spoken version (Woodbury 1987); and in M. Dale Kinkade's "Bluejay and His Sister," in which the line divisions of a Hymesian analysis are checked against the pauses heard in the tape-recorded original (Kinkade 1987). Some interesting criticism of the approaches of both Hymes and Tedlock is provided by Anthony Mattina in "Native American Indian Mythography" (1987), in which he questions, among other things, the assumption of both scholars that because they can divide the texts into lines, the texts must be poetry. [The reader may be interested to know that among those who have worked on the present volume there exists a diversity of opinion on this question. But it should be borne in mind that the lineation used in the texts presented in the present volume is based on analytical convenience, not poetic principles.] A recent and persuasive discussion of meter in a Native American story is John Dunn's "Aesthetic Properties of a Coast Tsimshian Text Fragment" (1988).

Because many of the stories studied by scholars of Native American literature are preserved only in transcriptions, performance analyses are relatively rare. Two interesting ones, however, are available: a recent performance analysis of a videotaped storytelling, Andrew Wiget's "Telling the Tale: A Performance Analysis of a Hopi Coyote Story" (1987), which discusses the contribution to the storytelling event of such things as gestures, the storyteller's laughter, and audience reaction; and Regna Darnell's "Correlates of Cree Narrative Performance" (1974), which brings information about the relationships between audience members and the storyteller into play to explain why a story is told in a certain way.

Several collections of essays about Native American traditional literatures are available: *Traditional American Indian Literatures: Texts and Interpretations* (Kroeber 1981), *Smoothing the Ground: Essays on Native American Oral Literature* (Swann 1983), and *Recovering the Word: Essays on Native American Literature* (Swann and Krupat 1987). All contain discussions of transcription and translation problems, as well as analyses of individual texts and suggestions for further reading. Additional literary commentary that includes some work on translations is available in *New Voices in Native American Literary Criticism* (Krupat

1993). A collection of translated texts accompanied by essays on the translation of Native American traditional literatures is *On the Translation of Native American Literatures*, edited by Brian Swann (1992).

## MARTHA LAMONT'S CHANGER STORY

### INTRODUCTION

In Lushootseed, as in other Northwest Coast literatures, stories about the Changer constitute a genre, and part of their function is to distinguish between the present time and a time long ago when there were not the separate categories "people" and "animals," but everyone was both. At some point in Lushootseed time, the Changer ***dukʷibəɬ*** appeared, stalking through the world and asking everyone, "What are you doing?" Depending on their responses, he then decided for them what their future characteristic activity in the world would be. A Changer story usually contains several short episodes told in parallel narration (like the third part of "Martha Lamont's Changer Story") with very little character development. The more involved characterizations in Mrs. Lamont's first two sections are unusual.

People in Lushootseed literature can also be changed from the way they were to the way they are now without the agency of ***dukʷibəɬ*** or any other character. In one story, for example, Raven, who is always greedy, gets some food caught in his throat; he flies up into the smoke hole, choking; his voice turns gravelly, the way it is today, and the smoke stains his white feathers black. If a character has a definite personality and a story is well-constructed, the character will display his typical flaws or virtues so that he seems to be felt to have earned the reward or punishment that may come to him. There is no need for a Changer to decide what should happen. Some stories, however, try to account for many people's being changed within a short time of each other, and in this case there is a need for a single agent who affects many different characters.

"Martha Lamont's Changer Story" is one that incorporates such a series of changes. Though the story is presented in this volume with graphic breaks demarcating three separate sections, it should be noted that as Mrs. Lamont tells it, there is virtually no pause between the first two sections: the last line of "Mink and Changer" and the first line of "Crow and Raven" are rendered as if they were one sentence. Between the last line of "Crow and Raven" and the first of "The Wolf Brothers" there is a slight pause, but not so long as a typical pause after ***huy gʷəl***. In a narrative whose parts are so closely knit together at the level of sound, one expects easily to identify some conceptual or formal unifying principle, such as narrative point of view. But narrative point of view is not a unifying principle in this story. In the first section, which is dominated by the personality of Mink, the point of view shifts between Mink and Changer a number of times; the second section is told from the point of view of Changer, who is watching, though he is scarcely even referred to in the narration; during the first half of the third section, Changer is still watching, but then he enters the story, and the point of view becomes that of the storyteller. When she finishes her narration of all three sections, Mrs. Lamont says "*gʷəl diɬ [...] tu(s)šaćs tiʔiɬ d(ə)čuʔ syəyəhub.*" ("And that [...] is the end of that one story.")

Like *dukʷibəɬ*, many other characters in "Martha Lamont's Changer Story" appear over and over again in other stories. Mink is one of the most important characters in Lushootseed literature. Like Raven and only a few others, he has developed a personality that exists independently of any one story. When a narrator mentions Mink's name, the audience already knows all about him. Although in the myth time everyone had supernatural powers, Mink stands out even in this company for his intelligence and practical ability, which includes expertise in impersonation, as well as in what might be called "magic": making things appear and disappear, for instance. As one might expect from a person with the abilities of a mink, he is an excellent broken-field runner: stories about his escaping from irate pursuers or absconding with stolen articles are numerous. Mink's love of female companionship repeatedly gets him into trouble. As distinct from Raven, whose tricks are frequently motivated by greed, Mink is most often moved to some mischief by a spirit of fun; and, while some stories show Mink engaged in activities for which we have no sympathy, he is most often seen as amiable. In encounters with the Changer—including Mrs. Lamont's—he is powerful enough almost to get the better of *dukʷibəɬ*.

Raven is the best-known character in Lushootseed literature. He is sometimes called "the Creator" and may be a coworker with *dukʷibəɬ*; an often-told story, for example, credits him with bringing daylight to the world (sometimes Mink is his partner; see Hilbert 1980:107–109). But, despite his importance, Raven is never shown as august. He is a miscreant, with gluttony his chief motive in life. Not only does he never share food (a very significant failing in terms of Lushootseed values); he never shares the credit for any accomplishment, especially if the credit really belongs to someone else. He is lazy, cowardly, irresponsible, vainglorious, and his manners are terrible. Unlike Mink, who uses his knowledge of other people in order to devise a way to trick them, Raven is basically uninterested in others. His fatuous, raucous way of speaking is easy to mimic, and storytellers do a lot of direct quoting of his words. His unregenerate character is so well known that he has only to promise to carry out a responsibility or to do a favor for someone and the audience will burst out laughing. His outrageous behavior in the second part of Mrs. Lamont's story needs no motivation beyond what people already know of him.

Whenever Raven and Mink appear, they are always male and always the same Raven or Mink who appeared the last time. The character of Crow is much less defined, probably because a crow character may be one of several different people. There is a male Crow who sometimes appears, and there are what seem to be a couple of different female Crows. One is a messenger and, like other birds who act as messengers, she has knowledge of the future. Another is a person with extraordinary powers for getting food (see text 3). This Crow may or may not be associated with Raven; but if she is, she is of higher rank than he. A third Crow is the one we see in this story: she is either Raven's wife or, as here, his sister, and may be badly treated by him. Though she is a cut above her brother, she is not of high rank, as we can see by the fact that she married Slug. (Although the status of myth-age people does not always correspond to the opinion people of the present day have about the animals that bear their names, we may assume Slug was not of high rank: a sure indication of this in the story is that his powers are not strong enough to enable him to complete successfully in even the most work-a-day task of gathering firewood.)

The other characters in the story appear somewhat abruptly in the third part and are not treated as fully as Mink, Raven, and Crow. We may suspect that in a longer telling of this story, Mrs. Lamont might have given us more detailed accounts of Deer, Flounder, and the Wolf brothers before she brought all the characters together in their encounter with ***dukʷibəɬ***. Flounder appears less frequently in the literature than any of the other characters. Unlike Deer and the Wolf brothers (the hunters and quarry around whom the final gathering takes place), she is not necessary to the plot. Her role in this third part of the story parallels the roles of Mink, Raven, and Crow; but, unlike them, she all but admits to the Changer that she has done wrong in sharing the deer meat. Perhaps she is meant to serve as a foil for the others.

Deer appears in the story only as food, more of a plot device here than a character. There is widely told in Lushootseed country another story about Deer, in which he meets but does not recognize ***dukʷibəɬ***. When asked, "What are you doing?" he replies that he is sharpening bones for spearpoints to use against the Changer. (This militant Deer is male, but Deer as quarry is, as in Mrs. Lamont's story, female.) ***dukʷibəɬ*** shoves the bones into Deer's forearms (this is why Deer has sharp bones in his forelegs) and tells him that from now on he will not be a killer, but quarry.

Wolves appear in stories most often as families or groups of brothers out hunting, and they may help hungry people by sharing their kill or by bestowing the power to hunt successfully. In stories in which they meet ***dukʷibəɬ***, they are often charged by him to help the coming generations of hunters. Narratives of their adventures frequently display the "youngest-smartest" pattern, in which the older brothers are killed or defeated but the youngest manages to succeed.

Martha Lamont is the dean of the breathless school of Lushootseed storytelling: once she gets going, she delivers long stretches of narration at breakneck speed without pausing for breath. Her delivery is so rapid, in fact, that some native speakers of Lushootseed have trouble understanding the tape recordings of her storytelling. Those who knew her recall her speaking in a traditional, measured way. Some elders have suggested that she may have spoken so rapidly because the tape recorder made her nervous. It is interesting to note that Mrs. Lamont's stories are among the most densely figured that we have and that this formal regularity was produced at high speed. When Mrs. Lamont does slow down, it is to sum up or quote what a character has said. For these speeches, she places her voice a little higher, lengthens syllables for emphasis (or, frequently, for comic effect) and makes more than usual use of rising and falling vocal inflections. When she wants one utterance to echo another, she will use the same inflection, even though the words may not repeat exactly. Contrary to the practice of other Lushootseed storytellers who seem to provide minor breakpoints in their narratives by using a pause followed by *gʷəl huy* or *huy gʷəl* ("and then"), Mrs. Lamont typically does not pause at all before *gʷəl huy* (which she pronounces as one word). Her pause comes afterward, and thus *gʷəl huy* has less the effect of marking a structural boundary than of providing a momentary suspension during which the story's momentum is not felt to change. For audible formal markers, Mrs. Lamont relies on changes of pitch, the prolonging of vowel sounds, and the repetition of words, phrases, and sound patterns. She does not rely on these more than other storytellers may, but she does rely on them more exclusively.

There were evidently periods in her life during which Mrs. Lamont did not tell the stories she knew. Leon Metcalf, who tape recorded information from her in the fifties, recalls that when Mr. Lamont would come into the room where they were taping, he would often comment that he had never heard his wife tell this or that story before. Yet, despite what may have been years of silence, Mrs. Lamont's delivery was rapid, and her work displays in abundance such features as part-variable repetition, parallel narration, circular and concentric structures, and traditional bridge patterns, preserving these conventions in some stories when other recorded versions have omitted or obscured them. In "Mink and Changer," for example, which is 132 lines long, approximately 67 percent of the lines are the constituents of identifiable narrative figures. One may suspect that Mrs. Lamont's unhesitating delivery depends in no small measure on her sure grasp of literary form.

## A Note on Further Reading

Changer stories are also told by the northern and southern neighbors of the Lushootseed. Like the Lushootseed, other literatures blend the Changer tradition with other creation narratives. An interesting example of the long, multi-episodic kind of Changer story is to be found in *The Faith of a Coast Salish Indian* (Jenness 1955). This story was told by Simon Pierre, one of the Katzie, a Halkomelem-speaking Salish people who live on the Fraser River in southern British Columbia. In Katzie tradition, Changer (Xaals) coexists with a human creative hero, Swaneset. To the south of Puget Sound, Changer's role is taken both by Moon (e.g., Adamson 1934:156–177) and by a culture hero named Xwani (in various spellings; see Adamson 1934:140–155 and 250–267; and Palmer 1925). Some stories told about Mink or Coyote by the Lushootseed are told about Xwani by the Chehalis (e.g., Adamson 1934:146–151) and the Cowlitz (Adamson 1934:263–264). The structure and rhetoric of "Mink and Changer" are discussed in Langen 1989b.

# MARTHA LAMONT'S CHANGER STORY

## EPISODE 1: MINK AND CHANGER

1 There was Mink.
2 Mink was there.
3 He was walking.
4 Yes, Mink was walking.
5 Mink was walking.

6 And then
he came upon someone.
7 As usual, he stole the salmon
that the old man was roasting, that Mink.
8 He stole that salmon
that he was roasting
on his fire.
9 And this old man was asleep.
10 And then
this guy came, this certain Mink.

11 Then he ate the salmon himself
that someone else was roasting.
12 And then, his food was gone.

13 And then
Mink was walking on.
14 He was walking.
15 He was walking everywhere.
16 He must have been walking along
the shore of the Sound.
17 There again he would be up along the bluff,
up along this bluff,
18 down along the water.

## EPISODE 1

1 ʔácəc tiʔíł bə́ščəb.
2 bə́ščəb t[ə ʔ]a; <tul...,>
3 tuləʔíbəš.
4 ʔi·, tuləʔíbəš tiʔíł bə́ščəb. →
5 ləʔíbəš tíʔəʔ bə́ščəb.

ᚁ

6 gʷəl (h)uy,
łčísəxʷ.
7 bəqádadidəxʷ [ʔə] tíʔəʔ [s]əsq̓ʷə́lb [ʔə ti] luƛ̕ →
ʔə tíʔəʔ sʔuládxʷ, tiʔíł bə́ščəb.
8 qádadid → [ʔə] tíʔəʔ [s]əsq̓ʷə́lb[s] →
ʔə tiʔíł sʔuládxʷ
ʔal tíʔəʔ huds. →
9 gʷəl → tuʔítutəxʷ <ti...,> tíʔəʔ luƛ̕. →
10 gʷəl (h)uy
łčíləxʷ tíʔəʔ gət, tíʔəʔ cədíł bə́ščəb.

11 huy → ləkʷ̓yídəxʷ [ʔə] tiʔə́ʔ cədíł tə[s]əsq̓ʷə́lb[s] →
ʔə tiʔíł sʔuládxʷ. →
12 gʷəl (h)ay, huy tíʔəʔ sʔə́łəds.

ᚁ

13 huy gʷəl →
bəʔíbəš tiʔíł bə́ščəb.
14 ləʔíbəš. →
15 ləʔíbəš bəkʷ̓ dxʷčad. →
16 xʷúʔələʔ →
[ʔa kʷi] səʔíbəš[s] ʔal tíʔəʔ liłʔílgʷił ʔə tə x̌ʷə́lč.
17 ʔa kʷi ƛ̕əbəsʔiłƛ̕áq̓ts,
liłʔál tiʔíł ʔiłƛ̕áq̓t. →
18 ʔa kʷi sʔiłčáʔkʷs.

ᚁ

19 Then he got thirsty.
20 He got thirsty.
21 And then
he drank everywhere.
22 He drank everywhere.

23 And then
he arrived at where he arrived.
24 And then
in one certain river,
he found that there were a lot of salmon.
25 Then again he caught a salmon.
26 Then he readied it.
27 Then he roasted it.
28 This certain Mink roasted where he was making
a sort of camp.

29 Then
he was walking along the shore.
30 Mink was all alone.
31 He was not together with *tətyíqa?*, his little younger brother.
32 He was all alone.

33 Then,
Mink slept.
34 And he slept.

19 huy → táqʷuʔəxʷ.
20 táqʷuʔəxʷ. →
21 gʷəl (h)uy,
bəqʷúʔqʷaʔ ʔal tiʔíɬ čad. →
22 bəqʷúʔqʷaʔ ʔal tiʔíɬ čad.

---

23 hay gʷəl
bəɬčíləxʷ dxʷʔal tiʔíɬ bədəxʷƛ̓číls. →
24 gʷəl (h)ay
b(əʔ)əÿdxʷəxʷ tiʔəʔ qa tiʔíɬ sʔuládxʷ →
ʔal tiʔíɬ cədíɬ dəč̓úʔ stúləkʷ. →
25 huy, → bəkʷədálikʷəxʷ ʔə tiʔəʔ sʔuládxʷ. →
26 huy → qʷíbidəxʷ. →
27 huy, → q̓ʷəldáxʷ.
28 q̓ʷəlbáxʷ tíʔəʔ cədíɬ bə́ščəb ʔal tíʔəʔ <dəxʷ. . . ,>
x̌əɬ ti ɬudəxʷq̓ə́lbs.

---

29 huy
ləʔíbəš liɬʔílgʷiɬ. →
30 dádiyəẏ tiʔəʔ bə́ščəb.
31 xʷiʔ gʷəsəsgʷáhtxʷs tiʔíɬ tətyíqaʔ súsuq̓ʷaʔs.
32 dádiyəẏ.

---

33 hay,
ʔítutəxʷ tíʔiɬ bə́ščəb. →
34 gʷəl ʔítutəxʷ.

---

35 It seems that Changer was walking now.
36 Changer was going along the beach.
37 He was walking along that very shore.
38 He was finding the people.
39 He was asking what they were doing.

---

40 And he came upon Mink.
41 He was asleep.
42 I guess this certain Changer had a thought,
43 "That Mink is roasting something really good."
44 This old Changer knew Mink well.

45 Then he had a thought,
46 "I guess I'd better steal what he is roasting
and I'll eat it.
47 for I am hungry."

48 Then he ate this now.
He helped himself to what Mink was roasting.
49 Changer ate now.
50 But I guess he left some trace of the salmon that was roasting.

---

51 And then this certain Changer walked on.
52 He went on ahead.
53 He was walking along the shore of the Sound.
54 There again he would be up along the bluff.
55 And again he would be down along the water,
along the shore.

---

35 gʷəháw̓əʔ ləʔíbəšəxʷ tíʔəʔ dúkʷibəł.
36 lədxʷdᶻálgʷəpəxʷ tíʔəʔ dúkʷibəł. →
37 <lə...,> ləʔíbəšəxʷ ʔal tiʔácəc liłʔílgʷił. →
38 ləʔə́y̓dxʷ tiʔíł ʔáciłtalbixʷ.
39 ləwíliq̓ʷid stab kʷi səshúys. →

---

40 gʷəl łčísəbəxʷ tiʔə́ʔ bə́ščəb.
41 ʔəsʔítut.
42 xʷúʔələ(ʔ) ʔəxʷcútəbitəb ʔə tíʔəʔ cədíł dúkʷibəł.
43 "dáy̓əxʷ (h)aʔł tiʔəʔ səsq̓ʷálb ʔə tiʔácəc bə́ščəb."
44 ʔəs(h)áydub [tiʔəʔ] bə́ščəb ʔə tiʔəʔ cədíł dúkʷibəł.

45 huy dxʷscútəbəxʷ. →
46 "xʷúʔələʔ ƛ̕ub čəd <ʔu...,> bəqádadid ʔə tiʔíł səsq̓ʷálbs
čədá gʷəʔə́łəd. →
47 huy čəd ʔəstágʷəxʷəxʷ."

48a huy, ʔə̀łədáxʷ ʔə tíʔəʔ.
48b kʷədálikʷəxʷ ʔə tíʔəʔ səsq̓ʷálb ʔə tíʔəʔ bə́ščəb.
49 ʔə̀łədáxʷ tíʔəʔ dúkʷibəł.
50 hay, → kʷáʔdəxʷ tiʔíł xʷúʔələ(ʔ) [kʷi] ʔəsʔəx̌íd təsəsq̓ʷálbs →
[ʔə tiʔił] sʔuládxʷ.

---

51 huy gʷəl (h)uy, bəʔíbəšəxʷ tíʔəʔ cədił dúkʷibəł. →
52 bəhíwiləxʷ.
53 ləʔíbəš liłʔílgʷił ʔə tíʔəʔ x̌ʷəlč.
54 <s...ʔu...,> ʔa [kʷi] ƛ̕əbə[s]liłt̕áq̓t[s]. →
55 gʷəl → ƛ̕əbəliłčáʔkʷ kʷi səʔíbəšs →
liłʔílgʷił.

Then Mink woke up.
Then he knew.
"Oh, it was Changer who came to me.
It was that no-good Changer who came to me.
And he ate that food of mine."

That old Mink knew well.
Because Mink was sort of clever.
He was sort of supernatural.
He knew that Changer would be walking about.
He had heard about it.
Changer was walking about.

Then he said,
"That is the one who stole from me.
He is the one who stole."

Mink ran up along the bluff of this place.
Away off there is Changer.
"So! He really was the one who ate that food of mine."

Then he went along up along the bluff.
And he was going.
And he was making water.
He made water.

It spilled down toward the sea.
He knew well.
That old Changer will be wanting water.
He will want water.
Because he had eaten the salmon.

56 huy qɬáx$^{w}$ tíʔəʔ bə́sčəb. →
57 huy, háydx$^{w}$əx$^{w}$.
58 "ʔu·, diɬ k$^{w}$i → dúk$^{w}$ibəɬ k$^{w}$[i ʔ]uɬčísəbš.
59 diɬ k$^{w}$i x$^{w}$iʔ ləháʔɬ dúk$^{w}$ibəɬ k$^{w}$[i ʔ]uɬčísəbš. →
60 g$^{w}$əl lək̓$^{w}$yíc ʔə tiʔiɬ sʔə́ɬəd."

61 ʔəs(h)áydub ʔə tiʔiɬ cədíɬ bə́sčəb. →
62 huy, <x̌əɬ ti bə...,> x̌əɬ ti bədx$^{w}$qáhig$^{w}$əd tiʔiɬ bəsčəb. →
63 x̌əɬ ti b(ə)asdúk$^{w}$il.
64 ʔəs(h)áydx$^{w}$ tiʔiɬ ƛ̕əsəʔíbəš ʔə tiʔiɬ dúk$^{w}$ibəɬ.
65 ʔəslúdx$^{w}$. →
66 ləʔíbəš ti dúk$^{w}$ibəɬ.

67 huy, cútəx$^{w}$. →
68 "diɬ [k$^{w}$i] ʔuqádadic. →
69 cədiɬ k$^{w}$i ʔuqádaʔ."

70 sáx$^{w}$əbəx$^{w}$ tíʔəʔ bə́sčəb liɬt̓áq̓t ʔə tíʔəʔ cədíɬ.
71 túdiʔ <təb...,> tə dúk$^{w}$ibəɬ. →
72 "təɬ cədíɬ háw̓əʔ tiʔiɬ ʔulək̓$^{w}$yíc ʔə tiʔiɬ dsʔə́ɬəd."

73 huy, → ʔúx̌$^{w}$əx$^{w}$ liɬt̓áq̓t. →
74 g$^{w}$əl ləʔúx̌$^{w}$. →
75 g$^{w}$əl → ləhúyud tíʔəʔ q$^{w}$uʔ.
76 húyud tíʔəʔ q$^{w}$uʔ. →

77 ʔuk̓$^{w}$ə́ɬ → dx$^{w}$čáʔk$^{w}$. →
78 ʔəs(h)áydx$^{w}$.
79 ɬ(u)astáq$^{w}$uʔ tiʔəʔ cədíɬ dúk$^{w}$ibəɬ. →
80 ɬutáq$^{w}$uʔ →
81 yəx̌i huy ʔuʔə́ɬəd ʔə tiʔəʔ <sə...,> sʔuládx$^{w}$.

82 And then
he went upland, up along the bluff.
83 And he went.
84 He went a little past him.
85 Then, he made water.
86 This water spilled down to the sea.
87 It wasn't much, just a "little water."
88 It would spill down to the sea.

89 Then he spoke.
90 He spoke
91 as soon as that certain one drank.
92 His throat was dry.
93 so he drank.
94 He drank with his face in the water.
95 Changer drank.
96 He really wanted water.

97 And then he said,
98 "Ha!
99 Somebody just drank some other guy's piss."

100 "Oh, that good-for-nothing.
101 Bad!
102 So I guess it must be him again who got to me."

103 That old Changer let it go.
104 And then he went on again.
105 He spit and spit again.
106 And he walked on.

107 He was far off again.

82 huy gʷəl
ʔux̌ʷ dxʷt̓áq̓t, liɬt̓aq̓t. →
83 gʷəl → ʔu·x̌ʷ. →
84 ləbíʔbəlx̌ʷəd.
85 huy <k̓ʷəɬ> húyudəxʷ tiʔəʔ qʷuʔ. →
86 k̓ʷɬáxʷ tiʔəʔ qʷuʔ dxʷčaʔkʷ.
87 x̌əɬ ti p̓áƛ̕aƛ̕ <*little...*,> *little water.*
88 ƛ̕uk̓ʷə́ɬ → dxʷčaʔkʷ.

89 huy cú(t)cuucəxʷ.
90 cú(t)cuuc →
91 yəx̌[í ʔ]uqʷúʔqʷaʔəxʷ tiʔəʔ cədiɬ. →
92 šábapsəbəxʷ.
93 huy, → qʷúʔqʷaʔəxʷ. →
94 tágʷusəbəxʷ ʔal tíʔəʔ qʷuʔ.
95 ʔuqʷúʔqʷaʔ tíʔəʔ dúkʷibəɬ.
96 cíck̓ʷəxʷ t(u)astáqʷuʔ. →

97 huy gʷəl cut.
98 "ši·. →
99 ʔuqʷúʔqʷaʔdid kʷi s[ʔə]x̌ʷáʔ ʔə kʷi sʔiɬləgʷəbs."

100 "ʔu· tə xʷiʔ ləháʔɬ.
101 saʔ. →
102 <də...,> bədíɬ əw̓ə sixʷ xʷúʔələʔ gʷuhúyuc."

103 bəkʷáʔtəb ʔə tiʔíɬ cədiɬ dúkʷibəɬ. →
104 gʷəl (h)uy bəʔúx̌ʷ. →
105 bətúʔtuʔad. →
106 gʷəl ʔíbəš.

107 bəlíl. →

108 And again he saw a nice trickling water.
109 Oh, it was nice.
110 From up along the bluff, the water came.
111 Oh, it was nice, a "little [water-]fall," the way it was made.
112 Then he drank so
113 for his throat was dry.

114 Mink spoke,
115 "Ha!
116 Somebody just drank some other guy's piss."

117 "Oh, that good-for-nothing.
118 It must be him again."

119 Then he had been following him.
120 He was making fun of Changer.
121 He was wanting to get the best of him
because he had stolen his salmon.

122 No one knew where Changer was going.
123 And then,
so then
Changer said to him.
124 "Oh, you are the one, Mink, and you are making fun of me.
125a You had better become just a mink,
be a nothing,
be scum
be there at the sea.

---

108 gʷəl bəšúdxʷ tíʔəʔ haʔɬ (ʔ)uk̓ʷík̓ʷəɬ qʷuʔ. →
109 ʔu· haʔɬ.
110 tuľťáq̓t tíʔəʔ suʔə́ƛ̓ ʔə tíʔəʔ qʷuʔ. →
111 ʔu· haʔɬ *little fall* tíʔəʔ səshúys. →
112 huy ʔuqʷúʔqʷaʔəxʷ sixʷ. →
113 huy ʔə(s)šábapsəbəxʷ.

---

114 bəcú(t)cuucəb ʔə tíʔəʔ bə́šč̓əb.
115 "ši· →
116 ʔuqʷúʔqʷaʔdid kʷ[i] s[ʔə]x̌ʷaʔ ʔə kʷi sʔiɬlə́gʷəbs."

117 "ʔu· tə xʷiʔ ləháʔɬ. →
118 bədíɬ əw̓ə sixʷ xʷúʔələʔ." →

---

119 <bələ...,> huy ləsčáladəxʷ.
120 <lə...,> ləhúyudəxʷ [x̌əɬ]ti sʔúkʷukʷ tiʔəʔ dúkʷibəɬ.
121 lədxʷsx̌ʷáľdxʷ[əb] dxʷʔal tíʔəʔ tusqádaditəbs
tíʔəʔ tusʔuládxʷs.

---

122 xʷúʔələ(ʔ) [lədxʷ]čádəxʷ kʷi səʔúx̌ʷ
ʔə tíʔəʔ dúkʷibəɬ. →
123 gʷəl (h)ay,
hay gʷəl
cút(t)əbəxʷ ʔə tíʔəʔ dúkʷibəɬ. →
124 "ʔu· dəgʷí bə́šč̓əb čxʷa ləhúyuc sʔúkʷukʷ.
125a ƛ̓úbəxʷ čəxʷ x̌ʷúľəxʷ ɬubə́šč̓əb,
ɬup̓áƛ̓aƛ̓, <ɬus...,>
ɬusdúkʷ
ɬuʔál túdiʔ čaʔkʷ.

125b The snags of driftwood are where you will wander,
you will paddle about,
and you will climb up."

126 He grabbed Mink.
127 And he threw him to the sea, to the water.

128 Mink is still swimmimg.
129 He became scum.
130 He became a mink.
131 "There among
the snags of driftwood
is where you will be seen once in a while."
132 So,
there was Mink.

## EPISODE 2: CROW AND RAVEN

1 And then this old Changer went on.
2 Yes. . . he found who was there, Crow and her brother.

3 It seems this Crow-woman was widowed.
4 Her husband had died.
5 Her husband had been Slug.
6 But that [man] had died.
7 Crow was widowed.

125b qəl̓qəládiʔ kʷi <ł(u)adsu...,>
ł(u)adsudᶻə́k̓ʷdᶻək̓ʷ,
ł(u)adsuʔúluł, →
ł(u)adsut̓áq̓tcut."

126 kʷədátəb tiʔíł bə́ščəb. →
127 gʷəl ʔíx̌ʷitəb dxʷčaʔkʷ dxʷʔal qʷuʔ.

128 t̓íčib uʔxʷ tiʔíł bə́ščəb. →
129 húyil sdukʷ. →
130 húyiləxʷ bə́ščəb.
131 "ʔáhəxʷ ʔal kʷi <stəb...,>
qəl̓qəládiʔ <stəb...,>
kʷi ł(u)adsuwəl[əl]íʔil."
132 hay,
ʔa· ti bə́ščəb.

## EPISODE 2

1 hay gʷəl ʔúx̌ʷəxʷ <ʔal...,> tiʔíł cədíł
<...tiʔíł bəščəb stəb...,> →
dúkʷibəł. →
2 ʔí:, bəʔə́y̓dxʷ t[s]iʔácəc <stəb stəb ʔi...,>
k̓áʔk̓aʔ ʔi tiʔəʔ ʔalšs.

3 gʷəháw̓əʔ ʔuq̓ʷíc̓il tsíʔəʔ cədíł k̓áʔk̓aʔ. →
4 ʔuʔátəbəd tíʔəʔ tusč̓ístxʷs.
5 <tu...,> tuq̓iyáƛ̕əd tiʔíł tusč̓ístxʷs.
6 gʷəl → dił ʔuʔátəbəd. →
7 ʔuq̓ʷíc̓il tsiʔəʔ → k̓áʔk̓aʔ. →

8 Then there was Raven, so, down at the shore.
9 And that poor Crow was walking.
10 She was going along mourning
11 because her husband had died.
12 She was widowed.

13 And then Crow was going along crying.
14 She was going along crying.
15 "My husband was *si?ab.*
16 My husband was *si?ab.*
17 My husband was *si?ab.*
18 He was like that, *si?ab.*"

19 Then Raven called out, so,
20 "Who was your husband?
21 Who was he, Crow?"

22 "Would his name be spoken—[you] good-for-nothing Splay-Foot
who would be thinking like that—if he had died?"

23 Poor Crow cried again.

24 He asked her again,
25 "Who was your husband anyway?
26 Who was he, Crow?"

27 "Oh, that good-for-nothing!
28 Would his name be spoken if he were one who had died?"

29 "Was he someone other than Slug?
30 Was he someone else?"
31 Bluntly he insulted the poor woman again:
32 "Slug was your husband!"

8 gʷəl → ʔa tíʔəʔ kaw̓qs sixʷ čaʔkʷ.
9 gʷəl → ʔíbəšəxʷ tsíʔəʔ <cədił. . . ,> cədił sʔušəbábdxʷ k̓áʔk̓aʔ.
10 lədᶻáqad. →
11 yəx̌i huy ʔuʔátəbəd tíʔəʔ sč̓ístxʷs. →
12 ʔuq̓ʷíc̓il.

13 huy gʷəl ləx̌á(hə)b tsiʔəʔ k̓áʔk̓aʔ.
14 ləx̌á(hə)b →
15 "tusiʔáb ti tudsč̓ístxʷ.
16 tusiʔáb ti tudsč̓ístxʷ.
17 tusiʔáb ti tudsč̓ístxʷ.
18 tusiʔáb tusʔístəʔ."

19 huy, qʷíʔadəxʷ sixʷ tíʔəʔ cədíł <bəščəb. . . ,>
tukáw̓qs. →
20 "tugʷiyát kʷi t(u)adsč̓ístxʷ. →
21 tugʷiyát, k̓áʔk̓aʔ."

22 "gʷədáʔatəb dᶻəł, tə xʷiʔ ləháʔł ʔəstəx̌tx̌ábšəd
kʷi dəxʷucútcut(t)əbs, gʷəʔátəbədəs."

23 bəx̌á(hə)b tsi sʔušəbábdxʷ k̓áʔk̓aʔ →

24 bəwíwiliq̓ʷid.
25 "tugʷiyát əw̓ə kʷi t(u)adsč̓ístxʷ. →
26 tugʷiyát, x̌ənimúlic̓aʔ."

27 "ʔu: tiʔəʔ xʷiʔ ləháʔł! →
28 gʷudáʔatəb dᶻəł gʷəcədíłəs kʷi gʷuʔátəbəd."

29 "ləlíʔ ʔu ʔə ti tuq̓iyáƛ̕əd.
30 ləlíʔ ʔu."
31 tíləbəxʷ bələq̓x̌ád tsiʔíł sʔušəbábdxʷ.
32 "q̓iyáƛ̕əd ti t(u)adsč̓ístxʷ!"

33 It wasn't much.
34 But he died.
35 I guess he was getting Douglas fir bark.
36 Then he tried something.
37 He broke the bark down from an old upright log.
38 And then it separated from the trunk.
39 And it came down on top of Slug.

40 What he was saying was the truth.
41 And so
her husband died; he was the late Slug.
42 Something collapsed on him while he gathered the firewood,
while he went for a little firewood.
43 So the truth is he got smashed;
that is why that poor woman cried.
44 And Raven insulted her, so.

## EPISODE 3: THE WOLF BROTHERS

1 They went there.
2 And then
[they] killed some game.
3 That certain one saw what it was that they did.
4 [They] killed Deer.

5 Then the poor fellow went.
6 Yes, that old Mink went.
7 Then he arrived.
8 Then "What are you doing?"
9 He wants to help butcher what is left of Deer.
10 He wants to help.

33 túx̌ʷux̌ʷ ʔutáb. →

34 gʷəl → yúbil.

35 <tu. . .,> xʷúʔələʔ <tu. . .,> tutáb ʔə kʷi <stəb. . .,> sčəbíd. →

36 gʷəl → ʔup̓áʔəd. →

ʔudᶻíx̌id tíʔəʔ sčəbíd ʔal tiʔíł luƛ̕ qʷłayʔ. →

38 gʷəl (h)uy → kʷáʔabacəxʷ. →

39 <huy. . .,> huy ləx̌ʷíǰəxʷ tiʔəʔ cədíł <tu. . .,> tuq̓iyáƛ̕əd. →

40 təł tiʔił dəxʷucútcuts.

41 huy gʷəl

ʔátəbəd tiʔəʔ sč̓ístxʷs, <tu. . .,> tuq̓iyáƛ̕əd.

42 ʔudᶻíx̌ič ʔal tíʔəʔ <ʔu. . .,> sučə́łs hud, suƛ̕áƛ̕čups. →

43 gʷəl → təł bíƛ̕il tiʔíł tədəxʷux̌á(hə)bsəxʷ tsiʔíł cədíł tusʔušəbábdxʷ.

44 huy → q̓x̌átəbəxʷ sixʷ ʔə tiʔəʔ kaw̓qs.

## EPISODE 3

1 ʔúx̌ʷəxʷ ə́lgʷəʔ ʔal tiʔił. →

2 gʷəl (h)uy,

bəčálqəxʷ.

3 šúdubəxʷ ʔə <tsíʔəʔ> cədíł tiʔíł tiʔíł ʔutáb.

4 <ʔu. . .,> ʔubəčálq ʔə tíʔəʔ sqígʷəc.

5 huy → ʔúx̌ʷəxʷ <tsiʔíł. . .,> tsiʔíł cədíł [s]ʔušəbábdxʷ.

6 ʔi → ʔúx̌ʷəxʷ tíʔəʔ cədíł bə́šč̓əb.

7 gʷəl → ləłčíl. →

8 gʷəl → "stab kʷ(i) adsuhúy."

9 ʔəxʷkʷáxʷadəbəxʷ tíʔəʔ ʔuk̓ʷíč̓ ʔə tíʔəʔ gʷəháw̓əʔ sqígʷəc.

10 ʔəxʷkʷáxʷadəbəxʷ. →

11 Yes, and then
he was [they were?] ready.
12 They finished their butchering.
13 All the pieces of meat were laid about.
14 Only the Deer's entrails and her parts—the kidneys and such—
these were left by the others.
15 Then this is what they said,
16 "You just take it,
You just take what's there, guy,
if you want to take it home."

17 Raven also got in on it again.
18 He arrived again.
19 And he got in on it again, on what was still there.
20 And then he took it.

21 That Flounder-woman arrived too.
22 There was only a little that was lying there for her.
23 There was just the entrails of Deer.
24 And [as for the parts] that Mink and Raven had taken,
theirs was a little better.

25 Now the ones who were killing game went on.

26 They were the ones called Wolves;
it was they who had killed the game.
27 They had killed Deer.
28 These certain ones were three full brothers.
29 These hunters were brothers to each other.
30 Wolf was their name.
31 They were Wolves.

11 ʔi:, gʷəl (h)uy,
húy[u]cut.
12 húyəxʷ tíʔəʔ sk̓ʷič̓s.
13 qʷátqʷatatəbəxʷ tíʔəʔ bək̓ʷ stab biác.
14 <dáy̓əxʷ tiʔíɬ stəb. . .,>
dáy̓əxʷ tiʔíɬ tuq̓ədᶻáx̌ ʔə tsiʔíɬ sqígʷəc ʔi ti stabs,
tusp̓us[s] stabs, tiʔiɬ qəlbíd ʔə tíʔəʔ cáadiɬ.

15 huy <díɬəxʷ ʔu. . .,>
díɬəxʷ ʔucút(t)əbəxʷ.
16 "x̌ʷúl̓əxʷ čəxʷ ʔukʷədád,
x̌ʷúl̓əxʷ čəxʷ ʔukʷədád gət →
t[ə ʔ]á gʷəx̌áƛtxʷəxʷ kʷi gʷəɬ(u)adst̓úk̓ʷtxʷ."

17 ƛál̓əxʷ bəc̓qʷíbəxʷ tíʔəʔ bəkáw̓qs. →
18 təbəɬčíləxʷ. →
19 gʷəl → <bə. . .,bə. . .,> bəc̓qʷíbəxʷ ʔə tiʔíɬ bəʔá.
20 huy gʷəl ʔúx̌ʷtubəxʷ ʔə tíʔəʔ cədíɬ.

21 ɬčíləxʷ tsíʔəʔ cədíɬ bəp̓uáy̓. <huy bə. . .,>
22 dáy̓əxʷ t(u)asqʷáqʷt(t)xʷ kʷsi ʔácəc.
23 x̌ʷúl̓əxʷ q̓ədᶻáx̌ ʔə tsiʔíɬ tusqígʷəc.
24 gʷəl díɬəxʷ ʔuʔúx̌ʷtub ʔə tíʔəʔ ʔi bə́ščəb ʔi tíʔəʔ kaw̓qs,
tiʔíɬ sgʷaʔs ə́lgʷəʔ ʔəsƛúƛubil.

25 ʔúx̌ʷəxʷ kʷaʔ tiʔíɬ ʔəsbəčálq ə́lgʷəʔ.

26 <diɬ..,> diɬ tíʔácəc ƛucút(t)əb <stəb. . .,> stiqtiqáyuʔ
tíʔəʔ ʔubəčálq. →
27 ʔubəčálq ʔə tsíʔəʔ sqígʷəc.
28 ɬíxʷixʷ tíʔəʔ cáadiɬ təlíxʷ súq̓ʷaʔ.
29 súq̓ʷsuq̓ʷaʔbitagʷəl tíʔəʔ cədíɬ dxʷsxʷíʔxʷiʔxʷiʔ.
30 stiqáyuʔ tiʔíɬ sdaʔs.
31 [s]tiqtiqáyuʔ.

32 And then
Flounder got in on it too.
33 She was the very last.
34 And then Flounder got in on the entrails.
35 The poor dear took them.

36 They said,
37 "You just do what you can with it.
38 You are Flounder.
39 That is what you get."

40 Then she took the entrails of Deer.
41 She fixed them up.
42 And then she backpacked them.
43 She backpacked them all.
44 Then she threw it on her back to this place here [gesturing].
45 Then there she was backpacking them.
46 This one had them.
47 The poor dear walked.

48 And then
Where did that one find them?
49 He came upon them.

50 "What are you folks doing, anyhow?"

51 "Oh, *si?ab*, we only killed this and we cut it all up.
52 Because we were starving.
53 We were hungry."

54 "Oh, you folks will just be wolves,
you will be nothing.
55 You folks will be hunters of deer
and other wild creatures."

32 huy gʷəl
ċqʷíbəxʷ tsíʔəʔ bəṗuáẏ.
33 <*she was*...,> díłəxʷ yuwáł ʔiłláq.
34 huy gʷəl → ċqʷíbəxʷ tsiʔíł ṗuáẏ ʔə tiʔił tuq̇ədᶻáx̌.
35 kʷədátəb ʔə tsiʔíł sʔušəbábdxʷ.

36 cút(t)əb.
37 "x̌ʷúl̕əxʷ čəxʷ ʔuháyayəd.
38 dəgʷíhəxʷ ṗuáẏ.
39 díłəxʷ stab adscqʷíb."

40 huy → kʷədádəxʷ tíʔəʔ sq̇ədᶻáx̌ ʔə tíʔəʔ sqígʷəc.
41 qʷíbidəxʷ.
42 gʷəl (h)uy → čəbáʔədəxʷ.
43 čəba:ʔədəxʷ.
44 gʷəl xʷəbáliǰbidəxʷ ʔal <kə...,> ʔəbíds ʔə ti.
45 gʷəl → ʔa ləsčəbá(ʔə)d.
46 ʔəstábad tiʔíł cədíł_______.
47 ʔíbəšəxʷ tsiʔíł sʔušəbábdxʷ.

48 huy gʷəl
čad kʷi sʔəẏdúbs ʔə tiʔəʔ cədíł.
49 łčísəb kʷaʔ tíʔəʔ caadíł. →

50 "ʔuʔəx̌íx̌əd čələp háẇəʔ."

51 "ʔu: tux̌ʷ, siʔáb, <ʔu...,> ʔubəčálq čəł →span
ʔə tsiʔacəc čła ʔuċəłqíwsəd.
52 yəx̌i huy ʔuyúbiləxʷ čəł. →
53 ʔutətágʷəxʷəxʷ."

54 "ʔu:, x̌ʷul̕əxʷ čələp łustiqáyuʔ,
łuṗáƛ̕aƛ̕əxʷ.
55 łudxʷsxʷíʔxʷiʔxʷiʔ čələp
<ʔu...,>ʔə kʷi sqígʷəc,
ʔə kʷi stab k̓ʷəč titčúlbixʷ."

56 He threw around what had been the game.
57 And he went.

58 And he quizzed Mink again.
59 He was just tossed away.

60 "You will be nothing,
61 you will be a mink,
62 you will be nothing,
63 just like scum.
64 Everywhere you will be running around by the water,
the snags of driftwood.
65 Sometimes you will be in a place up from the shore
where you will sometimes wander."

66 She was found too.
67 Flounder was still going along backpacking.
68 She was going.
69 She was on her way down to the shore.
70 Then that old Changer blocked her way.

71 And he said,
72 "What is that you are backpacking?"

73 "Oh, *si?ab*, I only got in on the entrails of the Deer
killed by those *si?ab*, the wolves.
74 That is how I happen to be backpacking this stuff
I got in on."

75 "Better those were just your entrails, Flounder,
as you will be made.
76 You will be food for later generations."

77 He threw her into the Sound.
78 So Flounder went.

56 ʔíx̌ʷduptəb tiʔíł tubəčálq. →
57 gʷəl → ʔux̌ʷ.

58 gʷəl bələwíwiliq̓ʷitəb <tsiʔəʔ...,> tiʔəʔ bə́ščəb. →
59 x̌ʷúl'əxʷ təbəxʷə́btəb.

60 "łup̓áƛ̓aƛ̓ čəxʷ →
61 łubə́ščəb
62 łup̓áƛ̓aƛ̓ →
63 x̌(ə)ł ti łusdúkʷəxʷ.
64 bək̓ʷ čád ł(u)ad(d)əxʷutəl'təláwil ʔal t[ə ʔ]a qʷuʔ,
qəl'qəládiʔ. →
65 diʔł čəxʷ bət̓áq̓t ʔal [ti] swátixʷtəd kʷi ł(u)adsudᶻə́k̓ʷ."

66 ƛ̓ál'əxʷ bəʔəy̓dúbəxʷ tsíʔəʔ.
67 bələsčəbáʔəxʷ tsíʔəʔ p̓uáy̓.
68 ləʔúx̌ʷ.
69 lək̓ʷít̓əxʷ.
70 gʷəl təqdúbəxʷ ʔə tíʔəʔ cədíł dúkʷibəł.

71 gʷəl cút(t)əb.
72 "stab tiʔíł adsəsčəbáʔ."

73 "ʔu:, c̓qʷib čəd, siʔáb, ʔə tiʔíł q̓ədᶻáx̌ ʔə tsiʔíł sqígʷəc
[s]bəčálq ʔə t[ə ʔ]á siʔiʔáb ʔi stiqáyuʔ.
74 dił cəxʷəsčəbáʔ [tiʔəʔ] dsəsc̓qʷíb tsíʔəʔ ʔúʔu."

75 "ƛ̓ub x̌ʷúl'əxʷ ł(u)adq̓ədᶻáx̌, p̓uáy̓, kʷi ł(u)adsəshúy.
76 łəsuʔə́łəd čəxʷ ʔə kʷi ʔiłláq ʔáciłtalbixʷ."

77 xʷə́btəb dxʷʔál x̌ʷəlč.
78 gʷəl ʔux̌ʷ tsi p̓uáy̓.

79 "Now those entrails will be her entrails,
the entrails that belonged to Deer."
80 This is why the entrails of Flounder are as they are.
81 That is what Changer did to her.

82 Certain others were found too.
83 And then
he spoke.
84 "What will be theirs, Crow's and Raven's?"

85 Then they just said,
86 "That is only what we got in on.
87 We only selected worthless stuff from there."

88 "Then you will just gather worthless stuff
down along the shore.
89 You, Crow,
90 And Raven are also the same:
91 You folks will be nobodies,
You will be made [as] things."

92 Then, "caw." This is what Crow said.
93 Raven went.
94 He was saying,
95 "qwa, qwa, qwa."
96 This is why he talks like that.
97 Crow is also the same.
98 "caw, caw, caw."

99 He just said to them,
100 "This is what you folks are to be doing.
101 You folks will pick up whatever you eat in the future."

79 <lə. . . ,> "díɬiɬəxʷ tiʔíɬ q̓ədᶻáx̌ ɬuq̓ədᶻáx̌səxʷ tsiʔíɬ.
gʷəɬ sqígʷəc q̓ədᶻáx̌."
80 tsiʔíɬ dəxʷ(ə)sʔístəʔ ʔə tiʔíɬ q̓ədᶻáx̌ ʔə tsiʔíɬ p̓uáy̓.
81 diɬ tushúyutəbsəxʷ ʔə tíʔəʔ dúkʷibəɬ.

82 təb(əʔ)əy̓dúbəxʷ tíʔəʔ cədíɬ ʔiɬkʷə́lq. →
83 gʷəl (h)uy,
cút(t)əb. →
84 "stab <kʷi gʷəs. . . ,> kʷi gʷəsgʷáʔs ə́lgʷəʔ ʔi k̓áʔk̓aʔ
<ʔi stəb. . . ,> ʔi kaw̓qs."

85 gʷəl → x̌ʷul̓ ʔucút. →
86 "diɬ bəsucqʷíb čəɬ tux̌ʷ c(əd)iɬ.
87 tux̌ʷ čəɬ p̓áƛ̓aƛ̓ <tu. . . ,> tukʷədálikʷ tul̓ʔá." →

88 "gʷəl x̌ʷul̓əxʷ čələp p̓áƛ̓aƛ̓ ɬudxʷbəxʷíqad liɬʔílgʷiɬ.
89 dəgʷí, k̓áʔk̓aʔ, →
90 ƛ̓al̓ b(ə)asʔístəʔ tiʔiɬ kaw̓qs.
91 <s. . . ,> xʷíʔəxʷ kʷi gʷátəxʷ,
stábəxʷ ɬusəshúyləp."

92 huy, "k̓a:" cut tsiʔiɬ k̓áʔk̓aʔ.
93 ʔux̌ʷ tiʔíɬ <stəb. . . ,> kaw̓qs.
94 cútcut.
95 "qʷaʔ, qʷaʔ, qʷaʔ."
96 dəxʷəscútucid ʔə tiʔíɬ cədíɬ. →
97 ƛ̓al̓ b(ə)asʔístəʔ tsiʔəʔ k̓áʔk̓aʔ.
98 "k̓a:, k̓a:, k̓a:."

99 x̌ʷúl̓əxʷ tucúuc. →
100 "ʔəsʔístəhəxʷ kʷi səhúyləp liɬʔílgʷiɬ.
101 <ɬubəkʷ. . . ,>
ɬubəkʷúcid čələp ʔə kʷi stab ɬusʔə́ɬədləp."

102 That is what Changer did.
103 He was changing the way Deer was.
104 And that was, I guess, when it was sometime later.
105 And that, I guess, is the end of that one story.

ꟷ

dił tushúy ʔə tiʔíł dúk$^{w}$ibəł.
lədúk$^{w}$udəx$^{w}$ tíʔəʔ tu(u)húy ʔə tíʔəʔ <s. . . ,> sqíg$^{w}$əc.
g$^{w}$əl ʔáləx$^{w}$ x$^{w}$úʔələʔ k$^{w}$i tudx$^{w}$láqəx$^{w}$.
g$^{w}$əl dił x$^{w}$úʔələʔ tu(s)šáċs tiʔíł dəčúʔ syəyəhúb.

# NOTES TO TEXT 1

Episode 1 (Text 1a)

1 *ʔacəc tiʔił bəščəb*. This is one of two traditional beginnings for a Lushootseed story that takes place in the myth time. The other is *ʔəsłałlil tiʔił bəščəb*: "Mink is (or was) living there." (See texts 2, 3, 6, and 7.)

1–5 Passages that introduce or link episodes often concern someone's traveling, and they often show incremental patterning. Here, lines 1 and 2 form a hysteron-proteron figure whose theme is "being," while 3–5 show incremental repetition and concern "walking." Frequent repetition of the name of the actor sets this passage off from what comes next, when Mrs. Lamont begins to narrate the action, using a series of verbs without stated agent.

6 As Mrs. Lamont delivers this, *gʷəl huy* sounds like part of line 5, and the word *łčisəxʷ* is isolated by pauses before and after it. As opposed to *łčił*, "to come upon," *łčis* has connotations of arriving in time for something or at the right time.

6–12 An example of circular figure with cap. By the time we get to line 10 (*łčiləxʷ*) we have circled back to where we started in line 6 (*łčisəxʷ*; this line also shows augmenting repetition). Within this circle of the narration of Mink's arrival, Mrs. Lamont has told how he stole roasted salmon from someone. In the cap lines (11–12), Mrs. Lamont tells how Mink ate what he stole, and she picks up here words from the lines in the center of the circular figure (line 7: *səsq̓ʷəlb e ti luƛ̓ ʔə tiʔəʔ sʔuladxʷ*; 8: *səsq̓ʷəlbs ʔə tiʔəʔ sʔuladxʷ*).

7 The *bə-* prefix ("again" or "anew") does not necessarily imply that Mink has stolen from this person before, but rather that Mink often steals. The *bə-* form of the verb is used to characterize the actor in this case, not the action [cf. the annotated text. -Ed.].

8 For roasting, the salmon was split and spread out with wooden splints; then the fish was mounted on roasting-sticks that were stuck into the ground near the fire.

13–18 Travel passage (bridge) with augmenting repetition based on *ʔibəš*. Note that Mink does not actually arrive anywhere until the beginning of the next episode (line 23); instead, the description of his typical way of traveling may be said to characterize him (see line 125 and text 1c, lines 64–65).

17–18 Except for the river delta, the coastline in Skagit country is made up of narrow beaches, points, and cliffs. Anyone traveling on foot along the shore will be forced periodically to leave the water's edge and travel along the top of the bluff, especially when the tide is in. The river courses are likewise lined with points, overhangs, and steep banks.

The direction terms that Mrs. Lamont uses have this characteristic in common (and in distinction to other terms for "toward the water" and "toward the land"): the motion in the direction specified does not need to stop at the shore. If you are going *dxʷčaʔkʷ*, then you may be either on land going toward the water, or on the water and heading further out. Likewise, *dxʷƛ̓aq̓t* can signify being on the water and coming toward land, or being on land and heading away from the water.

30–32 In the core of this little circular figure, Mrs. Lamont is referring to a frequently occurring situation in Lushootseed literature: Mink lures his younger brother (or cousin) *tətyiqaʔ* into mischief.

37 *tiʔacəc liłʔigʷił*. Literally, "the shoreline that was there," an emphatic way of referring to the shoreline, which draws attention to the echo of 29, when Mink was walking in the same place. This is the first of many times in the next part of the story (40–55) that Mrs. Lamont will use verbal echoes to remind the audience that Changer's behavior and Mink's are similar. Lines 29–32 and 35–39 are conceptually parallel: the two walk along the shoreline and are characterized by reference to other stories in which they appear (see next note).

39 According to the stories told about him, as Changer meets each person he asks "*stab kʷ(i)adsuhuy*" ("What are you doing?") (cf. text 1c, line 8), and whatever the person is doing becomes his characteristic action for all time once

he is changed. Often, then, the change is a kind of judgment on the person's way of life.

41 Cf. lines 33–34. Though the passage 33–41 is not structurally a circular figure, it illustrates the principle of Lushootseed storytelling that is embodied in circular narration: if there is a sequence of events A—B—C, after event B has been related the story will refer to the end of event A before going on with event C.

44 *ʔəs(h)aydub bəšč̓əb ʔə tiʔəʔ cədił dukʷibəł.* "Mink was known to Changer;" that is, Changer knew Mink's reputation as a thief. Note the emphatic reference in 43 to *tiʔacəc bəšč̓əb*, the Mink he has heard about.

50 Elders have explained that Changer leaves a few bits of food on Mink's lips, so that when he awakens, Mink will think he has already eaten.

51–55 Another bridge passage that combines a travel motif with the function of characterization. The first two lines simply inform us that Changer is on the move. Then Mrs. Lamont pauses. After the next line (53) she pauses again. So many pauses in a bridge (that is, nondramatic) passage are unusual: we may assume that 53 is being emphasized. It initiates a series of three lines (53–55) that echo the narrative of Mink's leaving the scene of his theft (16–18) and draw a parallel between his behavior and Changer's: Changer is becoming Mink-like, which is the opposite of what is supposed to happen. Notice that in Mrs. Lamont's narration of how Changer stole Mink's food, the verbal echoes of the narration of Mink's theft are unstructured—there are, for example, no syntactically parallel units. These verbal echoes seem to reflect only the similarity in subject matter between the two scenes. It is in the bridge passage, rather than in the scene, that Mrs. Lamont chooses to make her purposeful repetitions. (It should be noted that in Lushootseed there were available to Mrs. Lamont different ways of saying "to go down to the shore" or "to go away from the shore"; the verbal echoes were not forced upon her by the lexicon.)

57–69 Two overlapping circular figures (57–61, 61–64) with two-part cap (65–66 and 67–69). (The second circular figure is weighted.) The core of the first figure expresses what Mink knows and is repeated in the second part of the cap; the core of the second figure explains how he knows it and is repeated in the first part of the cap.

*haydxʷ* is the same verb used in 44, when Changer realizes that the thief is Mink. However, though both Changer and Mink have heard of each other, only Mink is able to figure out the situation without ever seeing his adversary.

*b(ə)asdukʷil* (63). A pause after this line puts emphasis on the word, as does the sound of *dukʷibəł*'s name, which occurs twice in the next three lines. The homophony strengthens the parallel being drawn between the two antagonists: the more equal they are in stature, the more exciting the contest. *dukʷ(u)* means to change or transform, and the suffix *-il* signifies becoming.

People who have heard that the Changer is coming usually respond in one of two ways: in hopes of escaping a disagreeable change, they are very respectful to any stranger they meet; or they try to arm themselves against him. The nature of Mink's response shows what an unusual person he is.

72 Note the echo of 60. Lushootseed narrative does not always overtly explain cause-and-effect relationships or the motivations of characters. Judiciously placed verbal echoes and word-group repetitions may serve this function, as here.

73–88 This portion of the story is constructed as two passages of parallel narration (73–77 and 82–88) joined by a one-plus-two pattern in lines 78–81 [the familiar *ʔəs(h)aydxʷ* followed by a bipartite statement of what he knew]. The two passages show the same organization, with the second passage showing amplification. Parallel lines show part-variable repetition. (This passage is analyzed more fully in the "Annotator's Introduction.")

75 *qʷuʔ* is fresh water, as opposed to salt water *(x̌ʷəlč)*. The connotation here is that this water is drinkable (cf. *ʔəstaqʷuʔ*, "to be thirsty," and *qʷuʔqʷaʔ*, "drink").

79 When she was telling the story, Mrs. Lamont said *bəščəb* instead of *dukʷibəł* here; but she corrected herself when the text was being transcribed.

85 When she was telling the story, Mrs. Lamont made a false start in this line and immediately corrected herself: *huy k̓ʷəł. . .huyudəxʷ tiʔəʔ qʷuʔ.*

87 "Little water" is Mrs. Lamont's English for "small stream." In Lushootseed, "little water" would be *qʷiʔqʷuʔ*.

89–97 Circular narration with interlaced core. Mink speaks—[interstitial material: "because" clause]—Changer is thirsty—he drinks—Changer is thirsty—he drinks—Changer is thirsty—Mink speaks. As in many figured passages, the first line talks about a time after the events or situation narrated in the middle lines, and the last line returns to the time of the first. This is one way Lushootseed narration handles the flashback or events that English might put into the past perfect tense.

*hay gʷəl cut* (97). No speaker is designated in the Lushootseed; but, because this line closes a passage of concentric narration, an audience familiar with the form would recognize that the speaker in line 97 is the same as the one in line 89, which opens the passage.

103–106 Four-statement travel passage bridging two scenes. (Mrs. Lamont's pause after *ʔibəš* (106) shows that 107 belongs with what follows it, not with the bridge passage.) Often, travel passages contain either four statements using verbs of travel or one introductory statement followed by three travel statements (see lines 1–5). In line 105, Mrs. Lamont varies the pattern by having Changer spit instead of travel. This variation on what was expected may have heightened the humor. Three of the statements employ the *bə-* prefix, which signifies a repeated action. In this version of the story, Changer only drinks from the "little water" twice, but in the old days, people tended to do things four times in Lushootseed stories. Mrs. Lamont's *bə-* may indicate her awareness that she has left out the first narration of Changer's drinking because she is shortening the story for this particular audience.

108–111 Though not structurally parallel, this passage is conceptually parallel to and meant to recall 86–88. This time, we see the waterfall from Changer's point of view. The humor arises from the fact that the audience, unlike Changer, knows Mink's point of view. The word *p̓aƛ̓aƛ̓*, "insignificant," line 87, which expresses the impression Mink hopes the waterfall will make on Changer, is replaced in this later passage with *haʔł* (good), which expresses what Changer thinks when he sees the little fall.

111 Note Mrs. Lamont's /b/ for /f/ in her pronunciation of the English word "fall." (There is, of course, a Lushootseed word for waterfall: *stəkʷab*.)

112–118 Parallel to 95–102. Note that Mrs. Lamont begins the parallel narration of the later passage only with the last half of the concentric pattern of 89–97: this is why Changer drinks before he is thirsty (112–113). The narration of Changer's two drinkings, we can now see, is organized in the same way as the narration of Mink's creating waterfalls: two parallel passages connected by a one-plus-two-repetition bridge passage (103–106).

The overall organization of the narration of Mink's trickery can be diagrammed as follows:

| (A) 73–77 | 78–81 | (A) 82–85 | 86–88 |
|---|---|---|---|
| Mink makes water | bridge | | (description) |
| (B) 95–102 | 103–106 | 108–111 | (B) 112–118 |
| Changer drinks | bridge | (description) | |

The A sections are parallel to each other, as are the descriptions of the water and the B sections, the first one (95–102) being ornamented with a circular figure (89–97); the bridge passages share the same pattern.

125 *łusdukʷ*. *dukʷ* here is a homophone of *dukʷ*, to transform, but it means something like "worthless" and thus overlaps the semantic field of *p̓aƛ̓aƛ̓*. Both *p̓aƛ̓aƛ̓* and *sdukʷ* have connotations of being insignificant and in the old days

were applied to people of low rank. *sdukʷ* is most often used, however, of things that are broken or don't work; with various suffixes it can indicate a disturbed state of mind—worry, anger, frustration—or be applied to something that has changed for the worse—weather or an illness. Mrs. Lamont's reiteration of the word in a parallel-constructed pair of lines later (129–130) shows that she wishes the audience to take note of it.

*dukʷibəɬ*'s series of predictions about Mink—all beginning with *ɬu-* and recited by Mrs. Lamont rhythmically, like a chant—shows *dukʷibəɬ* in the process of redefining what it will be to be a mink, and he is using words that recall Mink's former glory: *p̓aƛ̕aƛ̕* is the word Mink used to himself, thinking how harmless the waterfall would appear to *dukʷibəɬ* (87); *sdukʷ* recalls *dukʷil*, used to express Mink's cleverness (63); and *čaʔkʷ*, now no longer the place where both Changer and Mink walk (18, 55, etc.), has become *ʔal tudiʔ čaʔkʷ*, that shore over there, a place for the ostracized.

127 *ʔix̌ʷ(i)* is not just "to throw," but "to throw away." Notice the amplification of *dxʷčaʔkʷ* (toward the shore) with a phrase that reminds us of Mink's mischief: *dxʷʔal qʷuʔ*. (Mrs. Lamont had the option of using *x̌ʷəlč*, "salt water," as she did in 16.)

Episode 2 (Text 1b)

1 There is no pause between the last line of text 1a and the first line of text 1b. Mrs. Lamont delivers these as if they were part of one sentence.

1–2 The most common sort of bridge passage in Lushootseed literature is one that tells how someone traveled. Here, Changer (Mrs. Lamont says "Mink", but corrects herself), continuing on his tour of the area in order to check on people (cf. text 1a, line 38: *ləʔəy̓dxʷ tiʔacəc k̓aʔk̓aʔ*), comes upon Crow and Raven (*bəʔə́y̓dxʷ t[s]iʔácəc k̓áʔk̓aʔ...*). The audience is aware that Changer is watching Raven's misbehavior all along.

3–7 Concentric figure: Crow widowed—husband died—Slug—husband died—Crow widowed.

8 *sixʷ*. An intensifying particle that can mean "still" or "as usual." In this case, it does not refer to Raven's being at the shore as usual, but it characterizes Raven: we are to be treated to a sample of Raven-as-usual.

9–11 Mrs. Lamont's husband, Levi, explained that in the old days, when people lived together in large households, it was difficult for the bereaved to find a private place in which to grieve. A common solution was to rise early and walk along the shore away from the longhouse.

8–18 Concentric narration: Raven—[interstitial material: Crow walks]—Crow mourns—comment: Crow's husband is dead (two statements)—Crow mourns (two statements and a song)—Raven. (The last line also serves to launch the parallelism of the next passage.)

15–18 As we will see—and Mrs. Lamont's audience already knows—Slug was not a person of high rank. It is in the discrepancy between Crow's fond exaggeration and the truth that Raven sees the opening for his insults.

*siʔab*, which means "noble" or "powerful," contains within it the word for wealth—*ʔiʔab*. A person who was of high rank had guardian spirits who helped him in his activities, and his success made him wealthy. The most powerful spirits tended to ally themselves from generation to generation with the same families, so that competence and high rank came to be associated with one another. The story of the manner of Slug's death (33–43) thus casts doubt on Crow's claim that he was *siʔab*.

19–28 Two parallel-constructed passages clustered around line 23, the second set amplifying the first:

19 is conceptually parallel to 24 (speech introduction);

20 is parallel to 25 (which adds intensifier əw̓ə);

21 is parallel to 26 (Crow's personal name substituted for her generic name);

22 is parallel to 27–28 (order of elements changed).

20–21 "*gʷiyat*" is Raven's way of speaking: he says "who" (gʷat), but distorts the word so that it sounds like "*siʔab*": his mockery is delivered in the very rhythm of *k̓aʔk̓aʔ*'s song.

22 It is the Lushootseed custom not to mention the name of a person who has recently died. Since one purpose of the custom is to spare the bereaved the pain of hearing the name, Raven should be especially scrupulous when speaking to a new widow like Crow.

Not speaking the name is also a way of showing respect for the departed. Crow is saying that people would be respectful of Raven's name if he had died, even though he is not extending that courtesy to Slug. (When white settlers wanted to name their new town "Seattle" after the recently deceased Indian leader, *siʔaɬ*, they had no idea that they might be offending his family and tribe.)

26 *x̌ənimulic̓a* is a name, not a word meaning "crow," and the name is an old one: the earlier Lushootseed /m/ and /n/ have been replaced by /b/ and /d/, but proper names often preserve the old pronunciation. Crow is called by the name *x̌ənimulic̓a* in many stories, whether she is Raven's wife or, as here, his sister. All the myth-age characters had individual names, but only a few are remembered.

Before he says *x̌ənimulic̓a*'s name, Mrs. Lamont has Raven pause dramatically, making Crow wonder whether what is about to be said is her husband's name.

29–44 It is often said that storytellers do not make explanations. But of course they do. This passage, in which Mrs. Lamont brings her story to a close twice, contains one of the most common forms of Lushootseed authorial intervention, the flashback. The whole passage takes the form of two overlapping concentric organizations; and inside the A rings, (Raven insults Crow: A1, 29–32; A2, 40 [first figure]; A1, 40; A2, 44 [second figure]), we find the recapitulation of past events in the form of two more tiny circular organizations. The first one consists of "it didn't matter much, but Slug died" (B1, 33–34), he dealt with bark (core, 35–38), he died (B2, 39); and the second one consists of "Slug died" (B1, 41), he dealt with bark (core, 42), he died (B2, 43). The manner of Slug's death shows that he was not of high rank. In Lushootseed stories, bark-gathering is only done by slaves or children, never by those clearly marked as having *siʔaɬ* status.

43 Mrs. Lamont is joking here, using the anachronism of Slug's post-Change slowness of movement.

Episode 3 (Text 1c)

3 *tsiʔəʔ cədiɬ*: Crow.

4 Vi Hilbert suggests that since this story takes place in the myth time when Deer was a person, this killing is a murder.

8–11 The audience knows that Mink wants to "help" in order to secure some of the game for himself.

12–33 This late introduction of a new character into the story is handled with a certain amount of formality: Flounder arrives at the core of a passage of concentric narration (hunters—Mink—Raven—Flounder—Mink and Raven—hunters), and then her story is followed up, as if it were the pendant (32–47) to a figure.

26–31 Circular organization. Mrs. Lamont makes a point about the Wolf brothers by using circular organization to ornament this introduction of their name in the A2 ring of the concentric passage: they are of high rank (noted hunters are *siʔab*).

44 Mrs. Lamont indicated a spot on her back at the base of her neck. [This is Hess's observation. -Ed.]

46 After *cədiɬ*, Mrs. Lamont says something else, but it is unintelligible on the tape recording.

47 Dell Hymes has noted that in Kathlamet Chinook storytelling, the later run-throughs of pattern episodes are apt to be less detailed than the first one, a phenomenon he calls "fading explicitness" (1985:411). But what he goes on to describe is not "fading," but variations on a model as the storyteller elaborates,

omits, or changes the order of elements in the pattern. For the storytellers whose work is represented in the present collection, variation within a pattern—and this includes not having the first telling of the pattern be the most complete one—is a major expressive device, and the reader could miss much of what is being conveyed in the story by assuming that the fifth or tenth run-through were any less important than the first.

48–end The rest of the story is made up of scenes on this model: (A) Changer arrives and finds someone (e.g., 48–49); (B) Changer asks what is going on (e.g., 50); (C) the person answers, trying to put his activities in the best possible light, usually minimizing with the adverb ***tux̌ʷ*** the activity denoted by the verb (e.g., 51–53); (D) Changer announces the person's future status and characteristic activity, using the adverb ***x̌ʷul̓*** (e.g., 54–55); (E) Changer throws something (e.g., 56); (F) one of the participants in the scene leaves, thus ending it (e.g., 57). Part of the interest of this portion of the story lies in the variations that Mrs. Lamont makes in each version of the model.

48 In "Martha Lamont's Changer Story," the word *ʔəy̓dxʷ*, "to find something," is identified with Changer: we know that *tiʔəʔ cədił* is he. Note also in the next line another reference to his mission: *łčis*, "to arrive for a purpose," as opposed to *łčil*, "to arrive." (Compare text 1a, lines 38 and 40.)

51 ***tux̌ʷ*** is used to introduce a clause when what is being said is in contrast to or opposed to something, even though that something may remain unstated. ***tux̌ʷ*** may be translated "just," "only," "and yet," or "but." Its presence in people's answers indicates that what they say is running counter to some expectation or assumption of Changer's.

54 ***x̌ʷul̓***, like ***tux̌ʷ***, may be translated "only," but in the sense of "merely." Changer's announcements invariably concern reductions in status or scope for people's future lives. Note Changer's sarcastic echo of the Wolves' apologetic "*ʔu· tux̌ʷ, siʔab . . .*" (51) in his answer: "*ʔu· x̌ʷul̓əxʷ čələp . . . .*"

56 *ʔix̌ʷ(i)*. Literally, to throw away. (See text 1a, line 127.)

58–65 Because Mink's story has been told before, this episode is shortened: (A) is omitted; (B) is summarized; (C) is omitted; (E) is moved ahead of (D); and (F) is omitted. Notice that placing (E), what finally is done, ahead of (D), the description of the punishment, emphasizes (D), which is then dealt with in the greatest detail, including an echo (61–65) from the earlier "Mink" section of the story (text 1a, line 125).

66–79 In Flounder's story, (A) is elaborated in the form of a concentric organization: Changer finds her (66 and 70); how she traveled (67 and 69); she was going (68). What is added by means of the concentric development is detail about her backpacking, which receives attention at every step of her story (cf. 40–47). Flounder's reply (C) does not employ ***tux̌ʷ*** to minimize her role; instead, she uses her lowly social position for this, emphasizing the fact that she was given (*c̓qʷib*, "to be able to share in receiving something") her food by people of higher rank, among whom she evidently includes everyone else on hand ("*tə ʔa siʔiʔab ʔi stiqayuʔ*": all those nobles and wolves). 79–81 constitutes an addition to the model (we might think of it as a pendant to the model), another ornamental passage about her backpacking. (Flounder, as a bottom fish, has her intestines "on her back.")

82–101 Flounder made a point of saying that all she got was the least desirable portion of the deer meat. Changer's question here ("And what might Crow and Raven have?") is a sarcastic reference to Flounder's defensive tactic. The sarcasm continues as he mocks the birds' reply (87: "*tux̌ʷ čəł p̓áƛ̓aƛ̓*") in his sentencing of them (88: "*gʷəl x̌ʷul̓əxʷ čələp p̓aƛ̓aƛ̓ . . .*"). (This is the same tactic that he used with the Wolves; see lines 51 and 54.) Part F of this version of the model (92–98) is expanded in the form of a circular organization, the elaboration detailing Crow's and Raven's modern characteristics. (Mrs. Lamont's elaboration of part F of Flounder's story [what we have referred to as the pendant] is for the same purpose, though it does not employ circular narration.)

**86–88** Note the differences among *ćq*ʷ*ib* (86), a passive receiving of something given; *k*ʷ*ədalik*ʷ (87), an active taking of something one wants and *bək*ʷ (88) the circumscribed activity of taking what one is able to find.

**104–105** Vi Hilbert suggests that the idea of lines 104 and 105 taken together is "I guess that is the way it was when the story ended."

## TRANSCRIPTION OF CROW'S SONG

Lines 1b.16–18

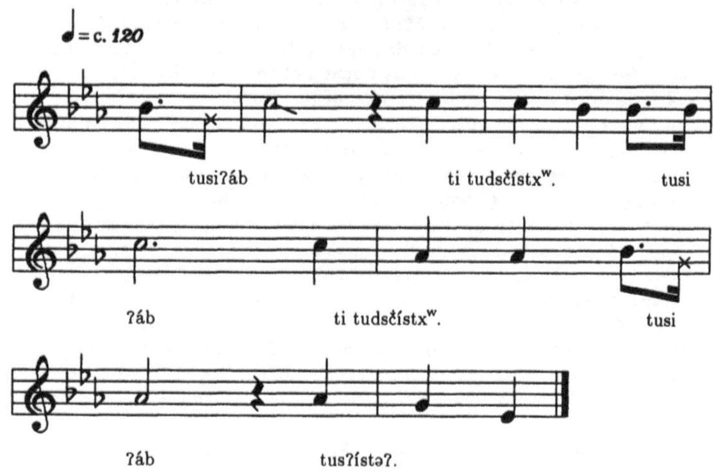


Transcription by Richard Crawford

# THE MARRIAGE OF CROW

## INTRODUCTION

The person called Crow in this story is obviously a very different crow from the *x̌ənimulič̓aʔ* of "Mrs. Lamont's Changer Story": one cannot imagine this Crow married to a lowly Slug. She is the daughter of a wealthy family and is very conscious of her *siʔab* rank. On the other hand, the audience of "The Marriage of Crow" remains conscious of the fact that in today's world Crow has very little prestige. This tension about the status of Crow shows itself in the variety of ways she is presented in the literature as a whole. In fact, some stories, such as "Crow Is Sick" (text 3), give her the characteristics of several social classes at once; and it may be that Mrs. Lamont is doing just that here, as well.

In "The Marriage of Crow," Crow's wealth testifies to her high rank. Her behavior in many ways also expresses this status. In the days when Lushootseed society flourished, daughters of high-ranking families were carefully protected until they were married: Crow is always accompanied by slaves, not just to show off her wealth, but because it would be improper for her to go anywhere alone. She seeks a husband from a village other than her own because village exogamy was the preferred form of marriage, especially for the first-born of high-ranking families. Not only was a marriage to any relative less than four degrees removed considered undesirable (Collins 1974:97), but in addition, marriage connections with different villages, and the resulting opportunities for cooperation and the exchange of property, were the fuel of prestige.

But there are aspects of Crow's behavior that are not proper. In the ordinary course of things, young ladies did not travel about announcing that they were husband-hunting. Marriages—especially first marriages—were arranged by the couple's families. The groom and his family came with gifts to the bride's village and asked for her, and only after the marriage did the bride go to the husband's village. Since it is the endowment with family—with knowledgeable and resourceful relatives, rather than with wealth alone—in which the Lushootseed concept of the *siʔab* resides, where, we ask, are Crow's relatives? She has only slaves to take her to her husband's village, and no one seems to know the way. The narrative underlines these inconsistencies by reiterating the verb *ʔuluƛ̕tub* ("was taken by water," a type of "passive" construction), to tell about the traveling of a woman who is taking the active course of setting out in search of a husband.

The blankets that figure so largely in Crow's wedding celebration were important at every major turning point in Lushootseed life—from birth, when swaddling clothes were ceremonially cut from larger weavings, through death, when a blanket would be used as a shroud. Important guests were welcomed by having a blanket put around their shoulders, and people receiving names or coming of age sat on piles of blankets when these events were celebrated. At potlatches, prestige could (and still can, to a certain extent) be reckoned by the numbers of blankets given away. Once women made blankets from mountain goat wool. During the nineteenth century, trading companies' machine-made blankets replaced hand-made blankets for all but the most prestigious and sacred ceremonial purposes.

The wealth and prestige of Shell is confirmed by the display of blankets laid down at Crow's arrival. In the mid–nineteenth century, a one-point Hudson's Bay blanket was worth sixty fresh salmon. It has been estimated that one mountain-goat-hair blanket (*k̓ʷastədulič̓aʔ*) was worth ten of the Hudson's Bay, or six hundred fish. Shell laid blankets down over Crow's entire path from water's edge to his house, certainly on level ground well above the winter high-water line. We are looking at a bridal walkway worth thousands and thousands of fish.

The form of "The Marriage of Crow" is simple: Crow sets off; various people come down to the shore to see whether they are her chosen bridegroom; Crow arrives at the right village. The hopeful-bridegroom episodes provide opportunities for parallel narration, increased by the repetitions of the songs of Crow and her slaves. In an earlier version of this story that Mrs. Lamont told some nine years before the one presented in this volume, there are ten suitors, as opposed to five. The episodes in which the suitors come down to the water are shorter than in the present version and are told with a much greater degree of parallelism.

The version presented here is, on the other hand, while formally less patterned, much more pointed. Here, Mrs. Lamont directs numerous remarks celebrating the beauty of the country and the people and the abundance of wealth and food in "this land of ours a long time ago": the calmness of the weather, which may be a mark of Crow's power, is reiterated here, and there are introductory remarks about how different life used to be long ago. In addition, several of the suitors are beautiful, not just the successful one; and the storytelling has become more ornate, the simple parallelism of the earlier version yielding to more complex techniques, such as interlace.

In Lushootseed literature, as in European, stories that concern people of wealth and rank are often vehicles for social criticism. It is almost as if a character's possession of wealth automatically brings to bear upon him the narrator's scrutiny as to his deportment and probity. But in this story, Crow's status—ambiguous because it is so different from her condition today—does not become the focus for social criticism; rather, it is the means by which Mrs. Lamont can invoke the grandeur of the past while not allowing us to forget the way things are in the present.

Her introductory remarks and authorial asides make it clear that she is thinking less about social tensions in the old days than about the possibilites of life for people in the time before Changer came, when Crow was not a despised scavenger, but the daughter of the best family; and when Lushootseed people could be fabulously wealthy simply by virtue of their position in their own community. It is interesting in this context to note the striking comparison with European royalty with which Ruth Shelton, a Tulalip elder a generation older than Martha Lamont, prefaced the description of marriage customs in the old days that she gave to Leon Metcalf in 1954, when she was about 100 years old:

> *tiʔəʔ ti tusʔəshuy ʔə ti tuʔaciłtalbix*$^{w}$. *tux̌*$^{w}$*ulab ʔə k*$^{w}$*i* king *ti tusʔəshuy ʔə t ʔə tiʔəʔ tuʔaciłtalbix*$^{w}$.
>
> (This is how the people of long ago used to do things. Almost as if they had been some sort of *kings* was the way people of long ago used to do things.)

Formally, "The Marriage of Crow" is a very satisfying story. By "form" here is meant the relationship between the story's parts, a pattern that can be understood in terms of a graph: at the beginning, Crow goes down to the water and at the end she goes ashore. In between, suitors repeat her journey on a smaller scale, going toward and away from the shore; but each one gives less of himself to the traveling than does Crow, whose journey in the water is longer than all of theirs put together—until she gets to Shell's village, where her last suitor has laid a path for her, the value of which is commensurate with the value she sets on her own activity.

What narrative strategies might be employed to embody this formal concept in a structure? Crow's trip toward and away from the water frames the part of the story involving the suitors, and we expect the two legs of the frame to relate to each other, either in parallel narration in which the mirroring elements contrast with each other, or else in some kind of circular relation in which the end of the story restates the beginning. Crow's activities while she is on the water are repetitions, and we would expect to see repetition of selected key elements in this part of the narrative. The suitor's activities we would expect to find given in parallel narration, because, while their activities are similar, the suitors themselves differ from each other. Mrs. Lamont's version employs all these strategies. Indeed, the fact that a significant portion of her repertoire is made up of stories whose "graphs" can be drawn this way suggests that the formal aspects of narrative meant a lot to her. But in "The Marriage of Crow," too, it is interesting to see how Mrs. Lamont has stretched the formal confines of the story with her remarks about how things used to be: we can see the circular figures growing elliptical under the weight of her nostalgia; bridge passages being made to lead not only into new dramatic units, but into a different time frame; and the report of the marriage feast elaborated in celebration of the plenty that once was.

## A Note on Further Reading

For further information about marriage customs among the Lushootseed and their neighbors, the reader may consult Haeberlin and Gunther (1930:50–52); Collins (1974:97–106) on the Skagit; Smith (1940:168–173) on the Puyallup and Nisqually; and Barnett (1955:180–196) on the Coast Salish peoples of southern British Columbia. For information on the network of in-laws and the continuing relationship of the bride with her parents, see Suttles (1960) and Bierwert (1979).

The earlier version of "The Marriage of Crow" referred to in the introduction above was recorded by Leon Metcalf on reel 38, now in the Metcalf Collection in the Thomas Burke Memorial Washington State Museum at the University of Washington. A transcription with a literal translation by Vi Hilbert is in the archives of Lushootseed Research, Inc., under the name "Crow and Her Seagull Slaves." (For another translation of this version, see Lamont forthcoming; for a discussion of the story, see Moses and Langen forthcoming.) Ruth Shelton's memoir was recorded by Leon Metcalf on reel 70, also in the Metcalf Collection. A transcription with gloss by Vi Hilbert is in the Lushootseed Research archives, under the title "Information from the Memories of Ruth Shelton."

Discussions of "The Marriage of Crow" incorporating matters of concern in translation theory and semiotics can be found in Bierwert (1991). The relation between Mrs. Lamont's two recorded tellings of the story is discussed in Langen (forthcoming).

# THE MARRIAGE OF CROW

1 People are living.
2 Many of them.
They are living.
3 Lots of them
in this world of ours a long time ago.

4 Crow and these—,
these seagulls are there.
5 The seagulls are Crow's slaves.
6 Her slaves are seagulls.

7 Crow was rather *siʔab*
when she was a person,
—that's how she is then—
in the first time of ours
in the world,
when a different world was yet laid out, at first.

8 It is the first time now,
when the world was created.

9 So then Crow travels on the water.
10 The day is very bright.
11 It is calm.
12 The day is intensely bright.
13 thus she travels.

14 The slaves are talking, the seagulls.
15 Lots of them.
Her slaves are the seagulls.
16 Just like seagulls always talking,
17 "**q$^{w}$əní, q$^{w}$əní, q$^{w}$əní, q$^{w}$əní, q$^{w}$əní**";
18 Thus just like that they "talked."

1 ʔəsłáłlil <tiʔíł. . . ,> tiʔíł ʔáciłtalbixʷ.
2 hi·kʷ
ʔəsłáłlil.
3 qa ʔál tiʔácəc swátixʷtəd ʔə tíʔəʔ gʷəł díbəł
ʔal kʷədíʔ tuhaʔkʷ.

4 tsíʔəʔ k̓áʔk̓aʔ <ʔi tíʔəʔ. . . ,>
ʔi tíʔəʔ <s. . . ,> kiyúuqʷs.
5 kiyúuqʷs tíʔəʔ <s. . . ,>
stú dəq ʔə tsíʔəʔ k̓áʔk̓aʔ.
6 <tiʔəʔ. . . ,> tiʔəʔ kiyúuqʷs stətúdəqs.

7a cick̓ʷ x̌əł ti siʔáb tsíʔəʔ k̓áʔk̓aʔ
<ti səshúys ʔal tíʔəʔ. . . ,>
7b ʔal kʷi c[əd]íł təsəshúys ʔáciłtalbixʷ
ʔal tíʔił tudᶻíxʷbid ʔə tíʔəʔ díbəłəxʷ
ʔal tíʔəʔ swátixʷtəd
ʔal kʷədíʔ təbəsəsbə́č ʔə kʷədíʔ təbələlíʔ swátixʷtəd tudᶻíxʷ.

8 dᶻíxʷbidəxʷ
ʔal kʷədíʔ tusqʷíbitəbsəxʷ ti → swátixʷtəd.

9 hay gʷəl ʔúlułəxʷ tsíʔəʔ k̓áʔk̓aʔ.
10 cick̓ʷ haʔł sləx̌íl.
11 ʔəsháʔləb.
12 pu·t (h)aʔł sləx̌íl.
13 huy ʔúlułəxʷ.

14 cúucəxʷ tíʔəʔ <ʔi. . . ,> stətúdəqs kiyúuqʷs.
15 qa·
tiʔíł kiyúuqʷs stətúdəqs.
16 x̌əł ti X̌(u)ucút tiʔíł kiyúuqʷs.
17 **“qʷəní qʷəní qʷəní qʷəní qʷəní.”**
18 huy x̌əł ti ʔugʷəcútad.

19 And then those seagulls prepared.
20 Thus they prepare their "*qíl̓b̓id*"—
their canoes.

21 And then they laid a mat, a sort of long long rug,
they made a woven path,
a place for Crow to walk
in order to get into the canoe.
22 It is spread out all the way to the canoe.
23 There must be a covering where she walks, that Crow.

24 Thus she is *siʔab*.
Crow is very *siʔab*
when she was a person.

25 Thus
her slaves put her on board.

26 Thus they take her.
27 They take her.
28 Her relatives are there.
Lots of them.
29 Her relatives are down at the shore just seeing her off.
30 They take her.

31 They take Crow.
32 Ye-s, it is perfectly still.

ılllr

33 Crow says,
34 **"I want you guys to take me,**
**to the son of** *x*$^{w}$*əyáliwa*.
35 **I want you guys to take me there."**

36 "*x*$^{w}$*əyáliwa* **is the name of the one, why she'll go,**
**why she goes,**
**why she goes, aha!"**

19 huy gʷəl gʷəqʷíbadəxʷ tiʔíɬ kiyúuqʷs.
20 huy qʷíbidəxʷ əlgʷəʔ tiʔíɬ <*canoes* əlgʷəʔ. . . ,>
q̓íl̓bids əlgʷəʔ.

21 huy gʷəl húyutəbəxʷ tiʔíɬ sɬágʷid,
cicəl̓šáad x̌əɬ ti,
<gʷə. . . ,> gʷədəxʷʔíbəš ʔə tsíʔəʔ k̓áʔk̓aʔ
ɬudəxʷq̓ílagʷil dxʷʔal tiʔíɬ q̓íl̓bid.
22 ʔəsɬə·x̌ dxʷʔál túdiʔ q̓il̓bid.
23 <ɬi. . . ,> yaw̓ ləscíl tiʔíɬ ǰásəds ʔal tiʔíɬ səʔíbəšs
tsiʔíɬ k̓áʔk̓aʔ

24 huy → siʔáb,
cick̓ʷ siʔáb tsi k̓áʔk̓aʔ
ʔal kʷi cədíɬ təsəshúys ʔáciɬtalbixʷ.

25 huy
ʔuq̓ílitəbəxʷ ʔə tíʔəʔ stətúdəqs.

26 huy ʔúluɬtubəxʷ.
27 ʔúluɬtubəxʷ.
28 qa tiʔíɬ ʔíišəds <əlgʷəʔ>.
29 x̌ʷul̓ ʔə(s)šúɬ tiʔəʔ ʔíišəds ʔəsk̓ʷít̓algʷiɬ.
30 ʔúluɬtubəxʷ.

31 ʔúluɬtubəxʷ tsíʔəʔ k̓áʔk̓aʔ.
32 ʔi·, ʔəslíqʷil.

33 cútcut tsiʔíɬ k̓áʔk̓aʔ. <dxʷʔál ti. . . , ʔal tiʔíɬ. . . ,>
34 **"dxʷʔál kʷi bədáʔ ʔə kʷi xʷəyáliwa**
**kʷi ɬusʔúx̌ʷtubšləp.**
35 **dxʷʔá kʷi ɬusʔúx̌ʷtubšləp."**

36 **"xʷəyáliwa tiʔiɬ sdaʔ ʔə tiʔíɬ ɬədəxʷʔúx̌ʷs,**
**dəxʷʔúx̌ʷs,**
**dəxʷʔúx̌ʷs háw̓əʔ."**

37 Thus the slaves take her.
38 There are lots of seagulls.
39 The seagulls are going along sort of talking.
They are taking dear Crow.
40 They are going along sort of talking.

41 All kinds of little animals hear about it.
42 Crow plans to travel to get a husband.
43 Now she wants to have a husband.
44 "Who will become her partner?"
45 and "Is this the one?"

46 Thus they announce to come down to the shore.
47 Just like the riff-raff to be first, I guess.
48 Ah—Raccoon is first.

49 Raccoon has prepared himself.
50 Since he has heard that Crow is going to get a husband—to. . . .
51 Who will become Crow's husband?
52 That Crow is very *si?ab*.
53 She is good.
54 And so Raccoon has prepared himself.

55 He paints up.
56 Raccoon paints his face.
57 He paints his face.
58 And how.
59 He paints his face with white and black
there on his face.
60 And he is ready.
61 Raccoon is all spruced up!
62 He really looks like somebody!

63 Thus he goes down to the water.
64 He goes down to the water as that Crow is coming.

37 huy ʔúx̌ʷtubəxʷ ʔə tíʔəʔ stətúdəq.
38 qa kiyúuqʷs.
39 x̌əł ti ləcút tíʔəʔ kiyúuqʷs
ləʔúlułtu tsíʔəʔ sʔúšəbabdxʷ k̓áʔk̓aʔ.
40 x̌əł ti ləcút.

41 lúdubəxʷ ʔə tíʔəʔ bək̓ʷ stab títčulbixʷ. <łu. . . ,>
42 łuʔíbəš kʷsi k̓áʔk̓aʔ l(ə)absčísčistxʷ.
43 x̌áƛ̓txʷəxʷ kʷi gʷəsəbsčístxʷils.
44 "gʷat kʷi <łusʔił. . . ,> łusʔiłhúygʷass."
45 gʷəl "dił ʔu tsi siʔáb."

46 huy, qʷíʔadəxʷ tíʔəʔ čágʷəxʷ.
47 xʷúʔələʔ ʔal kʷi dᶻixʷ tiʔíł <x̌əł ti,> p̓áp̓ap̓ƛ̓aƛ̓
48 ʔal → dᶻixʷ tíʔəʔ <stəb. . . ,> x̌áʔx̌alus.

49 qʷíbicutəxʷ tíʔəʔ x̌áʔx̌alus.
50 huy ʔəslúdxʷ l(ə)absčísčistxʷ tsíʔəʔ k̓áʔk̓aʔ
dxʷʔal kʷi łudəxʷ______.
51 gʷat kʷi dəxʷbəsčístxʷil ʔə tsiʔíł k̓áʔk̓aʔ.
52 cick̓ʷ siʔáb k̓áʔk̓aʔ tsiʔíł.
53 ʔəsƛ̓úbil.
54 huy gʷəl qʷíbicutəxʷ tíʔəʔ x̌áʔx̌alus.

55 [dxʷ]líq̓ʷusbəxʷ.
56 [dxʷ]x̌álusbəxʷ tiʔił <tiʔił stəb. . . ,> x̌áʔx̌alus.
57 [dxʷ]x̌álusəbəxʷ.
58 gʷəl ʔəx̌íd.
59 ʔə[xʷ]x̌álusəxʷ ʔə tiʔíł x̌ʷiqʷə́q̓ʷ ʔi tiʔíł x̌ibə́č
ʔal kʷədíʔ sʔácus(s).
60 gʷəl ʔəsqʷíb.
61 pútəxʷ haʔł tiʔíł x̌áʔx̌alus.
62 pútəxʷ x̌əł ti gʷat.

63 huy, k̓ʷít̓əxʷ.
64 k̓ʷít̓əxʷ ʔal tiʔíł cədíł səʔə́ƛ̓ ʔə tsiʔíł k̓áʔk̓aʔ.

65 She is going along singing, along by the shore,
along the shore
in the world
in the first time.
66 It is the first time now when the world was created
when everything was a person.

67 Thus Crow is going along singing as she travels on the water.
68 She is going along singing.
69 She is going along singing.
70 **"*káyəyə*'s going to marry,**
***káyəyə*'s going to marry,**
**the son of** $x^{w}$*əyáliwa* ,
$x^{w}$*əyáliwa*."
71 Crow is going along saying,
72 **"*káyəyə*'s going to marry,**
***káyəyə*'s going to marry,**
**the son of** $x^{w}$*əyáliwa*,
$x^{w}$*əyáliwa*."
73 Crow is saying it.

74 She is going along singing what she says.
75 She is going along to get a husband,
the son of $x^{w}$*əyáliwa*,
that Shell aha!: $x^{w}$*əyáliwa*.
76 He's the one she names.
77 He's a *siʔab* person.
He's why Crow goes.

78 Thus they take her.
79 **"Land it, folks!**
80 **Maybe he's the one."**
81 She and the seagulls land.

82 Suddenly Raccoon is at the shore.
He's going along all painted up.
83 That Raccoon is really very fine, the poor guy.
84 He thinks that he is the one Crow is going for.

65 ləƛ̕ílib ʔal kʷədíʔ sʔílgʷił,
ʔal tiʔéʔ sʔílgʷił
ʔal tiʔəʔ swátixʷtəd
ʔal kʷədíʔ tudᶻíxʷ.
66 dᶻíxʷbidəxʷ ʔə kʷi tədəxʷqʷíbitəbsəxʷ tíʔəʔ swátixʷtəd
[ʔal kʷi] təsəshúys əlgʷəʔ tuʔáciłtalbixʷ tiʔəʔ bək̓ʷ stab.

67 huy ləƛ̕ílib tsíʔəʔ k̓áʔk̓aʔ [ʔal] tiʔíł səʔúlułs.
68 ləƛ̕ílib.
69 <l. . . ,> ləƛ̕ílib.
70 **"ləbək̓íxʷk̓ixʷ káyəyə**
**ləbək̓ḷixʷk̓ixʷ káyəyə**
**dxʷʔal kʷi bədáʔ ʔə xʷəyáliwa,**
**xʷəyáliwa."**
71 ləcútcut tsiʔíł k̓áʔk̓aʔ.
72 **"ləbək̓íxʷk̓ixʷ káyəyə**
**ləbək̓íxʷk̓ixʷ káyəyə**
**dxʷʔal kʷi bədáʔ ʔə xʷəyáliwa,**
**xʷəyáliwa."**
73 cútcut tsíʔəʔ k̓áʔk̓aʔ.

74 ləƛ̕ílib tiʔəʔ səcútcuts.
75 l(ə)absč̓íšč̓istxʷs dxʷʔal tiʔił bədaʔ ʔə kʷi xʷəyáliwa,
tiʔił xʷč̓íłqs haw̓əʔ tiʔił xʷəyáliwa.
76 dił lədídaʔad.
77 siʔáb ʔáciłtalbixʷ <tiʔił. . . ,>
tiʔíł dəxʷəʔúx̌ʷs t[s]iʔíł k̓áʔk̓aʔ.

78 huy, ʔúlułtub.
79 **"<ła. . . ,> łáliltxʷ łi.**
80 **gʷədíł kʷədáʔ."**
81 łálil tiʔíł ʔi kiyúuqʷs.

82 diʔł kʷi sčaʔkʷ ʔə tíʔəʔ x̌áʔx̌alus
lə[dxʷ]x̌álus[əb].
83 pútəxʷ haʔł tiʔíł x̌áʔx̌alus, sʔušəbábdxʷ.
84 ʔəxʷ[s]cútəb cədíł kʷi dəxʷəʔúx̌ʷ ʔə tsíʔəʔ k̓áʔk̓aʔ.

85 However, they keep saying,
86 **"He's the wrong one, he is."**
87 **"Ah, wrong again, wrong again, wrong again,**
**wrong again, wrong again,"**
88 The seagulls say it.

89 **"Take it away from that guy, you folks!**
90 **Am I going for somebody painted up like that,**
**little paint-up face?"**
91 She insults poor Raccoon again.

92 He goes.
93 He goes up from the shore.
94 Raccoon is going along heartbroken.

---

95 Thus Crow is going on again, along the shore's edge.
96 She is traveling.
97 The day is bright.

98 It is calm.
99 She is still going along.

100 She's off again.
101 "***káyəyə*'s going to marry,**
***káyəyə*'s going to marry,**
**the son of** $x^{w}$*əyáliwa*,
$x^{w}$*əyáliwa*."

102 Still she goes.

---

103 Suddenly a fine man is again at the shore.
(What's this?)
It's Drake Buffelhead.

85 x̌ʷúl̕əxʷ bələcút(t)əb.
86 **"ləlí·ʔ tə ʔa."**
87 **"ʔa·, məlelíʔ məlelíʔ məlelíʔ**
**məlelíʔ məlelíʔ."**
88 cútcut tíʔəʔ kiyúuqʷs.

89 **"čaʔkʷtxʷ łi ʔə <tə...,> tə gədú.**
90 **cədił dᶻəł cəxʷəʔúx̌ʷ ʔəxʷx̌álus(s),**
**ʔəxʷx̌áʔx̌alusəd."**
91 bəqx̌átəb tíʔəʔ ʔušəbábdxʷ x̌áʔx̌alus.

92 ʔux̌ʷ.
93 čúbə.
94 ləsx̌ələł x̌əč tiʔíł x̌áʔx̌alus.

95 huy, bəhíwil tsíʔəʔ k̓áʔk̓aʔ ʔal tíʔəʔ liłʔílgʷił.
96 ləʔúluł.
97 haʔł sləx̌íl.

98 ʔəsháʔləb.
99 bələʔúx̌ʷ sixʷ.

100 bəhíwil.
101 **"ləbək̓íxʷk̓ixʷ kayəyə**
**ləbək̓íxʷk̓ixʷ kayəyə**
**dxʷʔál kʷi bədáʔ ʔə xʷəyáliwa,**
**xʷəyáliwa."**

102 bəʔúx̌ʷ sixʷ.

103 diʔł kʷi bəsčáʔkʷ ʔə tíʔəʔ ha·ʔł
<tiʔə́ʔ stəb...,>
tíʔəʔ s t̕ət̕tqʷíʔ.

104 He is very fine.
105 He kept changing.
106 His head kept changing.
There is something about how his hair is,
something about his hair.

107 He is very fine.
He kept changing.
108 It is every color:
109 blue,
sort of red inside,
sort of pink.
That's how it is.
110 sort of what? what would you say?
sort of yellowish-green.
111 That is fine.
His head kept changing,
that poor man.

112 Thus Crow says again,
113 **"Beach it, you folks!**
114 **Now this might be the one."**

115 The seagulls go up from shore again.
116 They are going along talking.
117 They're ashore.
118 They all go up the bank.

119 This Drake Buffelhead is coming down to the shore.
120 He is fine, "pretty."
Something about his little head is fine.
121 It was extremely so—
His hat, whatever it is, kept changing.

122 And then the seagulls say it again.
123 **"He is wrong; he's the wrong one.**
124 **He's wrong too.**
125 **He's wrong too."**
126 Thus, **"Take it away, you folks!"**

104 put haʔɬ <stəb. . . >.
105 ʔuləlalíʔcut.
106 ʔuləlalíʔcut tíʔəʔ sx̌əy̓úss
x̌əɬ ti səshúys sq̓ədᶻúʔs
gʷəsq̓ədᶻúʔsəs.

107 put haʔɬ
ʔuləlalíʔcut.
108 bəkʷ ʔəsʔəx̌ídəb:
109 x̌ʷiq̓ʷíx̌ʷ,
x̌əɬ ti ʔəxʷčcíligʷəd,
x̌əɬ ti *pink* kʷədíʔ
səshúy ʔə tíʔəʔ.
110 <x̌əɬ ti ʔəs. . . ,> stab <gʷəs. . . ,> gʷəscút(t)əbs,
x̌əɬ ti x̌ʷiqʷác.
111 ha·ʔɬ tiʔíɬ
suləlalíʔcut ʔə tíʔəʔ sx̌əy̓ús <ʔə tíʔəʔ. . . ,>
ʔə tíʔəʔ cədíɬ sʔušəbábdxʷ.

112 huy bəcút(t)əb ʔə tsiʔəʔ k̓áʔk̓aʔ.
113 **"dxʷt̓áq̓ttxʷ ɬi!**
114 **díɬəxʷ kʷədáʔ."**

115 bəčúbə əlgʷəʔ tíʔəʔ díʔəʔ kiyúuqʷs.
116 bələcútcut.
117 ɬálil əlgʷəʔ.
118 t̓át̓aq̓tagʷil.

119 ləkʷít̓ tsiʔíɬ st̓ət̓tqʷíʔ.
120 <háʔɬ *pretty*. . . ,>
haʔɬ kʷədíʔ sx̌íʔx̌əy̓ùs ʔə tíʔəʔ cədíɬ.
121 put yu tiʔəʔ <səsči. . . ,> suləlalíʔcut ʔə tíʔəʔ gʷəšíqʷs
gʷəstábs[əs].

122 huy gʷəl bəcút(t)əb ʔə tíʔəʔ kiyúuqʷs.
123 **"lalí·ʔ tə lə lalíʔ.**
124 **ƛ̓al' bəlalíʔ.**
125 **ƛ̓al' bəlalíʔ"**
126 hu·y **"dxʷčáʔkʷtxʷ ɬi!"**

127 Thus she goes again.

128 And they come to the next one she lands for.

129 This is Deer.
Everyone came down to the shore.
Something has been said.
130 Deer fixed himself up.
131 He made his antlers nice.
132 Everything is just so.
133 He is prepared.

134 No—.
135 He's the wrong one too again.
Deer.

136 There is Bear.
137 He thinks he is the reason Crow is traveling.
138 Again: Bear comes down to shore.

139 **"He's wrong too.**
140 **He's not the one."**

141 Bear is fine in the way he is prepared.
142 His fur is slicked and shiny: extremely fine.
143 Hanging his head—
hanging his head bashfully, Bear comes toward the water.

144 She just said this,
145 **"Take it away, folks.**
146 **He's wrong.**
147 **Now that would be something,**
**for me to be going for someone like him.**
148 **Ugly Stretch-eyes!"**

127 huy bəʔúx̌ʷ.

128 gʷəl ʔálil tiʔił cədił bədəxʷɬálils

129 tíʔəʔ sqígʷəc
bək̓ʷ tučáʔkʷ kʷədíʔ
ƛ̕ucút(t)əb.
130 ʔuqʷíbicut tiʔíł sqígʷəc.
131 háʔlid tiʔíł gʷádaʔkʷs.
132 put ʔəstábtxʷ.
133 ʔəsqʷíbtxʷ.

134 xʷi·ʔ.
135 ƛ̕al̕ bələlíʔ
tiʔíł <ləx̌ál, ʔi kiyúuqʷs, stəb,
kiyúuqʷs, huy stəb ʔi·. . . ,> sqígʷəc.

136 kʷi sčə́txʷəd.
137 dił ʔəxʷscútəb cədíł kʷədáʔ kʷi dəxʷəʔíbəš ʔə tsiʔíł k̓áʔk̓aʔ.
138 bəčáʔkʷ tíʔəʔ sčə́txʷəd.

139 **“ƛ̕al̕ bələlíʔ.**
140 **xʷiʔ lədíł.”**

141 haʔł kʷi səsqʷíb ʔə tíʔəʔ sčə́txʷəd.
142 put ʔugʷíličəb tíʔəʔ t̓ábids (h)aʔł.
143 <ləsdᶻəqíl. . . ,>
ləsdᶻíʔdᶻəqil̕ kʷi sək̓ʷít̓ ʔə tíʔəʔ sčə́txʷəd.

144 x̌ʷul̕ ʔucúcut(t)əb.
145 **“[dxʷ]ča·ʔkʷtxʷ łi.**
146 **ləlíʔ.**
147 **cədił dᶻəł kʷi**
**cəxʷəʔúx̌ʷ tə pútəxʷ ʔəstábtab.**
148 **ʔəxʷsʔút̓ʔut̓alus.”**

149 That poor Bear went.
150 His heart is crumbling.

151 The seagulls go.
152 Again they are traveling.
153 They are going along saying,
154 **"*káyəyə*'s going to marry,**
**_káyəyə_'s going to marry,**
**the son of** *$x^{w}$əyáliwa*,
*$x^{w}$əyáliwa*."
155 Again they are going along.

156 And again they are coming to land.

157 Again there is someone, and he came down to shore.
158 Again he is also fine.
159 This one has prepared himself.
He and others came down to shore.
160 It was duck who was last, I guess.
161 Mallard and these others.
162 So there, that's just how it was.
163 This duck came down to shore.

164 He's wrong too.

165 Again they go.
166 Again the seagulls push themselves off.
167 The seagulls are always going along screeching.
168 **"He's wrong too, nya, nya, wrong one,**
**wrong one, wrong one."**

149 ʔuʔúx̌ʷ tiʔíł sʔušəbábdxʷ sčə́txʷəd.
150 ləsx̌ə́łəł x̌əč.

151 ʔux̌ʷ ti kiyúuqʷs.
152 bələʔúluł əlgʷəʔ.
153 ləcútcut.
154 **"ləbək̓íxʷk̓ixʷ káyəyə**
**ləbək̓ixʷk̓ixʷ káyəyə**
**dxʷʔal ti bədáʔ ʔə xʷəyáliwa,**
**xʷəyáliwa."**
155 bələʔúx̌ʷ.

156 gʷəl → bələłálil əlgʷəʔ.

157 bəstábəxʷ tíʔəʔ b(ə)učáʔkʷ.
158 ƛ̕al̓ bəháʔł.
159 ʔəsqʷíbicut tíʔəʔ cədíł
ʔučáʔkʷ ʔi stábəxʷ.
160 xʷúʔələʔ tubúʔqʷəxʷ kʷi tuliłláq.
161 <ti dəxʷ. . . > x̌átx̌at ʔi kʷi təbəliłkʷə́lq.
162 tux̌ʷ (h)uy x̌ʷul̓ ʔəsʔístəʔ.
163 tiʔəʔ buʔqʷ kʷi tučáʔkʷ.

164 ƛ̕al̓ bəlalíʔ.

165 bəʔúx̌ʷ.
166 bəhíqicut tíʔəʔ kiyúuqʷs.
167 ƛ̕aləx̌áƛ̕il tíʔəʔ kiyúuqʷs.
168 **"ƛ̕a·l̓ məlalíʔ, məlalíʔ, məlalíʔ, məlalíʔ."**

169 That is the reason seagulls chatter.
170 Whenever they flew,
171 then they would just talk, sort of like that.
172 Whatever they're doing,
173 now they'll make a racket.

174 They screeched.

175 Thus they were that way,
when they were people.
176 Thus it was.

177 Crow had made them slaves.
178 Crow was rather *si?ab*,
when she was a person.

179 And then they come to the next one she lands for.

180 Thus someone over there talks about it,
"Crow is coming to get a husband."
181 Thus someone way over there knows about it.
It is Shell.
182 Thus, "My son is the one Crow is coming for.
183 Well, Crow is very *si?ab*."
184 Thus the people prepare themselves.

185 So the landing party was gotten ashore.
186 And the seagulls were talking,
187 **"That's the one! That's the one!**
**That's the one! That's the one!**
188 **That's the one! That's the one!**
**That's the one! That's the one!**
189 **So this is the place for our lady to land again."**

190 **"Land it, folks!**
191 **This is it according to you scoundrels."**
192 They landed.

169 diɫ tíʔəʔ dəxʷəscútucid ʔə tíʔəʔ kiyúuqʷs.
170 ʔəbíl̓əxʷ gʷus[áq̓ʷaq̓ʷ]saq̓ʷ.
171 gʷəl gʷucútcutəxʷ x̌ʷúl̓ab ʔə tiʔíɫ x̌əɫ ti diɫ.
172 ʔəbíl̓əxʷ əlgʷəʔ gʷuʔəx̌íd.
173 gʷəl ɫuƛələ́diʔ əlgʷəʔ.

174 ʔux̌áx̌aƛil.

175 <huy...,> huy diɫ təsəshúys əlgʷəʔ
ʔal kʷi təsəshúys əlgʷəʔ ʔáciɫtalbixʷ.
176 tuhúy.

177 t(u)ashúyutəb stúdəq ʔə tsíʔəʔ k̓áʔk̓aʔ.
178 <tu...,> tusʔíʔiʔəb tsiʔíɫ k̓áʔk̓aʔ
ʔal kʷi təsəshúys → ʔáciɫtalbixʷ.

179 hu·y gʷəl ʔálil kʷi cə[dí]ɫ dəxʷɫálils.

180 huy → cút(t)əbəxʷ ʔə kʷədiʔ di[ʔiʔ]
"ləʔəƛáxʷ tsi k̓áʔk̓aʔ l(ə)absč̓ísč̓istxʷ."
181 huy, → háydubəxʷ ʔə túdiʔ cə[dí]ɫ <dəbə́ɫ tiʔácəc...,>
xʷč̓íɫqs.
182 "huy, diɫ tiʔíɫ dbədáʔ kʷi dəxʷəʔə́ƛ ʔə tsi k̓áʔk̓aʔ.
183 huy, hikʷ siʔáb tsiʔíɫ k̓áʔk̓aʔ."
184 huy, qʷíbicutəxʷ tiʔíɫ ʔáciɫtalbixʷ.

185 hay, ʔúx̌ʷtubəxʷ tiʔíɫ ɫálil əlgʷəʔ.
186 <gʷə[l] →cu[t]...> cútcutəxʷ tiʔəʔ kiyúuqʷs.
187 **"ni·ɫ tə, ni·ɫ tə,**
**ni·ɫ tə, ni·ɫ tə.**
188 **ni·ɫ tə, ni·ɫ tə,**
**ni·ɫ tə, ni·[ɫ tə].**
189 **hay, → bədíɫəxʷ tiʔíɫ sʔəxʷɫálil[əb] ʔə tsiʔíɫ sixʷsiʔáb čəɫ."**

190 **"ɫáliltxʷ ɫi!**
191 **díɫəxʷ kʷəɫ ʔə tiʔəʔ xʷíʔ ləháʔhaʔɫ."**
192 ɫá·lil.

193 And, the *si?ab* people who lived there pulled them up.
194 And then, a walkway was made for Crow.
195 It was none other than a ceremonial blanket
which was spread up the beach
way up toward the house,
a grand house.
196 And so, Crow went to get a husband.

197 Her seagull slaves were dancing about.
198 **"He's the one, he's the one, he's the one,**
**he's the one, he's the one, he's the one,**
199 **he's the one, he's the one, he's the one."**

200 That is the reason seagulls chatter
just like seagulls, always screeching.
201 That is how I recognize them:
they'll make a racket.
That is what is said about them in the story.

202 So Crow and that one, that Shell, have a wedding.
203 Shell is *si?ab*.
204 The son of Shell is very fine.
205 He was quite iridescent
that's how he is
He glittered quite beautifully.
206 He is good looking in every way.
His clothing glitters.
that's him.

207 Thus Crow is pleased.
208 Thus they will be wed now.
209 She is seated beside that one, a Shell.

193 <gʷəl → lətáb tx̌ʷu. . . > tx̌ʷútəb əlgʷəʔ ʔə tiʔə́ʔ siʔiʔab ʔəsłáłlil.
194 huy gʷəl, ʔəshúyutəbəxʷ tíʔəʔ dəxʷcícəl̓šaadəbəxʷ ʔə tsiʔəʔ k̓áʔk̓aʔ.
195 x̌ʷúl̓ul̓ k̓ʷástədùliċaʔ tiʔíł
ʔułə́x̌təb dxʷƛ̓á·q̇t
dxʷʔal túdiʔ ʔálʔal,
hi·kʷ ʔálʔal.
196 huy gʷəl ʔúx̌ʷəxʷ tsi k̓áʔk̓aʔ <lə. . . > [l(ə)a]bsčísčistxʷ.

197 dᶻúbdᶻubalikʷəxʷ tíʔəʔ ʔikiyúuqʷs stətúdəqs.
198 **"ni··ł tə, ni·ł tə, ni·ł tə,**
**ni·ł tə, ni·ł tə, ni·ł tə,**
199 **ni·ł tə, ni·ł tə, ni·ł tə."**

200 [dił] tiʔíł ƛ̓ədəxʷucútcuts əlgʷəʔ
x̌əł ti ƛ̓ux̌áx̌aƛ̓il tíʔəʔ kiyúuqʷs.
201 <dił cəxʷ. . . > dił ƛ̓əc[əxʷ]ə(s)súxʷtəš
łuƛ̓əládiʔəs
tiʔił ƛ̓uscút(t)əbs ʔal ti <s. . . ,> syəyəhúb.

202 hay, bəlyíhəxʷ tsiʔíł k̓áʔk̓aʔ ʔi ti cədíł dəbə́ł tiʔíł xʷčiłqs.
203 siʔáb tiʔíł xʷčiłqs.
204 pu·t (h)aʔł tíʔəʔ bədáʔ ʔə tíʔəʔ xʷčiłqs.
205 put ʔuləl(ə)líʔcut
tíʔəʔ səshuys
suċəlqʷcúts put (h)aʔł.
206 bək̓ʷ (ʔ)əsʔəx̌íd haʔł šuł
suċəlqʷcúts tíʔəʔ sƛ̓álabacs
səshúys.

207 huy ǰúʔtəbəxʷ tsi k̓áʔk̓aʔ.
208 huy <łubəlyí. . . > łuhúygʷasəxʷ əlgʷəʔ.
209 gʷədíltub ʔəsq̇ʷúʔ ʔə tiʔəʔ cədíł dəbə́ł tíʔəʔ xʷčiłqs.

210 Thus, the people are pleased, according to custom.
211 And then they are pleased.
212 Crow has brought a loaded canoe.
There is lots.
smelt and everything,
herring and everything.
213 They always just went.
214 And they always helped themselves from the canoes.
215 And then they always just took that.
216 And they will help themselves from the piles,
from her feasting canoes.
217 Thus,
that is the reason everyone is pleased,
according to custom.

218 So Crow and that one, a Shell, are married.
219 And so everyone has been pleased.

220 So they have danced and danced now.
221 They are rapt as they always become when they sing.
222 They dance and dance.
223 They circled all around the fire.
224 Thus Crow was wed at the place she went in.

225 And that's the end of it,
that's it,
that's it, pertaining to Crow.

210 huy kʷaʔ ǰúʔiləxʷ tíʔəʔ ʔáciłtalbixʷ.
211 huy gʷəl ǰúʔiləxʷ.
212 təl(ə)abxʷq̓íl tsíʔəʔ k̓áʔk̓aʔ
tíʔəʔ qa· <...stəb...>
tíʔəʔ <s...,> šídᶻus, kʷi bək̓ʷ stab,
st̓úʔəl kʷi bək̓ʷ stab.
213 x̌ʷúl̕əxʷ ƛ̕uʔúx̌ʷ.
214 gʷəl ƛ̕utábad ʔal tiʔíł q̓íl̕q̓il̕bid.
215 gʷəl (h)uy x̌ʷul̕ ƛ̕uʔúx̌ʷtxʷ.
216 gʷəl łutábad ʔal tiʔił k̓ʷəłk̓ʷłád
[tul̕]ʔál tiʔíł q̓íl̕q̓il̕bid ʔə tsíʔəʔ <tiʔəʔ səs...,> səs.
217 huy
díłəxʷ kʷaʔ dəxʷǰúʔil ʔə tiʔíł cáadił.

218 hay bəlyí tsi k̓áʔk̓aʔ ʔi tíʔəʔ cədíł
[dábəł tiʔacəc] [xʷ]čiłqs.
219 gʷəl (h)uy tuǰúʔiləxʷ tíʔəʔ cáadił.

220 hay tudᶻúbdᶻubalikʷəxʷ əlgʷəʔ.
221 x̌áłəxʷ əlgʷəʔ ti ƛ̕ux̌ʷul̕ábil əlgʷəʔ ƛ̕utádᶻ.
222 dᶻúbdᶻubalikʷəxʷ.
223 ʔuqítqitid əlgʷəʔ tíʔəʔ hud.
224 huy, ʔuhúygʷasəxʷ tsíʔəʔ k̓áʔk̓aʔ ʔal tiʔəʔ <cə...,>
dəxʷhədʔíw̓s.

225 gʷəl → dił tu(s)šác̓s
tiʔíł <,...
tiʔíł, ʔə...,> dxʷʔal ʔádad k̓áʔk̓aʔ.

# NOTES TO TEXT 2

1 *ʔaciłtalbixʷ* means not only "people," but also Indian people, as opposed to other races.

34 *xʷəyaliwa* is a man's personal name and does not mean "Shell."

45 After this line on the original tape recording, Mr. and Mrs. Lamont speak to their dogs, who are interrupting the storytelling.

47 *p̓ap̓ap̓ƛ̓aƛ̓*, a reduplicated form of *p̓aƛ̓aƛ̓*. Some ethnographers report the use of *p̓aƛ̓aƛ̓* to refer to anyone who is not *siʔab*; others report that it referred to the very poor and to slaves. In any case, Raccoon is not the most desirable husband for Crow. The suitors become more noble as the story progresses.

53 *ʔəsƛ̓ubił* refers to Crow's reputation for virtue, as attested by her traveling with slaves and not alone, as well as to her magnificence; it may be tongue-in-cheek.

55 *liq̓ʷus[ə]b*. Literally, to paint one's face red, used to describe the preparations of people who are going to dance their spirit powers (see the introduction to text 3).

70 Crow, like Raven and the seagulls, has her own distinctive way of talking: "*k̓ixʷk̓ixʷ*" is her way of saying "*čisčistxʷ*," "to look for a husband."

70ff Songs in stories often have the effect of helping people get things done: in Susan Sampson Peter's Starchild story, for example, a homesick slave sings as he chops wood, and his family hears the song and rescues him (Hilbert 1980:8–9). In Lushootseed religion, singing is a way of expressing one's relationship to a guardian spirit or of mobilizing the power the spirit provides. The elevated diction in the lines surrounding Crow's singing indicates that hers is some sort of power song.

In stories whose protagonists are people who were later limited to their animal identities by the Changer, the power songs usually are not offered as authentic, but are recognizably parodies.

82 *tiʔəʔ*. Mrs. Lamont misspeaks and says "*tsiʔəʔ*" on the tape.

87 *mələliʔ*. Stylized speech equivalent to *bələliʔ*.

106 *sq̓ədᶻuʔ*, human hair. His hair when he was a person was as beautiful as his headfeathers are today.

135 In this line, Mrs. Lamont says "*ləx̌ál*" and "*kiyuuqʷs*" while searching for the word she really needs, "*sqigʷəc*."

Even though Mrs. Lamont does not say it is the seagulls who say the first two words here, one can tell this from the "seagull voice" she uses. This is also true of lines 139 in Bear's story and 164 in Mallard's.

178 Note reduplication in *siʔiʔab*, Crow is a little bit *siʔab*.

187–189 *nił təʔ*, the seagulls' way of saying *dił təʔ*. Notice how the cadence of the seagull's chant as rendered by Mrs. Lamont is carried over into the rest of their speech (which ends on 189), so that one can tell in line 190 that it is now Crow who is speaking, even though no change of speaker is announced.

193 Crow and her party sit in the canoe while it is brought up on shore, so that they do not even get their feet wet.

202–204 The concept of "shell" itself carries in it notions of wealth, power, and beauty. The generic word for oyster nowadays is *ƛ̓ux̌ʷƛ̓ux̌ʷ*. But *xʷčilqs* is specifically a large native oyster-like shell that was formerly used much as money is used today. In addition, iridescent shell (chiefly mother-of-pearl and abalone) was used on ceremonial objects to represent the presence of spirit power. The son of Shell may also have chosen the glittering colors of his clothing to reflect the spirit power that he has—just as today, people will wear certain colors or drive a car of a certain color as a way of nurturing their relationship with their spirit helpers (Bierwert 1986:445).

224 *dəxʷ(h)ədiẃs*. Literally, the place of her (going or being received) inside. The word is used as a metaphor for being accepted into a family of note.

225 *dił (s)šac̓s*. That is the ending of it, a traditional way to end a story. Mrs. Lamont's inclusion of *tu-*, emphasizing that it was a long time ago, is unusual.

# TRANSCRIPTION OF CROW'S SONG

Line 70 (Line 72 is a close variant)

Transcription by Tara Browner

## CROW IS SICK

### INTRODUCTION

"Crow Is Sick" is a story about social relations, which are especially problematic when it comes to the management of spirit power. In one sense, the story is a variant of the "bungling host" genre. (The bungling host invites a guest for whom he tries, and humorously fails, to provide food by supernatural means.) In "Crow Is Sick," the occasion is not a feast, but one of the most revered of Lushootseed institutions, the winter dance; and the host is not Crow, but her family.

The winter dance is a gathering at which people ceremonially dance to songs that have been given to them personally by their guardian spirits. In the autumn, at the beginning of the ceremonial season, people who have such songs become "sick"—troubled by a need to dance. An important part of maintaining the good relationship between people and their spirit helpers is dancing regularly during the winter season.

People who will be singing their songs for the first time are often especially troubled, and there is a prescribed way of managing such a crisis. When Mrs. Lamont's audience heard "Crow Is Sick," they had a model with which they could compare Crow's and Raven's behavior in the story. First, an Indian doctor is called in to determine the cause of the sickness. (For more on Indian doctors, see text 4, "Shaman Cure.") When it has been determined that it is a song that is troubling the person, the doctor helps to bring out the song and its dance; and, during the course of this work, details about the costume and face paint the new dancer is to wear may be revealed. When the song has been brought out, relatives host a gathering at which the new dancer will dance in public while the new song is being sung and drummed by other members of the community. At this time, the dancer may be given a new name.

In Lushootseed practice, a winter-dance gathering, even when hosted by one family, is not an event for the benefit of one person only. Many people usually dance their powers at a gathering, not just the new dancer; and the whole community has a chance to help make a home for all the spirit helpers by coming together and giving their attention and support. Failure to take proper care of this duty can result in hardship, not only for people whose powers are not recognized, but also for the community.

The way Raven helps his sister when she begins to be troubled by her song does not conform to common practice, of course; but then, whenever it comes to food—and with Raven, everything comes down to food—Raven's interpretations are always idiosyncratic. For example, people have to tell Raven that he needs to find out what is wrong with his sister. (Presumably any real adult would have lived through enough winter seasons not to need telling.) Raven does know, however, that what he ought to do is call in an Indian doctor: we know this, because what he does is to "doctor" his sister himself. A real *dxʷdaʔəb* would sing a song to call his spirit helpers, but Raven's song is useful only to lend a doctor-like authority to his own "diagnosis": that people are making his sister sick because they have designs on her supply of winter provisions. This appears to be step one in a plan to trick *x̌ənimulića?* out of her food, especially as Mrs. Lamont caps the "doctoring" incident with the obviously sarcastic comment, "*x̌ʷax̌ʷaq̓ʷəxʷ tiʔił kaw̓qs dxʷʔal tsiʔəʔ ʔalš̓s ʔəsx̌əł.*" ("Raven was troubled about his sister, who was sick.")

Another discrepancy with customary practice is Crow's agreeing to let Raven take the food out to people, instead of having them eat at her house. In Lushootseed literature, when Raven offers to take care of the berries someone has gathered or the salmon they have caught, the audience bursts into laughter because they know that Raven will eat up all that has been entrusted to him as soon as the owner's back is turned. *x̌ənimulića?* in this story has a very powerful wealth-giving spirit power; it is a mystery how she can be so gifted and yet so dumb: perhaps she did not pay attention when her grandmother told Raven stories.

In the last part of the story (line 58 on), Mrs. Lamont seems to slow down the narrative pace (that is, the rate at which new ideas or actions are introduced, rather than the rate at which words are delivered, which is in fact speedy here) and to dwell on the one fact that Raven is stealing the food his sister has prepared for her guests. (Note that here again, as in text 2, it seems to be Crow herself who is providing the food, when one would expect her relatives to do this.) The reader needs to keep in mind that the audience would be laughing here, and each time that Mrs. Lamont has another serving dished up, they would laugh again. This kind of narrative, in which much depends on the storyteller's facial expression, tone of voice, and gestures all fueling and responding to audience reaction, is the kind that suffers most from being reduced to writing.

The reader will also notice that Mrs. Lamont closes her story by retelling part of it. There are a couple of possible explanations for this. When a storyteller is not satisfied with how the story has gone, he or she may append an explanation or recapitulation of its salient features at the end. We see this often when people are telling stories in English to collectors and are afraid that the point of the story may not be getting across. Another possibility is this: there is a form of closure in Lushootseed literature that recapitulates the main incidents of the story in reverse order at the end, so that the story ends exactly where it begins. (See Dora Solomon's "Star Story" in Hilbert 1980:5–13 and text 7 in this volume.) This is a beautiful and difficult thing to bring off, and Mrs. Lamont seems to have had something like it in mind for

"Crow Is Sick."

Aside from the ending, however, we find few formal structures in this story; and even the conventional introduction and alternation of bridge and scene are not fully exploited: the introduction is one line long, as is the only bridge passage with a travel motif. We find passages of commentary acting as bridges between scenes, and we find scenes juxtaposed without bridging; we find a long passage of summary narration that might be considered a bridge, except that it intervenes between a scene and the final passage of authorial commentary. In fact, the first thing one notices about this story is that there is more comment than there is drama. Mrs. Lamont is up to something different here, and she relies almost exclusively upon the technique of rhythm to accomplish it.

This story, in which Raven several times takes food, goes away with it, and returns, might have been developed in passages of parallel narration, but Mrs. Lamont has avoided this; although narration of Raven's activities is repeated, the order of the elements is varied and the syntax almost never paralleled. Mrs. Lamont seems to want to save repetition for another purpose, for use as a component of rhythm, by which is meant the varied repetition at irregular intervals of symbols, concepts, or actions in such a way that they accrue meaning. This accrual can come from the changing contexts in which the repeated element is introduced, or it can come from slight changes in the element itself. (The term "rhythm", then, does not apply to repeated words, groups of words, or syntactic patterns that are used the same way every time they recur or that recur at proportioned or regular intervals.)

The most obvious rhythms in the first part of the story involve concepts collecting around *ƛ̕ub*, *x̌əɬ*, *x̌ʷax̌ʷaq̓ʷbid* and the words for verbal communication: *cut* and *ʔil(i)*.

We see *ƛ̕ub* ("in good order," "practicable," "healthy") first as used to talk about what would be helpful to do; people are always telling Raven, "*ƛ̕ub čəxʷ*..." ("It would be a good idea if you...") We see it also used in the form *ƛ̕ubil* ("getting better") for the result desired, Crow's recovery. Then Raven appropriates *ƛ̕ub* for his own plans ("It would be better if you just dished up the food...."), and what seems a good idea to him is, of course, a bad idea. Finally, it becomes an emblem of Crow's stupefied state: "*bəƛ̕ub,*" she says, agreeing once more to something that someone wrongly thinks would be a good idea. The opposite of *ƛ̕ub* at the beginning of the story is *x̌əɬ* ("sick"), and all of the good ideas are designed to combat sickness. But by the end of the story, *ƛ̕ub*'s opposite has become *saʔ* ("bad"), the judgment on what Raven has done to carry out the good ideas.

Likewise, *x̌əɬ* is used at first for Crow's illness, and *x̌ʷax̌ʷaq̓ʷbid* ("troubled") for Raven's worried state of mind. Line 7 accepts them equally as legitimate. After Raven has sung his doctoring song comes a line very similar to line 7, only now we know that Raven's trouble is not legitimate, while Crow really is sick. Finally, just before Crow sings her song, she is described as "troubled" (*x̌ʷax̌ʷaq̓ʷbid)*, but Raven's discomfort is never so real that he can be called "sick" (*x̌əɬ*).

The action in the first part of the story consists of what people say to each other: *cut*. People give advice, and Raven warps it to his own purposes. Each step forward in the plot is triggered by people talking to Raven. In the second part of the story, when Raven's scheme is in full swing, another group of words and phrases is used rhythmically, this time on a more strictly comic level (*cilitəb*, "dished up"; *páq̓atəb*, "distributed"; *ʔúx̌ʷtxʷ*, "take away"; and *líʔlil*, "a little way off"). At the end, in a brilliant circular figure, Mrs. Lamont reintroduces *ƛ̕ub* and *cut* in a new context: *ƛ̕ub* as contrasted with *saʔ*, as we have noted; and *cut* (what was said) contrasted with *huyud* (what was done).

## A Note on Further Reading

A fascinating and reliable work on the religion of the northern Lushootseed people is Amoss (1978). For an earlier description specifically of the winter dance among the Skagit, see Collins (1974:171–189); it should be remembered, however, that Collins did most of her fieldwork in the 1940s, when the winter dance was considered—mistakenly, as it turns out—to be becoming a thing of the past. Jilek, a psychiatrist, documents what he identifies as the therapeutic value of winter dancing (1982), based on his experience as a medical doctor among the Halkomelem-speaking Salish people of the Fraser Valley in British Columbia. For a study that places winter dancing in the context of the year-round ceremonial life of a Salish village (Musqueam, near Vancouver, B.C.) see Kew (1970).

## CROW IS SICK

1 They are dwelling where they are.

2 Then Crow is sick.
3 Crow is sick for a long time.
4 She is not well.

5 But she [will] be all right.

6 He is worried about his sister, Raven is.
7a He is worried about his sister
for a way to cure her.
7b She was sick.
8 She was not getting well.
9 And so Raven is worried.

10 They say to him,
11 "You had better attend your sister.
12 Maybe you are the one who understands her."

13 So Raven goes.
14 Then he says to her,
15 "I will sing about what is happening to you,
about how those people your neighbors are making you sick."

16 Then he sings for her,
17 "They must want to eat for themselves from Crow
her dried dog salmon and her dried king salmon.
18 Oh, ho, ho, ho, ho, ho, ho."

19 Raven says,
20 "They must want to eat for themselves from Crow
her dried dog salmon and her dried king salmon.
21 Oh, ho, ho, ho, ho, ho, ho."

22 Raven is worried about his sister
who is sick.

1 ʔəsłáłlil álgʷəʔ ʔal tiʔíł dəxʷʔás.

2 gʷəl → ʔəsx̌áł tsiʔəʔ k̓áʔk̓aʔ.
3 hágʷəxʷ tux̌áł tsiʔíł k̓áʔk̓aʔ.
4 xʷíʔəxʷ [gʷə] shaʔłs.

5 gʷəl (h)uy ƛ̕ub.

6 (ʔu) x̌ʷáx̌ʷaq̓ʷbitəbəxʷ ʔə tiʔəʔ ʔalš[s], kaw̓qs.
7a x̌ʷáx̌ʷaq̓ʷbidəxʷ tsiʔəʔ ʔalšs →
dxʷʔal kʷi gʷədəxʷ(h)əlíʔils
7b ʔux̌áł.
8 xʷi·ʔ kʷi suƛ̕úbils.
9 huy gʷəl, x̌ʷáx̌ʷaq̓ʷəxʷ tíʔəʔ kaw̓qs.

10 cút(t)əbəxʷ.
11 "ƛ̕úbəxʷ čəxʷ ʔuháy̓əd ts(i) adʔálš.
12 huy čəxʷ [x̌ə]ł ti ʔəsgʷəháydxʷ."

13 huy ʔúx̌ʷəxʷ tiʔəʔ kaw̓qs.
14 huy, cú(t)cuucəxʷ.
15 "łuʔílid čəd tiʔácəc ad(d)əxʷəshúyutəb, <adəxʷəs. . . ,>
ad(d)əxʷəsx̌áł ʔə tiʔəʔ ʔáciłtalbixʷ (ʔ)ə díłił adq̓ʷúʔax̌ad."

16 huy ʔílyidəxʷ.
17 "ʔəxʷslək̓ʷdxʷyítəməm dᶻəł tsə x̌ə̀nimúlic̓aʔ
ʔə tə słuʔəməs, t̓əlúʔuməs.
18 ʔu huʔ huʔ huʔ huʔ huʔ huʔ."

19 cútcut <tiʔił. . . ,> tiʔił kaw̓qs.
20 "ʔəxʷslək̓ʷədxʷyítəməm dᶻəł tsə x̌ə̀nimúlic̓aʔ
ʔə tə słuʔəməs, t̓əlúʔuməs.
21 ʔu huʔ huʔ huʔ huʔ huʔ huʔ."

22 x̌ʷáx̌ʷaq̓ʷəxʷ tiʔił kaw̓qs dxʷʔál tsiʔəʔ ʔalšs
ʔəsx̌áł.

23 Then the people say,
24 "You have only talked.
Crow had better sing her power song,
25 because that is probably why she is sick."

26 Then Crow said,
27 "It is better for you folks to be hosted,
28 for Raven to invite the people."

29 Then "It is better for them to eat there, right where they are."
30 said Raven,
31 "I'm not inviting the people.
32 It is better that you just dish up the food
and I will just run with it
and I will give the food to them.
33 I will distribute it among the people."

34 She says,
35 "It's all right that way, I guess."
36 Because she thought
37 Raven was truthful.

38 Then the sister Crow sang because she was troubled.
39 "Don't call me Crow now, folks.
40 Just call me *dx*$^{w}$*hiʔidə* (one with wealth power).
41 Just call me *dx*$^{w}$*hiʔidə* (one with wealth power).
42 Caw, Caw, Caw, Caw, Caw, Caw, Caw, Caw, hey."
43 Crow was saying.

23 huy, cútəxʷ tiʔił ʔáciłtalbixʷ.
24 "x̌ʷul̕ č əxʷ ʔucút,
ƛ̕úbəxʷ ʔuʔílitəb ʔə tsiʔił x̌ə̀nimúlic̓aʔ
kʷi sqəlálituts,
25 yəx̌i dił dəxʷəsx̌ə́łs háw̓əʔ."

---

26 huy, ʔíləxʷ tsiʔəʔ k̓áʔk̓aʔ,
27 "ƛ̕ub x̌ʷul̕ čələp ʔuʔábyib.
28 ʔugʷí(h)itəb ʔə tiʔəʔ kaw̓qs kʷi ʔáciłtalbixʷ.

29 gʷəl ƛ̕ub <ʔuʔə́łəd. . . ,>
łuʔə́łəd ʔa ʔal tiʔəʔ dəxʷʔás ə́lgʷəʔ."
30 huy cútəxʷ tiʔəʔ kaw̓qs.
31 "<xʷiʔ kʷi gʷəds. . . ,> xʷiʔ gʷədsgʷí(h)id tiʔił ʔáciłtalbixʷ.
32 ƛ̕ub čəxʷ x̌ʷul̕ łuləcílitəb tiʔəʔ sʔə́łəd
čəda x̌ʷul̕ łuləsáxʷəbtxʷ, čəd[a] łuləłíl(y)id.
33 łuləpáq̓yid čəd tə ʔáciłtalbixʷ."

34 <ʔucúuc čəxʷ. . . ,>
cútəxʷ tsiʔił.
35 "bəƛ̕úb ʔas xʷúʔələʔ."
36 yəx̌í huy ʔəxʷscútəbitəb
37 təł tiʔəʔ kaw̓qs.

38 hay ʔíləxʷ tsiʔəʔ k̓áʔk̓aʔ, (ʔ)alš[s], <x̌ʷáx̌ʷaq̓ʷət. . . ,>
d(xʷ)x̌ʷáx̌ʷaq̓ʷacut.
39 "xʷíʔəxʷ łudídaʔacləp ʔə kʷi k̓áyək̓a.
40 x̌ʷúl̕əxʷ dxʷhíʔidə kʷi łudídaʔaclayiyəp
41 x̌ʷúl̕əxʷ dxʷhíʔidə kʷi łudídaʔaclayiyəp
42 x̌aw x̌aw x̌a·w x̌aw x̌aw x̌aw x̌aw x̌aw, hay."
43 cútcutəxʷ tsiʔił k̓áʔk̓aʔ.

---

Then he is told,
"Now the food better be distributed.
So distribute it now."
It is dished up.

Then he takes some dried king salmon that was dished up.
That Raven distributes it.
He himself is in charge of the food.
Next he takes it now.
Raven goes just a little way off,
And he is going along eating the food.
just a little way off,
And he will return again.
And it will be dished up for him again.
"There is another house where I must go."
He goes again,
just a little way off again,
and he is going along eating again.

So Raven is very ill bred.
He is an ass,
a big stink,
a huge eater.

Then that is how he deprived his sister of her feast.
* [Asterisks denote text added by Levi Lamont. See footnotes.]

The people are who living over there do not know.*
"What's the matter with Crow?
What's up?
Is there to be a feast * —
Or not?"

---

* 66 He was just going along eating the food, that one.
* 67 . . .what Raven is doing.
* 70 . . .Crow is giving the people. . .

huy cút(t)əbəxʷ.
"ƛ̕úbəxʷ ʔupáq̓atəbəxʷ <ʔə tiʔił. . . ,> tiʔił sʔə́łəd.
gʷəl páq̓adəxʷ."
cíl̕cilitəbəxʷ.

huy ʔúx̌ʷtub ʔə kʷi tust̕əlúb ʔal tiʔił ʔəscíl̕cil.
páq̓atəbəxʷ ʔə tiʔəʔ díłił kaw̓qs.
ʔudíłdiłcut dxʷʔal tiʔił sʔə́łəd.
huy, ʔúx̌ʷtxʷəxʷ.
x̌ʷul̕ ƛ̕ələlíʔlil tiʔəʔ kaw̓qs,
gʷəl ƛ̕ələlə́k̓ʷəd tiʔił sʔə́łəd.
x̌ʷul̕ → ləlíʔlil,
gʷəl łubələbə́lkʷ.
gʷəl łubələcílyitəb. <gʷəl łu. . . ,>
"mədíłəxʷ ti dəčágʷtxʷəxʷ kʷi łubəcəxʷʔúx̌ʷ."
bəʔúx̌ʷ.
x̌ʷul̕ bələlíʔlil,
gʷəl bələlə́k̓ʷəd.

huy ci·ck̓ʷ (ʔ)əsc̓áp̓ tiʔəʔ kaw̓qs.
ʔəscə́qʷ.
hi·kʷ saʔ.
hikʷ dxʷsʔə́łəd.

hay, dił dəxʷhúyuds ʔušəbabdxʷ tsiʔəʔ ʔalš[s] ʔə tiʔəʔ suʔəłádəps.
*

xʷiʔ gʷəs[əs](h)áydubs ʔə túdiʔ ʔáciłtalbixʷ ʔəsłáłlil. *
"ʔuʔəx̌íd tsiʔəʔ x̌ə̀nimúlic̓aʔ.
ʔəsčál.
ʔuʔəłádəp ʔu— *
xʷiʔ ʔu?"

---

* 66 x̌ʷúl̕əxʷ əw̓ə lələ́k̓ʷəd tiʔəʔ sʔə́łəd, cədił.

* 67 tiʔił sʔuhuy ʔə tiʔił kaw̓qs.

* 70 tsiʔəʔ x̌ə̀nimúlic̓aʔ ʔə tiʔəʔ ʔáciłtalbixʷ

72 Yet again he is gobbling.*
73 He is seen by his younger sister, by Crow.
74 Raven is just going again.
75 And he is going along eating the food dished up for the others.
76 He is going just a little way.
77 And he eats it,
78 He is going just a little way.
79 And he eats it again.

80 Nothing arrived safely to the people.
81 Then that no-good Raven, with [his] flared nostrils, got in trouble.

82 They called Raven names.

83 So that is what Raven was doing.
84 That's what he was up to while his sister was sick.
85 Upon finding out, the people felt sorry.
86 There is just no food for which they had been invited.
87 He had said he had better distribute it himself.
88 *
89 Then he simply ruined Crow's feast.

90 *x̌ənimúlićaʔ* is the name of Crow,
her name when she is sick.

91 That's the end of my story.

---

* 72 Raven eats the food himself.

* 88 Then the food to be distributed only disappeared.

72 gʷa·ʔ bəx̌ʷúl̓əxʷ ləčə́tx̌ʷt[əb].*

73 ʔə(s)šúucəb ʔə tsiʔəʔ súʔsuq̓ʷaʔ, ʔə tsiʔəʔ k̓áʔk̓aʔ.

74 x̌ʷul̓ ə́ẃə sixʷ ləʔúx̌ʷ tiʔəʔ kaẃqs.

75 gʷəl lələ́k̓ʷəd tiʔił <ʔəs,tiʔił...,> ləcucílyi(a)likʷ sʔə́łəd.

76 x̌ʷul̓ lədíʔil.

77 gʷəl bələlə́k̓ʷəd.

78 x̌ʷul̓ lədíʔil.

79 gʷəl bələlə́k̓ʷəd.

80 xʷiʔ gʷəsutə́łəłs dxʷʔal tə ʔa ʔáciłtalbixʷ.

81 huy ʔusáʔil əẃə sixʷ tiʔəʔ xʷiʔ ləháʔł kaẃqs, ʔəxʷk̓ʷə́lx̌qs <ʔəxʷk̓ʷə́lx̌qs...>.

82 q̓x̌ábactəbəxʷ tiʔił kaẃqs.

83 hay, dił tushúy ʔə tiʔəʔ kaẃqs.

84 [dił əẃə sixʷ] tushúyucuts sixʷ ʔal tiʔácəc <təsə...,> təsəsx̌ə́ł ʔə tsiʔəʔ ʔalš́s.

85 x̌ʷúl̓əxʷ ʔə́ẏdxʷ ti tux̌əłəł x̌əč tiʔəʔ ʔáciłtalbixʷ.

86 x̌ʷul̓ xʷiʔ gʷəsʔə́łəds tugʷí(h)itəb ə́lgʷəʔ.

87 ʔucút ƛ̓ub x̌ʷul̓ łupáq̓ad cədíł.

88 *

89 hay, x̌ʷúl̓əxʷ ʔuhúyud saʔ tiʔił tusʔəłádəp ʔə tsiʔəʔ ʔušəbábdxʷ k̓áʔk̓aʔ.

90 x̌ə̀nimúlic̓aʔ tə sdaʔ ʔə tsiʔił k̓áʔk̓aʔ
sdáʔs ʔal tiʔəʔ səsx̌ə́łs.

91 dił suhúys tiʔił dsyəyəhúb.

---

* 72 -əb ʔə tiʔəʔ kaẃqs tiʔəʔ sʔə́łəd.

* 88 hay, x̌ʷul̓ ləgʷəšəbád tiʔił sʔə́łəd tupaq̓atəb.

# NOTES TO TEXT 3

1 Possibly the most traditional way to open a Lushootseed story is to say that someone "dwelled [there]." Not typical, however, is the lack of repetition. This is virtually a one-line introduction.

10 ***cut(t)əbəxʷ***. Literally, "it is said:" everyone in the village is talking about this and finally someone says it to Raven's face. He should have done something long ago.

11 ***hay̓əd***, to try to learn something, apply the intellect to something.

12 ***haydxʷ***, to find out. See text 4, line 43, where the word is used for what a doctor does. Raven's neighbors are perhaps suggesting the kind of help he should get for his sister.

15 Lushootseed has many words for "sing." *ʔil(i)* is not only "to sing," but "to repeat and interpret"; it may also be used of singing a power song (see line 24). In text 4, when the doctor's wife is singing to help the work, the word used for this is ***t̕ilib***, "sing." Specifically, "to sing a power song" is ***yawdəb***.

One interpretation of this passage is that Raven is singing his sister's song for her so that she may dance her power and be comforted. Another, supported by the lexical spread of *ʔil(i)* and by the words of the song, is that Raven is, for reasons of his own, pretending to doctor her. A comparison of this procedure with the procedure told about in text 4 shows that, though songs are used in curing, the announcement of the cause of the illness is delivered in speech.

17 "Oh, ho . . . " These are vocables used in song refrains and are not associated, as in English, with laughter.

The time when the spirits return and people begin to be troubled is late fall, after the salmon runs. During the summer, Crow was evidently able to put up a lot of dried fish, and people noticed.

***słuʔəm*** is Ravenese for ***słuʔəb***, a Skagit word for "chum" or "dog salmon." ***st̕əluʔəb*** is alder-smoked dried fish.

25 *əw̓ə*, emphatic. Here, something like "for Pete's sake," implying that Raven ought to know this already.

39 ***hiʔidəʔ*** is a wealth spirit who looked like a human being (see Collins 1974:152 and Haeberlin and Gunther 1930:73). The name ***dxʷhiʔidəʔ*** means one who is associated with this spirit. People who assumed the names of their guardian spirits did not do so at large gatherings; such names were kept secret (Collins 1974:220). This song of Crow's, then, like most power songs found in stories, is a parody.

66–67 Material given in the footnotes here and at lines 70, 72, 80, and 88 represents Levi Lamont's commentary (in Lushootseed) as he was assisting in the transcription of the story.

91 ***dił shuys*** (that's the end of it) is a typical story ending.

## TRANSCRIPTION OF RAVEN'S SONG

Lines 20–21

## TRANSCRIPTION OF CROW'S SONG

Lines 39–42

Transcriptions by Tara Browner

## SHAMAN CURE

### INTRODUCTION

With "Shaman Cure" we leave the time of myth and enter the time that can be remembered. "Shaman Cure" is a memoir by Edward (Hagen) Sam about his grandfather *sʔádacut*, a Snohomish *dxʷdaʔəb*, or Indian doctor, who helped many people during his years of practice. *sʔádacut* and his wife, *sk̓ʷúyał*, were consultants for Hermann Haeberlin in 1916–17, when the anthropologist was collecting the material that later was published in *The Indians of Puget Sound* (Haeberlin and Gunther 1930). The book refers to them by their English names, Little Sam and Annie Sam, and contains a photograph of *sk̓ʷúyał*.

As it did for all Lushootseed children, *sʔádacut*'s spiritual training began when he was a little boy, and even when he was quite young he was able to endure hardships that tested him both physically and mentally. When he was still very small, *sʔádacut*'s grandfather showed him how to make a pheasant trap, but in order to use the trap one had to obtain pheasant power. The little boy went into the woods and fasted for several days before finding a pheasant. He then stayed for two nights more in the woods with the bird until *sʔádacut*'s grandfather came looking for him and carried him home. *sʔádacut* was ill for a little while, but when he recovered, he found that the pheasant had given him her power (Haeberlin and Gunther 1930:48–49, 69–70).

It is interesting to note that in this instance *sʔádacut*'s training was provided, not by someone he has identified to Haeberlin as a blood relative, but by an interested person of his grandparent's generation. (See the discussion of the term *ʔíbac*, "grandchild," in the notes to this text.) As a child evinced signs of talent, efforts would be made by many adults, blood relatives or not, to help him fulfill his promise.

A person became an Indian doctor by obtaining one or more of those spirit powers called *xʷdaʔəb*. These powers enabled the doctor to cure people; some of the powers also enabled a doctor to harm another person if he wished.

The situation in "Shaman Cure" is one that seems to have recurred from time to time in the old days: a doctor—probably an older man—has had his offer of marriage rejected by a young woman and has taken revenge by making her ill. A well-attested method of causing illness was for a shaman to take a small material object and work on it so that it was capable of doing harm and then to transport it by means of spirit power so that it lodged in a victim's body. Illnesses caused in this way were fatal if not cured, and only a doctor whose powers were as strong as those of the malevolent shaman could hope to locate the foreign object and remove it, or at least nullify its power. The doctor who performed a cure was able to identify the shaman responsible for the illness; in Mr. Sam's memoir, it is evident that everyone knows who the offending shaman is.

In contrast to *syəyəhub*, in which the techniques of narrative art are used to direct the audience's interpretation of the narrative, history or memoir uses the techniques of narrative to testify to the circumstantial veracity of the facts narrated. "Shaman Cure" is a somewhat formal set piece that makes use of various rhythmic devices inside a frame of personal witnessing. We notice the absence of those short opening and closing formulas customary in *syəyəhub*. We notice also that events are presented in an order more chronological than that employed in *syəyəhub*. Mr. Sam interrupts the linear progress of events only twice: once to insert a validating passage just before telling about the healing ceremony and once to repeat his narrative of the moment when the patient wakes up cured.

Within the speeches made by participants in the incident that Mr. Sam records there are circular figures, and some speeches stand in a relation of rough parallelism to each other: but these devices remain at the rhetorical level and are not used to regulate the order in which events are presented. The chronological momentum of the narrative stops at line 53, when the healing ceremony is begun. Mr. Sam tells us nothing of what was actually done, because this information is sacred and not to be discussed. Instead, he tells us how he and the young woman's relatives felt as the ceremony was going on; though he is being discreet, his narration remains vivid. The one detail of what happened that he can share—the sound of the enemy shaman's voice—is embellished with a concentric figure.

It is when there remains only one event to tell, the moment when the young girl shows that she is cured, that Mr. Sam abandons chronology altogether. The effect of what he does is to frame his narration of that moment with two roughly parallel passages testifying to his bona fides as a witness and to his grandfather's greatness as a doctor. It is true that between the enemy shaman's speaking and the girl's waking up cured, there occur more events that Mr. Sam cannot relate, and the first witnessing section does stand in the stead of chronological time that cannot be narrated. If "Shaman Cure" were fiction or art-narrative, we might be better able to suggest that Mr. Sam had in mind the notion of frame for this narrative moment. We simply cannot say how intentionally or conventionally he used the frame to bridge the sacred and therefore secret aspects of the ceremony. Indeed, the overt purpose of Mr. Sam's first witnessing passage is to lend veracity to the narrative of the moment when the cure becomes visible, so that that narrative in turn will buttress the claims about *s?ádacut*'s greatness made in the second witnessing passage. Framing, then, may have been the farthest thing from Mr. Sam's mind when he was constructing what comes across as a frame to a reader.

Because text 4 is a memoir and not a *syəyəhub*, it has been printed in paragraphed, rather than lineated, form. In this format, the rhetorical figures may be harder to see, but they are there.

## A Note on Further Reading

There is no book-length treatment of Lushootseed Indian doctoring, but most ethnographies contain brief discussions. Lists of shamanic spirits and their capabilities can be found in Haeberlin and Gunther (1930:79–80) for the general Puget Sound region and in Smith (1940:68ff.) for the Puyallup and the Nisqually. Reports of the feats of noted doctors are given in Collins (1974:194–205) for the Skagit and in Smith (1940:83–86). There is some information on methods of healing in Barnett (1955:209–216) for the Coast Salish peoples of British Columbia, northern neighbors of the Lushootseed; in Haeberlin and Gunther (1930: 77–78); and in Smith (1940:75–83, 87–90). These works also discuss ways in which shamans could make people ill. Smith's is the most detailed account, but it should be remembered that her focus is on the Southern Lushootseed and that some of her emphases, particularly on the rivalry between doctors and on the pervasive fear of sorcery, are not appropriate for the northern peoples. An account of the ways other than healing in which Indian doctors help people may be found in Amoss (1978:20, 44–45, 52–56, 84–86). This work also discusses beliefs about ghosts, which may interest readers of "Shaman Cure." The most recent publication (Miller 1988) on Lushootseed shamanism is a book-length study on the spirit-canoe ceremony, in which a group of shamans would journey to the land of the dead. Kew and Kew (1981) provide an account, which is both personal and academic, of a fairly recent curing by a well-known Lummi doctor.

Illuminating discussions on Lushootseed kinship are to be found in Miller (1985) and in Collins (1974: chap. 6). The reader will find Lushootseed texts of Edward (Hagen) Sam in the *Lushootseed Reader with Introductory Grammar: Four Stories from Edward Sam*, compiled by Thomas M. Hess (1995).

1 I remember my grandfather and my grandmother who raised me. 2 My grandfather's name was *sʔádacut.* 3 And my grandmother's name was *sk̓ʷúyał.*

4 A man came to us with his wife and children. 5 He was in trouble when he came to see us. We were living far off near Quilceda.

6 The man spoke with his wife by his side. 7 "Ooh, I am in trouble. 8 My daughter has become a wraith. She is sick and I thought of you, my uncle. 9 This is why we have come. 10 This is why we have traveled from a long way off. 11 I am asking help from you, *siʔab sʔádacut.* 12 I want you to help my daughter. 13 She is sick. 14 She is weak. 15 Have pity on us, *siʔab.* 16 You could help my daughter."

17 Then my grandfather, *sʔádacut*, spoke. 18 "What is wrong with your daughter?"

19 "Ooh, an Indian doctor far away wants her. 20 He wants to take her. 21 He wants to settle down with her, 22 and make her his wife. 23 But she said no. 24 Your grandniece said no. 25 Because of this, the shaman 'shot' her with his killing power when she said no. 26 In this situation, we thought of you. 27 I discussed it with my wife, and I said, 28 'There is *sʔádacut.* 29 He would help us.' 30 This is the reason we came, *siʔab.* 31 Have pity on us."

32 Ooh, my grandfather and grandmother agreed. 33 They prepared themselves. 34 *sʔádacut* washed his hands. 35 And he prepared himself for curing the sick woman. She was his grandniece who was sick; she was his own blood, his grandniece. 36 My grandmother sang as usual. 37 Then he knew. 38 The back of her head was where she'd been 'shot.' 39 And it lay up above her eye.

40 My grandfather said, 41 "I can help your daughter. 42–43 In just a few years, it will destroy, 44 and her eye would die. 45 She would not be able to see. 46 Only one eye would be good."

47 Then her father said that should not be. 48 "Go ahead. 49 Help your grandniece. 50 Your relative and I agree. 51 Go ahead."

52 Then my grandfather began the healing.

1 ...čəda tuláx̌dxʷ tiʔíł tudscápaʔ təcəxʷulúƛ̕il ʔi tsiʔíł tudkiáʔ.
2 sʔádacut tiʔíł tusdáʔ ʔə tiʔíł tudscápaʔ. 3 gʷəl sk̓ʷúyał ti tusdáʔ ʔə
tsiʔíł dkiáʔ.

4 tułčísəb čəł ʔə tiʔə́ʔ stubš [ʔi] tsiʔíł čəgʷás(s) ʔi tiʔíł bədbədáʔs.
5 tułčísəb čəł ʔə tiʔił ʔəsʔušəbábdxʷil dxʷʔal túdiʔ tədəxʷəsłáłlil čəł
čítbid ʔə tiʔíł qʷəl̓sídəʔ.

6 tucútəxʷ tíʔəʔ stubš ʔi tsiʔíł čəgʷás təsəsq̓ʷúʔs. 7 "ʔu· [ʔu]ʔušəbáb-
dxʷil čəd. 8 skáyuhəxʷ tsíʔəʔ dbədáʔ. 9 ʔəsdúkʷəxʷ čəda láx̌dubicid,
dəgʷí dyəláb, tiʔə́ʔ dəxʷəłčíl čəł. 10 tul̓ʔál túdiʔ tulíl, tə dəxʷuʔíbəš čəł.
11 ləʔùšəbtədábut čəd dxʷʔal dəgʷí, siʔáb sʔádacut. 12 x̌áƛ̕txʷ čəd
kʷi gʷadskʷáxʷad tsiʔíł dbədáʔ. 13 huy ʔəsdúkʷəxʷ. 14 ʔəsc̓údəxʷ.
15 ʔúšəbitubuł čəxʷ, siʔáb. 16 gʷəkʷáxʷdxʷ čəxʷ <tiʔił dbədáʔ...>
tsiʔíł dbədáʔ."

17 hay gʷəl tucútəxʷ tiʔə́ʔ dscápaʔ, sʔádacut. 18 "ʔəs[ʔə]x̌íd ts(i)
adbədáʔ."

19 "ʔu· tux̌áƛ̕ildub ʔə tiʔíł dxʷdáʔəb stubš ʔal túdiʔ lil. 20 x̌aƛ̕[txʷ]
kʷi gʷətuskʷədátəbs. 21 gʷətusgʷədíls dxʷʔal tiʔə́ʔ. 22 gʷəl gʷətuhúyutəb-
əxʷ čəgʷás. 23 gʷəl t(u)asxʷíʔəd. 24 t(u)asxʷíʔəd ts(i) adʔíbac. 25 díłəxʷ
tədəxʷƛyáʔtəbsəxʷ ʔə tíʔəʔ dxʷdáʔəb ʔal tiʔíł tusxʷíʔəds.

26 ʔal tiʔíł sláx̌dubicid čəł. 27 gʷádadgʷad čəd ʔi tsiʔíł čəgʷas čədá
cútəxʷ. 28 'ʔa tiʔíł sʔádacut. 29 gʷəkʷáxʷdubuł.' 30 tiʔḷəʔ dəxʷəłčíləxʷ
čəł, siʔáb. 31 ʔúšəbitubuł."

32 ʔu·, ƛ̕úbəd tiʔił dscápa(ʔ) ʔi tsiʔíł dkiáʔ. 33 qʷíbicutəxʷ álgʷəʔ.
34 c̓ágʷači(ʔ)b tiʔəʔ sʔádacut. 35 gʷəl qʷíbicut [d]xʷʔal łudəxʷbáłads
tsíʔəʔ słádəyʔ ʔəx̌ə́ł, ʔíbacs tsiʔíł ʔəsx̌ə́ł, sgʷaʔs stúligʷəds ʔíbac[s].

36 tuƛ̕ílibəxʷ sixʷ tsiʔíł dkiáʔ. 37 gʷəl tuháydxʷ. 38 tuləqábac ʔə
tiʔíł sx̌əy̓ús tiʔił dəxʷəsłyáʔs. 39 gʷəl ʔəsbə́č dxʷʔal tiʔəʔ šəq ʔə tiʔił
šəqbíd ʔə tiʔíł qəlúbs.

40 tucútəxʷ tiʔíł dscápaʔ, 41 "gʷəkʷáxʷdxʷ čəd ts(i) adbədáʔ.
42 túx̌ʷəxʷ ʔal kʷi k̓ʷìdəládxʷəxʷ. 43 gʷəl <łux̌...,> łuxʷíʔil.
44 <...tiʔíł...> gʷəl łuyúbil tiʔíł qəlúbs. 45 xʷ(iʔ)əxʷ kʷi łəbəšúłal-
buts. 46 day̓əxʷ tiʔíł dəčúʔ kʷi łuháʔł."

47 hay gʷəl tucútəxʷ tiʔíł bads, kʷ[i xʷ]íʔəs kʷi łədəxʷəsʔístə(ʔ)s.
48 "yəháw̓txʷ. 49 ts(i) adʔíbac kʷáxʷad. 50 ʔəsƛ̕úbildxʷ čəł ts(i)
<ad...,> adsyəyáʔyaʔ ʔi ʔəcá. 51 yəháw̓txʷ."

52 huy tubáłatəbəxʷ ʔə tiʔíł dscápaʔ.

53 I was scared; I was just a child. 54 I was peeking through the door with a little girl next to me. 55 I was crouching down. 56 I was always forbidden by my grandfather. 57 "You are forbidden to look. 58 You stay in the bedroom."

59 Then this woman was helped. 60 She was not very old. 61 She was still a child. 62 And her father, her mother, and her older sister were afraid. 63 They were all just afraid.

64 And at that point the child was possessed. 65 She laughed at my grandfather. 66–67 "No, you won't get me out, *sʔádacut*. 68 No, you won't get me out. 69 I'm in here. 70 No you won't get me out." 71 The woman just laughed again. 72 The woman sounded just like the shaman.

73 I heard this when I was a child; that's how I know what my grandfather did. 74 Because he was a shaman. 75 So I believe with all my mind, with all my heart, to this day. 76 Now I am a man. 77 I'm getting older, I am, and that's why I know. 78 This is no story. 79 This the truth of what I know, what I saw of my grandfather who raised me.

80 And the woman awoke. 81 My grandfather helped her. 82 She sat up. 83 And she spoke to her mother and father. 84 "Ooh, I'm hungry. 85 I want to eat." 86 The woman brushed back her hair. 87 She sat up. 88 "I'm hungry, mother. 89 I'm hungry. 90 Where in the world am I?"

91 Her mother said, 92 "You are at the house of *sʔádacut* and your grandmother."

93 I saw this with my own eyes, *siʔab* friend, and I heard this with my own ears. That is why I know. 94 I was raised with this, and I knew my grandfather. 95 He was a great shaman. 96 He was a great man.

97 That is all there is to tell you, *siʔab*. 98 I have finished.

53 x̌ʷúl̓əxʷ čəd t(u)asx̌ə́c ʔə tiʔíɬ tudsč̓áč̓as. 54 t(u)ask̓ʷíləxʷ
čəd ʔə tiʔíɬ šəgʷɬ ʔi tsiʔíɬ č̓áč̓as tudsəsq̓ʷúʔtub. 55 [ʔəsx̌k̓ʷúcut čəd]
56 tux̌əx̌aʔx̌áʔtub čəd ʔə tiʔíɬ dscápaʔ. 57 "x̌áʔx̌aʔ kʷ(i) adsk̓ʷíl.
58 ʔal[cut] čəxʷ [ʔal] tiʔíɬ xʷpíitali."

59 hay kʷáxʷatəbəxʷ tsíʔəʔ sɬádəyʔ. 60 xʷiʔ ləhəláʔb luƛ̓. 61 č̓áč̓as
uʔxʷ. 62 gʷəl tux̌ə́c2 tiʔíɬ bads ʔi tsiʔíɬ sk̓ʷuys ʔi tsiʔíɬ sqas. 63 x̌ʷúl̓əxʷ
ʔux̌ə́cx̌əc ə́lgʷəʔ.

64 gʷəl ʔáləxʷ tiʔíɬ tuskʷədáxʷ ʔə tsíʔəʔ č̓áč̓as. 65 tux̌áyəbid ti
dscápaʔ. 66 "xʷiʔ gʷadsƛ̓íqdubš. 67 [xʷiʔ gʷadsʔəx̌íx̌tubš], sʔádacut.
68 xʷiʔ gʷadsƛ̓íqdubš. 69 ʔəcá tíʔəʔ ʔəsdə́kʷ. 70 xʷiʔ gʷadsƛ̓íqdubš."
71 x̌ʷul̓ ƛ̓əbəx̌áyəb tsíʔəʔ sɬádəyʔ. 72 pu·t x̌ʷúl̓ab ʔə ti dxʷdáʔəb tiʔíɬ
suƛ̓əládiʔ ʔə tsiʔíɬ sɬádəyʔ.

73 ʔəslúud čəd ʔal tíʔəʔ dq̓ʷəládiʔ ʔal tiʔiɬ tudsč̓áč̓as cəxʷəs(h)áydxʷ
cək̓ʷ tiʔíɬ təsəshúy ʔə tiʔíɬ tudscápaʔ. 74 yəx̌í huy tudxʷdáʔəb. 75 gʷəl
ʔəstɬíldxʷ čəd tul̓ʔál bək̓ʷ dx̌əč, tul̓ʔál bək̓ʷ dsc̓áliʔ dxʷʔal tiʔəʔ sləx̌íləxʷ.
76 stúbšəxʷ čəd. 77 ləlúƛ̓əbəxʷ čəd, [ʔə]cá, tiʔíɬ cəxʷəs(h)áydxʷ.
78 xʷiʔ ləsyəyəhúb tiʔə́ʔ. 79 tux̌ʷ həláʔb syə́cəb tul̓ʔál kʷi dsəs(h)áydxʷ
tədsə(s)šúuc tiʔíɬ tudscápaʔ təcəxʷəlúƛ̓il.

80 gʷəl tuhəlíʔdubut tsíʔəʔ sɬádəyʔ. 81 tukʷáxʷdub ʔə ti dscápaʔ.
82 tugʷədíləxʷ. 83 gʷəl tíləb tucúuc tsiʔíɬ sk̓ʷuys ʔi tiʔíɬ bads. 84 "ʔu·
ʔəstágʷəxʷ čəd. 85 x̌aƛ̓txʷ čəd kʷi gʷədsʔə́ɬəd." 86 ʔup̓t̓úsəbəxʷ tsíʔəʔ
sɬádəyʔ. 87 ʔəsgʷədíl. 88 "ʔəstágʷəxʷəxʷ čəd, dk̓ʷúyəʔ. 89 ʔəstágʷəxʷəxʷ
čəd. 90 čádəxʷ ə́w̓ə tíʔəʔ dsʔa."

91 cút(t)əbəxʷ ʔə t[siʔ]íɬ sk̓ʷuys, 92 "ʔal čəxʷ tíʔəʔ ʔálʔal ʔə tiʔíɬ
sʔádacut ʔi ts(i) adkiáʔ."

93 tušúdxʷ čəd, siʔáb dsyáʔyaʔ, dxʷʔal tíʔəʔ dqəl̓qəlúb čədá t(u)as-
lúu·d ʔal tíʔəʔ dq̓ʷəl̓q̓ʷəládiʔ cəxʷəs(h)áydxʷəxʷ. 94 ʔa· ds(ʔ)iɬəlúƛ̓il
dsəs(h)áydxʷ tiʔíɬ tudscápaʔ. 95 tuhíkʷ tudxʷdáʔəb. 96 həláʔb tustúbš.

97 húyəxʷ, siʔáb, ti dsyəcəbtúbicid. 98 húyəxʷ čəd.

# NOTES TO TEXT 4

In the unnumbered lines just before the memoir begins, Mr. Sam gives permission for this information to be repeated by the person to whom he is telling it. The incident that was about to be related was well known in the community at Tulalip.

1 *tudscápaʔ*. My grandfather, who is now dead. Note the frequency of the use of "*tu-*" to place the events in the historical past. In *syəyəhub* "*tu-*" appears relatively infrequently and is not crucial to creating a sense of the past.

6 Note that though the speaker is the husband, he is speaking equally for his wife. In making every decision he consults with his wife (lines 27 and 50), as does *sʔádacut* (line 32).
The father's speech shows circular narration: description of daughter's illness (8); appeal to relationship (9–10); request for help (11–12); description of illness (13–14); with cap: request for help (15–16).

8 *skáyuʔ*. This word can mean "corpse" or "ghost." Since people become ghosts when they first die, the statement means that the young woman is all but dead. Spirit sickness manifests itself in an inability to eat or drink, a lack of energy that may develop into an inability to move at all, and an impairment of cognitive faculties that may precede unconsciousness. The young woman is in a coma and has suffered serious loss of weight.
*skáyuʔ* is also the name of a spirit power that has the appearance of a skeleton. This power can be sent by a shaman to lodge inside of and gradually kill a victim. One of the symptoms of such spirit intrusion is that the victim begins to talk and act like the shaman who has sent the *skáyuʔ* (Collins 1974:195).

9 *yəlab*. Used of one's parents' brothers and sisters and their spouses when one's parents are dead. (*ʔəpus*, "aunt," and *qsiʔ*, "uncle," are the terms used while one's parents are living.) *yəlab* also includes everyone who in English terminology would be known as cousins of one's uncles or aunts. Lushootseed kinship terminology tended to refer not just to a specific relative, but to all relatives in that generation.

24 *ʔibac*. Grandson or granddaughter, grandnephew or grandniece. This term was used not only by one's grandparents and but also by the siblings of one's grandparents, their spouses, and their cousins. The young woman who is ill would call *sʔádacut* "*scápaʔ*," ("grandfather"), even though he is a sibling or a cousin of her grandfather. Notice how the young woman's father is escalating his appeal to *sʔádacut*, referring to the young woman no longer as "my daughter," but now as "your *ʔíbac*."

35 To acknowledge someone as *ʔíbac* was to acknowledge an obligation, to take some responsibility (see Collins 1974:96–97).

36 *sk̓ʷúyał* sings her husband's power songs so that his spiritual helpers will come and assist him to discover the cause of the illness. The songs are not diagnoses (compare Raven's "curing strategy" in text 3), but a way of enlisting the help of spirit powers.

47 The father of the sick girl affirms his belief that *sʔádacut* is stronger than the enemy shaman and is being too modest in his predictions of success.

55 Mr. Sam added this sentence later when helping to transcribe the text.

57 Mr. Sam was born in 1907; if he was about seven years old (young enough to have been excluded from the ceremony, but old enough to have understood and remembered it) when this incident took place, then we can date the event to c.1914.

58 Native houses did not have bedrooms or interior doors; *sʔádacut* is evidently living in a European-style house.

65–71 The spirit of the malevolent shaman possesses the young woman: it is his voice that speaks through her mouth while she is still unconscious.
Line 67 was added later by Mr. Sam, and at his request a repetition of line 68 was omitted.

73 Mr. Sam began this sentence in second person, using *čəxʷ* and *ad-*; then halfway through he switched to first person, *d-* and *cəxʷ-*. He intended first person throughout, as written here.

75 *tuľʔál bək̓ʷ dsčaliʔ*. Probably influenced by the English expression "with all my heart."

# THE LEGEND OF THE BOY WHO COULD NOT WALK

## INTRODUCTION

> The imaginative construction of personhood is the best, and perhaps the only kind of life, as N. Scott Momaday suggests when he writes that "an Indian is an idea which a given man has of himself." —Paula Gunn Allen

"The Legend of the Boy Who Could Not Walk" is not a *syəyəhub* like "The Marriage of Crow" or "Martha Lamont's Changer Story," for it is set neither in the myth time nor during the Change, and the protagonist is just a human being. Nor is the legend a historical text like "Shaman Cure," because the time in which it is set, "long ago," is a time outside the scope of the individual storyteller's memory and indeed seems to antedate the limits of family tradition, for the characters have no names. "The Legend of the Boy Who Could Not Walk" is recounted by storyteller Emma Conrad as having happened at a specific place, just as storytellers from other places who tell their own versions of this legend locate it within their own territories. Though it may be a standard, the legend tempts us to believe that we can see behind it the record of something historically specific, something that actually did happen somewhere in this world to a real person who had something wrong with his legs.

Certainly, one way to understand Mrs. Conrad's story is to see it as a quest. Some decades ago, Jackson Harvey, a Skagit elder living on the Sauk River, told anthropologist June Collins about sending his son out to fast in preparation for a spirit-power quest. One spirit that people could receive, he said, lived in a longhouse under water. The person questing for this spirit would tie a rope around his waist with a rock at one end and then jump from a raft into deep water:

> He doesn't hang on to the rock but on to the rope. Grass grows about ten feet high on the bottom of the lake. He doesn't land on the bottom. The rock hits the house. He is awake until he hits the house; then he becomes unconscious. The chief of the house sends his hired man out to ask who is coming.
>
> "Indian is here."
>
> "Is he clean? Does he have food in him yet?"
>
> "He is clean."
>
> "Bring him in the house." (Collins 1974:177)

The parallels between this information and the plot of Mrs. Conrad's "Legend" are many, and they raise for non-Indian readers the question of what might be the difference between legend and history.

Mr. Harvey's information is given as fact, and a reading of text 5 shows that such fact might be used in a legend. Unlike Mr. Harvey, however, Mrs. Conrad nowhere prefaces her narrative with the statement that this is what could happen or did happen on a spirit quest; in fact, she never says in so many words that the boy went on a quest at all. The Lushootseed audience would know that when the boy goes away by himself, grieving, he is replicating for himself a situation that includes several components of the quest (solitude, physical and emotional or mental stress); and when the man in the house sends out a messenger to report on who has arrived, the audience would know that the boy has found a certain kind of spirit helper. Perhaps one difference between "information" and "legend" is shown by the fact that Mrs. Conrad leaves this sort of generic information for the audience to supply and narrates only the particular events (though, as the notes will point out, the style and organization of the narrative is certainly generic).

Let us return, then, to the difference between what we are calling "legend" and ***syəyəhub*** or "myth." (Lushootseed storytellers use the term "legend" or "legend-story" interchangeably with ***syəyəhub***.) Behind the screen of the story in legend the audience can discern reference to what may be seen as someone's individual experience, whereas behind the screen of story in ***syəyəhub*** the focus is on custom or condition, about which a point of view is being presented, often paradoxically and humorously, as in text 2. Texts 5 through 7 present an itinerary of sites along a legend-myth continuum. The stories all seem to deal in some way with the quest for spirit power. Text 6 seems to be a combination of two different quest stories and to show some influence from outside Lushootseed literature. Text 7 may or may not refer to a specific spirit quest: the ingredients are all there, as they are in text 5 (the problem that prompts the quest, the traveling by water, the fasting, the encounter with spirit helpers, and the return home with power), but the magic seal and the war between the ducks and the dwarfs are motifs that occur in many ***syəyəhub***.

The spirit-quest narrative may be considered the Lushootseed literary formulation of passage into maturity. In the past, no Lushootseed person would attempt to undertake the responsibilities of adult life without the aid of supernatural helpers. In some cases, a relationship with spirit helpers would be inherited, and in others, it would develop spontaneously during a period of grief or serious illness; but generally it was established by encounters in the wilderness between spirit helpers and young persons who had prepared themselves to go out and search.

Almost from infancy, Lushootseed children were trained for spirit-questing:

> Young children from the age of five or six years were

> brought up in a tradition of personal cleanliness and self-discipline. Daily bathing in the river was the cornerstone of this regime. Old people who were trained this way told of bathing in the Nooksack River when there was ice on it. Bathing was designed to prepare the young person for a lonely quest for supernatural power at or before adolescence.
>
> ...Children were trained by a combination of "instruction"—verbal explanations and moral lectures—and carefully designed ordeals. The ordeals were not ordinarily physical suffering, but more often exercises in overcoming fear.... Trainers, usually grandparents but sometimes other experienced and concerned adults, sent the children out at night to find a token which the trainer had put on a distant hill or near a lake where dangerous supernaturals were known to be. Through these and similar devices the children were taught to control their fear. (Amoss 1978:13)

The physical and mental cleanliness required of the seeker after an encounter with a spirit also entailed fasting. Small children in training were encouraged to go without one of their meals each day; as children grew older, their periods of fasting were lengthened. When a young person was ready to begin questing, emetics might be used (Amoss 1978:13).

The supernatural being whom the boy in Mrs. Conrad's legend meets is one of the most powerful wealth-giving spirits about whom we have information. *tiyułəbax̌ad* was known to every tribe along the shores of Puget Sound. (In fact, various forms of his name seem to be known in an area extending from Musqueam in British Columbia to Kalapuya in Oregon [Suttles 1987a].) He was considered to be greater than *dxʷhiʔidəʔ*, the wealth power mentioned in "Crow Is Sick." Some Upper Skagit elders have said that *tiyułəbax̌ad* lived in a house at the bottom of the Skagit River near the present town of Concrete (Collins 1974:146, 151–152), while other tribes place his dwelling closer to themselves, not even necessarily under water (e.g., Smith 1940:71 and the present text). *sʔádacut*, the Snohomish doctor who is the subject of text 4, obtained this spirit by inheritance from an ancestor who had dived for it (Haeberlin and Gunther 1930:74). Skagit tradition reports that *tiyułəbax̌ad* could cure people of physical disabilities, as well as give them the power to bring game right to their doorstep, where it would fall down dead, ready to butcher (Collins 1974:152).

In practice, when a young person returned from a successful quest there was usually a period of several years during which his acquired powers did not manifest themselves, especially if the child were very young. When it came time for the spirit power to become a part of the person's daily life, an Indian doctor helped the person to learn how to manage the power, and a winter dance was held at which the power was cared for by performing its dance and song (see the introduction to "Crow Is Sick"). In story, however, the person returning from a spirit encounter already has his powers under control; if there is a period of waiting before he exercises them, it is short.

Texts 5 and 6 are told by Emma Conrad, who traced her descent from the Sauk-Suiattle people, who live along two far-upriver tributaries of the Skagit. We do not yet know enough about the dialects of Lushootseed to be able to say which features of Mrs. Conrad's distinctive way of speaking are attributable to her Sauk-Suiattle heritage and which are idiosyncratic; but listeners to the tape recording will soon notice her pronunciation of *əlg*$^{w}$*əʔ as ʔəg*$^{w}$*əʔ*, which is an upriver trait.

In contrast to Martha Lamont, who spoke more quickly when she was telling stories than she did in everyday speech, Mrs. Conrad spoke more slowly. In part, this may be because it is a Lushootseed tradition in public speaking to go slowly. But Mrs. Conrad spoke slowly in everyday speech, whether in English or in Lushootseed. Mrs. Conrad's delivery tends to be measured and a little sing-song, almost as if she is reciting or at least telling once again something she has told many times before in exactly the same way. She makes particular use of the innate rhythms of Lushootseed, and her way of emphasizing something is not to repeat it or speak more loudly, but to slow down and bring out dactylic, anapestic, or iambic patterns in the phrases. Especially distinctive is her use of "supernatural narration," a delivery making use of particular pitches and accents that signals the presence of a supernatural or spiritual component in the events she is telling about.

## A Note on Further Reading

A good general account of the spirit quest among the southern British Columbia neighbors of the Lushootseed, as well as a series of paraphrases of personal narratives that display the differences that may obtain among the practices of neighboring tribes, is given in Barnett (1955:141–149, 152, 160–161, 167–169). See also Smith for the Puyallup and the Nisqually (1940:189–194); Haeberlin and Gunther for Puget Sound (1930:67–71, 73–74); and Elmendorf for the Twana, western (Hood Canal) neighbors of the Lushootseed (1960:491–496).

Unfortunately, we have not been able to find space in any of the introductions to texts in this volume to include a discussion of myth formation, a question that also arises in connection with texts 6 and 7. Jarold Ramsey, in his interesting account of the literary history of an anecdote about Simon Fraser (1976), takes the euhemeristic view of this process—that is, that all myths begin as history. Another theoretical model is the "myth-ritual" theory, which holds that myth, far from being a creative development from another kind of narrative, is in fact the product of a degeneration of ritual. (See Gaster 1954 and the discussion in the introduction to text 6 in the present volume.) Langen (1990), in a discussion involving text 5, takes the view that "mythification" and "documentation" are a matter of narrative choice, not development.

A recent overview of myth scholarship is provided by Dundes's anthology, *Sacred Narrative* (1984). Readers of Lushootseed literature, however, will note at once the Old-World bias of all of the essays in Dundes's collection, even the ones that cite American Indian material. (Any definition of myth, for example, that requires the presence of gods and heroes, is not applicable to Lushootseed tradition.)

A common-sense approach to the whole question of the role in real life of the story that is told, not read, is Leslie Marmon Silko's *Storyteller* (1981), a collection of personal narratives, photograph annotations, poems, short stories, myths, and anecdotes that from very different perspectives illustrate the social valency of oral narrative. The narrators' point of view is one that students of "myth" need to keep in mind. A demonstration of Silko's beliefs about story may also be found in this collection.

An outline preceding this text and text 7 shows the spirit-quest format used in both stories and also indicates the large formal features. It is hoped that these outlines will facilitate an appreciation of these stories as sites on the legend-myth continuum mentioned in the introduction to this text. (Line numbers in the left-hand column refer to line numbers in the Lushootseed text. Narrative figures named in the right-hand column are defined in the "Annotator's Introduction." The vertical series of bullets [•] mark the spans of lines in which labeled figures occur. Each figure continues until a bullet is underlined [•̲].)

Schematic Analysis of Text 5

| | | |
|---|---|---|
| I | Introduction (1–14) | |
| | (1–7) People lived there | • circular |
| |     (8–13) One child was crippled | • narration |
| | (14) People lived there | •̲ |
| II | Motivation for quest (15–30) | |
| | (15–18) Time of year | •̲ circular figure |
| |     (19–23) People's activities (summer) | • circular |
| |         (24–28) Mother's speech and son's reaction | • narration |
| |     (29–30) People's activities (fall) | •̲ |

IIIa Journey into the wilderness (31–44)
 (31–34) He goes
 (35–39a) He swims
 (39b–44) He camps (cf. 57–66) • parallelism

IVa Parents discover the boy is gone (45–56)
 (45–46) They are moving • circular
  (47–52) They look for him • narration
 (53–54) They stop moving • with cap
  (55–56) They look for him •

IIIb Journey into the wilderness (57–66)(39b–44)
 (57) He is still camping
  (58–62) Crawling • overlapping
   (63) His destination • circular
  (64) Crawling (duration; arrival) • figures
   (65) His destination •
  (66) Crawling (duration; arrival) •

IVb His parents give up (67–70)
IIIc Journey into the wilderness (71–73)
 (73) Arrival (66)

Sections III and IV • interlace

Va Quest—further purification (74–96)
 (74–76) The spirit power sends someone to look at the boy (93) • parallelism
 (77–79) The messenger does so (94) •
 (80–84) The boy's condition is reviewed (95–96) •
  (85–92) The boy becomes cleaner

Vb Quest—cure (97–136)
 (97–98) The spirit power sends someone to fetch the boy (cf. 109–111) • loose
 (99–102) The messenger does so (112–116) • parallelism
  (103–104) The power is *tíyułəbàx̌ad*
 (105–108) The boy's condition is reviewed (117–128) •
 (109–111) The spirit power instructs his helpers to cure the boy •
 (112–116) The helpers do so •
 (117–128) The boy's new condition is reviewed •

| | |
|---|---|
| Vc Quest—envoi (129–136) | |
| (129–130) The spirit power sends someone outside with the boy | • loose parallelism |
| (131–136) He instructs the boy | •̲ (cf. 74–84, 93–96, etc.) |
| VI The boy returns home (137–184) | |
| 137–144 He travels to his village | |
| (145–146) His parents are sad | • circular |
| (147–152) His mother does not recognize him | • organization |
| (153–159) His mother does not recognize him | • with parallel |
| (160–166) His mother sees "a person" | • scenes at |
| (167–171) His parents are sad | •̲ the core |
| (172–176) His father does not recognize him | •̲ cap of circ. org. |
| (177–184) His mother decides to believe the boy is her son; he instructs her | • pendant of circ. org. |
| VII Validation of spiritual power (185–240) | |
| (185–195) The mother invites people and finds the two orphans | |
| (196) The boy sings his power | • circular |
| (197–202) He tells of his experience | • figure |
| (203) The boy sings his power | •̲ |
| (204) The boy sings his power | • concentric |
| (205–208) The animals arrive | • narration |
| (209–210) Land animals | • |
| (211–213) Fish | • |
| (214) The animals arrive | •̲ |
| (215) He comes home | • circular |
| (216–217) with what has been given him when he was disabled | • figure |
| (218) The boy sings his power | ••̲ overlapping * |
| (219) He arrived | • circular |
| (219–225) He instructs people | • figures |
| (226–227) They follow his instructions | • |
| (227) before he sings | • |
| (228) After he sings, | •̲ |
| (229–240) the people are well off | •̲ pendant |

* The concentric narration (204–218) and the circular narration (218–228) overlap. The circular figure in 215–219 interlocks with both of the other figures.

# THE LEGEND OF THE BOY WHO COULD NOT WALK

1 There were some people long before us. 2–4 Their village was way upriver beyond the bend. 5–7 Through the seasons, they traveled about, camping here and there on the lands near their village, gathering food, traveling about.

8–9 Among them were their children; they had children. 10 And the oldest boy was crippled. 11 He was crippled: 12 he had no use of his legs 13 and he used his hands to move.

14 During the summer, his parents lived way upriver, beyond the bend in the river. 15 As fall came, 16 the salmon came upstream there; those were dog salmon. 17 There the people dried the salmon and the meat they had hunted.

18–21 When it began to grow cold, they would return to the place near the mouth of "Muddy River" where their village was. 22 Then they would take their belongings to the bend in the river. 23 So they moved their things one morning.

24 And the mother of the crippled boy spoke. 25 She said, 26 "Son, it's time to be traveling. 27 (And this one is such trouble.)" 28–30 (She didn't know she had hurt her son's feelings as they moved their things downstream.)

31 But the crippled son prepared himself. 32 He took one blanket and his moccasins. 33 And he crawled. 34 All he could do was crawl with his hands. 35 And he crawled upstream, upstream along the river. 36 And he swam upstream; 37 he swam, 38 biting his blanket as he went. 39 And he went ashore upstream, crawling up and 40 crawling up, until he came to a clearing. 41 He spread out the soaked blanket 42 and stayed there. 43 And night came, 44 and he camped.

45 His parents were down below, 46 having gone down and back with their things. 47 But he was nowhere to be seen. So they looked for him. 48 They tracked where he seemed to have gone. 49 Where was he? 50 They tracked him down to the river. 51–52 He seemed to have gone in and drowned in the river. 53 Then there they were. 54–55 They just looked for him; they did not move to the village. 56 But they could not find where he had gone.

57 And over there, he camped until his blanket dried. 58 Then he crawled. 59 And he crawled. When he reached the end of his blanket, 60 then he'd pull it ahead again, 61 and then he'd spread it out again. 62 So he crawled like that.

1 tíʔəʔ díʔəʔ ʔáciłtalbixʷ ʔal tiʔíł tuháʔkʷ dᶻíxʷbid čəł. 2 gʷəl
t(u)asłáłlil ʔal túdiʔ sq̓xʷábac. 3 d(í)ləxʷ tuʔúx̌ʷ. 4 tułáłlil. 5 gʷəl
ƛ̕uxʷíʔxʷiʔ. 6 gʷəl dił tədəxʷʔúx̌ʷs ə́lgʷəʔ. 7 gʷəl tułáłlil ə́lgʷəʔ.

8 gʷəl absbədbədáʔ ə́lgʷəʔ. 9 absbədbədáʔ ə́lgʷəʔ. 10a gʷəl tiʔíł
ʔiłlúƛ̕ bədáʔs ə́lgʷəʔ 10b gʷəl ʔəsq̓ʷúp̓q̓ʷup̓. 11 ʔəsq̓ʷúp̓q̓ʷup̓. 12 xʷiʔ
gʷəǰə́səds gʷədəxʷuʔíbəšs. 13 gʷəl day̓ tíʔəʔ čáľčaləss.

14 t(u)asłáłlil tiʔəʔ yəľyəlábs ʔal tudíʔ q̓ixʷ sq̓xʷábac ʔal tiʔəʔ
pədhə́dəb. 15 gʷəl lət̕síl. 16 gʷəl ʔálil tiʔíł ƛ̕usq̓íl ʔə tíʔəʔ diʔəʔ sʔuládxʷ,
tíʔəʔ díʔəʔ ƛ̕xʷayʔ. 17 tuľʔá gʷəl ləšábalikʷ ə́lgʷəʔ ʔə tiʔíł <bəl. . .>
bələsʔuládxʷ [ʔi tə] biács suxʷíʔxʷiʔs ə́lgʷəʔ.

18 gʷəl ʔáliləxʷ ti səč̓ítils dxʷʔal kʷi sət̕síls. 19 <gʷəl. . .,> gʷəl
łuʔəƛ̕áxʷ ə́lgʷəʔ. 20 łubəbəlkʷáxʷ ə́lgʷəʔ dxʷʔal tíʔəʔ díʔəʔ č̓it łq̓úcid
ʔə tiʔəʔ diʔəʔ sʔílucid ʔə dxʷqəlb. 21 ʔa kʷ[əd]íʔ təsəsłáłlils ə́lgʷəʔ.
22 tuľʔá gʷəl, gʷəl ʔəƛ̕txʷáxʷ ə́lgʷəʔ tíʔəʔ stabs ə́lgʷəʔ ʔal tíʔəʔ dádatu.
23 gʷəl ʔuʔábgʷasəxʷ ə́lgʷəʔ ʔal tíʔəʔ q̓xʷábac ʔal tiʔəʔ stkʷáb.

24 tuľʔá gʷəl cút(t)əbəxʷ ʔə tsíʔəʔ díʔəʔ słádəyʔ tíʔəʔ bədáʔs
<ʔəs. . .> ʔəsq̓ʷúp̓q̓ʷup̓. 25 ʔucúucəxʷ. 26 “dəxʷʔúluł[s] sixʷ tiʔəʔ
dbədáʔ. 27 gʷəl x̌ʷuľ cədíł kʷi səsx̌ʷáq̓ʷ.” 28 gʷəl, xʷiʔ gʷəsəs(h)áydxʷs
gʷəx̌ə́łəłəs x̌əč tiʔəʔ bədáʔs. 29 x̌ʷuľəxʷ ə́lgʷəʔ ʔuʔə́ƛ̕. 30 ʔuqʷíctxʷ ə́lgʷəʔ
tə stabs ə́lgʷəʔ sʔábgʷas(s) ə́lgʷəʔ.

31 tuľʔá gʷəl húyucutəxʷ tíʔəʔ diʔəʔ c(ə)díł bədáʔs ə́lgʷəʔ ʔəsq̓ʷúp̓-
q̓ʷup̓. 32 kʷədádəxʷ tíʔəʔ d(ə)č̓úʔ sʔíc̓əbs ʔi tíʔəʔ sq̓áʔšəds. 33 tuľʔá
gʷəl [tu]dᶻəqíl. 34 dił day̓ suhúys ti sudᶻəqíls. 35 gʷəl dᶻəqíləxʷ dxʷʔal
tíʔəʔ t̕(a)q̓tábac, ti st̕(a)q̓tábac stútələkʷ. 36 gʷəl t̕íčib dxʷt̕(a)q̓túcid.
37 t̕íčibəxʷ. 38 gʷəl ləsx̌ə́ƛ̕əd tíʔəʔ sʔíc̓əbs. 39a gʷəl łálil dxʷt̕(a)q̓túcid
39b gʷəl dᶻəqíl dxʷt̕aq̓t. 40a dᶻəqíl dxʷt̕aq̓t 40b gʷəl łčil dxʷʔal tíʔəʔ
ʔəsgʷígʷəq̓. 41 gʷəl tíx̌id tíʔəʔ sʔíc̓əbs ʔułə́qʷ. 42 <gʷəl. . .,> gʷəl ʔácəc
ʔal tiʔíł. 43 gʷəl łáx̌il. 44 gʷəl q̓əlb.

45 q̓iləxʷ tíʔəʔ yəľyəlábs. 46 t(u)asʔábgʷas. 47 gʷəl xʷiʔálusbitəbəxʷ
gʷəl gʷəč̓təbáxʷ. 48 k̓ʷədtəbáxʷ dxʷčad kʷi sʔux̌ʷs, 49 dxʷčad <kʷi s. . .,>
kʷi s[ʔux̌ʷs]. 50 ʔukʷədtəbáxʷ gʷuk̓ʷít̕əs. 51 gʷəl gʷət̕əbáʔ. 52 gʷəl
gʷəp̓ə́q̓ʷ ʔal ti stúləkʷ. 53 tuľʔá gʷəl ʔácəc. 54 xʷíʔəxʷ gʷəsʔúľ(ʔ)uľułs
ə́lgʷəʔ. 55 x̌ʷuľəxʷ ə́lgʷəʔ ʔugʷə́č̓əb. 56 gʷəl xʷiʔ gʷədəxʷkʷə́d(d)xʷs
ə́lgʷəʔ ʔal tiʔíł dəxʷʔux̌ʷs.

57 gʷəl ʔáhəxʷ ʔəsq̓ə́lb dxʷʔal (s)šab ʔə tiʔəʔ sʔíc̓əbs. 58 tuľʔá gʷəl
dᶻəqíləxʷ. 59 gʷəl dᶻəqí·l gʷəl łušac̓ tíʔəʔ sʔíc̓əbs. 60 gʷəl ƛ̕əbətx̌ʷúd.
61 gʷəl ƛ̕əbəłə́x̌əd. 62 gʷəl liłʔá tiʔíł sədᶻəqíls.

63 There was a mountain around there called "Little Beds." That was where he was going. 64 He went for a month, crawling and resting until he arrived at the place they call "Little Beds." 65 (The mountain was shaped like sleeping platforms.) 66 And he reached there after he had been going along for one month, crawling.

67 His parents gave up. 68 And they went down to their village. 69 And they looked down there with the other people, 70 until they all gave up.

71 And over there was the crippled young man. 72 He came near the house of the people of the mountain. 73 And he camped.

74 One of the people said, 75 "Someone has come near the house. 76 You folks go out and see what is happening." 77 The messengers went out, 78 and they saw the person, 79 and they went back in 80 and said, 81 "A person has come, 82 but his *(h)əliʔ* is very bad. 83 He is crippled 84 and there is something there inside of him."

85 He stayed there all day, 86 and again another day. 87 He was there for two days, 88 and then something came out of him. 89–90 What had been there, what had been inside of him, came out. 91 He had been traveling for a month, crawling. 92 Finally, what had been inside of him came out.

93 The messenger went again to see, 94 and saw him, 95 and said, 96 "He's fine now; he's clean."

97 The messenger was told, 98 "Go ahead. Go to him and bring him in." 99 He went to the young man and 100 brought him in. 101 He brought him in.

102 And they sat him down in the middle of the ***sqəlálitut*** house. 103 This one is called ***tíyuɬəbàx̌ad***. 104 That is the ***sqəlálitut*** that caused the young one to come in.

105 He was pitiful. 106 He was crippled. 107 He could not walk. 108 He only used his hands.

109 Then the leader of the *sqəlálitut* said, 110 "You will help him. 111 You will stand him in the middle of the house." 112 They massaged his deformities. 113 Twice, they rubbed him while he slept. 114 Then he was no longer crippled. 115–116 While he slept, while he was in there, his legs became well.

63 tádiʔ sbádil q̓xʷabac ƛ̕udáʔatəb <ʔal...,> lìlil̓wáʔsəd dəxʷʔá ti səʔúx̌ʷs. 64 dəč̓ú·ʔ sɬukʷálb tiʔíɬ səʔúx̌ʷs, sədᶻəqíls ʔal tiʔíɬ ləq̓ə́lq̓əlb dxʷʔa·l sɬčils dxʷʔal tiʔəʔ cədíɬ ƛ̕udáʔatəbəxʷ lìlil̓wáʔsəd. 65 sləlalwáʔs təsəshúy ʔə tə sbádil. 66 dxʷʔal gʷəl ɬáʔəxʷ dxʷʔa ʔə tiʔíɬ d(ə)č̓úʔils sɬukʷálb səʔúx̌ʷs sədᶻəqíls.

67 tud(xʷ)x̌ʷál̓igʷədəxʷ tíʔəʔ yəl̓yəlábs. 68 huy tuqʷícəxʷ ə́lgʷəʔ t̓úk̓ʷəxʷ dxʷʔal ti dəxʷəsɬáɬlils. 69 gʷəl ʔáhəxʷ kʷi səgʷə́č̓əbs ə́lgʷəʔ ʔi tíʔiɬ ʔiɬkʷáalq ʔáciɬtalbixʷ dxʷʔáləxʷ sd(xʷ)x̌ʷál̓igʷəds ə́lgʷəʔ. 70 gʷəl gʷəƛ̕əlád ə́lgʷəʔ. 71 ʔáhəxʷ tíʔəʔ díʔəʔ č̓áč̓as stubš ʔəsq̓əy̓q̓əyúʔus. 72 ɬčíləxʷ dxʷʔal tíʔəʔ díʔəʔ čəgʷálatxʷ[bid] ʔə kʷi ʔáciɬtalbixʷ ʔal tiʔíɬ sbádil. 73 gʷəl q̓əlb.

74 cút(t)əb ʔə tíʔəʔ ʔáciɬtalbixʷ. 75 "ʔácəc kʷəd[iʔ ʔ]uɬčíl čəgʷálatxʷ. 76 híwil ɬi šúuc." 77 šədᶻál tíʔəʔ sčsád. 78 ʔə(s)šúucəb tíʔəʔ ʔáciɬtalbixʷ. 79 gʷəl ʔux̌ʷ hədʔíẇ. 80 gʷəl cut. 81 "ʔáciɬtalbixʷ tíʔiɬ ʔuɬčil. 82 gʷəl tux̌ʷ <[ʔ]əs...,> ʔəsdúkʷ (h)əliʔ. 83 ʔəsq̓əy̓q̓əyúʔus. 84 gʷəl tux̌ʷ ʔa, absbə́q̓."

85 ʔáhəxʷ dxʷʔal ti sləx̌íls. 86 ʔáləxʷ bəd(ə)č̓úʔ sləx̌íl. 87 ʔáləxʷ cəbdát kʷi sʔas. 88 gʷəl ƛ̕iq kʷədíʔ cədíɬ; 89 tuʔá huʔxʷ; 90 t(u)asbə́q̓əd. 91 ʔa dxʷʔal tíʔəʔ díʔəʔ dəč̓úʔ sɬukʷálb səʔíbəšs sədᶻəqíls, 92 túx̌ʷəxʷ ʔuƛ̕íq tiʔíɬ (ʔ)a tul̓ʔal kʷədíʔ sʔácigʷəds.

93 bəčsátəbəxʷ tiʔíɬ tušúuc. 94 gʷəl šúucəbəxʷ. 95 gʷəl cút(t)əbəxʷ. 96 "háʔɬəxʷ ʔəsxʷcáxʷ."

97 cút(t)əbəxʷ tíʔəʔ cədíɬ tučsátəb. 98a "híwiləxʷ 98b ʔux̌ʷc čxʷa hədʔíẇəd." 99 ʔúx̌ʷcəbəxʷ tíʔəʔ díʔəʔ lə́gʷəb. 100 gʷəl hədʔíẇtəbəxʷ. 101 hədʔíẇtəb.

102 gʷəl gʷədíltub ʔal tíʔəʔ ʔúdəgʷabac ʔə tíʔəʔ <s...,> ʔálʔal ʔə tiʔəʔ sqəlálitut. 103 diɬ kʷi ƛ̕udáʔatəb tíyuɬəbàx̌ad. 104 tíʔəʔ sqəlálitut dəxʷhədʔíẇ ʔə tíʔəʔ <s...,> sqáqagʷəɬ.

105 ləsʔušəbábdxʷil. 106 [ʔəs]q̓əy̓q̓əyúʔus. 107 xʷiʔ gʷəsuʔíbəšs. 108 day̓ay̓ čál̓čaləs kʷi ƛ̕(u)ǰə́ctxʷ.

109 tul̓ʔá gʷəl cút(t)əbəxʷ ʔə tíʔəʔ cədiɬ sdᶻixʷqs ʔə tíʔəʔ sqəlálitut. 110 "ɬukʷáxʷad čələp. 111 ɬukíistxʷ čələp ʔal tiʔíɬ ʔudəgʷábac." 112 tášatəbəxʷ tiʔíɬ səsbáʔkʷɬs. 113 cəbáb kʷi stášatəbs ʔə kʷi səsʔítuts. 114 gʷəl xʷíʔil tiʔíɬ <səs, səs...,> səsq̓əy̓q̓əyúʔus. 115 həlíʔil tiʔəʔ ǰə́sǰəsəds ʔal kʷədíʔ səsʔítuts, 116 səshədʔíẇtubs ʔal tiʔíɬ.

117 Then someone said, 118 "You will see the kind of people you
have come into. 119 See the dried game, the fresh game, the salmon: all
kinds of salmon: king, steelhead, dog salmon, silvers, all the fish of the
sea." 120 Everything was there. 121 All the fruit of the world was there.
122–123 The things made from animals were there: 124–125 the people's
blankets called *k̓ʷàstədúličaʔ.* 126 It was all there. 127 It was all piled
up. 128 That all would belong to him.

129 This is what they said to him, 130 "You take him outside."
131 The *sqəlálitut* said, 132 "Go home and go back to your parents.
And take this to where your parents are. 133 They must get clean.
134 And then take these two young girls with no family. 135 These will
be your helpers, 136 and they will be your two wives."

137 He went on. 138 He traveled downstream. 139 But he wanted
to stay where he had gone in, until he found a log lying across the river.
140 That is how he crossed over to the other side. 141 And that is how
he got to the other side. 142 And he came downstream until he came to
the edge of the land ridge. 143 He came to the edge of where his people
were living. 144 And then he came to the place of his relatives.

145 They were sleeping, 146 lying head to foot, 147 and they were
sleeping. 148 And he went to his mother. 149 And he touched her, he
jiggled her foot. 150 And the old women just said, 151 "Ooh, that must
be *sqíx̌əd* always bothering my foot. 152 Shoo! Shoo! Get away!"

153 A little later, 154 he went to her again. 155 And again he
touched her feet, her toes. 156 Again she said, 157 "What did you do?
158 Get away, dog. 159 Why are you bothering me?"

160 So again he went to his mother. 161 And again he jiggled her
foot. 162 She looked then. 163 And she saw a person, he was a different
person. 164 He was standing near her. 165 Suddenly the old lady sat
up. 166 And she spoke to her husband.

167 They were sleeping head to toe and toe to head 168 while they
mourned their missing son, 169 because they had given him up. 170 And
they had just cried as they searched along the river where it seemed he
had fallen in and 171 drowned.

117 tulʔá gʷəl cút(t)əbəxʷ. 118 "łušúuc čəxʷ tíʔəʔ səshúy ʔə tíʔəʔ
ad(d)əxʷhədʔíw̓ tiʔəʔ ʔáciłtalbixʷ. 119 łušúuc čəxʷ t[ə ʔ]a díʔəʔ, tíʔəʔ
tátačulbixʷ ʔəsšáb, tiʔəʔ tatačúlbixʷ ʔəsc̓íkʷ, tíʔəʔ díʔəʔ bək̓ʷ <s...,>
tiʔəʔ sʔuládxʷ, tíʔəʔ bək̓ʷídup sʔuládxʷ, tíʔəʔ díʔəʔ yúbəč, tíʔəʔ díʔəʔ
<s...,> qiw̓x̌ʷ, tíʔəʔ díʔəʔ ƛ̕xʷayʔ, tíʔəʔ díʔəʔ skʷxʷic, tíʔəʔ sʔuládxʷ
ʔal tíʔəʔ x̌ʷəlč." 120 bək̓ʷ ʔa. 121 tíʔəʔ sq̓ʷəláłəd ʔə tíʔəʔ swátixʷtəd bək̓ʷ
ʔácəc. 122 tíʔəʔ díʔəʔ t̓ábid ʔə tíʔəʔ tátačulbixʷ ƛ̕əlahúyutəb, 123 gʷəl dił
ʔa. 124 sʔíc̓əb ʔə tiʔíł ʔáciłtalbixʷ. 125 ƛ̕udáʔatəb sdaʔ <k̓ʷastəd...,>
k̓ʷàstədúlic̓aʔ. 126 ʔəsʔístəʔ. 127 ʔəspúkʷpukʷəb. 128 díłəxʷ łusgʷáʔils,
bək̓ʷ.

129 díłəxʷ scút(t)əbs. 130 "łušədᶻáltxʷəxʷ čələp." 131 cút(t)əbəxʷ
ʔə tíʔəʔ sqəlálitut. 132 "łut̓uk̓ʷ čəxʷ čxʷa łułčíl dxʷʔal adyəlyəláb čxʷa
łukʷədád ti dəxʷʔá ʔə tiʔíł adyəlyəláb. 133 łuhaʔlid álgʷəʔ. 134 gʷəl
tulʔá łukʷədád kʷi s[ə]sáʔliʔ dxʷłəgʷəlígʷədəb słáałədəyʔ. 135 gʷəl dił
ł(u)adsixʷyáyus. 136 gʷəl dił ł(u)adčáagʷəs s[ə]sáʔliʔ."

137 tuʔúx̌ʷəxʷ. 138 tuʔíbəšəxʷ (ʔ)al tiʔíł ləsqʷícəxʷ. 139a gʷəl
ləsx̌á(hə)bidəxʷ tiʔəʔ dəxʷhədʔíw̓s 139b dxʷʔal tusʔə́y̓dxʷs kʷi scqʷúləs
šáqʷiləb ʔal tiʔíł stúləkʷ. 140 díłəxʷ dəxʷdᶻəlúcids. 141 gʷəl łaʔ
dxʷ[ʔə]ƛ̕úcid. 142 gʷəl ʔəƛ̕áxʷ dxʷqʷícəxʷ dxʷʔal tíʔəʔ díʔəʔ [ʔə]ƛ̕yáx̌ad-
əxʷ ʔal tíʔəʔ díʔəʔ ʔal tíʔəʔ q̓íxʷ[us] swátixʷtəd. 143 [ʔə]ƛ̕yáx̌ads tiʔíł
sʔa ʔə tiʔíł ʔáciłtalbixʷ ʔəsłáłlil. 144 dxʷʔá(hə)xʷ kʷi słčils dxʷʔal tiʔíł
dxʷʔá ʔə tiʔíł yəlyəlábs.

145 gʷəl ʔəsʔítʔitut. 146 dxʷyəlyəláqid ti səstáadᶻils. 147 gʷəl
ʔəsʔítut álgʷəʔ. 148 gʷəl ʔux̌ʷc tsi sk̓ʷuys. 149 gʷəl *touched*, dᶻákʷad ʔal
kʷədíʔ ǰə́sədz. 150 gʷəl x̌ʷul ʔucút tsiʔíł luƛ̕, 151 "ʔu·, dił kʷədáʔ sixʷ ti
sqíx̌əd kʷədíʔ ƛ̕(ə)ləbápac ʔal kʷədíʔ dǰə́səd. 152 ša·, ša·, lílcut."

153 ʔa gʷəl háʔa(ʔ)kʷ. 154 gʷəl bəʔúx̌ʷc. 155 gʷəl bə*touch*ədáxʷ
tiʔíł ǰə́sədz, č̓ətq(s)šádz. 156 bəcúuc. 157 "ʔuʔəx̌íd ə́w̓ə čəxʷ. 158 lílcut
sqix̌a[ʔ]. 159 ʔəx̌íd əw̓ə t(ə) ad(d)əxʷubápac."

160 tulʔá gʷəl bəʔúx̌ʷcəxʷ tsi sk̓ʷuys. 161 gʷəl bədᶻákʷšadid.
162 tíləbəxʷ ʔušúł. 163 gʷəl ʔušúdxʷ ti diʔəʔ ʔáciłtalbixʷ, ləlíʔ ʔáciłtalbixʷ.
164 ʔəskíis č̓ítbids. 165 tíləbəxʷ ʔugʷədíl tsiʔíł luƛ̕. 166 gʷəl ləcúuc tiʔíł
sč̓istxʷs.

167 ʔəxʷdíʔaqid kʷədiʔ səsʔítʔituts álgʷəʔ, 168 ʔal kʷ[əd]íʔ ƛ̕əsu-
x̌á(hə)bs álgʷəʔ ti sxʷiʔalusbids álgʷəʔ tiʔíł bədáʔs álgʷəʔ. 169 d(xʷ)x̌ʷál-
igʷədsəxʷ álgʷəʔ. 170 gʷəl dáy̓əxʷ sux̌á(hə)bs álgʷəʔ ʔə kʷi sugʷə́č̓əbs
álgʷəʔ liłʔal ti stúləkʷ <gʷə...,> gʷut̓əbáʔəs, 171 gʷəl gʷəp̓áq̓ʷ.

172 So she told her husband to wake up. 173 "There is a person standing near us." 174 The old man woke up. 175 And he looked. 176 And he didn't recognize their son either.

177 The old lady questioned him then. 178 And her son said, 179 "It's me who has come back to you again. 180 It's me who has come back. I have come home and I have news for you to share with your friends. 181 They had better come to your house. 182 You get ready. 183 Get the two girls with no family, bring those two young ones here, 184 and they will prepare the house."

185 The old lady ran to all the neighboring houses. There were lots of people. 186 And she told them the news. 187 "Our son has come. 188 And he is different, he is a different person. 189 And he wants you to gather at our place this evening."

190 And this is what she did. 191 She looked for those two girls. 192 And she brought them back. 193 Then the girls worked. 194 They swept the house. 195 They made it clean.

196 And this is what the young man did: he sang the *sqəlálitut*, what he had found, what had come to him. 197 And he showed what the *sqəlálitut* had made of him, 198 what *tìyułəbáx̌ad* had brought him into. 199 And it cleansed him, 200 and it healed his deformities, 201–202 and it sent him home to sing the *sqəlálitut*.

203 The young man sang. 204 He sang his *sqəlálitut*. 205 And the creatures came down. 206 They came to that land. 207 All of [the creatures] came down. 208 The creatures that he had seen on the mountain came down. 209 There were deer, bear, "grizzly bear", "all" the small creatures, every—, those—_____, mink, everything, all the _____, grouse, quail, everything. 210 And this is what came to the side of the house there: everything.

211 The salmon came from downstream. 212 The little fish came leaping from down below. 213 The river was jammed. 214 This is what came. 215 He was home. 216–217 He was bringing together at home what had been given to him when he arrived there in his pitiful form, crippled, without legs.

172 tuľʔá gʷəl cúucəxʷ tiʔíł sq̓ʷuʔs łuqəłcút[əs]. 173 "ʔáciłtalbixʷ tíʔəʔ ʔəskíis čítbid čəł." 174 qłáxʷ tiʔíł luƛ̕. 175 gʷəl šuł. 176 gʷəl xʷiʔ gʷəbə(s)súxʷtəšs tíʔəʔ díʔəʔ bədáʔs álgʷəʔ.

177 túx̌ʷəxʷ ʔuwíliq̓ʷəxʷ tsíʔəʔ luƛ̕. 178 gʷəl cút(t)əbəxʷ ʔə tíʔəʔ bədáʔs. 179 "bəʔəcá tułčísbułəd. 180 [ʔə]cá tíʔəʔ ʔułčíl, ʔut̓úk̓ʷ čxʷa łuyə́cəbtxʷ kʷ(i) adʔíišəd. 181 gʷəl ƛ̕ub łuʔə́ƛ̕ dxʷʔal tíʔəʔ adʔálʔal. 182 łuqʷíbid čəxʷ. 183 łuʔúx̌ʷc čəxʷ kʷi s[ə]sá[ʔ]liʔ słáałədəyʔ dxʷłəgʷłəgʷəlígʷədəb čxʷa łuʔə́ƛ̕txʷ. 184 gʷəl łuqʷíbid álgʷəʔ tíʔəʔ adʔálʔal."

185 təláwiləxʷ tsi luƛ̕ dxʷʔal tiʔíł dəxʷdíʔax̌əd <ʔə...,> qa ʔáciłtalbixʷ. 186 gʷəl ləyə́cəb. 187 "ʔułčíl tiʔíł bədáʔ čəł. 188 gʷəl t[u]x̌ʷ ləlíʔəxʷ, ləlíʔəxʷ ʔáciłtalbixʷ. 189 gʷəl x̌aƛ̕txʷ kʷi gʷəsq̓ʷúʔləp dxʷʔal tiʔíł dəxʷʔá čəł ʔal tiʔəʔ səłáx̌il."

190 gʷəl dił sʔux̌ʷs, 191 [s]gʷə́č̓əds tíʔəʔ c[əd]ił s[ə]sá[ʔ]liʔ słáałədəyʔ. 192 gʷəl ʔəƛ̕txʷ. 193 huy gʷəl yáyus tiʔíł słáałədəyʔ. 194 ʔíq̓ʷid álgʷəʔ tíʔəʔ ʔálʔal. 195 háʔlid álgʷəʔ.

196 gʷəl díʔłił sʔux̌ʷ ʔə tíʔəʔ díʔəʔ lə́gʷəb sʔílids tíʔəʔ sqəlálitut tələsʔə́y̓dxʷ, ləsʔə̀y̓gʷásbid. 197 gʷəl yə́cəd tíʔəʔ shúyutəbs ʔə tíʔəʔ sqəlálitut, 198 hədʔíw̓təbs ʔə tíʔəʔ tìyułəbáx̌əd. 199 gʷəl c̓ágʷatəb. 200 gʷəl həlíʔtub tiʔíł <səs...,> səsq̓ʷúp̓q̓ʷup̓s. 201 gʷəl čsátəb [łu]t̓úk̓ʷəs 202 gʷəl łuʔílid tíʔəʔ sqəlálitut.

203 tuʔíləxʷ tíʔəʔ díʔəʔ lə́gʷəb. 204 tuʔílidəxʷ tíʔəʔ sqəlálituts. 205 gʷəl tučágʷəxʷ tíʔəʔ cədíł tátačulbixʷ. 206 tułčís ʔal tiʔíł swátixʷtəd. 207 tučáʔkʷ tíʔəʔ bək̓ʷ ______ . 208 tuʔəƛ̕á(h)əxʷ tíʔəʔ tátačulbixʷ <tu...,> tu(s)šúłtubs ʔal iʔəʔ sbádil, 209 tíʔəʔ díʔəʔ sqígʷəc, tíʔəʔ díʔəʔ sčə́txʷəd, tíʔəʔ díʔəʔ *grizzly bear, all* dxʷʔal tíʔəʔ bək̓ʷ <s...,> wíw̓suʔ tátačulbixʷ, tíʔəʔ bək̓ʷ..., tíʔəʔ díʔəʔ <stə...,> q̓ʷ(ə)łtəbáy̓, tiʔəʔ díʔəʔ <stə...> bəščəb, tíʔəʔ díʔəʔ bək̓ʷ stab, tíʔəʔ díʔəʔ bək̓ʷ ______ , ti stə́xʷəb, tíʔəʔ sə́səq̓ʷ, tíʔəʔ bək̓ʷ. 210 díłəxʷ bək̓ʷ tułčíl ʔilálatxʷ ʔə tíʔəʔ díʔəʔ ʔálʔal ʔal tíʔəʔ díʔəʔ.

211 tuq̓íləxʷ ti sʔuládxʷ tuľčáʔkʷ. 212 tugʷádiləxʷ ʔal tiʔəʔ sčágʷəbs álgʷəʔ tíʔəʔ wiwíw̓su sʔuládxʷ, 213 put tupə́łt ʔal tə stúləkʷ. 214 díłəxʷ tuʔə́ƛ̕. 215 tut̓úk̓ʷ. 216 ləsq̓ʷuʔ ʔə cədíł ʔal tiʔíł tust̓uk̓ʷs təsəsʔabádəbs ʔə tíʔəʔ tədəxʷłčíls ʔal tiʔíł təsəshúys sʔušəbábdxʷ. 217 t(u)asq̓ʷúp̓q̓ʷup̓, ʔəsxʷə́ł ǰə́səd.

218 He sang his spirit song for four days. 219 He had arrived. 220 He had told the people, 221 "You will kill the animals before our singing opens up, and dry them, and tan the bear hides, the mountain goat hides, the hides of all those things. 222 Their hair is good for making the ceremonial blankets."

223 Yes the salmon were there. 224 He told his relatives to kill the salmon 225 and to dry it. 226 They preserved the small fish. 227 And they took them home before the singing opened up. 228 It was done before the singing started.

229 So they slaughtered the creatures. 230 And they preserved them. 231 And the wives he had taken worked making garments, blankets which they made from the hides of the animals. 232 They made lots of things. 233 The women made lots of yarn for blankets. 234 They worked the yarn. 235 They wove with the mountain goat wool and the other animal fur. 236 And they made their blankets. 237 The wealth grew. 238 They had plenty of everything. 239 They were *siʔab* when it was done.

240 And that's the end.

218 tupígʷədəxʷ ʔal tiʔíɬ dxʷʔal tushúys buusəɬdát. 219 tuɬčíləxʷ tíʔəʔ díʔəʔ. 220 ʔucúucəxʷ tíʔəʔ ʔáciɬtalbixʷ. 221 "ɬugʷəlálalikʷəxʷ čələp ʔə tiʔíɬ tátačulbixʷ dᶻixʷbídəxʷ ʔə tíʔəʔ <ɬus. . . ,> ɬusʔə́q̓ʷ ʔə tíʔəʔ díʔəʔ supígʷəd čəɬ, čələpa ɬušábad, čələpa ɬuʔúləx̌əd tiʔíɬ k̓ʷəlúʔs tíʔəʔ sčə́txʷəd, tíʔəʔ sx̌ʷíƛ̓əyʔ, tíʔəʔ cədíɬ stəbtábəl̓. 222 gʷəl diɬ haʔɬ tiʔíɬ cədíɬ sč̓áʔads dəxʷsčəɬ[s] ti cədíɬ <k̓ʷás, k̓ʷəs, k̓ʷəsdúlic̓aʔ. . . ,> k̓ʷástədùlic̓aʔ."

223 ʔi tiʔíɬ sʔuládxʷ, 224 tuhílidəxʷ tiʔíɬ ʔíišəds ɬuləgʷəlálalikʷəs ə́lgʷəʔ ʔə ti sʔuládxʷ. 225 gʷəl ɬušábad ə́lgʷəʔ. 226 ʔúləx̌ədəxʷ ə́lgʷəʔ tíʔəʔ wiw̓su sʔuládxʷ. 227 <gʷəl. . . ,> gʷəl t̓úk̓ʷtxʷəxʷ ə́lgʷəʔ dᶻixʷbídəxʷ ʔə tíʔəʔ sʔə́q̓ʷ ʔə tíʔəʔ diʔəʔ spígʷəds. 228 tuhúyəxʷ ʔal tiʔíɬ tushúysəxʷ tiʔíɬ spígʷəds.

229 gʷəl tux̌ʷádᶻalikʷəxʷ ʔə tíʔəʔ díʔəʔ tátačulbixʷ, 230 gʷəl tuʔúləx̌ədəxʷ. 231 gʷəl tuhúyutəbəxʷ ʔə tiʔəʔ čaagʷəsils tíʔəʔ cədíɬ sčəɬs ə́lgʷəʔ sʔíc̓əb sčəɬs ə́lgʷəʔ sƛ̓álalic̓aʔ tul̓ʔál tíʔəʔ <stə. . . ,> k̓ʷəlúʔ ʔə tíʔəʔ tátačulbixʷ. 232 tuqəl̓qəlíləxʷ ə́lgʷəʔ tustáb. 233 tuqəl̓qəl̓íləxʷ [kʷi] sʔíc̓əb [əʔ] tsiʔíɬ sk̓ʷuys. 234 tuyáyusəxʷ ʔə tiʔəʔ cədíɬ. 235 ɬáqadəxʷ ə́lgʷəʔ tíʔəʔ díʔəʔ cədíɬ <sa. . . ,> sx̌ʷíx̌ʷƛ̓əyʔ [ʔi] tiʔəʔ tátačulbixʷ. 236 gʷəl húyudəxʷ ə́lgʷəʔ sʔíc̓əbs ə́lgʷəʔ. 237 tuʔíʔabil̓əxʷ. 238 tuqá(h)igʷsiləxʷ. 239 tusiʔábəxʷ ʔáciɬtalbixʷ ʔal tiʔíɬ tushúys.

240 gʷəl diɬ (s)šac̓s.

# NOTES TO TEXT 5

1ff Note the documentary tone of the opening. The information—that people lived there—is the same as what is given at the beginning of a *syəhub*, but here there is more circumstantial detail about the location and the seasonal activities of the people. The traditional opening word, *ʔəsłáłlil*, does not come until the second line.

14 In the summer, people moved to temporary camps as they went about collecting food for the winter. When the weather turned cold, people moved back to their permanent winter villages where the longhouses were.
Dog salmon would be running in the Skagit River in the fall, the run peaking in October. The further upstream the salmon were taken, the less fat they were and the better, therefore, for preserving.

20 *dxʷqəlb*. This was the name for Baker River, but also could be any fast-running, muddy river. (*qəlb* is "rain.") Several Skagit winter villages were also called *dxʷqəlb*: evidently, it was a name frequently given. Skagit elder Jim Enick suggested that in the context of a story the name could even be considered generic.

27 It is unlikely that the mother said this aloud. Perhaps she thought about the trouble involved in moving her son and he sensed what she was thinking.

29–30 Fall is not only the time when the people return to their winter homes, but also the time when the guardian spirits return for the ceremonial season. The people who are to be troubled by spirits now begin to get sick (see text 3), and people who are already troubled in mind, as this boy is, are especially susceptible to spiritual influence.

31ff *húyucut*, he made himself ready. On the surface of the story, it may seem that the boy just runs away; but *húyucut* implies a sense of purpose, not just impulse. The swim in the river may be seen as referring to (encoding) the practice of bathing for purification. Note that later (line 63), Mrs. Conrad speaks of the boy's having a destination: the mountain where the spirit power lives. Many people get their guardian spirits during times of grief; here, the story conflates passive and active means of coming into contact with the supernatural.

59–62 In the past, when this story takes place, the ground was covered with dense undergrowth. Elders consulted about the meaning of this passage suggest that the boy puts his blanket on top of the brush, making a surface he can crawl over. When he gets to the end of the blanket, he throws it ahead of him and again crawls across.

63 *lìliľwáʔsəd*. According to information given to Sally Snyder by Louise and Charley Anderson (Vi Hilbert's parents), "*lelewased*" is a hill approximately four miles below Bedal Creek on the south side of the Skagit River. The hill had snow on top all year round. On the west end of the hill is a high, round elevation called "*besed*" (Jack Mountain). The "beds" in the English translation are geological formations that look like the sleeping platforms in the traditional longhouses.

84 The young man needs to fast for a longer period of time; he is not yet in a pure enough state to encounter the spirit power.

111–116 The events in the young man's cure (being placed in the middle of the house, being made to stand up, being massaged, losing consciousness) all occur in ceremonies of curing and of taking new winter dancers into the longhouse.

118 *ad(d)əxʷhədʔiẁ*. "Where you entered (a house)" here has the sense of being made a sharer in. The young man is being told that he now has the power to procure all these things. Cf. text 2, line 224, where *hədʔiẁ* means "being taken into a family."

132–133 Getting the house ready could require ceremonial measures to make it clean enough for the spirit to visit, not just cleansing it of dirt.

134–136 Having more than one wife required wealth. Most wealthy men, however, would marry women from prominent families, not orphans. There may be a hint here that this young man is to share his good fortune with two people who, as orphans in a society in which family connections are of crucial importance, faced a hard time.

People who had *tiyułəbax̌ad* as a guardian were known for their hospitality, and a household with more than one wife would have been a great advantage for someone who often fed large numbers of people.

145–184 This "nonrecognition" scene is almost standard in stories that deal with people returning after an absence of some length. For variations, see text 6, lines 132ff. and text 7, lines 693ff.

146 It is possible to infer from the story that sleeping head-to-foot may be a customary practice for a couple in mourning, but it has not been possible to verify this.

189ff The last part of the story is not easy to follow. It may be helpful for the reader at this point to take a look at the ending of "The Seal Hunters" (text 7), which has the same elements as the present story, but in a more straightforward order. It is the inclusion of the boy's instructions to his people (actually an element from a slightly different kind of story) that complicates the narration here.

207 At this point the tape was inadvertently erased. The missing word is *tátačulbix̌ʷ*.

209 Translation for the word *q̓ʷ(ə)ƛ̓təbáy̓* is unknown.

218 Four days. Four is a number with special meaning for the Lushootseed, as three is in Christian tradition. Probably it is not literally four days that is meant here, but the length of time that had to pass in order for the young man to learn to manage his power.

240 *dił (s)šac̓s*. Traditional closing statement at the end of a *syəhub*; used even though this is a "legend."

# THE ALL-YEAR-AROUND STORY

## INTRODUCTION

In "The All-Year-Around Story," we seem to be encountering the representative of a genre different from the ones we have looked at before. This story does not seem to be a history, either personal or social, nor can one readily see history behind it at some remove, except perhaps in its first part. It does not seem to be a myth, for the protagonist, only human, never rises to the stature of Mink or Raven or even of a seemingly human myth-character such as Swaneset (see the introduction to text 1): these characters are all bigger than the individual stories in which their deeds are told, whereas the hero of "The All-Year-Around Story" exists only as an actor in it. Neither is this story a member of that genre that tells of events during or before the Change and seems to have social criticism or a reconsideration of values as part of its purpose. To a far greater extent, it seems, than any other story in this volume, "The All-Year-Around Story" is meant simply as entertainment.

Further, the surface of the story displays many traces of European influence: thimbles, steamboats, spyglasses; and, at a slightly deeper level, we find the hero wandering from adventure to adventure in a manner familiar from European fairy tale—he does things, but we never come to know him. Contrast, for example, the clarity and intimacy of Martha Lamont's portrait of Crow in text 2 with the absence of individualizing traits in the portrait of the hero of "The All-Year-Around Story." We hear Crow's very voice; we see her servants' attitude toward her; we take note of the discrepancies between her purported status and her actual demeanor; and our response to this character from long ago is complicated by Mrs. Lamont's reminders—in language and tone that call for special attention—that the memory of the old days is precious. The hero of "The All-Year-Around Story" has no individual voice, nor does he stand for anything larger than himself; Mrs. Conrad's chanting delivery tells us from time to time that something happening in the story involves agencies that are not human, but this fact does not control or contribute to the audience's response to her main character. In fact, the second part of "The All-Year-Around Story" is more like the European wondertale than it is like any other story in this volume.

Readers of texts 5 and 7 will notice that text 6 seems to combine two kinds of story. The first part—in which the protagonist is set adrift by his father-in-law, arrives at a far-off shore where he is given supernatural gifts, and returns back home unrecognizable because of his new powers—seems to be constructed on the model of the spirit-quest story that we see in "The Legend of the Boy Who Could Not Walk" and "The Story of the Seal Hunters." But there is something different about this hero's gifts: the young man of text 5 returns home able to feed his people, and he becomes an important person for the coming generations; the seal hunters of text 7 return home able now to hunt whales, as well (and, by implication, to feed even more people than they did before), and their return restores a moral balance in their village. The hero of text 6 comes home with wives; and, though there are many stories in which supernatural wives are a great help to their husband's people, nothing is said about that possibility in text 6. In failing to follow his supernatural wife's instructions about when she is to be revealed, the hero provides the opportunity for the storyteller to add another narrative, the hero's search for his vanished wife. And it is this second narrative, which springs from the disruption of the old model, which strikes us as most like the wondertale.

The preeminent analyst of the content of the European wondertale has been Vladimir Propp, whose *Morphology of the Folktale* (1968) is a standard work. Propp's premise that "morphologically, a tale... may be termed any development proceeding from Villainy or Lack, through intermediary functions to Marriage, or to other functions employed as a denouement" (Propp 1968:92) has been applied to the plots of American Indian stories by Alan Dundes (1964). The term "folktale" is too broad a translation of Propp's *ska'zka*, which refers only to the fairy tale or wondertale (see the discussions in Wagner 1968:ix–x and in Liberman 1984:ix). The genre "wondertale" is described by Propp in *The Historical Roots of the Wondertale* as follows:

> A wondertale begins with some harm or villainy done to someone (for example, abduction or banishment) or with a desire to have something (a king sends his son in quest of the firebird), develops through the hero's departure from home and encounters with the donor, who provides him with the magic agent that helps the hero find the object of the search. Further along, the tale includes combat with an adversary.... Later [the hero] escapes, is subjected to a trial by difficult tasks, and becomes a king and marries, either in his own kingdom or in that of his father-in-law. (1984:102)

We can see that, allowing for the Lushootseed love of reduplication (both of Propp's typical beginnings are present in text 6, and there are two donors, if one counts advice as a magic agent), the plot of Mrs. Conrad's narrative of the hero's search for his wife in "The All-Year-Around Story" bears a certain resemblance to Propp's outline.

Propp believed that most of the familiar wondertale motifs came originally from rites of initiation into hunters' secret societies as such rites were practiced by European peoples during the period when hunting was their most important souce of food (1984:116–117). During these initiations, Propp theorizes, tales of how one's forebears acquired hunting skill were not only told but also reenacted as part of a process of conferring the skill on a new initiate and of instructing him in proper behavior: "If one envisions everything that happens to the initiate and narrates it in sequence, the result will be the compositional basis of the wondertale" (117).

If one accepts "sea" and "far-away island" as equivalent in Lushootseed terms to the European primeval forest, then among the eleven "initiation-complex motifs" listed by Propp (116), seven are present in "The All-Year-Around Story": abduction by a supernatural agent connected with the forest, a house in the forest, a provisional contract, receiving magical help, disguise, a teacher in the forest, and sorcery. The initiation rite of which Propp speaks involved not only hunting themes, but also some sort of social and sexual rite of passage that he terms "the wedding"; and of the ten motifs he lists as deriving from "the period before the wedding and the moment of return" (116), five are to be found in "The All-Year-Around Story": the big house, a table set inside it, a beautiful woman in an enchanted place, the husband at his wife's wedding, and the forbidden pantry.

And yet, despite these correspondences, it cannot be denied that the feel of European wondertale—its tone, intent, and context—is alien to the feel of Lushootseed story. It is not just that Propp's notions about initation are Eurocentric and even in those terms now dated. The fact is that, as far as we know, the Lushootseed had and have no concept of initiation along these lines—and, more specifically, no puberty rite for boys (Smith 1949:17). The European emphasis on individual prowess for its own sake, too, seems not to fit Lushootseed ways of thinking about spirit power or worldly success.

Further, in the purely historical terms that Propp proposes, Lushootseed story—no matter what the genre—does not correspond to the wondertale. Propp theorizes that when hunting was displaced in Europe as the main source of livelihood, the rites of initiation into hunters' secret societies fell into disuse. The tales continued to be told, but divorced from their ritual context; and sacred literature became mere entertainment: the wondertale is by definition "not the product of the social order in which it is current" (120). The effect of its marginal position on the wondertale has been described by Claude Lévi-Strauss in an essay about Propp's *Morphology of the Folktale*:

> "[Tale] is less strictly subjected than [myth] to the triple consideration of logical coherence, religious orthodoxy, and collective pressure. The tale offers more possibilities of play, its permutations are comparatively freer and with time they acquire a certain arbitrary character." (1973 [1976]:326)

The sacred journey becomes an adventure; and its episodes, no longer set into a matrix of belief, are told so as to amaze and no longer ring true. One wonders whether Mrs. Conrad would have accepted this as a description of the status of the second part of her story. It cannot be a coincidence that "The All-Year-Around Story" was a favorite one to bring out (and to tell in English—see Harry Moses's "Legend of the Seasons" in Hilbert 1985:111–117) when enquirers from the dominant culture came into Sauk-Suiattle country in search of Indian stories.

With that one possible exception, the Lushootseed literature represented in this volume never suffered that relegation to the irrelevant that Propp and Lévi-Strauss describe. Most of the stories that we have on tape, in fact, were collected twenty to thirty years ago from elders who maintained certain traditional ways despite the misgivings of white friends and even on occasion of younger relatives—living in a relatively isolated spot in a house without modern conveniences, for example; or bathing in the Skagit River in the winter; or refusing to speak English. It seems obvious to us looking back that these elders were maintaining a holding action, giving the stories over to the tape recorder so that someone in the future could take them on, but meanwhile persevering in exemplary daily behavior in case the future should unexpectedly overlap the present. And the hopefulness of these elders may be in the process of being vindicated. The ancestral religion of Puget Sound, deemed extinct thirty years ago, now flourishes again, and with it there begins to be a demand that tribes provide, at least for winter dancers (among whom perhaps are to be found the legatees of the tape recorder), some instruction in the ancestral language. These stories, then, grow out of and carry in them the most serious beliefs and values of the society in which they are rooted.

### A Note on Further Reading

Two versions of "The All-Year-Around Story" told in English are available: one, called "The Story of the Big Box," was given by "someone at Conrad's" (probably Emma; see Cary 1977) and one, called "Legend of the Seasons," was given by Harry Moses (Hilbert 1985:111–117). In each case, it is interesting to see how little figured the English-language version is as compared with the Lushootseed—though to what extent this may be due to editorial activity is not clear.

An accessible discussion of Propp's model for the wondertale and of its modifications at the hands of his successors may be found in chapter 4 of Wallace Martin's *Recent Theories of Narrative* (1986). Discussion of the appropriateness of the application of Propp's ideas to American Indian narrative are Jacobs (1959b) and Langen (1989a).

A thorough consideration of the acceptance of foreign tales into Indian literary tradition has yet to be made. Among the few available essays covering parts of this broad field are Thompson (1919) (European tales), Beck (1958) (Old World traditions), and Ramsey (1977) (Bible stories).

Some collections in which acculturated stories may be found are Teit (1916) (Upper Thompson), Parsons (1918) (Tewa), Jacobs (1945) (Kalapuya), and Thompson (1919) (various). Anthony Mattina's *The Golden Woman* (1985) is a book-length presentation of a Colville storyteller's formulation of a tale including marvels and anachronisms comparable to those in Mrs. Conrad's tale. It offers a Colville-language transcription with enough grammatical information to enable a non-Colville-speaker to follow it, as well as interlinear and free translations and a glossary.

## THE ALL-YEAR-AROUND STORY

[The following comments, audible on the tape, preceded this story.]

(This white person wants a story, a story.)
(You folks will eat before. . . )
(*I'm going to put it there.*)
(Just watch my cooking.)
(You folks eat and then return.)
(*Oh, okay.*)
(Do you understand? *heh*!)

1 This story is about the way people were long ago.

2 And the people were settled.
3 They were lined up side by side.
4 It was good where the houses were lined up,
where the people were settled.

5 And this was their leader, a *siʔáb*.
6 He was their head man.
7 And he had a child, a young daughter.

8 And there were others.
9 They were settled next door.
10 And they had a child, a young son.

11 And they were settled there.
12 For a long time they have been there.

13 And the children both grew older.
14 And in time they wanted to get married.
15 And this young man took the daughter of the *siʔáb*.
16 And he intended to make her his wife.

17 And he was disliked by the parents of the girl
18 because his parents were poor.

( x̌aX̌tub ʔə k$^{w}$i pastəd k$^{w}$i s[y]əyəhúb, s[y]əyəhúb.)
( <łu. . . dił. . . > łux̌ic čələp d$^{z}$ix$^{w}$bid ʔə k$^{w}$i łu–. . . )
( *I'm going to put it there.*)
( x̌$^{w}$ulʔəx$^{w}$ čələp łuʔəswatchbid k$^{w}$i łudsk$^{w}$úk.)
( łuʔəsx̌ic čələp čələpa łubəlk$^{w}$.)
( *Oh, okay.*)
( ʔəsləqalbut čəx$^{w}$ ʔu. *heh!*)

1 tə syəyəhúb təsəshúy ʔə k$^{w}$i ʔáciłtalbix$^{w}$ ʔə k$^{w}$ədíʔ tuháʔk$^{w}$.

2 g$^{w}$əl t(u)asłáłlil tíʔəʔ ʔáciłtalbix$^{w}$.
3 t(u)asƛ̓ədáx̌ad.
4 tuháʔł dəx$^{w}$əsƛ̓ə́d ʔə tiʔíł ʔálʔal →
tədəx$^{w}$əsłáłlil ʔə tiʔíł ʔáciłtalbix$^{w}$.

5 g$^{w}$əl tíʔəʔ sd$^{z}$íx$^{w}$qs(s) ə́lg$^{w}$əʔ siʔáb.
6 six$^{w}$siʔábs ə́lg$^{w}$əʔ.
7 g$^{w}$əl absbədáʔ ʔə tsíʔəʔ čáčas sládəyʔ.

8 g$^{w}$əl ʔácəc tíʔəʔ díʔəʔ ʔiłk$^{w}$aalq.
9 tíʔəʔ díʔəʔ ʔəsłáłlil dəčág$^{w}$tx$^{w}$.
10 g$^{w}$əl absbədáʔ ə́lg$^{w}$əʔ ʔə tíʔəʔ stubš čáčas.

11 g$^{w}$əl ʔal tiʔíł səsłáłlils ə́lg$^{w}$əʔ.
12 haʔk$^{w}$ ʔa:l tiʔíł dəx$^{w}$ʔás ə́lg$^{w}$əʔ.

13 g$^{w}$ə(l) ləlúX̌luX̌il ti stáwix$^{w}$aʔł.
14 g$^{w}$əl ʔálil tiʔíł g$^{w}$əsx̌áX̌tx$^{w}$s ə́lg$^{w}$əʔ →
[k$^{w}$i] g$^{w}$əsk$^{w}$ədátag$^{w}$əls ə́lg$^{w}$əʔ.
15 g$^{w}$əl k$^{w}$ədátəbəx$^{w}$ ʔə tíʔəʔ díʔəʔ čáčas stúbš
tsíʔəʔ díʔəʔ bədáʔ ʔə tíʔəʔ siʔáb.
16 g$^{w}$əl łuhúyud čəg$^{w}$áss.

17 g$^{w}$əl sáʔtub ʔə tíʔəʔ díʔəʔ yəl̓yəláb ʔə tsi čáčas.
18 yə́x̌i s[ʔ]ušəbábdx$^{w}$ tíʔəʔ yəl̓yəlábs. →

19 And the *siʔáb*, the father of this young woman,
said to his daughter,
20 "Don't marry him,
because he is poor."
21 And she did not listen to that.

22 This man took it,
23 Then he took that cedar.
24 And he built a box.
25 He made this box.
26 It was big enough for the two who will be inside.
27 And he made it solid.
28 It was made so that no water could get inside the box.

29 And he took his son-in-law and his daughter,
30 and he put them in that box.
31 He nailed on the lid.
32 He took it.
33 And he carried it.
34 And he took it down.
35 He took it down to the water.
36 And he sank it.
37 This box sank down.

SCENE 1

38 And it went.
39–40 It drifted through this world
in the water
spinning around,
beaching.
41 This box was doing everything.
42 For one month they were going by water.

43 And there was a woman.
44 She was settled way out in the great sea.
45 She was settled alone in a nice little place.
46 (You know the gravel along the shore.)

19 gʷəl siʔáb tíʔəʔ diʔəʔ bad ʔə tsíʔəʔ díʔəʔ č̓áč̓as słádəyʔ
tədəxʷcúucs tsíʔəʔ bədáʔs. →
20 “xʷiʔ gʷadshúygʷastxʷ →
yə́x̌i s[ʔ]ušəbábdxʷ.”
21 gʷəl ʔal tiʔíł xʷiʔ gʷəslə́qs.

22 kʷədádəxʷ <tíʔəʔ díʔəʔ...>
tíʔəʔ díʔəʔ stubš.
23 gʷəl kʷədád tíʔəʔ díʔəʔ x̌páyʔ.
24 gʷəl šə́łəxʷ wə́q̓əb.
25 húyudəxʷ tíʔəʔ wə́q̓əb. →
26 ʔəshíkʷ [s]ʔiƛ̓úb dxʷʔal tíʔəʔ s[ə]sá[ʔ]liʔ łudə́kʷ.
27 gʷəl húytxʷ ƛ̓əq̓ʷ. →
28 ʔəsʔístə[ʔ ʔə] kʷi sxʷiʔs gʷəqʷúʔ gʷudə́kʷ dxʷʔal tíʔəʔ wə́q̓əb.

29 <tulʼʔá...,> →
gʷəl kʷədádəxʷ tíʔəʔ <s...,> sx̌áʔx̌aʔs ʔi tsíʔəʔ bədáʔs, →
30 gʷəl
dəgʷášəxʷ ʔal tiʔíł wə́q̓əb.
31 c̓súcidəxʷ.
32 kʷədádəxʷ. →
33 gʷəl q̓ílid. →
34 gʷəl ʔúx̌ʷtxʷ dxʷčáʔkʷ.
35 čágʷədəxʷ (d)xʷʔal tiʔíł qʷuʔ.
36 gʷəl dxʷbə́čəbəd.
37 dxʷbə́čəb tíʔəʔ díʔəʔ wə́q̓əb.

## SCENE 1

38 gʷəl ʔux̌ʷ
39–40 p̓əq̓ʷ ʔal tíʔəʔ swátixʷtəd
ʔal tíʔəʔ qʷuʔ
kʷi səsə́:lps,
kʷi səp̓ədí:ls
41 bək̓ʷ ʔəsʔəx̌íd səhúys tíʔəʔ wə́q̓əb.
42 dxʷʔal dəčúʔ słukʷá:lb
ti səʔúx̌ʷs liłʔál tíʔəʔ díʔəʔ qʷuʔ.

43 gʷəl ʔa tsiʔił słádəyʔ.
44 ʔəsłáłlil lil čaʔkʷ ʔal tíʔəʔ hikʷ x̌ʷəlč.
45 ʔəsłáłlil dáy̓ay̓ ʔal tíʔəʔ haʔł swáw̓tixʷtəd.
46 ʔəs(h)áydxʷ čəxʷ tíʔəʔ <stəb...> či[či]čƛ̓aʔ liłʔílgʷi:ł.

47 And upland it was a nice place.
48 It was very hazy-blue, "everything."
49 And that was where the box was going.
50 It was going along drifting.
51 And it beached on that sweet island where the woman was.
52 It stayed.
53 Just how long was it there?

54 And that woman spoke.

55 Three women were her workers.
56 One was her cook.
57 And one was her housekeeper.
58 And one was her dishwasher.
59 They were the hired hands of this woman.

60 From the making of this world,
she has been settled there.
61 She didn't go anywhere.

62 And she said to her children,
63 "We had better go for a stroll together.
64 We stroll along the shore of the water."
65 They went strolling about.

66 I don't know why she picked up a little hatchet and a—
What is that called, *hamə*? hammer. hammer.
67 They got there.
68 And they walked.
69 The four of them went for a stroll.
70 And they were going far along the shore of the water.
71 The little rocks were nice.
72 That is how they saw this box.
73 It was beached.

74 Then she said to the children.
75 "What is that thing which has beached?"

47 gʷəl tíʔəʔ díʔəʔ t̕aq̓t haʔɬ swátixʷtəd.
48 pu:t ʔəsq̓ʷixʷil, *everything*.
49 gʷəl díɬ səʔúx̌ʷ ʔə tíʔəʔ wə́q̓əb. →
50 ləp̓ə́q̓ʷ.
51 gʷəl p̓ədíl dxʷʔal tsiʔíɬ sčəgʷúcid dəxʷʔá ʔə tsiʔíɬ sɬádəyʔ.
52 ʔuʔáhəxʷ. →
53 x̌ʷul̓ ʔəsʔəx̌íd kʷi s(ə)ʔa:s.

54 gʷəl ləcút tsiʔəʔ sɬádəyʔ.

55 ɬíxʷixʷ tíʔəʔ díʔəʔ sixʷuyáyuss.
56 díičuʔ tsiʔíɬ sixʷukʷúks.
57 gʷəl díičuʔ tsíʔəʔ díʔəʔ ʔəsyáyusbid tíʔəʔ ʔálʔal.
58 gʷəl díičuʔ tsíʔəʔ díʔəʔ sixʷuc̓agʷúlč.
59 sʔílax̌ad ʔə tsíʔəʔ sɬádəyʔ.

60 tul̓ʔál kʷi tushúy ʔə tíʔəʔ swátixʷtəd
sʔas ʔəsɬáɬlil.
61 xʷiʔ gʷəsəʔúx̌ʷs dxʷčad.

62 gʷəl cúucəxʷ tíʔəʔ díʔəʔ <stə. . .,> stáwixʷaʔɬs,
63 "ƛ̕úbəxʷ čəɬ ʔugʷáx̌ʷ.
64 ʔugʷáx̌ʷ čəɬ liɬʔál ti ʔílgʷiɬ ʔə tíʔəʔ díʔəʔ qʷuʔ."
65 gʷáx̌ʷax̌ʷgʷax̌ʷ.

66 <su. . .,> xʷiʔ gʷədsəs(h)áydxʷ səsčál kʷi dəxʷkʷədáds →
tíʔəʔ díʔəʔ sk̓ʷík̓ʷqʷəb míʔmad
ʔi tíʔəʔ <stabəxʷ kʷi sdaʔs tiʔíɬ c(əd)íɬ stəb *hamə*,
šq́áčiʔd. . .,> šq́áčiʔd. šq́áčiʔd.
67 ɬáʔəxʷ. →
68 gʷəl ʔíbəš.
69 gʷax̌ʷ əlgʷəʔ bəbúʔs.
70 gʷəl li:l ti səʔúx̌ʷs əlgʷəʔ liɬʔílgʷiɬ ʔə tiʔiɬ qʷuʔ.
71 ha:ʔɬ či[či]čƛ̕aʔ.
72 díɬəxʷ kʷi [s]šúdxʷs ə́lgʷəʔ tíʔəʔ díʔəʔ wə́q̓əb.
73 ʔəsp̓ədíl.

74 huy cúucəxʷ tíʔəʔ stáwixʷaʔɬ.
75 "stábəxʷ tiʔíɬ ʔəsp̓ədíl."

76 And they went on.
77 And they were drawing closer,
78 And they made out a box.
79 They kept going
and they arrived at it.

80 She said to the children,
81 "This is a box
And it is a very nice one.
82 We will salvage it.
83 We will find out about it
and we will open the lid of this box."

84 She took that little hammer.
85 And
she hit it.
86 She took the hatchet.
87 And she lifted.

88 She saw these two people who were there.
They were inside the box.
89 When she took the box,
90 and she opened the lid,
91 then she saw these people.

92 And she said to her children.
93 "We had better take this man
and we will take him home."
94 They took the woman.
95 And they returned her.
96 They pushed her off.
97 Whatever the reason they pushed her off,
98 she went home.

99 They took the man home.
100 And they had him there.
101 He was their worker.
102 The man just stayed on.
103 He was a good worker in everything.

76 gʷəl ʔúx̌ʷ ə́lgʷəʔ. →
77 gʷəl ləč̓ítil, →
78 gʷəl ʔəscə́k̓ʷdxʷ wə́q̓əb.
79 [lə]cuʔúx̌ʷəxʷ →
gʷəl łčis.

80 cúuc tíʔəʔ stáwixʷaʔł. →
81 "tíʔəʔ wə́q̓əb. →
gʷəl cick̓ʷ haʔł. →
82 łuʔúləx̌əd čəł.
83 łudxʷs(h)áydxʷəb čəł čła łuʔ[ə]q̓ʷúcid tíʔəʔ díʔəʔ wə́q̓əb."

84 kʷədádəxʷ tíʔəʔ díʔəʔ šišqáči(ʔ)d. →
85 gʷəl
tə́səd.
86 kʷədádəxʷ tsi sk̓ʷík̓ʷqʷəb.
87 gʷəl šə́qəd.

88 ʔə(s)šúdxʷəxʷ tíʔəʔ s[ə]sá[ʔ]liʔ ʔáciłtalbixʷ ʔa →
ʔəsdə́kʷ ʔal tíʔəʔ wə́q̓əb, stúbš ʔi tsiʔ—.
89 ʔáləxʷ kʷi tuskʷədádsəxʷ tiʔíł wə́q̓əb, →
90 gʷəl tuʔ[ə]q̓ʷúcid, →
91 gʷəl tušúdxʷ tíʔəʔ díʔəʔ c[əd]ił ʔáciłtalbixʷ.

92 gʷəl tucúucəxʷ tíʔəʔ c[əd]íł stáwixʷaʔłs.
93 "X̌ub čəł łukʷədád tíʔəʔ díʔəʔ stubš →
čła łut̓úk̓ʷtxʷ."
94 kʷədádəxʷ ə́lgʷəʔ tsíʔəʔ słádəyʔ. <gʷəl. . . ,>
95 gʷəl bə́lkʷtxʷ ə́lgʷəʔ.
96 híqid ə́lgʷəʔ.
97 ʔəsčál kʷi tədəxʷhíqids.
98 tut̓úk̓ʷ.

99 tut̓úk̓ʷtxʷəxʷ ə́lgʷəʔ tíʔəʔ stubš.
100 gʷəl tuʔátxʷəxʷ ə́lgʷəʔ.
101 sixʷuyáyuss ə́lgʷəʔ.
102 x̌ʷul̓əxʷ tuʔáʔiləxʷ ti stubš, →
103 haʔł tiʔíł suyáyuss dxʷʔal tiʔíł stab.

104 And she took him
105 and she made him her mate.
106 This man was now her husband.
107 And the four women were all his wives while he stayed there.
108 That was nice, the way it was, when he stayed.

109 There this man was until it came to be the month of *July*.
110 This is the way it was.
111 Then from the first coming of spring,
112 so it came to be the month of *July*.

113 This woman said to her hired hands,
114 "We had better give back this man
and we will see his parents."
115 They prepared for their water-trip.
116 She did not know if her boat was there, that steamboat.
117 And that is what they boarded.
118 They just got themselves ready.
119 And this woman took these four;
these are "peanuts."
120 She took them.
121 And she put them in the pockets of this man.
122 Two are in one pocket:
the younger one,
123 and the older one.
124 This middle one
125 and this one
are in one pocket.

126 They spoke to this man.
127 "You are not to reveal us.
128 No matter may happen,
129 or what you hear, you are not to reveal us.
130 Simply go ahead when the day comes
that we reveal you to your parents
then we will reveal ourselves."

104 gʷəl tukʷədádəxʷ →
105 gʷəl tuhúyudəxʷ sq̓ʷuʔs.
106 sč̓ístxʷsəxʷ tíʔəʔ stubš.
107 gʷəl bək̓ʷáxʷ čáagʷəss tiʔiʔəʔ díʔəʔ bəbúʔs ʔal tiʔíɬ tusʔáʔilsəxʷ.
108 diɬ shaʔɬs kʷi səshúys ʔal tiʔíɬ tədəxʷʔáʔils.

109 tuʔaːhəxʷ tíʔəʔ díʔəʔ stubš dxʷʔal tíʔəʔ díʔəʔ
təsəʔáʔils tíʔəʔ díʔəʔ *July* sɬukʷálb.
110 tíʔəʔ tushúys. →
111 gʷəl tul̕ʔál kʷi dᶻixʷ səx̌qʷùlílbs.
112 gʷəl ləʔáliləxʷ tíʔəʔ díʔəʔ *July* sɬukʷálb.

113 tucút(t)əbəxʷ ʔə tsíʔəʔ sɬádəyʔ tíʔəʔ c[əd]íɬ sʔílax̌ads.
114 "x̌úbəxʷ čəɬ ɬuʔábaqəd tíʔəʔ díʔəʔ stubš
čɬa ɬušúdxʷ kʷi yəl̕yəlábs."
115 tuqʷíbicutəxʷ ə́lgʷəʔ dxʷʔal ɬusʔúluɬsəxʷ ə́lgʷəʔ.
116 xʷiʔ gʷəsəs(h)áydxʷs gʷəʔáhəs tíʔəʔ q̓íl̕bids,
tíʔəʔ díʔəʔ hùdálgʷiɬ.
117 gʷəl díɬəxʷ tədəxʷq̓ílagʷils ə́lgʷəʔ.
118 x̌ʷul̕ ə́lgʷəʔ tuhúyucut. →
119 gʷəl tukʷədátəb ʔə tsíʔəʔ sɬádəyʔ tíʔəʔ díʔəʔ, <əh. . . ,> buus →
tíʔəʔ díʔəʔ *peanuts*.
120 tukʷədád. →
121 gʷəl tudəgʷáš <*put it. . . ,*>
ʔal tiʔíɬ [xʷ]dəgʷígʷsali ʔə tíʔəʔ stubš.
122 sáliʔ ʔal tíʔəʔ dəčuʔ xʷdəgʷígʷsali,
tsíʔəʔ ʔiɬƛ̓ísu. →
123 gʷəl tsíʔəʔ ʔiɬɬúx̌.
124 tsíʔəʔ díʔəʔ ʔiɬʔəgʷsátəd
125 gʷəl cədíɬ ʔal tíʔəʔ díʔəʔ dəčuʔ xʷdəgʷígʷsali.

126 cúucəxʷ tíʔəʔ stubš.
127 "xʷiʔ kʷi ɬ(u)adswəlíʔtubuɬ.
128 p̓ax̌ax̌ gʷəʔáhəs kʷi ʔəsčál ɬuhúy →
129 gʷə(l) ləqdxʷ čəxʷ gʷəl xʷiʔ kʷi ɬ(u)adswəlíʔtubuɬ.
130 tux̌ʷ yaw̓ ɬuʔálil kʷi sləx̌íl
ɬuswəlíʔcid čəɬ dxʷʔal tiʔíɬ adyəl̕yəláb
čɬa ɬuwəlíʔcut."

131 They traveled with the man until they got him there.
132 They reached his parents.
133 He was not recognized.
134 He was not known as the very one he was.
135 He simply had to introduce himself when he went in.

136 And his parents were blinded
by his very great beauty; he was transformed.
137 And
they could not see for a long time.
138 It was a long time before they could see their son.
139 But they did not recognize him.
140 He simply had to introduce himself to his parents.

141 So they found out.

142 And right away his father went.
143 He told his neighbors, those people,
about the arrival of their son.
144 He must not have died.
145 He had arrived.
146 He had returned.
147 But now he is simply different, he was transformed.

148 As soon as the people found out,
149 then they went.
150 And they looked at him.
151a The people could not see for a long time, being blinded
by the person, by his difference;
151b he was transformed.
152 He was beautiful now; he was transformed;
he was a brilliant person.

131 tuʔúx̌ʷtxʷəxʷ ólgʷəʔ tiʔəʔ stubš dxʷʔal tusłčíltxʷs ólgʷəʔ.
132 tułčíl dxʷʔal tiʔíł yəl̓yəlábs.
133 xʷ(iʔ)áxʷ gʷət(u)səsúxʷtəbs.
134 xʷ(iʔ)áxʷ gʷəsəs(h)áydubs gʷəcədíłəs.
135 túx̌ʷəxʷ tuláʔcut ʔal kʷədíʔ tushədʔíw̓s. →

136 gʷəl tuc̓xʷc̓xʷáy̓s tíʔəʔ yəl̓yəlábs
ʔal tíʔəʔ scí:ck̓ʷsəxʷ haʔł tíʔəʔ səshúys.
137 gʷəl <tu. . . ,>
xʷiʔ gʷətu(s)šúłdubuts dxʷʔal haʔkʷ.
138 hágʷəxʷ gʷəl tušúdxʷ ólgʷəʔ tíʔəʔ bədáʔs.
139 gʷəl xʷ(iʔ)áxʷ gʷət(u)səsúxʷtəšs.
140 túx̌ʷəxʷ tuláʔcutbid tíʔəʔ yəl̓yəlábs.

141 gʷəl tuháydub.

142 gʷəl tíləbəxʷ tuʔúx̌ʷ tíʔəʔ díʔəʔ báds.
143 tuyə́cəb dxʷʔal tíʔəʔ díʔəʔ t̓ədáx̌ads ólgʷəʔ ʔáciłtalbixʷ
ʔə tiʔíł słčil ʔə tiʔíł bədáʔs ólgʷəʔ.
144 xʷiʔ əw̓ə gʷəsʔátəbəds.
145 ʔułčíl. →
146 ʔubə́lkʷ. →
147 gʷəl tux̌ʷ ləlíʔəxʷ tiʔíł səshúys.

148 x̌ʷúl̓əxʷ ʔuháydub ʔə tiʔíł ʔáciłtalbixʷ, →
149 huy ʔúx̌ʷəxʷ. →
150 gʷəl šúucəb.
151a xʷ(iʔ)áxʷ gʷəsušúdubs dxʷʔal haʔkʷ kʷi ƛ̓usc̓xʷáy̓s →
ʔə tíʔəʔ ʔáciłtalbixʷ ʔə tíʔəʔ sləlíʔsəxʷ →
151b tíʔəʔ səshúys.
152 háʔłəxʷ tíʔəʔ səshúys →
t(u)asgʷəqíl ʔáciłtalbixʷ.

153 Then that *si?áb* man of the people found out that he had arrived;
their daughter had already arrived.
154 Therefore he said,
155 "I'd better go see him."
156 He went.
157 And he arrived there.
158 But he could not see the young man.
159 For a long time he was there.
160 Then he saw him sitting down.

161 And right away he said to this man.
162 "Oh, you are very different now in your transformed being.
163 You are very beautiful in your transformed being.
164 You'd better take my daughter."

165 The man said,
166 "No!
167 I won't take her."

168 That other man argued for a long time.

169 He wouldn't listen.
170 He wouldn't even say "Oh!"

171 He just still wanted to get the boy.
172 He wanted him to return to his former wife.

173 But the man said no until he yielded.

174 He took the youngest who had been hidden,
who had been pocketed.
175 He took it.
176 And he rolled it.
177 And it rolled.
178 And she stood up.
179 The people who were there could not look at her.
180 They could not see her for a long time
because this woman was quite brilliant.

153 huy, háydubəxʷ ʔə tíʔəʔ cədíɬ siʔáb ʔə tíʔəʔ ʔáciɬtalbixʷ
kʷi sƛ̓čil ʔə tiʔíɬ tuɬčíl kʷaʔ tsíʔəʔ bədáʔs álgʷəʔ.
154 tuľʔál gʷəcútəxʷ. →
155 "ƛ̓ub čəd ʔuʔúx̌ʷ ʔušúuc."
156 tuʔúx̌ʷəxʷ. →
157 gʷəl tuɬčíl dxʷʔal tíʔəʔ díʔəʔ.
158 gʷəl xʷiʔ gʷə(s)šúdxʷs tíʔəʔ díʔəʔ <ƛ̓. . . ,> čáč̓as stubš.
159 há:ʔkʷ kʷədíʔ sʔa:s. →
160 gʷəl ləšúdxʷ tiʔíɬ səsgʷədíls.
161 gʷəl tíləbəxʷ tucúuc tíʔəʔ díʔəʔ stubš.
162 "ʔu: cick̓ʷəxʷ ləlíʔəxʷ tiʔíɬ adsəshúy.
163 "cick̓ʷəxʷ čəxʷ haʔɬ tiʔíɬ adsəshúy.
164 "ƛ̓ub čəxʷ ɬukʷədád tsiʔíɬ dbədáʔ."
165 tucút tíʔəʔ stubš. →
166 "xʷiʔ.
167 xʷiʔ gʷədsəkʷədád."
168 tux̌íx̌q̓əxʷ tíʔəʔ díʔəʔ stubš dxʷʔal haʔkʷ.
169 xʷiʔ gʷəsləqs.
170 xʷiʔ gʷəscúts "ʔu!"
171 x̌ʷuľ ʔiɬ(ʔə)xʷskʷəd(d)xʷáb tíʔəʔ díʔəʔ čáč̓as.
172 x̌áƛ̓txʷ kʷi gʷəsbálkʷs dxʷʔal tsiʔíɬ <tsiʔíɬ,təb. . . ,>
tučəgʷáss.
173 gʷəl ləxʷíʔəd tíʔəʔ stubš dxʷʔal sx̌ʷaľs.

-ıllı-

174 kʷədádəxʷ tsíʔəʔ díʔəʔ <ʔiɬ. . . ,> ʔiɬƛ̓ísu tusʔáyitəbs,
tusdəgʷyítəbs.
175 kʷədádəxʷ. →
176 gʷəl tə́ǰəd.
177 gʷəl təč.
178 gʷəl kiis.
179 tiʔíɬ ʔa ʔáciɬtalbixʷ xʷiʔ gʷəšúɬdubuts.
180 xʷiʔ gʷəšúɬs álgʷəʔ dxʷʔal haʔkʷ kʷədíʔ scick̓ʷs →
ʔəsgʷəqíl tsíʔəʔ sɬádəyʔ.

181 It was a long time.
182 Then they could see her.
183 The woman was very beautiful to look at.

184 The old fellow only said even more,
185 "My daughter is more beautiful.
186 You'd better take her; she has returned."

---

187 The man took that next one, older than this one.
188 And he let it go.
189 It rolled on the floor until she stood up again.
190 The same thing happened again.
191 For a longer time the people looked
before they could see her.
192 She was best; the woman was again more beautiful.

193 But that old fellow did not give up.
194 He only argued even more for his daughter
that she was more beautiful
than this woman.
195 "She is better to look at."

196 He argued with this young man for a long time.
197 Then
he gave up.

---

198 He took their cook.
199 And he rolled it.
200 She stood up.
201 She was even better, more beautiful.

[Note: the tape was changed here and something was likely omitted]

181 hágʷəxʷ. →
182 gʷəl šúdxʷ ə́lgʷəʔ. →
183 ci:ck̓ʷ haʔł šuł słádəyʔ.

184 x̌ʷul̓ bəʔiłcút tíʔəʔ díʔəʔ luƛ̓.
185 "tsiʔíł dbədáʔ gʷəl ʔiłháʔł.
186 ƛ̓ub čəxʷ ʔukʷədád, ʔubə́lkʷ."

187 bəkʷədátəbəxʷ ʔə tiʔəʔ stubš tíʔəʔ díʔəʔ c(əd)ił <ʔił. . . ,>
ʔiłlúƛ̓, tul̓ʔal tsíʔəʔ.
188 gʷəl bəkʷáʔəd.
189 təč ʔal tiʔíł x̌łídup dxʷʔal bəskíiss.
190 ƛ̓al̓ b(ə)asʔístə(ʔ) kʷədíʔ shuys. →
191 ʔiłhagʷəxʷ kʷi ssuł ʔə tiʔíł ʔáciłtalbixʷ
dxʷʔal kʷi səšúdxʷs ə́lgʷəʔ.
192 dᶻíxʷəxʷ bəʔiłháʔł słádəyʔ.

193 huy, xʷiʔ gʷəsx̌ʷál̓ ʔə tíʔəʔ díʔəʔ luƛ̓.
194 x̌ʷul̓ ʔiłx̌íx̌q̓ tsiʔíł bədáʔs →
gʷəl ʔiłháʔł tul̓ʔal tsíʔəʔ díʔəʔ słádəyʔ.
195 "ʔiłháʔł šuł."

196 x̌ix̌q̓ tíʔəʔ díʔəʔ č̓áčas stubš dxʷʔal haʔkʷ.
197 gʷəl
bə[dxʷ]x̌ʷál̓igʷəd.

198 kʷədádəxʷ tsíʔəʔ díʔəʔ kʷuks ə́lgʷəʔ.
199 gʷəl tə́ǰəd.
200 kíis.
201 ʔiłdᶻíxʷəxʷ ʔiłháʔł. <čad. . . ,>

[Note: the tape was changed here and something was likely omitted.]

202 The man was there.
203 And he lost his wives because he had revealed them.
204 The day had not come when he was told to reveal his wives.
205 But he did reveal them.

206 So this woman went home.
207 She took her crew home.

208 And there was the man.
209 And he didn't know
210 how he would manage.
211 And he wanted to get back his wife.
212 And he just was very heart-broken.

## SCENE 2

213 And he walked.
214 He walked this way to the world upriver.
215 It was upriver that he walked.

216 He didn't go that way.

217 He walked to that far land.
He walked until he arrived at the first place where he arrived.

218 These people had been playing since the making
of the world there was this:
it was called a hoop.
219 It was rolling from up above on a mountain, a beautiful mountain.
220 It was a very blue mountain.
221 So that is where these people were.

222 They were playing.
223 They were rolling this hoop downward.
224 And there are their little spears.
225 And there they are chasing that hoop.

202 ʔa <ti stə. . .> tiʔił stubš.
203 gʷəl x̌ʷil̓álcbidəxʷ tiʔił čáagʷəss ʔal tiʔił swəlí(ʔ)ids.
204 xʷiʔ ləʔál kʷi sləx̌íl tuscút(t)əbs łuswəlí(ʔ)ids
tiʔił čáagʷəss.
205 gʷəl wəlí(ʔ)id.

206 gʷəl t̓uk̓ʷ tsə słádəyʔ. →
207 ʔut̓úk̓ʷtxʷ tiʔił sʔílax̌ads.

208 gʷəl tíʔəʔ stubš.
209 gʷəl xʷ(iʔ)áxʷ gʷəsəs(h)áydxʷs. →
210 ʔəsčáləxʷ kʷi łushúys
211 gʷəl gʷəbálkʷdxʷ tsiʔił čəgʷáss.
212 gʷəl x̌ʷul̓əxʷ ʔux̌áłəł x̌əč. →

## SCENE 2

213 gʷəl ʔíbəšəxʷ.
214 ʔíbəšəxʷ dxʷʔístə(ʔ) ʔal tiʔəʔ swátixʷtəd dxʷq̓(i)xʷúlgʷədxʷ.
215 [dxʷ]q̓(i)xʷúlgʷədxʷ tiʔił sʔíbəšs. →

216 xʷiʔ gʷəsʔúx̌ʷs dxʷdíʔiʔ.

217 tuʔíbəšəxʷ ʔal tiʔił li:l swátixʷtəd. <tus. . .> →
tuʔíbəš dxʷʔal tusłčíls dxʷʔal tíʔəʔ dᶻixʷ tədəxʷƛ̓číls.

218 tíʔəʔ díʔəʔ ʔáciłtalbixʷ ləcuʔúkʷukʷ tul̓ʔál kʷi tushúy →
ʔə tíʔəʔ swátixʷtəd tíʔəʔ díʔəʔ <s. . .>
ʔudáʔatəb sbəbíʔ.
219 ləcutə́č tul̓šə́q ʔə tiʔił sbádil, haʔł sbádil. <put. . .>
220 put x̌ʷiq̓ʷíx̌ʷ sbádil.
221 gʷəl dił dəxʷʔá ʔə tíʔəʔ ʔáciłtalbixʷ. →

222 ləcuʔúkʷukʷ. →
223 ləcutə́ǰəd ə́lgʷəʔ tíʔəʔ sbəbíʔ dxʷgʷəd.
224 gʷəl ʔa tíʔəʔ čičič̓sáyʔs ə́lgʷəʔ.
225 gʷəl ʔa tíʔəʔ ləsčálad tíʔəʔ cədíł sbəbíʔ.

226 And the one who can put the spear through the hoop
before it gets down to the foot of the mountain,
227 then that one will win.
228 And they were rolling it.
229 Until it—[sentence unfinished].

230 From the day they started that game,
231 then no one had speared the hoop.
232 There they had been playing this way as the year would go.
233 And the next year came again.

234 This was where this man arrived.
235 He was walking.
236 And he just watched those who were playing.

## SCENE 3

237 And he turned back.
238 He walked some more.
239 He went to a far off land where he walked.

240 Then
he came to this person.
241 He too was on a mountain,
242 and the mountain was beautiful.
243 He was sitting on the mountain.

244 And he had a pipe.
245 And he was smoking.
246 He would just smoke his pipe,
his pipe was this long.
247 And it reached down to the foot of the mountain.
248 And he just smoked.
249 And smoke would come over the world.
250 and the clouds would come.

251 This was where this man arrived.
252 And he was just there visiting.
253 He watched what this old man was doing
until he left him again.

226 g$^{w}$əl diɬ [k$^{w}$i] g$^{w}$at ɬucíqdx$^{w}$ tíʔəʔ sbəbíʔ d$^{z}$ix$^{w}$bíd ʔə tíʔiɬ ɬusbə́čs
dx$^{w}$ʔal di sbədšəd ʔə tíʔəʔ sbádil.
227 g$^{w}$əl diɬ ɬuc̓əlálik$^{w}$.
228 g$^{w}$əl ləcutə́ǰəd ə́lg$^{w}$əʔ.
229 ʔa:l dx$^{w}$ʔal tiʔíɬ ʔa, <tus, tus stəb, ʔa...>

230 tuľʔál sləx̌íl <tus, tus...> tushúyuds ə́lg$^{w}$əʔ tiʔíɬ sʔúk$^{w}$uk$^{w}$
231 g$^{w}$əl x$^{w}$iʔ k$^{w}$i g$^{w}$at g$^{w}$ələcucíqdx$^{w}$ tíʔəʔ sbəbíʔ.
232 ʔa: ləcuʔúk$^{w}$uk$^{w}$ ʔəsʔístə(ʔ) ʔə k$^{w}$i ƛ̕usʔúx̌$^{w}$s tíʔəʔ dəč̓ag$^{w}$áldx$^{w}$.
233 g$^{w}$əl ʔálil k$^{w}$i bədəč̓ag$^{w}$áldx$^{w}$.

234 díɬəx$^{w}$ tədəx$^{w}$ɬčíl ʔə tíʔəʔ díʔəʔ stubš.
235 tuləʔíbəš.
236 g$^{w}$əl x̌$^{w}$uľ t(u)a(s)šúuc tiʔiʔíɬ ləcuʔúk$^{w}$uk$^{w}$.

## SCENE 3

237 g$^{w}$əl təbəbə́lk$^{w}$.
238 bəʔíbəš.
239 tuʔúx̌$^{w}$əx$^{w}$ ʔal tiʔíɬ li:l swátix$^{w}$təd ƛ̕ədəx$^{w}$ʔíbəšs.

240 g$^{w}$əl <tuɬčísəx$^{w}$ tíʔəʔ díʔəʔ>
tuɬčísəx$^{w}$ tíʔəʔ díʔəʔ ʔáciɬtalbix$^{w}$. → <ʔal tu...,> →
241 ƛ̕aľ bəʔál tíʔəʔ sbádil,
242 g$^{w}$əl tuháʔɬ sbádil.
243 ʔəsg$^{w}$ədíl ʔal tíʔəʔ sbádil.

244 g$^{w}$əl absp̓aʔk$^{w}$.
245 g$^{w}$əl ləcubádəš.
246 x̌$^{w}$uľ ƛ̕ubádəš ʔə tiʔíɬ p̓aʔk$^{w}$s,
tiʔíɬ haac tíʔəʔ p̓aʔk$^{w}$s.
247 g$^{w}$əl ʔəsbə́dšəd dx$^{w}$ʔal tíʔəʔ sbədšəd ʔə tíʔəʔ sbádil.
248 g$^{w}$əl x̌$^{w}$uľ ƛ̕ubádəš,
249 g$^{w}$əl ƛ̕uʔəƛ̕ ti ƛ̕usg$^{w}$əpq̓$^{w}$ád ʔə tíʔəʔ swátix$^{w}$təd. →
250 g$^{w}$əl ƛ̕uʔə́ƛ̕ tíʔəʔ sq̓áƛ̕.

251 díɬəx$^{w}$ bədəx$^{w}$ɬčíl ʔə tíʔəʔ stubš.
252 g$^{w}$əl x̌$^{w}$uľ ʔuʔá ʔəsd$^{z}$əx̌əx̌bíd.
253 ʔə(s)šúuc tiʔíɬ suhúy ʔə tíʔəʔ díʔəʔ luƛ̕ stubš
dx$^{w}$ʔal təbəsɬə́g$^{w}$ɬs.

## SCENE 4

254 He went again.
255 He walked again in a far off land
which is where he went,
256 where he walked until he arrived at three
young men.
257 Their older brother had left them.
258 Their older brother had died.
259 And a beautiful garment had been his garment.

260 And that is what they have laid down as their goal
at the top of the mountain.
261 And that is it; the garment of their older brother is
what they are arguing about.
262 They have been claiming it.
263 "I am the one who will take the garment
of my older brother."
264 And another one would speak.
265 "No.
266 I am the one who will take it."
267 That is what they have done since their older brother died.
268 They have been there since the world was made.
269 And that is what they have done.

270 And the day came that this one who was walking arrived at them.
271 He arrived at those who have been arguing about the garment.
272 And the young men told him what they were doing.
273 And he said to these young men,
274 "I will tell you folks what you can do
so someone gets the garment of that one,
your late older brother.
275 It is not good that you folks have just been arguing."
276 He will take this "ball,"
277 just like this big "ball."

## SCENE 4

254 təbəʔúx̌ʷəxʷ.
255 təbəʔíbəšəxʷ li:l swátixʷtəd →
tiʔíł ƛ̕ədəxʷʔúx̌ʷs.
256 ƛ̕ədəxʷʔíbəšs dxʷʔal tusłčíss tíʔiʔəʔ díʔəʔ łíxʷixʷ
ʔa č̓áč̓as stúbubš.
257 tułə́gʷəldub ə́lgʷəʔ ʔə tíʔəʔ sqas ə́lgʷəʔ. →
258 ʔuʔátəbəd tiʔəʔ sqas ə́lgʷəʔ. →
259 gʷəl absƛ̕álabac ʔə tíʔəʔ haʔł sƛ̕álabac.

260 gʷəl díłəxʷ <ʔəs...,> ʔəsbə́čtxʷ ə́lgʷəʔ <ʔə...,> sláʔus(s) ə́lgʷəʔ →
ʔal tiʔíł šəq ʔal tiʔíł sbádil.
261 gʷəl <...ʔəl gʷəl...,> díłəxʷ dəxʷux̌íx̌q̓s ə́lgʷəʔ
tíʔəʔ sƛ̕álabac ʔə tíʔəʔ sqas ə́lgʷəʔ.
262 ləcut̓ayad ə́lgʷəʔ. →
263 "ʔəcá kʷi łukʷədád ti sƛ̕álabac ʔə tiʔíł dsqa." →
264 gʷəl ƛ̕əbəcút tiʔíł díič̓uʔ. →
265 "xʷi:ʔ. →
266 ʔəcá kʷi łukʷədád."
267 dił suhú:ys ə́lgʷəʔ tul̓ʔál kʷi tusʔátəbəd →
ʔə tiʔíł sqas ə́lgʷəʔ. →
268 ʔa tul̓ʔál kʷi tushúy ʔə tíʔəʔ swátixʷtəd.
269 gʷəl dił suhúys ə́lgʷəʔ. →

270 gʷəl ləʔálil tiʔíł sləx̌íl słčísəbs ə́lgʷəʔ ʔə tiʔíł cədíł ləʔíbəš.
271 łčísəxʷ tiʔiʔíł ləcux̌íx̌q̓bid tíʔəʔ sƛ̕álabac.
272 gʷəl yəcəbtúbəxʷ ʔə tiʔiʔəʔ stúutubšs tiʔíł shuys ə́lgʷəʔ.
273 gʷəl cúucəxʷ tíʔəʔ díʔəʔ stúutubš.
274 "łucúucbułəd čəd ʔəsʔəx̌íd gʷəshúyləp čələpa →
gʷəkʷə́d(d)xʷ tiʔíł sƛ̕álabac ʔə tiʔíł →
tusqáləp →
275 xʷiʔ ləƛ̕úb tiʔíł sx̌ʷul̓(l)əp ləcux̌íx̌q̓."
276 łukʷədádəxʷ tíʔəʔ díʔəʔ <stə...> *ball*,
277 x̌ʷúl̓ab ʔə tíʔəʔ díʔəʔ hikʷ *ball*.

278 He said,
279 "I will roll this and you all will chase it.
280 And the one who gets it before it falls way down to
the foot,
281 then that one will win the garment."

282 The boys tumbled down right behind the rolling "ball."
283 No one could get it.
284 And it reached the bottom.
285 They got it; one of them got it.
286 And they climbed up arguing.
287 "I am the one who got the 'ball.'"
288 "No!
289 I am the one who got it."
290 They were always saying this over and over
until they reached the summit where that one was.
291 He was waiting.

292 From there,
then he said to them.
293 "No one got this "ball."
294 So I will roll it again and you all will chase it again."
295 He took it again.
296 And he rolled it again.
297 And it rolled.
298 And the boys went.
299 They were tumbling down behind it to the bottom.
300 No one got it.
301 From there
then it was taken again by one of them.
302 And they returned there again.
303 They were arguing.
304 They said,
305 "I am the one who got it."
306 The other one said,
307 "No.
308 I am the one who got it."
309 They were saying this until they reached the summit again
where that one was waiting.

278 cúuc. →
279 "ɬutə́ǰəd čəd tíʔəʔ díʔəʔ čələpa ɬučálad.
280 gʷəl díɬ gʷat ɬukʷədádəxʷ dᶻixʷbíd ʔə kʷi ɬusbə́čs →
dxʷʔal túdiʔ sbə́dšəd.
281 gʷəl diɬ ɬuc̓ə́ldxʷ tíʔəʔ sƛ̕álabac."
282 dᶻáq̓əxʷ ti stúutubš liɬləqbíd ʔə tíʔəʔ diʔəʔ *ball* lətə́č.
283 xʷiʔ kʷi gʷat gʷukʷə́d(d)xʷ. →
284 gʷəl bə́dšəd.
285 kʷədádəxʷ ə́lgʷəʔ kʷədiʔ díičuʔ kʷəd(iʔ) ʔukʷədád. →
286 gʷəl kʷátač ə́lgʷəʔ ləx̌íx̌q̓. <tsi. . . ,>
287 "ʔəcá tiʔíɬ ʔukʷə́d(d)xʷ tiʔíɬ *ball*."
288 "xʷi:ʔ!
289 ʔəcá tiʔíɬ ʔukʷə́d(d)xʷ ti."
290 ck̓ʷaqid səcutcuts ə́lgʷəʔ dxʷʔa:l bəsq̓íluss ə́lgʷəʔ →
dxʷʔal ti dəxʷʔá ʔə tiʔəʔ cədiɬ.
291 <ʔəs. . . ,> ʔəsʔáʔsil.

292 tuľʔá →
gʷəl bəcút(t)əb ə́lgʷəʔ. →
293 "xʷiʔ kʷi gʷat gʷukʷə́d(d)xʷ tiʔíɬ ʔa *ball*.
294 gʷəl bətə́ǰəd čəd čələpa ɬəbəčálad."
295 bəkʷədádəxʷ. →
296 gʷəl bətə́ǰəd. →
297 gʷəl təč.
298 gʷəl ʔux̌ʷ tíʔəʔ díʔəʔ stuutubš. →
299 lədᶻáq̓ liɬləqbíd ʔə tíʔəʔ díʔəʔ dxʷʔal gʷəsbə́dšəds. →
300 xʷiʔ kʷi gʷat gʷukʷə́d(d)xʷ.
301 tuľʔá →
gʷəl bəkʷədátəb ʔə kʷədiʔ díičuʔ. →
302 gʷəl bəbə́lkʷ ə́lgʷəʔ ʔa:. →
303 ləx̌íx̌q̓ ə́lgʷəʔ. →
304 ləcút. →
305 "ʔəcá tiʔíɬ ʔukʷə́d(d)xʷ."
306 ʔucút kʷədiʔ díičuʔ. →
307 "xʷiʔ. →
308 ʔəcá tiʔíɬ ʔukʷə́d(d)xʷ."
309 ləcútcut ə́lgʷəʔ dxʷʔal bəsq̓ílus ə́lgʷəʔ →
dxʷʔal tiʔəʔ dəxʷʔá ʔə ti cədíɬ ʔəsʔáʔsil.

310 From there
then they were told again.
311 "No one of you got it.
312 I will roll it again."
313 It was rolled again.
314 And they went again.
315 And he just rolled that thing there.
316 And the boys went.
317 They ran.

318 He took that garment.
319 And he put it on.
320 It was exactly right for him.
321 He took it.
322 And he pulled it off
323 and he laid it down.

324 From there
then those boys came.
325 This time also they were arguing again as they
reached the summit again for the third time.

326 Then, there for the fourth time, he said,
327 "I will roll it again and you all will chase it again."
328 This is the fourth time now.
329 "And the one who will get the 'ball'—"
[Note: the tape was changed here and something was not recorded.]
330 *
331 There for the fourth time those boys went.
332 They tumbled down.
333 They chased that "ball."

---

* [that one will win this garment.]

310 tulʼʔá →
gʷəl bəcút(t)əb ə́lgʷəʔ. →
311 "xʷiʔ kʷi gʷat gʷukʷə́d(d)xʷ ʔə gʷəlápu tiʔíɬ.
312 ɬubətə́ǰəd čəd."
313 bətəčtəbáxʷ tiʔíɬ. →
314 gʷəl bəʔúx̌ʷ ə́lgʷəʔ.
315 gʷəl x̌ʷúlʼəxʷ <ʔu...,> ʔutə́ǰəd tiʔíɬ (ʔ)a. →
316 ʔuʔúx̌ʷ tiʔíɬ stúutubš. →
317 ʔudᶻaq̓. →

318 gʷəl kʷədádəxʷ tiʔíɬ sƛ̕álabac. →
319 gʷəl ƛ̕alš.
320 pu:t ʔiƛ̕úb dxʷʔal cədíɬ.
321 kʷədád. →
322 gʷəl ʔúq̓ʷud →
323 gʷəl ɬáq̓ad.

324 tulʼʔá →
gʷəl ʔəƛ̕áxʷ tiʔíɬ stúutubš. →
325 ƛ̕alʼ bələx̌íx̌q̓ dxʷʔal bəsq̓ílus ɬixʷáɬəxʷ.

326 gʷəl ʔáləxʷ tíʔəʔ sbúusaɬils cuuc. →
327 "ɬubətə́ǰəd čəd čələpa ləbəčálad."
328 tiʔá(ʔəxʷ) sbúusàɬs. →
329 gʷəl diɬ kʷi gʷat <ɬu...,> ɬukʷə́d(d)xʷ tiʔíɬ *ball*
[Note: the tape was changed here and something was not recorded.]
330 * 331ʔáləxʷ tiʔíɬ sbúusàɬsəxʷ sʔúx̌ʷəxʷ ʔə tiʔíɬ stúutubš. →
332 ʔudᶻáq̓. →
333 ʔučálad tiʔíɬ cədíɬ *ball.*

* [gʷəl diɬ ɬučə́ldxʷ tíʔəʔ sƛ̕álabac.]

334 Then the man took the garment.
335 And he put it on.
336 Those boys tumbled down until they got to the bottom again.
337 And no one got that thing.
338 It continued rolling until one of them went after it again.
339 And he got it.
340 And they brought it back.
341 There they are
then arguing as they were coming.

342 And they arrive.
343 And there was no man.
344 He was not there.
345 And there was no garment.

346 And the older one spoke.
347 "Where did he go?
348 Where is the garment?"
349 The younger one said,
350 "Oh, for a while I thought about this.
351 He would do it this way.
352 He would take that garment.
353 This is why he did this thing to us."

354 And there he was standing.
355 He was listening.
356 He was wearing the garment.

357 The garment was simply put on,
358 And you would not be visible.
359 You would not be visible while wearing the garment.

360 That is what they were arguing about.
361 Each one wants to get it.
362 And there they were.
363 They continued talking.

334 gʷəl kʷədátəbəxʷ ʔə tíʔəʔ stubš tíʔəʔ sƛ̕álabac. →
335 gʷəl ƛ̕alš.
336 dᶻáq̓əxʷ tiʔíɬ stúutubš dxʷʔal bəsbədšəds əlgʷəʔ.
337 gʷəl xʷiʔ kʷi gʷat gʷ(ə)kʷəd(d)xʷ tiʔəʔ cədíɬ.
338 ləcutəčtəb dxʷʔal bəsʔúx̌ʷcəbsəxʷ ʔə kʷədiʔ díičuʔ. →
339 gʷəl kʷədád.
340 gʷəl ʔəƛ̕txʷáxʷ əlgʷəʔ.
341 ʔa
gʷəl ləx̌íx̌q̓ ʔal kʷədiʔ səʔəƛ̕s əlgʷəʔ. →

342 gʷəl ɬčil əlgʷəʔ.
343 gʷəl xʷíʔəxʷ tíʔəʔ díʔəʔ stúbš.
344 xʷ(iʔ)áxʷ gʷəsʔás.
345 gʷəl xʷ(iʔ)áxʷ tíʔəʔ sƛ̕álabacs.

346 gʷəl cútəxʷ tiʔíɬ ʔiɬlúƛ̕.
347 "<ʔə. . . ,> dxʷčádəxʷ kʷi sʔux̌ʷs. →
348 dxʷčádəxʷ ti sƛ̕álabac."
349 cútəxʷ tíʔəʔ ʔiɬƛ̕ísu,
350 "ʔu: haʔkʷ čəd ʔəxʷcútəbid. →
351 ɬuhúyud ʔəsʔístəʔ. →
352 tiʔíɬ sƛ̕álabac ɬukʷədád.
353 tíʔəʔ dəxʷuhúyutubuɬs ʔə tíʔəʔ diʔəʔ stáb."

354 gʷəl ʔa ʔəskíis. →
355 ʔəsləq. →
356 ʔəsƛ̕áltxʷ ti sƛ̕álabac.

357 x̌ʷul̕ ƛ̕uƛ̕álib tiʔəʔ sƛ̕álabac,
358 gʷəl xʷ(iʔ)áxʷ gʷadsəswəlíʔ.
359 xʷ(iʔ)áxʷ gʷadsəswəlíʔ gʷəƛ̕álšəxʷ tíʔəʔ sƛ̕álabac.

360 diɬ dəxʷux̌íx̌q̓bids əlgʷəʔ. →
361 x̌áƛ̕tub ʔə kʷi díičuʔ gʷəskʷəd(d)xʷs.
362 gʷəl ʔáhəxʷ əlgʷəʔ. →
363 ləcu<cu. . . ,>gʷáagʷad. →

364 He left.
365 He went again.
366 He walked again.

367 There he was wearing the garment.
368 He walked again into a far off land—

369 It was then that cold weather was coming again.

## SCENE 5

370 Eventually he arrived at this woman.
371 He arrived at this house.
372 But it is not a very big house.

373 And he went.
374 And he looked at what was there.
375 And only an old woman was there.
376 She was huddled on her little mat.

377 He asked the old woman.
378 And he was told,
379 "Don't you go on with your walking.
380 You will stay here.

381 "My grandchildren are powerful.
382 My grandchildren are powerful.
383 If you were walking around here,
you would meet them, and you would freeze.
384 They are powerful ones, my four grandchildren."

385 She said,
386 "I will take you and you will be behind me."
387 She covered him.
388 And there she lay face down when the oldest came.

364 gʷəlɬəgʷɬáxʷ.
365 bəʔúx̌ʷəxʷ. →
366 bəʔíbəš.

367 ʔáhəxʷ ləsƛ̕áltxʷ tiʔíɬ sƛ̕álabac.
368 bəʔíbəšəxʷ dxʷʔa:l kʷi líləxʷ swátixʷtəd.

369 díɬəxʷ səʔə́ƛ̕s dxʷʔal kʷi bəsƛ̕sílsəxʷ.

## SCENE 5

370 dxʷʔa:l sɬčíssəxʷ tsíʔəʔ díʔəʔ, →
371 ɬčil dxʷʔal tíʔəʔ díʔəʔ ʔálʔal. →
372 gʷəl tux̌ʷ xʷiʔ ləhíkʷ ʔálʔal.

373 gʷəl ʔux̌ʷ.
374 gʷəl šúuc kʷədíʔ ʔa.
375 gʷəl dáy̓ tsíʔəʔ luƛ̕ tsíʔəʔ ʔa. →
376 ʔəsx̌k̓ʷúcut ʔal kʷədíʔ sɬáʔɬəgʷids.

377 ʔuwíliq̓ʷid tsi luƛ̕.
378 gʷəl ləcút(t)əb.
379 "xʷiʔ kʷi ɬ(u)adsʔúx̌ʷ ʔal tíʔəʔ adsəʔíbəš.
380 ɬudíʔaʔ čəxʷ."

381 "x̌áʔx̌aʔ tiʔíɬ dʔíbibac.
382 x̌áʔx̌aʔ tiʔíɬ dʔíbibac.
383 gʷəʔíbəš čəxʷ ʔal ti →
čxʷa gʷəʔəy̓gʷásbid čxʷa gʷəq̓áxʷ.
384 x̌áʔx̌aʔx̌aʔ tiʔíɬ dʔíbibac ʔal bəbúʔs."

385 cúucəxʷ. →
386 "ɬukʷədácid čəd čxʷa <ɬu...,> ɬuʔál tiʔəʔ dʔalq̓ʷbíd."
387 gʷəx̌áčij̓əd.
388 gʷəl ʔa ʔəsx̌k̓ʷúsəb dxʷʔal sʔəƛ̕ ʔə <tiʔəʔ diʔəʔ...,>
tiʔəʔ diʔəʔ <ʔiɬ...,> ʔiɬlúƛ̕.

389 He is the one who came.
390 But that chill in the house as he came near
wasn't very strong.

391 And the old woman said,
392 "My grandson is coming now."
393 The older one will come.
394 And they really shiver when these grandchildren come with
their killing cold weather.

395 That one was also the same as he came along the road
and entered.
396 And "Humm. There is a human smell that I'm smelling."

397 The old woman said,
398 "Where would a human come from?
399 I'm all alone here."

400 And that one went.
401 And he was standing until the cold weather was there.
402 And he was there for one month.

403 And that next one arrived again.
404 This one was there for a cold month.

405 The old woman said again,
406 "The older one is coming again."
407 And she said,
408 "This is a stiffer cold."
409 He nearly froze.
410 She just hunched over.
411 And his face was covered with a blanket.
412 He really shivered, this grandson who was coming.

413 When he arrived again,
he too said again what was said,
414 "Humm. There is a human smell that I smelled."

389 diɬ ʔuʔə́ƛ̕.
390 gʷəl tux̌ʷ xʷiʔ lətíb
ti?ə? sƛ̕il ʔə tíʔəʔ díʔəʔ ʔálʔal dxʷʔal ti səʔə́ƛ̕s səčítils. →

391 gʷəl cút(t)əb ʔə tsíʔəʔ luƛ̕. →
392 "lə(ʔə)ƛ̕áxʷ tiʔíɬ dʔíbac."
393 ɬulčíləxʷ ʔiɬlúƛ̕. →
394 gʷəl pu:təxʷ ƛ̕(u)učə́dəb ʔal tiʔíɬ ƛ̕usɬčíls tiʔíɬ ʔibibac
təš sƛ̕əss.

395 ƛ̕al' b(ə)asʔístəʔ tíʔəʔ cədíɬ ʔal kʷədíʔ səʔə́ƛ̕s ʔal tiʔíɬ šəgʷɬ
shədʔíw̓bs. →
396 gʷəl "lə hə́m:, ʔáciɬtalbixʷàləqəp kʷi ləcu[ʔə]ƛ̕áləqəp."

397 cútəxʷ tsíʔəʔ luƛ̕. → <ʔáciɬ. . .,> →
398 "gʷətul'čádəxʷ kʷi ʔáciɬtalbixʷ gʷəɬčíl. →
399 dáy̓ay̓ čəd ʔal tíʔəʔ cəxʷʔá."

400 gʷəl ʔúx̌ʷ tíʔəʔ cədíɬ. →
401 gʷəl ləkíis dxʷʔal kʷi ƛ̕ədəxʷʔás tíʔəʔ sƛ̕əs.
402 gʷəl haʔkʷ dəčaʔílc sɬukʷálb tiʔíɬ sʔas. →

403 gʷəl bəɬčíl ti cədíɬ diičuʔ.
404 tə c(əd)iɬ ʔa sƛ̕əs sɬukʷálb.

405 <bə. . .,> bəcút(t)əbəxʷ ʔə tsíʔəʔ luƛ̕.
406 "bəʔəƛ̕áxʷ tiʔíɬ <ʔiɬ, ʔiɬ. . .,> ʔiɬluƛ̕."
407 gʷəl <c. . .,> cút(t)əbəxʷ ʔə tsíʔəʔ. →
408 "<diɬ. . ., diɬ ʔiɬqʷíq̓ʷəxʷ sƛ̕əs."
409 tux̌ʷəxʷ stab gʷəq̓áxʷəs <tiʔəʔs. . .>.
410 x̌ʷul'əxʷ ʔəsx̌k̓ʷúcut. →
411 gʷəl ʔəsxʷəlk̓ʷúsəb ʔə tiʔíɬ sʔíc̓əbs.
412 pútəxʷ ʔučə́dəb ti sʔəƛ̕ ʔə tiʔíɬ ʔíbacs.

413 dxʷʔal bəsɬčíls <gʷə. . .,>
ƛ̕al' b(ə)ascút kʷədiʔ scuts,
414 "hə́m:, ʔáciɬtalbixʷàləqəp kʷi ʔu[ʔə]ƛ̕áləqəp."

415 The old woman said,
416 "From where would a person arrive?
417 I'm alone here."

418 He went over here.
419 And he put himself where he would be
when warm weather would come.
420 There were two of them now.

421 This next one came.

422 This man was there.
423 He was waiting until the next month came again.

424 And that one came again.
425 He was the third one now.
426 He came.

427 The old woman said,
428 "My grandson comes again."
429 That one there is coming.
430 It grows cold.
431 A stiff cold is what would come.
432 This one is just called 'Adhere.'
433 'Adhere' is this month.
434 And he is powerful.

435 And this one is there until the next arrives again.
436 We are getting short until this man arrives again.

437 He came until he entered again by the door.
438 He too again said what was said,
439 "Humm. There is a human smell that I'm smelling."

440 The old woman said,
441 "No.
442 From where would a person reach me?
443 I'm alone."

415 cút(t)əb ʔə tsíʔəʔ luƛ̓. →
416 "gʷətuľčádəxʷ kʷi ʔáciłtalbixʷ gʷułčíl. →
417 dáy̓ay̓ čəd ʔal tíʔəʔ díʔaʔ."

418 ʔux̌ʷ tíʔəʔ díʔəʔ. →
419 gʷəl ləʔácut ʔal kʷədíʔ ƛ̓ədəxʷʔás ʔə tíʔəʔ →
łusʔə́ƛ̓ ʔə ti ƛ̓usq̓ʷəlíls.
420 s[ə]sá[ʔ]liʔiləxʷ.

421 [ʔə]ƛ̓áxʷ tíʔəʔ díʔəʔ.

422 ʔa tíʔəʔ díʔəʔ stubš. →
423 ʔəsʔáʔsil dxʷʔal bəsʔə́ƛ̓ ʔə tíʔəʔ dəčúʔ słukʷálb.

424 gʷəl bəʔə́ƛ̓ ti cədíł.
425 słíxʷixʷsəxʷ.
426 ləʔəƛ̓áxʷ.

427 cút(t)əb ʔə tsíʔəʔ luƛ̓. →
428 "bəʔəƛ̓áxʷ tiʔíł dʔíbac."
429 ʔəƛ̓áxʷ tiʔíł ʔa. →
430 t̓sil. →
431 qʷiq̓ʷ st̓əs tiʔíł ƛ̓usʔə́ƛ̓s.
432 tux̌ʷ tíʔəʔ díʔəʔ ƛ̓udáʔatəb ƛ̓iq̓s.
433 ƛ̓iq̓s tíʔəʔ słukʷalb.
434 gʷəl tíʔəʔ x̌áʔx̌aʔ.

435 gʷəl tíʔəʔ díʔəʔ dxʷʔá:ləxʷ bəsłčíls.
436 ləq̓iq̓x̌ʷuʔiləxʷ čəł dxʷʔal bəsłčíl ʔə tíʔəʔ díʔəʔ stubš. →

437 ləʔə́ƛ̓ dxʷʔal bəshədʔíw̓s tiʔíł šəgʷł.
438 ƛ̓aľ b(ə)ascút kʷədíʔ b(ə)ascúts.
439 "hə́m: ʔáciłtalbixʷàləqəp ti ləcu[ʔə]ƛ̓áləqəp."

440 cút(t)əb ʔə tsíʔəʔ luƛ̓.
441 "xʷi:ʔ. →
442 gʷətuľčádəxʷ kʷi ʔaciłtalbixʷ gʷəłčísəbš.
443 dáy̓ay̓ čəd."

444 He went over there where he would be.
445 He too is there.
446 And that man waited for another month.
447 For four months he was there.

448 The old woman said,
449 "Now my youngest grandson will come."
450 This is "Croaking Frog."

451a That is the one who sits down.
451b That is the one who has warmth.
452 That is his work in all things
453 which are frozen by his older brothers.
454 He is the one who repaired everything, these people.
455 They will only arrive,
456 And tell of their broken arms,
their broken heads,
their broken ears,
their broken legs.
457 of why they would come:
458 the killing ice,
the cold.

459 And the cold months, the men who were named, have passed.
460 It would grow cold when they would walk through the world.
461 The great cold would descend,
the wind,
that snow,
that ice,
462 and rivers would get filled with floating ice
because that is how those men are made.
463 And they are passed now.

444 ʔux̌ʷ dxʷʔal kʷədiʔ c(əd)ił ƛ̕ədəxʷʔás.
445 ƛ̕aľ ʔa. →
446 gʷəl ʔáʔsiləxʷ tíʔəʔ díʔəʔ stubš dxʷʔal [də]čuʔ słukʷálb.
447 buus słukʷálb tíʔił sʔas.

448 cút(t)əbəxʷ ʔə tsíʔəʔ luƛ̕.
449 "łuʔəƛ̕áxʷ tiʔíł ʔiłt̕ísu dʔíbac."
450 tíʔəʔ díʔəʔ wəxʷsús.

451a díłəxʷ sgʷədíls. →
451b díłəxʷ sq̓ʷəlíls. →
452 díłəxʷ səyáyussəxʷ tiʔəʔ bək̓ʷ stab. →
453 ƛ̕uq̓áxʷatəb ʔə tíʔəʔ səxʷsqátəds.
454 díłəxʷ ʔuhúyudəxʷ tíʔəʔ bək̓ʷ stab,
tíʔəʔ díʔəʔ ʔáciłtalbixʷ. <bək̓ʷ ʔal łu. . . ,>
455 x̌ʷuľ łułčíl tíʔəʔ cáadíł. →
456 gʷəl ƛ̕uyə́ccut ʔə kʷi sət̕ət̕q̓ʷáčiʔs,
kʷi sət̕ət̕q̓ʷqí:ds,
kʷi sət̕ət̕q̓ʷəldíʔ, →
kʷi sət̕ət̕q̓ʷšád[s], →
457 ʔə tíʔəʔ díʔəʔ ƛ̕ədəxʷəʔə́ƛ̕s, →
458 təš sq̓axʷ,
t̕əs.

459 gʷəl bəlx̌ʷáxʷ tiʔíł st̕əs słukʷálb
stúbubš ʔəsdáʔ.
460 ƛ̕ut̕síl ʔal tiʔíł ƛ̕usgʷáx̌ʷs ə́lgʷəʔ ʔal tíʔəʔ swátixʷtəd.
461 ƛ̕ubə́č tí ʔəʔ hikʷ st̕əs, →
tíʔəʔ šə́xʷəb, → <tíʔəʔ díʔəʔ, s. . . ,>
tíʔəʔ díʔəʔ báqʷuʔ, →
tíʔəʔ díʔəʔ <s. . . ,> sq̓áxʷ,
462 gʷəl ƛ̕udxʷp̓ə́q̓ʷ tíʔəʔ stúləkʷ ʔə tíʔəʔ sq̓axʷ
dxʷʔal tiʔíł səshuy ʔə tiʔíł stububš
gʷəl ʔal tiʔíł. →
463 gʷəl ləbəlx̌ʷáxʷ.

464 It is getting to the time of good weather in the world.
465 It is the month of "Croaking Frog," the youngest,
brother of these men.
466 He will be coming now.
467 And he will heal this world.
468 He helps everything with broken arms,
with broken legs,
with broken ears,
with broken necks that ice has killed
because of how those three men are made.

469 And this is their younger brother.
470 And he is good.
471 He is warm.
472 He will come now.
473 He will heal
everything in this world.
474 He would come and the world would grow green.
475 It turns fair when that one comes, the youngest.

476 He will arrive soon for a while, his work is coming.
477 He will arrive at the place of his older brothers
and their grandmother.
478 She is the one alone there at their place,
their grandmother.
479 From there he will arrive.

480 Their grandmother said,
481 "My grandson is coming now."
482 And they felt it growing warm
at their place
as the youngest grandson
of the old woman drew near.
483 It was then she said,
484 "My grandson has arrived now."
485 That one is growing very warm.

464 ʔáliləxʷ tíʔəʔ <łus...,> łusháʔłiləxʷ ʔə tíʔəʔ swátixʷtəd.
465 ti słúkʷalb wəxʷsús ʔiłt̓ísu súq̓ʷaʔ →
ʔə tíʔəʔ díʔəʔ <stu...,> stúbubš.
466 łuʔəƛ̓áxʷ. →
467 gʷəl łuháʔlid tíʔəʔ díʔəʔ swátixʷtəd.
468 ʔukʷáxʷadəxʷ tíʔəʔ bək̓ʷ ƛ̓ut̓ət̓q̓ʷáčiʔ, →
ƛ̓ut̓ət̓q̓ʷšád, →
ƛ̓ut̓ət̓q̓ʷəldíʔ,
ƛ̓u[dxʷ]pkʷápsəb təš
tíʔəʔ sq̓axʷ tíʔəʔ səshúy ʔə tíʔəʔ díʔəʔ słixʷixʷ stúbubš.

469 gʷəl tíʔəʔ súq̓ʷaʔs ə́lgʷəʔ. →
470 gʷəl haʔł. →
471 dxʷsq̓ʷəl. →
472 łu[ʔə]ƛ̓áxʷ. →
473 gʷə(l) łuháʔlidəxʷ →
tíʔəʔ bək̓ʷ stab ʔal tíʔəʔ swátixʷtəd.
474 ƛ̓u[ʔə]ƛ̓áxʷ tíʔəʔ ƛ̓usq̓ʷíx̌ʷiləxʷ ʔə tíʔəʔ swátixʷtəd. →
475 ƛ̓usháʔłilsəxʷ
ʔal tiʔíł ƛ̓us[ʔə]ƛ̓áxʷ ʔə tíʔəʔ, tiʔíł ʔiłt̓ísu.

476 łułčíləxʷ ʔə kʷi xʷ(iʔ)áxʷ ləháʔkʷ kʷi səʔəƛ̓s səyáyuss.
477 łułčíləxʷ dxʷʔal tiʔíł dəxʷʔá ʔə tiʔíł dəxʷsqátəds,
tsiʔíł kíaʔs ə́lgʷəʔ.
478 dił dáy̓ay̓ ʔa, ʔal tiʔíł dəxʷʔás ə́lgʷəʔ, →
tsiʔíł kíaʔs ə́lgʷəʔ.
479 tul̓ʔáləxʷ tiʔíł łusłčílsəxʷ. →

480 cút(t)əbsəxʷ ʔə tsiʔíł c(əd)ił kíaʔs ə́lgʷəʔ. →
481 "ləʔəƛ̓áxʷ tiʔíł dʔíbac."
482 gʷəl ʔəsx̌ə́yd(d)xʷəxʷ ə́lgʷəʔ tíʔəʔ sq̓ʷəlíləxʷ →
ʔə tíʔəʔ dəxʷʔás ə́lgʷəʔ →
ʔə tíʔił səč̓ítiləxʷ <ʔə tiʔíł...,>
ʔə tiʔił c(əd)ił ʔiłt̓ísu
ʔíbac ʔə tsíʔəʔ luƛ̓.
483 díłəxʷ kʷədíʔ scútsəxʷ.
484 "ʔułčíləxʷ tiʔíł dʔíbac."
485 c[ic]k̓ʷáxʷ ʔudxʷsq̓ʷəlíləxʷ tíʔəʔ díʔəʔ.

486 She said to that man she had covered,
487 "You had better get up now
488 for the world is getting warm."
489 The man got up.

490 They just looked at him, the older ones
who had come in first.
491 They still spoke no greeting.
492 Because they moved on again—.

493 As he moves forward again,
it grows warm again
in this world.
494 And that one arrives again.

495 He too said again what was said,
496 "Humm. There is a human smell that I smelled."

497 The old woman said,
498 "No.
499 From where would a human—?
500 I'm alone where I stay."

501 That one entered now.
502 And he looked at this man who was there.
503 Then
they met one another.
504 They became good, close friends.

505 And they got to talking.
506 He got to talking with this man
about how his brothers were made,
what they would do
when they would go,
when they would walk about.

486 cúucsəxʷ tíʔəʔ díʔəʔ stubš ʔəsx̌aċíčtxʷ. →
487 "ƛ̕úbəxʷ čəxʷ ʔugʷədíləxʷ.
488 dxʷsq̓ʷəlíləxʷ tiʔəʔ swátixʷtəd."
489 [ʔu]gʷədíləxʷ ti stubš.

490 x̌ʷuľəxʷ ʔə(s)šúucəb ʔə tíʔəʔ cáadił ʔiłlúƛ̕luƛ̕
ƛ̕ələhədʔíẇ liłdᶻíxʷ.
491 xʷ(iʔ)áxʷ gʷəsčáləxʷ gʷəbəsʔídigʷatsəxʷ. →
492 yəx̌i huy bədᶻə́x̌əxʷ gʷəbə— .

493 gʷəbəsúlacutəs →
dxʷsq̓ʷəliləxʷ →
ʔə tíʔəʔ swátixʷtəd.
494 gʷəl bəłčíləxʷ tiʔíł cədíł. →

495 ƛ̕aľ b(ə)ascút tiʔíł bəscúts. <*he says...,*>
496 "hə́m:, ʔáciłtalbixʷàləqəp kʷi ʔu[ʔə]ƛ̕áləqəp."

497 cút(t)əb ʔə tsíʔəʔ luƛ̕.
498 "xʷi:ʔ. →
499 gʷətuľčádəxʷ kʷi gʷəʔáciłtalbixʷ.
500 dáẏaẏ čəd ʔal tiʔəʔ cəxʷʔácəc."

501 hədʔíẇəxʷ tíʔəʔ cədíł,
502 gʷəl šuuc tíʔəʔ díʔəʔ stubš ʔácəc.
503 huy,
ʔəẏdágʷələxʷ.
504 háʔłəxʷ ə́lgʷəʔ təlíxʷ syáʔyaʔ.

505 gʷəl gʷáagʷadəxʷ ə́lgʷəʔ.
506 gʷaagʷa(d)txʷəxʷ tíʔəʔ díʔəʔ stubš →
dxʷʔal tíʔəʔ suhúy ʔə tíʔəʔ [də]xʷsqátəds,
tíʔəʔ ƛ̕ushúys ə́lgʷəʔ →
ʔə tíʔəʔ ƛ̕usʔúx̌ʷs ə́lgʷəʔ, →
ƛ̕usgʷáx̌ʷs ə́lgʷəʔ. →

507 And it would grow cold.
508 And they would freeze everything
in the world.
509 They would destroy people.
510 They would make them die from the killing cold,
from the ice.

511 There is snow.
512 It would snow.
513 And it would pile up very high.

514 This is what he told this man.
515 "That is my work and I am very tired
as I am coming,
coming home,
as I am healing everything
they would destroy."

516 Then
he asked that man where he was going,
what he was doing there.
517 The man said,
518 "I am going along looking for my wife."
519 This was the wife he had lost.
520 There were four with her hired hands,
521 three others.
522 "They are the ones I am going along looking for."

523 And that Croaking Frog spoke to him.
524 "There is a woman over there.
525 She is going to be married.
526 She's to be married later on today.
527 And a feast will be given at midnight tonight.
528 And lots of people will be fed."

529 This man was told.
530 "You go quickly.
531 Because later today she'll be married,
they marry today.
532 And a feast will be given at night, at midnight."

507 gʷəl <ƛu. . . ,> ƛut̓síl. →
508 gʷəl → ƛuq̓áxʷad ə́lgʷəʔ tíʔəʔ díʔəʔ bək̓ʷ stab →
ʔal ti swátixʷtəd.
509 ƛux̌ʷádᶻad ə́lgʷəʔ tíʔəʔ ʔáciłtalbixʷ. →
510 ƛušúbali(d) təš st̓əs, →
təš sq̓axʷ.

511 tiʔəʔ báqʷuʔ. →
512 ƛuqʷát. →
513 gʷəl → ƛupúkʷəb ci(c)k̓ʷ liłšə́q.

514 díłəxʷ s(u)yə́cəbtxʷs tíʔəʔ díʔəʔ stubš.
515 "gʷəl díłəxʷ dsəyáyus čədá cíck̓ʷəxʷ ləsxʷák̓ʷil →
ʔal tiʔəʔ dsəʔə́ƛ,
dsət̓uk̓ʷ
tiʔíł dsəháʔlid tiʔíł bək̓ʷ stab →
ƛux̌ʷádᶻad ə́lgʷəʔ."

516 huy,
wíliq̓ʷidəxʷ tíʔəʔ stubš gʷələdxʷčádəs, →
gʷəsčáləs tiʔíł dəxʷʔás ʔal tiʔíł.
517 cút(t)əbəxʷ ʔə tiʔəʔ stubš.
518 "ləgʷə́č̓əd čəd tsiʔíł dčəgʷás."
519 tíʔəʔ čəgʷás(s) sx̌ʷil̕álcs.
520 bəbúʔs sʔílax̌ads. →
521 tiʔíł łíxʷixʷ,
522 "gʷəl dił čəd ləgʷə́č̓əd."

523 cút(t)əbəxʷ ʔə tíʔəʔ cədíł <ʔə. . . ,> wəxʷsús.
524 "ʔácəc tsi słádəyʔ ʔal tiʔəʔ diʔəʔ ʔístəʔ.
525 łuhúygʷas.
526 ʔuhúygʷas ʔal kʷi tíl̕x̌i.
527 gʷəl łuʔələdálikʷ ʔal kʷi čəx̌gʷás słax̌.<gʷəł. . . ,> →
528 gʷəl qá ʔáciłtalbixʷ kʷi łuʔəłtúb."

529 cút(t)əbəxʷ tiʔəʔ stubš. → <ʔə. . . ,>
530 " łuʔúx̌ʷ čəxʷ ʔə kʷi ʔał.
531 yəx̌i ʔal kʷi tíl̕x̌i kʷi łusbəlyís,
bəlyi ʔal tiʔəʔ sləx̌íl. →
532 gʷəl łuʔələdálikʷ ʔal kʷi łax̌, čəx̌gʷás słax̌."

533 This man walked on.

534 He searched for his wife,
for his four wives.
535 One was the housekeeper.
536 And one did the cooking.
537 And one washed the dishes.
538 That was the job of the youngest one.
539 The women were the hired hands of that woman.

540 This man walked.
541 On and on he walked from morning until midnight.

## SCENE 6

542 And he arrived where his wife was to be married.
543 And
he saw what was inside.
544 He was wearing the garment.
545 He went inside.
546 No one could see him.
547 The people were gathered.
548 At the table, they were fed by the woman to be married.

549 He was there.
550 He was standing behind his wife.
551 On the other side of the table was the man she will marry.

552 And they were talking.
553 They got to talking.
554 And that one spoke.—
555 He had arrived.
556 And he took the "coffee" of (his) wife.
557 And he drank it.

533 łuʔíbəšəxʷ tiʔəʔ diʔəʔ stubš. →

534 gʷəčədáxʷ tsiʔił čəgʷáss
bəbúʔs tiʔəʔ čáagʷəss.
535 díičuʔ tsiʔəʔ diʔəʔ ʔəsyáyus ʔal tiʔəʔ ʔálʔal.
536 gʷəl díičuʔ tsiʔəʔ ləcukʷúkcut.
537 gʷəl díičuʔ tsiʔəʔ ləcuc̓ágʷad tiʔəʔ diʔəʔ č̓àwəyʔúlč.
538 dił suyáyus ʔə tsiʔəʔ díičuʔ ʔiłƛ̓ísu.
539 tiʔəʔ słəládəyʔ sʔílax̌ad ʔə tsiʔəʔ sládəyʔ.

540 ʔíbəšəxʷ tiʔəʔ stubš. → <ʔal dxʷʔal tiʔíł. . . ,>
541 ƛ̓áľaľ tuʔál dádatu kʷi sʔíbəšs dxʷʔal tiʔił čəx̌gʷás słax̌. →

SCENE 6

542 gʷəl łčil dxʷʔal tiʔəʔ <dəxʷ. . . ,> dəxʷʔá ʔə tsiʔəʔ čəgʷáss ʔubəlyí.
543 gʷəl
šuł dxʷʔal tiʔił ʔəshədʔíw̓. →
544 ləsƛ̓áltxʷ ti sƛ̓álabac.
545 hədʔíw̓.
546 xʷiʔ kʷi gʷat gʷəšúdxʷ.
547 q̓ʷúʔq̓ʷuʔ ʔáciłtalbixʷ. →
548 ʔuʔə́łəd ʔal tiʔíł *table* sʔəłədálikʷ ʔə tsi sládəyʔ ʔubəlyí.

549 ʔa:.
550 ƛ̓ukíis ləqbíd ʔə tsi čəgʷáss.
551 diʔílc tiʔił <s. . . ,> stubš sʔiłbəlyís.

552 gʷəl → gʷáagʷad ə́lgʷəʔ.
553 ʔugʷáagʷad ə́lgʷəʔ.
554 gʷəl díłəxʷ kʷədiʔ scuts.
555 tułčíl. →
556 gʷəl tukʷədád tíʔəʔ díʔəʔ *coffee*
ʔə tsiʔəʔ čəgʷás. →
557 gʷəl qʷúʔqʷadid.

558 And the woman spoke,<br>
559 "Oh, didn't you give me any 'coffee'?"<br>
560 There was the girl, her hired hand.<br>
561 And she came.<br>
562 And<br>
she took a cup for her.<br>
563 And she filled it with "coffee" for her.

564 And there she was<br>
and she got to talking with her fiancé.<br>
565 The man took this "coffee."<br>
566 And he drank it again.<br>
567 And<br>
there she was.<br>
568 She got to talking with the other man, her fiancé.

569 It was then that she missed her "coffee" again.<br>
570 That was the third time.<br>
571 She said again,<br>
572 "Didn't you give me any 'coffee'?<br>
573 Because I asked for some.<br>
574 And I still have no 'coffee.'"<br>
575 That hired hand said,<br>
576 "I have been giving you the 'coffee,'<br>
577 but you were not drinking it."<br>
578 And now it is the third time.

579 And<br>
she felt something was there<br>
that somehow her husband was making this happen,<br>
580 that this was his doing.<br>
581 Her "coffee" was poured for her again.

582 There she was,<br>
583 And she was talking with her fiancé.<br>
584 She didn't stop talking.

558 gʷəl cútəxʷ tsiʔəʔ słádəyʔ.
559 "ʔu: xʷiʔ əw̓ə ʔu kʷi t(u)adsʔábyic ʔə kʷi *coffee*."
560 tsiʔíł słáłdəyʔ sʔílax̌ads.→
561 gʷəl ʔəƛ̕. →
562 gʷəl <ʔə. . . ,>
kʷədyítəb ʔə tiʔəʔ *cup*. →
563 gʷəl ləč̓yitəb ʔə tíʔəʔ *coffee*.

564 gʷəl ʔa
gʷəl ʔugʷáagʷa(d)txʷ tíʔəʔ díʔəʔ → shúygʷass.
565 kʷədátəbəxʷ ʔə tíʔəʔ stubš
tíʔəʔ díʔəʔ *coffee*. →
566 gʷəl bəqʷúʔqʷadid. <tul̕ʔá. . .>
567 gʷəl
ʔa. →
568 ʔugʷáagʷa(d)txʷ tiʔəʔ diʔəʔ stubš shúygʷass.

569 tul̕ʔá gʷəl <bə. . . ,>
bəxʷiʔálusbid tiʔíł *coffees*.
570 <*That's the third*. . . ,> łíxʷałəxʷ.
571 bəcútəxʷ. →
572 "xʷiʔ əw̓ə ʔu kʷi t(u)adsʔábyic ʔə kʷi *coffee*. →
573 gʷə(l) t(u)ugʷíhalikʷ čəd.
574 gʷəl → xʷiʔ uʔxʷ gʷəd*coffee*."
575 cút(t)əbəxʷ ʔə tiʔəʔ diʔəʔ c[əd]íł sʔílax̌ads.
576 "ləcuʔábyicid čəd ʔə tiʔíł *coffee*, →
577 gʷəl xʷiʔ kʷ(i) adsuqʷúʔqʷadid."
578 gʷəl ʔáləxʷ tiʔíł słixʷáłils. →

579 gʷəl <gʷəl, dxʷtu. . . ,> →
ʔuptídgʷasəb gʷəʔáhas <gʷəs. . . ,>
ʔəsčál gʷəshúy ʔə tiʔíł sč̓istxʷs,
580 gʷədíłəs tiʔəʔ ləcuhúy.
581 bək̓ʷəłyítəbəxʷ ʔə tiʔəʔ *coffees*.

582 tuʔá, →
583 gʷəl gʷáagʷa(d)txʷ tiʔəʔ diʔəʔ shuygʷassəxʷ.
584 xʷiʔ gʷəsgʷəƛ̕əláds gʷəsugʷáagʷads.

She looked at her "coffee" a fourth time.
Again it was empty.
"You still haven't given me any 'coffee,'
and I asked many times."

---

She stood.
She went immediately to her bedroom.
She searched immediately for a looking-glass.
Now she came.
And she looked.
She looked around.
But she could not see him.

She returned it to the bedroom.
From there she brought another one.
And she looked.
She looked.
She could not see that one.

From there she took that one back.
She came again with another one.
This was the third time.
From there she looked again.
This time too, she didn't see anything.

She returned that one.
And she brought back a big one.
Now she saw her husband.
Her husband was standing behind her.
He kept drinking her "coffee."

Immediately she sent away the other man.
And she went running to him.
And she hugged him.

That's the end.

585 <tu. . . , gʷəl. . . ,>
ʔə(s)šúucəxʷ tíʔəʔ *coffees* búusałiləxʷ.
586 ƛ̕aľ uʔxʷ b(ə)a[sdxʷ]xʷcáb.
587 <xʷiʔ uʔxʷ xʷiʔ gʷə. . . ,>
"xʷiʔ uʔxʷ háẇəʔ ʔugʷadsʔábyic ʔə kʷi *coffee*, →
588 gʷəl čəd tugʷíhalikʷ qáhaʔłəxʷ."

589 kíisəxʷ. →
590 tíləbəxʷ ʔuʔúx̌ʷ dxʷʔal kʷədiʔ piitálʔtxʷs.
591 tíləbəxʷ ʔugʷə́č̓əd tíʔəʔ díʔəʔ səxʷšúł.
592 ʔəƛ̕áxʷ. →
593 gʷəl šuł.
594 gʷəč̓əlúsəb. →
595 gʷəl xʷiʔ gʷədəxʷšúdxʷs.

596 ʔubə́lkʷtxʷ tiʔəʔ dxʷʔal tiʔíł piitálʔtxʷ.
597 tuľʔá gʷəl bəʔə́ƛ̕txʷ dəč̓uʔ.
598 gʷəl → šuł.
599 tušuł.
600 xʷiʔ gʷədəxʷšúdxʷs tíʔəʔ díʔəʔ.

601 tuľʔá gʷəl bəbə́lkʷtxʷ tiʔíł.
602 bəʔəƛ̕áxʷ ti dəč̓uʔ.
603 łixʷáłəxʷ.
604 tuľʔá gʷəl bəšúł.
605 ƛ̕aľ xʷiʔ kʷi bə(s)šúdxʷs.

606 ʔubəlkʷtxʷáxʷ tiʔíł.
607 gʷəl ʔəƛ̕txʷáxʷ tíʔəʔ hikʷ. <čə, líkʷ, tuľʔal. . . ,>
608 šúdxʷəxʷ sč̓istxʷs.
609 sč̓istxʷs tíʔəʔ ʔəskíis ləqbíds. →
610 ləcuqʷúʔqʷadid tíʔəʔ *coffees*.

611 tíləbəxʷ ʔučsád tíʔəʔ díʔəʔ. →
612 gʷəl ləsáxʷəbid. →
613 gʷəl ləqʷúlud. <da. . . , > →

614 díłəxʷ (s)šaćs.

# NOTES TO TEXT 6

In the introduction to text 5, mention was made of Mrs. Conrad's technique of "supernatural narration," a chantlike delivery with which she signals the presence of a spiritual component in the events of which she is telling. In "The All-Year-Around Story" Mrs. Conrad uses this technique to such an extent that parts of the narrative are almost unintelligible unless the audience is aware of the form of delivery. Since space limitations preclude annotation of each occurrence of "supernatural narration," the reader is urged to listen to the tape recording.

31 Because the question of whether a specific implement represents Lushootseed or white culture in this story becomes important later on, we should point out now that the verb *ćsuʔcidəxʷ*, "nailed," does not indicate whether metal nails or wooden pegs were used.

62 *stáwixʷaʔɫs*, literally "children," here refers to people younger than the woman, but not necessarily her offspring. They are her helpers, not her equals; but they are not of a different social class.

66 Since one way Mrs. Conrad informs us about the otherworldly status of this woman is by emphasizing her command of non-Lushootseed goods, the reader should bear in mind that hammer and hatchet both existed in pre-contact culture. A hammer was a rock of a certain shape (see Charley Anderson's story "Boil and Hammer" [Hilbert 1985:15]), and any number of bone or stone and wood implements could have qualified as a hatchet.

*sk̓ʷík̓ʷqʷəb* is the diminutive of *sk̓ʷ(ə)qʷəb*, "axe," and so already meant "little axe" before Mrs. Conrad added the word *míman* ("little").

89–91 The tape reel had just been turned over, and Mrs. Conrad is summarizing what she said at the end of the previous side.

109–112 When people stay for a "month" in the spirit world, they may find on their return home that they have been away for much longer than that. Striking here is the use of the loanword "July" to encode that otherworldly duration. The Lushootseed word for the time of year around July is *pədʔagʷəd*, "blackberry time."

130 A person is not supposed to reveal what spirit helpers he has. Though Mrs. Conrad never identifies these women as spirit powers, these instructions replicate the instructions given by spirit powers in the model quest story that underlies the present narrative here (cf. text 5, lines 131–136).

165–173 Vi Hilbert explains that "*stubš*" in this episode refers to the young man. The person who won't listen in 169–170, then, is the old man, and the reason for this is given in 171–172. "*xʷiʔ gʷəscuts ʔu*" is a traditional way of saying that someone will not even acknowledge what is being said to him. In 173, the young man gives in to the temptation of showing his father-in-law in a convincing way why he will not return to the marriage (*x̌ʷal'* is "to lack control"; cf. 196–197).

202–205 Only three wives have been revealed. It is possible that due to the tape change after line 201, which bothered Mrs. Conrad, some of the story was lost—possibly the account of the fourth wife. It is also possible that the woman took her helpers away before she herself could be revealed.

211 *čəgʷáss*: the woman who has the helpers.

216 *dxʷdiʔiʔ* seems to refer to the direction in which the supernatural woman's island lies.

218 ff *sbəbiʔʔ*. A popular game of skill in much of the Northwest, it involved throwing a spear through a small rolling hoop. Ruth Shelton mentions that when her people first encountered hardtack they found it inedible and played *sbəbiʔʔ* with it instead (Shelton 1988).

276 Many kinds and sizes of balls were used by the Lushootseed in the old days. Small ones of yarn or wood might be covered with skin. Larger balls were made entirely of buckskin.

384 Who are these grandchildren? Elders differ: some identify them as the winds; others, as the four winter months. Nooksack elder Louise George used to say that every time you told this story, it would snow the next day.

394 Vi Hilbert explains that it is the grandchildren who are shivering; they shiver with their cold natures, just as something hot radiates its heat.

513 On the tape recording, Mrs. Conrad says *liłx̌ə́q*, but this is a slip of the tongue. *dxʷx̌əq* is the proper word here. (*liłx̌ə́q* means "up high" like an airplane, not like a tall pile.)

579 *sč̓istxʷs*, the hero of the story, not the new fiancé.

611 *tiʔəʔ diʔəʔ*, the new fiancé.

614 *dił (s)sac̓s*. Traditional ending for a *syəyəhub*, even one with a steamboat and peanuts in it.

## THE STORY OF THE SEAL HUNTERS

### INTRODUCTION

"The Story of the Seal Hunters" is Martha Lamont's version of a story that was told in many variants all over the Northwest Coast. In most of these variants, the seal hunters are sent on their enchanted journey by a member of their family who has been offended by what he perceives as their lack of respect. From time to time, the episode of the enchanted cedar seal turns up as a story all by itself or as part of another story altogether. Cedar seals frequently figure in stories that hinge on quarreling, either within a family or among a group of people who are settling new territory. In her story of the Swinomish flood (Hilbert 1980:1–4), Dora Solomon says about the new people who have been re-created from the bones of those who drowned: "But these people were not friendly, because they could not understand each other. They had different languages. They were always quarreling. Some were making cedar seals who could come to life and swim." This is all Mrs. Solomon says, so it is evident that her audience was familiar with cedar seals being used in the prosecution of a quarrel.

In most versions of the seal hunters' story, as in Mrs. Lamont's, the adversary is a canoe maker who is highly talented but dependent on his relatives for food production. In fact, sea mammal hunting and canoe making were both highly respected professions, specialties in a society that had little career specialization. The fact that the main characters in the story are all members of a professional elite may account for the theme of rivalry that runs through many versions.

The ability to hunt sea mammals was the gift of certain spirit powers, and the pursuit of this vocation required a degree of self-discipline. Before the hunt, as before a spiritual quest, the hunters bathed, fasted and refrained from sexual activity. Seals might be taken with a net or, as in this story, with a harpoon. The hunters—a steersman aft and a harpooner in the bow—set out in a small canoe that was kept ritually clean and used for this purpose only. In silence they approached within striking distance; the harpooner struck the seal, who typically did not sound deeply and could be drawn alongside the canoe and clubbed.

Though there were women who became noted hunters of land animals, women did not hunt sea mammals; in fact, they were prohibited from touching any of the gear and from riding in the canoe, even when it was not being used in the hunt. Many Northwest Coast tribes also prescribed special, very circumspect, behavior for wives when their husbands were away on a sea mammal hunt: if the wife were to make a loud noise or forceful movement, the seal might take fright and escape. Perhaps this uneasiness about the effect of women's behavior on the sea mammal as quarry underlies the episode at the end of Mrs. Lamont's story, when the whale is adversely affected by the stare of a menstruating woman. In any case, the power represented by menstruation is felt to be inimical to the power represented by the successful hunter: if his wife were menstruating, for example, a Twana seal hunter did not go after seals.

The whale in Mrs. Lamont's story is looked at by a young woman who is not following the rules for a menstruating woman. When a girl reached puberty, she was sequestered in a small house or tent built for her use at this time. She observed certain disciplines, including fasting, and was instructed by the women of her family. Imbued with great power at this time, she was not supposed even to look out of the tent; in fact, she was regarded as so powerful on certain days that she wore a hood over her face so that no one could accidentally meet her gaze (Collins 1974:225–227).

Another thing that some readers may wonder about is why Mrs. Lamont's canoe maker is so angry with his brothers-in-law for not providing food for his household. In Lushootseed society, this older man had every right to expect such service from the young people: he is married to the seal hunters' sister, and not only were relatives-in-law expected to share food, but brothers were also expected to provide food for their sisters' families. In addition, successful hunters were expected to feed people—the whole village when their catch was large, or just the old people when the catch was small.

The younger brothers in Mrs. Lamont's story behave in an exemplary fashion, not only giving away food, but cooking it first: the implication is that they are outstanding hunters, for only when their catch was large were hunters expected to give a feast, as opposed to simply portioning out raw food. We notice, however, that they do not send their sister around to people with gifts of food, as was often done, for female members of a hunting household were expected to participate in their family's generosity. Instead, we see Mrs. Lamont's young woman only as she piles her own plate high.

Although the Upper Skagit did not count the meat of sea mammals as a major part of their diet, there were some noted seal hunters from upriver (Collins 1974:52). Hair seal and porpoise were the two sea mammals hunted by the Skagit. In preparation for cooking, the seal's hair was singed and the skin scraped before butchering began. The fat was removed through an incision on the dorsal side; and the entrails, through an incision on the ventral. The meat was cut into small pieces, laid directly on stones heated in the fire, and covered with mats for cooking (Haeberlin and Gunther 1930:22–23; Elmendorf 1960:133–134).

The canoe maker, like the seal hunter, received from a guardian spirit the ability to practice his profession. He was given special songs for each phase of the task, from felling the tree to caulking the finished vessel; and he practiced certain physical disciplines as well. He preferred to work alone, away from the village, because his spirit helpers would not manifest themselves in a place frequented by people. Perhaps it is the canoe maker's customary seclusion that accounts for the fact that Mrs. Lamont's old man does not know how generous his brothers-in-law have in fact shown themselves to be.

Lushootseed canoes were dugouts made from the trunks of cedar trees burnt out, adzed to a precise form—not the final canoe form but one ready to be shaped—and then filled with water in which hot stones were placed so that the cedar was softened by steaming, spread, and then fixed in a bowed position with inserted thwarts. Several kinds of canoes were made, varying in size from shallow-drafted, one-person river vessels to large, multipaddler craft for use in open sea.

Like the seal hunter, the canoe maker devoted most of his time to his vocation. Not only did he make canoes, but he made paddles as well. He also manufactured all of his own tools and made up the pigments needed if a canoe were to be painted (Smith 1940:141). A canoe maker worked to order and was paid for his work. Since he brought income into the family group, he was not expected to provide food. Rather, he and his wife and children had food provided for them by the relatives who shared the prosperity resulting from the sale of his handiwork.

## A Note on Further Reading

The most detailed accounts of Coast Salish sea mammal hunting available do not deal with the Lushootseed, for sea mammals were not an important part of the Lushootseed diet. About the Twana, Hood-Canal neighbors of the Lushootseed, however, Elmendorf provides information on the role of spirit power and ritual in sea mammal hunting (1960:85–86, 100–102), on equipment and techniques (1960:102–106), and on the customary ways of distributing the catch (1960:106–107, 141–143). For the Coast Salish of British Columbia, see Barnett (1955:92–95, 104–105) on quest and ritual; see Barnett (1955:98–99, 102–103) on equipment and techniques and Suttles (1952).

Information on canoes and canoemakers may be found in Barnett (1955:109–118) for the Coast Salish of British Columbia and in Elmendorf (1960:170–192) for the Twana. Rev. Myron Eels, missionary to the Twana at the turn of the century, includes in his discussion of their modes of transportation two accounts of what it was like to travel with them by canoe (1985:181–195). More specifically for the Lushootseed, see Collins (1974:64–66); Haeberlin and Gunther (1930:34–35); Smith (1940:288–292); and Waterman and Coffin (1920).

Other readily available versions of the story of the seal hunters include Adamson (1934:77–81) (Chehalis), Ballard (1927:77–81) (Southern Lushootseed), and Jacobs (1958:207–226) (Clackamas Chinook). In

Domanic Charlie's account of the origin of the Squamish (Charlie 1966), the seal hunters' story is told to show how people came to settle at Kuper's Island and Cowichan Bay. Wayne Suttles's discussion of Coast Salish sea mammal hunting mentions Domanic Charlie's story, as well as Penelekuts, Musqueam and Katzie versions, and provides an interesting context for them (1952 [1987]:238–239). Two versions, both titled "Seal Hunter and Canoe Maker," were told by two Skokomish brothers, Henry and Frank Allen (Elmendorf 1961:106–117). Frank Allen's story shows how motifs may be elaborated: his little people are attacked by many kinds of birds in turn, and on their way home the seal hunters stop at the villages of seven different tribes of salmon and trout before even meeting the whale.

Schematic Analysis of Text 7

(See p. 159 for explanation of chart.)

| | | |
|---|---|---|
| I | Introduction (1–14) | |
| | (1) Pheasant and his brothers-in-law lived there | |
| | (2) The brothers-in-law were hunters | • overlapping |
| |     (3–5) Where and what they hunted | • circular |
| | (6a) They were hunters | • figures |
| |     (6b) They were brothers of his wife | • |
| |     (7a) They were brothers of his wife | • |
| | (7b) They were hunters | • |
| | (8) This man worked wood | • juxtaposed |
| |     (9) He had grown old working wood | • circular |
| | (10) He worked wood | • |
| | (11) He worked wood | • figures |
| |     (12–13) what he made | • |
| | (14) He worked in cedar | • |
| II | Motivation of Journey (quest) (15–198) | |
| | (15–31) The brothers provide food (70–81) | • loose |
| | (32–33) They tell their sister to | parallelism |
| | save some for her husband | • |
| | (34–43) She and her children eat it (91–92) (117) | • |
| | (44–52) She puts ashes on their faces (93–95) | • |
| | (53–56) The husband arrives and | |
| | asks about food (83–86) (114) | • stricter |
| | (57–62) She lies (87–90) (115–116) | • parallelism |
| | (63–69) He reacts (96–113) (118–123) | • |
| | (122–189) The old man tries out the seal four times | |
| | (190–198) He sends the brothers after it | |

| IIIa | The Journey: Water (199–277) | |
|---|---|---|
| | (199–205) They board the canoe | • juxtaposed, |
| | (206–211) It is a real seal | concentric, |
| | (212–214) They go after it | overlapping |
| | (215–218) They spear it | • and simple |
| | (219–226) They spear it | • circular |
| | (227–230) It dives down | • figures, |
| | (231–236) It runs off with them | some with |
| | (237–248) One's hand is stuck | • pendants |
| | (249–253) They were taken | • |
| | (254–258) They were taken | • |
| | (259–263) They were taken | • |
| | (264–267) It is foggy | • |
| | (268–270) They arrive | |
| | (271–277) Log becomes visible | - |

| IIIb | The Journey: Hunger (278–408) | |
|---|---|---|
| | (278) Edge of the world | |
| | (279–285) It is different | • circular figure |
| | (286–298) They hide | |
| | (299–307) A canoe is coming | • two circular figures |
| | (308–312) They are hidden | |
| | (313) Dwarf arrives | • pendant to 305–307 |
| | (314–321) He stops | • reduplicated circ. fig. |
| | (322) He is below them | • pendant |
| | (323–324) He dives (334–335) | • parallel |
| | (325) Question with *ʔəx̌id* (338) | • narration |
| | (326–327) The brothers' thoughts (336–337) | • of |
| | (328) Dwarf emerges (339) | • first two |
| | (329) He has fish (340, 342) | • dives |
| | (330–332) He throws it into canoe (341, 343–4) | • |
| | That is what he did (333) | • explanatory remark |
| | (345–352) Brothers plan | |
| | (353–355) Dwarf dives, stays under | |
| | (356–358) Brothers plan | |
| | (359–360) Dwarf emerges, [dives], stays under | • interlace |
| | (361–372) Brothers steal fish | |
| | (373–374) Dwarf emerges, puts fish into canoe | |
| | (375–394) Dwarf finds them out | |
| | (395–408) He takes them away | |

| IV | What They Saw (409–634) |
|---|---|
| | (409) Brothers become slaves |

| | |
|---|---|
| (410–415) They perceive dwarf's power | • circular figure |
| (416) They become slaves | |
| (417–421) They are hungry and lost | |
| (422–423) Many lived there in houses | • circular figure |
| (424) Many people | |
| (425) They speak of them | |
| (426b) This is where he brought them | • concentric |
| (427) They are dwarfs, little people | • figure |
| (428) They are old | • |
| (429) Little people, dwarfs | • |
| (430) This is where he brought them | • |
| (431) Dwarf is old | • cap |
| | |
| (432–3) 434–6] Dwarfs' food is uncooked | |
| (437–442) Dentalia are piled up | |
| (443–447) Brothers are seated | |
| (448–454) There they are | • circular figure |
| (455–456) Dwarfs' food is raw | |
| | |
| (457–482) Dwarfs attacked by ducks | |
| (483–490) Brothers fight off ducks | |
| (491–501) Ducks defeated | |
| | |
| (502–506) Brothers find out what is wrong with dwarfs | |
| (507) One dwarf comes to | |
| (508) He sits up | • concentric |
| (509–510) The rest are cured | • figure |
| (511) They sit up | • |
| (512) They come to | |
| (513–514) Brothers find out what is wrong with dwarfs | |
| | |
| (515) Dwarfs come to | • pendant in form |
| (516–517) Ducks are dead | • of juxtaposed |
| (518) Dwarfs come to | • circular figures, |
| (519) Dwarfs come to | • the second |
| (520–521) They are glad | • with a |
| (522) They know | • reduplicated |
| (523) They were protected | • core |
| (524) They know | • |
| (525–526) Ducks killed them | • |
| (527) They come to | • |
| (528) They are okay | • cap |
| | |
| (529–531) Dwarfs told to see to brothers | |
| (532–537) Dialogue about cooking | |
| (538) Brothers understand a little | • circular figure |

(539–544) Dialogue about cooking
(545–551) Brothers cook ducks
(552) Good ducks
(553–557) Brothers eat ducks • circular figure
(558–560) Good ducks
(561) Dwarfs told...
(562–563) Brothers understand a little • circular figure
(564–568) ...to see to brothers
(569) Brothers eat • pendant to
(570–571) They get better • 552–560 (cf. 921ff.
(572–579) They gather dentalia
(580–588) Dwarfs asked to take care of brothers
(589) Whale is coming
(590–604) Brothers instructed • circular figure
(605–608) Whale is coming
(609–613) Dentalia loaded
(614–621) Brothers embark
(622–634) Whale instructs them

V Family Mourns (635–651)
(635–644) Mother and grandmother mourn
(645–646) Family mourns • circular
(647) Weather is good • figure
(648–651) Whale tells them family mourns •

VI Arrival Home and Validation of Powers (652–936)
(652–659) They disembark • circular
(660–664) Fate of the whale • figure
(665–666) Dentalia spilled • with
(667–672) They disembark • concentric
(673–676) Dentalia spilled • core
(677–683) Fate of the Whale •
(684–689) Dentalia spilled • cap of concentric figur
(690–692) They disembark

(693) They are there • interlace
(694–695) Boy is seen •
(696–697) They are there •
(698) Boy comes •

(699–704) They recognize their brother • parallelism
(705–719) They instruct him (739–742) •
(720–733) He is/is not believed (743–758) •
(734–738) Brother reports to them -

(759–760) House is prepared

- (762–768) Conversation between brothers and elders
- (769–771) People lead them up — • bridge passage

VII The Brothers' Story (772–930)

- (772–779) Motivation for journey
  - (780–792) The journey (water)
  - (793–926) What they saw
    - (793–834) Ducks attack
      - (835–841) Brothers gather food — • interlace
    - (842–869) Brothers help dwarfs
    - (870–873) Dwarfs confer about helping brothers
      - (874–887) Dialogue about cooking
    - (888–905) Dwarfs help brothers
      - (906–910) Brothers prepare to cook ducks
        - (913–916) Dwarfs' food is raw — • circular figure
        - (917–918)They die
      - (919–920) Brothers cook ducks
        - (921) They eat — • pendant
        - (922) They get better — • (cf. 569ff.)
        - (923–925) They gather dentalia
      - (926–927a) Formal close of brothers'story
- (927b–930) Motivation for journey

VIII Closing

- (931–935) What happened to the sister
- (936) Formal close of Mrs. Lamont's story

# THE STORY OF THE SEAL HUNTERS

1 Pheasant dwelled [there]
and his brothers-in-law
[and] others.
2 They were hunters.
3 They would hunt out on the water.
4 They would hunt up in the forest.
5 They killed deer, bear, [etc.]

6 His brothers-in-law were expert hunters,
the cross-sex sibling(s) of his wife.
7 The brothers of his wife were hunters.

8 And as for him,
he just made canoes.
9 This old man made canoes—it seems he was old,
it seems he was now an old person.
10 He made canoes.
11 He made canoes.
12 He always crafted canoes,
13 anything, he could make everything.
14 He made canoes out of red cedar.

15 And they went.
16 His brothers-in-law would hunt.
17 And they would arrive.
18 And they would steam cook the game [and] whatever.
19 Then that food would be prepared by his brothers-in-law.
20 They would prepare it by cutting [it] up into little pieces.

21 Then they would tell her,
22 "Bring your platter.
23 What's been prepared will be there.
24 The food is cooked.
25 It is steam cooked."
26 What was it? Perhaps that's what it was. It was seafood.
What it was was hair seal, it was, whatever.
27 That is what was cooked, so it seems.

1 ʔəsłáłlil tiʔił <...ʔəsłáłlil tiʔił...> →
ʔi sgʷəlúb <...sgʷəlúb...> →
ʔi tiʔił x̌ə́łx̌əłtəds, <...x̌ə́łx̌əłtəds...> →
tiʔəʔ ʔiłkʷə́lq.
2 dxʷsxʷíʔxʷiʔxʷiʔ. <ƛ̕u...,>
3 ƛ̕uxʷíʔxʷiʔ álgʷəʔ dxʷčaʔkʷ.
4 ƛ̕uxʷíʔxʷiʔəxʷ álgʷəʔ dxʷƛ̕áq̓t. →
5 ʔubəčálq əlgʷəʔ ʔə kʷi sqígʷəc, <stəb...> sčə́txʷəd <stəb...>.

6 dᶻəgʷáʔ →
dxʷsxʷíʔxʷiʔxʷiʔ tiʔił x̌ə́łx̌əłtəds, <sč̓ístxʷs, stəb...> →
ʔalš ʔə tsiʔəʔ čəgʷass.
7 ʔálalš ʔə tsiʔəʔ čəgʷass tiʔił dxʷsxʷíʔxʷiʔxʷiʔ.

8 gʷəl cədíł, →
gʷəl
x̌ʷul̓ ʔup̓áyəq.
9 ʔup̓áyəq tiʔəʔ luƛ̕, gʷəluƛ̕əs, →
gʷəluƛ̕əxʷəs ʔáciłtalbixʷ.
10 ʔup̓áyəq. →
11 ʔup̓áyəq. →
12 (c)k̓ʷáqid ʔuhúyalikʷ ʔə tiʔəʔ q̓íl̓bid. →
13 tiʔəʔ stab, dił stab gʷuhúyud.
14 ʔup̓áyəq ʔə tiʔił x̌páyʔ.

<gʷəl...,>
15 gʷəl ʔuʔúx̌ʷ tiʔił. →
16 ƛ̕uxʷíʔxʷiʔ tiʔił cáadił x̌ə́łx̌əłtəds.
17 gʷəl ƛ̕ułči·l̩l tiʔəʔ c(əd)ił.
18 gʷəl ƛ̕uq̓ə́lstəb t[ə ʔ]a sxʷíʔxʷiʔ, stab. →
19 hay, ƛ̕uhúyutəbəxʷ<ʔə tə ʔa...,>
ʔə tiʔəʔ c(əd)ił x̌ə́łx̌əłtəds tiʔił sʔə́łəd.
20 ƛ̕uhúyudəxʷ álgʷəʔ dxʷʔal kʷi gʷəsłíłič̓s.

21 hay, ƛ̕ucút(t)əbəxʷ. →
22 "ʔə́ƛ̕txʷ kʷ(i) adłaʔx̌.
23 łuʔá t(u)ashúyəxʷ. →
24 ʔəsq̓ʷə́l tiʔəʔ sʔəłəd.
25 ʔəsq̓ə́ls."
26 stab ʔəbíl̓ bədíł tiʔacəc. tul̓čáʔkʷ stab sup̓qs stab.
27 dił <słi...> ləsq̓ʷəlás gʷəbədíłəs.

28 And then she took her platter.
29 And it was dished up.
30 The meat of the hair seal was cooked well.
31 So everything they fed her was [already] prepared.

32 "Save some for when your husband arrives,
and feed it to him."
33 It was their sister they told this to.

34 How many little children [lit., litter] did she have?
35 Were there two?

36 And then the woman took home this what was cooked.
37 It was brought [to her].
38 Then they arranged to bring it.

39 And then they ate, [she] and her little children.
40 She was taking the cooked food they had been given.
41 And she and her children had it all.
42 Then they finished it all up.
43 There was nothing left for her husband
that she was saving.

44 She took her little children.
45 And she grayed their noses.
46 She grayed the little ones with ashes from the fire.
47 She told them to pretend that there was nothing.
48 They had nothing to eat.
49 They got dirty [with ashes].
50 This was the thing: the food got [them] greasy.
51 It couldn't be noticed when she grayed their noses with ashes.
52 And it was the same for her.

53 Her husband arrived.
54 And he was asking.
55 "Did they finally arrive?
56 What happened to your brothers?"

57 "They arrived, *siʔáb*.
58 They arrived.
59 Whatever those people [ironic] were doing.

28 huy gʷəl, ʔúx̌ʷtxʷəxʷ tiʔəʔ łaʔx̌s. →
29 gʷəl ləcílitəb.
30 haʔł ʔəsq̓ʷəl tiʔəʔ biác ʔə tiʔəʔ sup̓qs.
31 hay, bək̓ʷ ʔəsqʷíb sʔəłtúbs. →

32 "łux̌ədíd kʷi łułčíl ʔə tiʔəʔ <čístxʷ ʔə...,>
ad(s)čístxʷ
čxʷa łuʔə́łtxʷ ʔə tiʔił."
33 ʔálšs ə́lgʷəʔ tsiʔəʔ ʔucu[t]cúuc.

34 absbíbədbədáʔ ʔə kʷi tuk̓ʷídid. 35 səsáʔli ʔu.

36 huy gʷəl, t̓úk̓ʷtubəxʷ ʔə tsiʔəʔ słádəyʔ tiʔəʔ cədił ʔəsq̓ʷə́l.
37 ləłčíldub.
38 huy, łčíldxʷəxʷ ə́lgʷəʔ. →

39 gʷəl (h)uy ʔə́łədáxʷ ə́lgʷəʔ ʔi tiʔəʔ bíbədbədáʔs. →
40 ləkʷədáxʷ tiʔəʔ <s...,> tusłíltəbs ə́lgʷəʔ t(u)asq̓ʷə́l. →
41 gʷəl → bə́k̓ʷdxʷ → ʔi tiʔəʔ bíbədbədáʔs.
42 huy, tubək̓ʷíldxʷ. →
43 xʷíʔəxʷ kʷi bəstáb gʷətugʷə́ł tiʔił sčístxʷs <tu...,>
təsəsx̌ədíds.

44 kʷədádəxʷ tiʔəʔ bíbədbədáʔs. →
45 gʷəl dxʷ šúk̓ʷìlqsədəxʷ.
46 šúšk̓ʷìldəxʷ ʔə tiʔił X̌uxʷ(h)údad ʔal kʷi X̌uhúd.
47 cut łuk̓əyíłas p̓áX̌aX̌. → <tux̌ʷəs...,>
48 xʷiʔ kʷi stab gʷət(ə)suʔə́łəds.
49 <ʔəs, ʔəs..., stab> sčiq̓ʷil. →
50 dił kʷi gʷəsəsc̓úx̌ʷil ʔə tiʔił sʔə́łəd.
51 t(u)aswəlíʔ kʷi dəxʷšúk̓ʷílqsədəxʷs ʔə tiʔíł xʷ(h)údad.
52 X̌ál̓əxʷ b(ə)asʔístəʔ tsiʔił. →

53 łči·l tiʔił c(əd)ił sčistxʷs. →
54 gʷəl ləwiliq̓ʷ.
55 "tułčíləxʷ ʔu sixʷ.
56 tuʔəx̌ídəxʷ kʷ(i) adʔálalš."

57 "tułčíl, siʔab. →
58 tułčíl. → <gʷəl ʔəsʔəx̌íd kʷi...,> →
59 stab kʷi X̌əsuhúy ʔə kʷi ʔáciłtalbixʷ.

60 We don't know.
61 They are around here, though.
62 Your brothers-in-law have arrived."

63 This old man seemed to think this,
64 "She might have been given a little food by her brother[s]
so I could eat."
65 The poor man just kept on.

66 And he went again.
67 He made canoes again. [He returned to his canoe making.]
68 He made canoes somewhere far off to the side [of the village].
69 Yes.

---

70 Again the brothers brought food for her
when they had finished cooking it.
71 It was [all] ready.

72 Again she got her platter.
73 And again she took it.
74 It was dished up.

75 They would give her a lot of food.
76 It was very well 77 cooked,
including that certain sea[food], hair seal.
78 What was it?
79 Perhaps that's what it was.
80 That was the food she was given.

81 And then
unabashedly she would take it.

82 Oh, doesn't poor Pheasant bring down [any] game?

83 And then
again that man finally arrived.

60 xʷiʔ gʷəsəsgʷəháydxʷ čəł.
61 ƛ̕(u)asčál <kʷi ƛ̕u...,> díʔaʔəxʷ kʷaʔ.
62 ƛ̕ułčíl t(i) adx̌ə́łx̌əłtəd."

63 <ʔu...,>
gʷəxʷcútəb tiʔəʔ luƛ̕. →
64 "gʷəƛ̕ułiłəltəb kʷədáʔ tsiʔəʔ ʔə ti ʔalšs
čəda łuʔə́łəd."
65 x̌ʷul̕ ləstáb kʷi sʔušəbábdxʷ. →

66 gʷəl bəʔúx̌ʷ. → <bə...,>
67 bəp̓áyəq.
68 ʔup̓ayəq ʔal kʷədíʔ čad lílax̌ad.
69 ʔi·.

70 bəłčíltxʷyitəb ʔə tiʔəʔ ʔálalš ʔə tiʔəʔ sʔə́łəd →
ƛ̕ushúys kʷi ƛ̕usq̓ʷə́lds ə́lgʷəʔ. →
71 ləshúy.

72 bəkʷəd[ád] kʷi łaʔx̌s. →
73 gʷəl → bəʔúx̌ʷtub.
74 cílitəb. →

75 qa tiʔəʔ ƛ̕usłíltəbs əlgʷəʔ. →
76 dáy̓əxʷ (h)aʔł. 77 ʔəsq̓ʷə́l
ʔi tiʔəʔ cədił tul̕čáʔkʷ sup̓qs.
78 stab. →
79 ʔəbíl̕ dił tiʔił bəstáb.
80 dił ƛ̕usłíltəbs. →

81 gʷəl huy
wəlíʔ ƛ̕uwáw̓əxʷ. →

82 ʔu· ƛ̕uc̓qʷíb ʔu tiʔił sʔušəbábdxʷ <stəb...,> sgʷəlúb.

83 hay gʷəl
bəłčíl sixʷ tiʔił cədił. →

84 And again he asked.
85 "What has happened, have your brothers arrived?"

86 "No.
87 They have arrived, *siʔáb*.
88 But we don't know what they are doing.
89 Your children are really, really starving!
90 What is happening to us?"

91 But she would eat the good food that was brought.
92 The woman and her little children would eat it.
93 Then she make them powdered over with something
so there was nothing that could be seen.
94 The children were really covered with dust
95 as if there was nothing for them to eat.

96 Then this man became angry.
97 He became angry.
98 He was upset with his brothers-in-law.
99 The canoe maker became angry.
100 "Whatever are those hunters doing?
101 There is not even a little to eat."
102 This one thought; he came up with a plan [used his mind].
103 "I should carve a hair seal.
104 Because hair seal is what they hunt.
105 And porpoise is what they hunt.
106 That is what they spear."
107 [So] it is: he will carve a hair seal now.

108 That old fellow went.
109 And then he carved somewhere off to another side.
110 Yes.
111 He did not tell his wife.
112 He carved.
113 And then
he finished this thing of his.

84 gʷəl bəwiliq̓ʷ. →
85 “ʔuʔəx̌íd <kʷi...,>, ƛ̕ułčíl ʔu tiʔił adʔálalš.”

86 “xʷiʔ. →
87 ƛ̕ułčíl, siʔab. →
88 tux̌ʷ (h)uy xʷiʔ gʷəstáb gʷəƛ̕əsəs(h)áydxʷ čəł.
89 pútəxʷ ʔəsyúbil tiʔəʔ adbədbədáʔ, pútəxʷ.
90 stab kʷi gʷəƛ̕usʔəx̌íd čəł?” →

<gʷəƛ̕u...,>
91 gʷa·ʔ ƛ̕(u)ulə́k̓ʷəd tiʔəʔ ƛ̕ułčíltub háʔł sʔə́łəd.
92 ƛ̕ulə́k̓ʷtəb ʔə tsiʔəʔ słádəyʔ ʔi tiʔəʔ bíbədbədáʔs.
93 huy, ƛ̕uhúyud pədíǰədə[s] ʔə kʷi stab łuxʷ(iʔ)as ləšúdub tiʔił.
94 put ʔəsp̓əlx̌ʷíč tiʔəʔ wíw̓su.
95 gʷəl xʷiʔ kʷi stab suʔə́łəds.

96 huy, x̌íciləxʷ tiʔəʔ cədił stubš.
97 x̌íciləxʷ. →
98 dúkʷtxʷəxʷ tiʔəʔ x̌ə́łx̌əłtəds.
99 x̌íciləxʷ tiʔəʔ dxʷsp̓áyəq.
100 “stábəxʷ kʷi səshúy ʔə kʷi dxʷsxʷíʔxʷiʔxʷiʔ. →
101 xʷiʔ ləgʷədəxʷ[u]ʔíʔłəd[s].”
102 [dxʷs]cút(t)əbəxʷ tiʔəʔ cədił ł(u)abx̌ə́čs.
103 “ƛ̕úbəxʷ čəd łup̓áyəqəxʷ ʔə kʷi sup̓qs.
104 yəx̌i dił sxʷíʔxʷiʔs əlgʷəʔ tiʔił sup̓qs.
105 dił sxʷíʔxʷiʔs əlgʷəʔ ʔi tiʔił qʷsyuʔ.
106 dił ƛ̕əsucácq̓s ə́lgʷəʔ.”
107 súp̓qsəxʷ tiʔił łusp̓áyəqs.

108 ʔúx̌ʷəxʷ tiʔił luƛ̕. →
109 gʷəl (h)uy p̓áyəqəxʷ ʔal kʷi díʔax̌ad. →
110 ʔi·. →
111 xʷiʔ gʷəsyə́cəbtxʷs tsiʔəʔ čəgʷás(s).
112 p̓áyəqəxʷ. → <huy gʷəl...,> →
113 hay gʷəl
huy kʷi stabs.

114 And he arrived.
115 He is still given no food.
116 There is no one who gave food to him.
117 Instead she would just eat it.
118 Then at that point he just thought,
119 "So be it."

120 And then, he went again to his carving.
121 He would try out his carving, the hair seal,
this is what he was making.

122 He had finished his carving.
123 That old fellow was an expert carver.

124 He would tell this hair seal what it should [do]:
bend itself part way back,
just as [a real one] would be doing,
just like [one] in the water,
on a rock, on some rock, a big rock that is flat.

125 Then
he put it up there [on the rock].
126 Then it was bending itself part way back.
127 It was made of red cedar.
128 It was truly a kind of hair seal.
129 But not yet,
I guess, was it done [quite right].

130 He took it up again.
131 And he carved it again.
132 Yes.
133 He made it again.
134 He redid it.
135 And then he fixed it again.

114 gʷəl ɬčil.
115 xʷiʔ sixʷ gʷəsɬíltəbs. →
116 xʷiʔ [kʷi] gʷat t(u)ułíligʷəd tiʔił. →
117 tux̌ʷ (h)uy x̌ʷul̓ ƛ̓ulək̓ʷəd.
118 hay ʔáhəxʷ x̌ʷul̓ ʔəxʷcútəb. →
119 "ƛ̓ub ʔəsʔístəʔ."

120 hay, huy bəʔúx̌ʷc tiʔił sp̓áyəqs.
121 ƛ̓up̓áʔad tiʔəʔ (s)p̓áyəqs, sup̓qs, tiʔəʔ suhúyalikʷs.

122 ʔuhúyud sup̓ayəqs. →
123 dᶻəgʷaʔ dxʷsp̓áyəq tiʔəʔ cədił luƛ̓.

124 ƛ̓uhílidəxʷ tiʔəʔ sup̓qs łuƛ̓úbəs <ʔu. . . ,>
ʔuk̓ʷálalk̓ʷálč̓cut x̌ʷul̓áb ʔə kʷi ƛ̓əbəsəshúys →
x̌ʷul̓áb ʔə tiʔił ʔal qʷuʔ,
ʔal ti č̓ƛ̓aʔ, ʔal kʷi č̓ƛ̓aʔ, hikʷ č̓ƛ̓aʔ ʔəsp̓íl. →

125 huy
t̓agʷtədəxʷ ʔa. →
126 huy k̓ʷálalk̓ʷálč̓cutəxʷ. →
127 tiʔił x̌páyʔ ʔəshúytxʷ.
128 ta·ł x̌əł ti ti sup̓qs.
129 tux̌ʷ xʷiʔ uʔxʷ →
ləxʷúʔələʔ dił səshúys.

130 bəkʷədád. →
131 gʷəl → bəp̓áyəqbid. →
132 ʔi·. →
133 bəqʷíbid.
134 bəhúytxʷ →
135 gʷəl (h)uy bəqʷíbid. →

136 And he put it back again.
137 It bent itself back.
138 Then it bent itself part way back.
140 And then it would sort of flop.
141 It would shake itself just as a [hair seal] would [...].
142 And then it barked.
143 It barked just like a hair seal.
144 It barked.
145 That hair seal barked.
146 No.
147 His throat was still not right.

148 He took it back again.
149 And he fixed it again.
150 He went at it again.
151 He did it again.
152 He fixed it.
153 He fixed it.
154 It was made of red cedar.
155 And then he made a person [out of it; he made it animate].
156 He made a hair seal.
157 "Let it live!"

158 So he went at it again.
159 And he fixed it again.
160 This old fellow planned to do them in,
the brother-in-law of the hunters,
brothers of this woman,
161 And so he went to the hair seal again.
162 And he says again.
163 "so bark.
164 You bark."
165 That one barked.
166 Its bark was good.
167 It's really a seal now.

136 gʷəl → bəʔáʔəd.
137 k̓ʷálč̓cut. →
138 huy k̓ʷálalč̓cut. → [There is no line number 139.
140 huy gʷəl ƛ̓uflop x̌əɬ tihəxʷ.
141 ƛ̓udᶻákʷacut x̌ʷul̓áb ʔə tiʔiɬ ƛ̓us [sentence unfinished].
142 huy gʷəl q̓ʷáʔq̓ʷabəxʷ. →
143 q̓ʷáʔq̓ʷabəxʷ tiʔiɬ x̌əɬ ti x̌ʷul̓áb ʔə tiʔiɬ sup̓qs.
144 q̓ʷáʔq̓ʷab.
145 q̓ʷáʔq̓ʷab tiʔiɬ cədiɬ sup̓qs.
146 xʷiʔ. →
147 ʔəsdúkʷ uʔxʷ tiʔiɬ q̓əyuq̓ʷs.


148 bəkʷədád. →
149 gʷəl bəqʷíbid. →
150 bəʔúx̌ʷtxʷ. →
151 bətábad.
152 qʷíbid. →
153 ʔuqʷíbid. →
154 huy x̌payʔ. →
155 gʷəl tux̌ʷ →
(h)uy ʔuhúyud ʔáciɬtalbixʷ.
156 ʔuhúyud sup̓qs. →
157 "ʔəsƛ̓úb ɬuhəlíʔ."


158 hay, bəʔúx̌ʷtxʷ. →
159 gʷəl bəqʷíbid.
160 x̌ʷəyálqəbəxʷ tiʔəʔ c(əd)iɬ luƛ̓,
x̌ə́ɬtəd ʔə tə ʔa dxʷsxʷíʔxʷiʔxʷiʔ,
ʔálalš ʔə tsiʔəʔ sɬádəyʔ.
161 huy gʷəl bəʔúx̌ʷtxʷ tiʔəʔ sup̓qs. →
162 gʷəl <bə. . . ,> bəcúuc. →
163 "hay q̓ʷáʔq̓ʷab.
164 q̓ʷáʔq̓ʷab čəxʷ."
165 q̓ʷáʔq̓ʷab tiʔiɬ cədiɬ. <ʔə kʷi. . . ,>
166 haʔɬ kʷi sq̓ʷáʔq̓ʷabs.
167 ti həláʔbəxʷ sup̓qs.

168 So it bent itself part way back on that rock.
169 Then that certain hair seal carried on like a really
true hair seal.
170 What was happening?
171 It bent itself part way back.
172 Oh, and then it will bark.
173 It will bark [just] as a seal would sound
when it is on top [of a rock].

174 Then
he says to the hair seal.
175 "You are just right now.
176 You are just right now where you are.
177 I will put you where you are, you Hair Seal,
and you will speak [i.e., bark like a seal].
178 Perhaps you will see them when they travel.
179 Those brothers-in-law will come after you.
180 When they come in their canoe,
you will be doing something like that.
181 You thrash about.
182 You will sort of thrash yourself.
183 You will bend yourself backward over and over
and you bark.
184 You bark the way the hair seal does.
185 When they come, it will be by water.
186 Clearly there would be two
in their canoe for hunting,
their special hunting canoe."

187 And then
he left it.
188 And he says.
189 "Indeed you are just right."

190 Then this man who is old went home.
191 And he informed the brothers-in-law at the house.
192 "That is your game, my brothers-in-law,
what is bending itself back;
it's right there.

168 hay, → k̓ʷálalk̓ʷálč̓cut ʔal tiʔił <stəb. . .,> čƛ̓aʔ.
169 huy, → tábabəxʷ tiʔił cədił sup̓qs x̌ə́łəxʷ ti
tə həláʔbəxʷ təł sup̓qs.
170 ʔu[ʔə]x̌ídid. →
171 ʔuk̓ʷálalk̓ʷálč̓cut.
172 ʔuhay gʷəl łuq̓ʷáʔq̓ʷab. →
173 łuq̓ʷáʔq̓ʷab x̌ʷul̓áb ʔə tiʔił ƛ̓əsucú(t)cut ʔə kʷi sup̓qs
səst̓ágʷtəs.

174 hay
cúucəxʷ tiʔəʔ sup̓qs
175 "ʔəsƛ̓úbiləxʷ čəxʷ.
176 ʔəsƛ̓úbiləxʷ čəxʷ ʔal tiʔił ad(d)əxʷʔá.
177 łuʔácid čəd ʔal tiʔəʔ ad(d)əxʷʔá dəgʷí sup̓qs
čxʷa łucú(t)cut.
178 ʔəbíl̓ čəxʷ łušúdxʷ tiʔił łələgʷáx̌ʷ,
179 łu[s]ʔəƛ̓cbícids [tiʔił] sx̌ə́łx̌əłtəd.
180 łələʔəƛ̓ás ə́lgʷəʔ ʔə tiʔił q̓íl̓bids ə́lgʷəʔ
čxʷa łuʔístab ʔə tiʔił. →
181 ʔuč̓áxʷacut.
182 łuč̓áxʷaxʷacut čəxʷ. →
183 łuk̓ʷálk̓ʷalč̓cut čəxʷ →
čxʷa ʔuq̓ʷáʔq̓ʷab.
184 ʔuq̓ʷáʔq̓ʷab čəxʷ x̌ʷul̓ab ʔə tiʔił ƛ̓əsəshúy ʔə tiʔił sup̓qs.
185 łələʔəƛ̓áxʷəs ə́lgʷəʔ łələʔúluł. →
186 wəlíʔ <ƛ̓u, ƛ̓u. . .,> ƛ̓usəsá[ʔ]liʔ →
ʔal tiʔił ƛ̓uq̓íl̓bids sxʷíʔxʷiʔs ə́lgʷəʔ →
xʷíʔxʷiʔadads."

187 huy gʷəl
łəgʷłáxʷ. →
188 gʷəl cúucəxʷ. →
189 "ʔəsƛ̓úbiləxʷ čəxʷ t[ə ʔ]a."

190 huy t̓úk̓ʷəxʷ tiʔəʔ cədił stubš luƛ̓. →
191 gʷəl ləyə́cəbtxʷ tiʔəʔ x̌ə́łx̌əłtəds ʔal ʔálʔal.
192 "dił ti sxʷíʔxʷiʔləp, dx̌ə́łx̌əłtəd, →
ti ʔuk̓ʷálk̓ʷálč̓cut
ʔal tə ʔa.

193 There is a rock over there.
194 Your game is on top of it.
195 There is a hair seal right there."
196 "Ah, *si?áb*, perhaps we will go after [it].
197 There it is, it bends itself back part way.
198 It has climbed on top of that rock."

199 Then they went.
200 They went after it.
201 The canoe was lightened by jettisoning [all nonessentials].
202 And they went after it again.
203 And they set it down on the water.
204 And they got in.
205 And they go, the two hunters,
brothers of this woman,
wife of the old canoe maker.

206 [Then] they went
over there to where it was bending itself part way back
on yonder rock.
207 That one was bending itself back.
208 It was bending back.
209 It barked.
210 That is truly a hair seal.
211 It is truly the game.

212 These hunters went after it.
213 Suddenly
that hair seal threw itself down into the water.
214 Then it partially emerged again.
215 Then those hunters speared it.
216 It extended itself so they could spear it.
217 It was pretending.
218 [So that] they will spear it.
219 Then
just as soon as it will be speared,
220 then it will leap down.

193 č̓ƛ̕aʔ ʔístəʔ. <ʔəs, ʔəstəb...> →
194 t̓ágʷt tiʔił sxʷíʔxʷiʔləp.
195 ʔa ti sup̓qs ʔal tə ʔa.”
196 “ʔa· siʔab, bədíł łuʔúx̌ʷc čəł.
197 ʔa ʔal tiʔił ʔuk̓ʷálalk̓ʷálč̓cut.
198 ʔəst̓ágʷtagʷil ʔal tiʔił č̓ƛ̕aʔ.”

199 huy, ʔúx̌ʷəxʷ álgʷəʔ. →
200 ʔúx̌ʷtub tiʔəʔ. →
201 q̓ʷác̓atəbəxʷ tiʔəʔ sdəxʷíł. →
202 gʷəl ləʔúx̌ʷtub.
203 gʷəl ləbəčátəb ʔal tiʔił qʷuʔ. →
204 gʷəl ləq̓ílagʷil əlgʷəʔ.
205 gʷəl ʔux̌ʷ dxʷsəsá[ʔ]liʔ dxʷs xʷíʔxʷiʔxʷiʔ →
ʔálalš ʔə tsiʔəʔ słádəyʔ, →
čəgʷás ʔə tə luƛ̕ dxʷsp̓áyəq.

206 ʔúx̌ʷ <gʷəl ƛ̕...,>
túdiʔ tə suk̓ʷálalk̓ʷálč̓cuts ʔal túdiʔ č̓ƛ̕aʔ.
207 k̓ʷálk̓ʷálč̓cut tiʔił cədił. →
208 ʔuk̓ʷálk̓ʷálč̓əb. →
209 ʔuq̓ʷáʔq̓ʷab.
210 sup̓qs tiʔił təł.
211 sxʷíʔxʷiʔ təł.

212 ʔúx̌ʷcəbəxʷ ʔə tiʔəʔ cədił dxʷsxʷíʔxʷiʔxʷiʔ.
213 tíləbəxʷ<ʔu,ʔu...,>
ʔuxʷəbágʷiləxʷ dxʷʔal tə qʷuʔ tiʔił cədił sup̓qs.
214 huy bəƛ̕íqiqəxʷ.
215 huy cáq̓atəbəxʷ ʔə tiʔəʔ cáadił dxʷsxʷíʔxʷiʔxʷiʔ.
216 ʔábcutəxʷ dxʷʔal kʷi gʷəscáq̓atəbs. →
217 k̓áyił.
218 łucáq̓atəbəxʷ. →
219 hay,
díʔłił łuscáq̓atəbs, →
220 hay łusáxʷəb dxʷgʷəd.

221 "You will leap down
and you will go wherever you will go.
222 It will be far,
toward the edge of the world,
that you will cause them to be.
223 You are a hair seal."
224 This one who was angry spoke.

225 Then it happened like this.
226 These [men] speared that which the old fellow over there
had said was their game.
227 They speared this seal.
228 Then it went down.
229 It dove down.
230 And it went again.

231 It ran off with them.
232 One was just [managing to] steer
with a paddle held over the stern [like a rudder].

233 Then they were taken.
234 He was holding this
which was his own,
the rope used
when hurling their two-pronged harpoon.
235 It lurched forward with them.
236 And the one in the stern was just about yanked off balance.
[i.e., when the canoe lurched forward.]

237 This hunter's hand is stuck.
238 He would let go [if he could].
239 And his companion would speak to him.
240 "Let go!
241 Let go!
242 It is running [too] far with us."
243 He would let go [if he could].
244 [But] he could not let go.
245 He could not let go.

221 “łusáxʷəb čəxʷ dxʷgʷəd →
čxʷa łuʔúx̌ʷ dxʷʔal kʷi ƛ̕(u)ad(d)əxʷʔúx̌ʷ.
222 dxʷlil kʷi <łu...,>
dxʷʔal kʷi sbəčáx̌ad ʔə tə swátixʷtəd →
kʷi ƛ̕(u)adsdxʷʔátxʷ.
223 dəgʷí sup̓qs.” →
224 cút(t)əb ʔə tiʔəʔ c(əd)ił ʔux̌ícil.

225 huy, húyəxʷ ʔəsʔístəʔ. →
226 cáq̓atəbəxʷ ʔə tiʔəʔ cáadił tiʔił ʔucút(t)əb ʔə túdiʔ luƛ̕
sxʷíʔxʷiʔs əlgʷəʔ.
227 cáq̓atəbəxʷ tiʔəʔ sup̓qs. →
228 huy ʔúx̌ʷəxʷ dxʷgʷəd. →
229 ʔúsiləxʷ dxʷgʷəd.
230 gʷəl bəʔúx̌ʷ. →
231 təláwiltub tiʔəʔ cáadił.
232 x̌ʷul̓əxʷ ləsx̌áƛ̕alap tiʔəʔ diičuʔ. →

233 huy ʔúx̌ʷtubəxʷ. →
234 ləskʷə́d ʔə tiʔəʔ cədił <tiʔəʔ...>
gʷətusgʷáʔs <səs, gʷəstabs, ʔə...,> →
gʷət̓əbíłəd ʔə tiʔəʔ cədił
dəxʷəscáq̓alikʷs stáʔłs əlgʷəʔ.
235 sáxʷəbtubəxʷ. →
236 gʷəl x̌ʷúl̓əxʷ ləƛ̕čábcut tiʔəʔ cədił <ʔił...,> ʔiłʔíl(l)aq.
237 ƛ̕íq̓ačiʔəxʷ tiʔəʔ cədíł dxʷsxʷíʔxʷiʔ.
238 ƛ̕ukʷáʔədəxʷ. →
239 huy, ʔucút(t)əb ʔə tiʔəʔ ʔáy̓əds. →
240 “kʷáʔədəxʷ čəxʷ. →
241 kʷáʔədəxʷ.
242 ʔusáxʷəbtub čəł dxʷlil.”
243 ƛ̕ukʷáʔəd. →
244 xʷíʔəxʷ gʷəskʷáʔdxʷs.
245 xʷi·ḷʔəxʷ gʷəskʷáʔdxʷs.

246 Then his hand was stuck to their hunting tackle,
the rope of that one.
247 He could not let go.
248 It had stuck to his hand.
249 Then they were taken.
250 His companion was just [managing to] steer
with a paddle held over the stern.
251 It [went on] the same.
252 It seems that all he could do was
just steer with a paddle held over the stern.
253 Then they were taken.

254 And then they were taken.
255 It would dive.
256 And this hair seal went on again.
257 And it went again to somewhere.
258 Then they were taken.
259 And the land was foggy,
260 this land that used to have very nice weather.
261 It became foggy.
262 It became foggy.
263 Then they were taken.
264 For many days they were run off with by the hair seal.
265 It is foggy.
266 They could not see for many days.
267 Maybe it was for five days
they were run off with.
268 And then they ran aground.
269 They were way out when this one stopped
who ran off with them.
270 There the fog was sort of gone.
271 Something appeared:
the thing was the odd, big cedar log that ran off with them.
272 The cedar log was floating [there dead in the water].
273 There were a lot of limbs.

246 huy, ʔuƛ̓íq̓ačiʔəxʷ ʔal tiʔəʔ <səs, ʔus. . . ,> sə[xʷ]xʷíʔxʷiʔs ə́lgʷəʔ →
t̓əbíɬəd ʔə tə ʔa cədíɬ.
247 xʷíʔəxʷ gʷəskʷáʔdxʷs. →
248 ʔuƛ̓íq̓əxʷ ʔal ti čálə[ss]. →

249 huy → ʔúx̌ʷtubəxʷ. →
250 x̌ʷúl̓əxʷ ləsx̌áƛ̓alap tiʔəʔ cədíɬ ʔáy̓əds.
251 ƛ̓ál̓əxʷ. →
252 x̌ʷul̓əxʷ x̌əɬ ti bədáy̓əxʷ gʷəsəshúys tiʔiɬ →
sx̌ʷúl̓səxʷ ləsx̌áƛ̓alap.
253 huy, → ʔúx̌ʷtubəxʷ əlgʷəʔ. →

254 gʷəl (h)uy, ʔúx̌ʷtubəxʷ əlgʷəʔ. <ƛ̓u. . . ,>
255 ƛ̓uʔúsil. →
256 gʷəl → ɬəbəʔú·x̌ʷ tiʔəʔ cədiɬ ti sup̓qs.
257 gʷəl → ɬəbəʔúx̌ʷ ʔal kʷi čad. →
258 huy, ʔuʔúx̌ʷtubəxʷ əlgʷəʔ.

259 gʷəl qʷšáabəxʷ ti swátixʷtəd. →
260 ƛ̓(u)asháʔləb yu tiʔəʔ swátixʷtəd.
261 qʷšáabəxʷ. →
262 ʔuqʷšáabəxʷ. →
263 huy, ʔúx̌ʷtubəxʷ.

264 qa sləx̌íl kʷi tu(s)saxʷəbtubs əlgʷəʔ <ʔə tiʔəʔ. . . ,>
ʔə tiʔəʔ sup̓qs.
265 ʔəsqʷšáab. →
266 xʷíʔəxʷ kʷi stabəxʷ gʷəƛ̓(u)asšúdxʷ əlgʷəʔ
dxʷʔal kʷədiʔ tuk̓ʷidəɬdát. →
267 xʷúʔələʔ ʔəsʔəx̌íd cəlác sləx̌íl <ʔi kʷi ʔə. . . ,>
kʷədiʔ tu(s)sáxʷəbtubs.

268 hay gʷəl t(u)asp̓ədíltub. →
269 ʔəsčaʔkʷ əlgʷəʔ kʷi səsgʷəƛ̓əltubs əlgʷəʔ ʔə tiʔəʔ cədiɬ
ləsáxʷəbtxʷ.
270 díɬəxʷ x̌əɬ ti sliʔlil ʔə tiʔəʔ sqʷšaab.
271 ʔuwəlíʔiləxʷ
(s)tab hi·kʷ əw̓ə x̌páyʔac tiʔəʔ ləsáxʷəbtxʷ əlgʷəʔ.
272 ʔəsp̓úsəbəxʷ tiʔiɬ x̌páyʔac. →
273 ʔəsqa· sč̓ásč̓ast. →

274 It was very ugly, [very] bad.
275 It was a bad cedar log.
276 There it was what had kidnapped them.
277 He [the carver] had changed it.

278 Away off, over there far at the edge of the world
was where they were put.
279 It was a foreign land.
280 It was foreign.
281 And then they spoke.
282 "What shall we do?"

283 There they are there where
they are put ashore at this certain land.
284 It was land and yet it was sort of very [gloss unknown].
285 It was a strange land to which they had been brought.

286 When they were ashore they spoke.
287 "We will go up from shore [i.e., up the bank]."
288 They went up from shore.
289 They carried their special hunting canoe.
290 And they took it up from shore.
291 And they hid it up inland.
292 They were very tired.
293 Then there they are, there.

294 And these hunters, these young men, felt bad.
295 What will they do now?
296 Where is the land that they have been taken to?

297 They hid now.
298 That was in case something might happen.

274 put x̌ik̓ʷ, saʔ.
275 sa·ʔ → sx̌páyʔac.
276 tə ʔa tusáxʷəbtxʷ əlgʷəʔ. →
277 ʔudúkʷud.

278 ʔáləxʷ kʷədiʔ li·l, díʔiʔ lil, sbəčáx̌ad ʔə tiʔił swátixʷtəd
tiʔił sʔaʔildubs əlgʷəʔ. →
279 ləlíʔ swátixʷtəd.
280 ləlíʔ.
281 huy gʷəl cútəxʷ əlgʷəʔ.
282 "ł(u)asčáləxʷ kʷi łushúy čəł."

283 ʔáhəxʷ əlgʷəʔ ʔal kʷədíʔ <dəxʷx̌əłtis əlgʷəʔ...,>
ʔəsťagʷts əlgʷəʔ ʔal tiʔəʔ cədił swátixʷtəd
284 swátixʷtəd gʷəl tux̌ʷ put x̌əł ti ʔəsbəx̌ʷúbad.
285 ləlíʔ swátixʷtəd tiʔəʔ dəxʷłčíldubs.

286 ʔáləxʷ kʷi tusťáq̓t[s] tuscútsəxʷ. →
287 "łučúbəhəxʷ."
288 čúbə. →
289 xʷácadəxʷ əlgʷəʔ tsiʔəʔ <tsiʔəʔ...,>
sxʷíʔxʷiʔads əlgʷəʔ, q̓íl̓bids əlgʷəʔ.
290 gʷəl → ləčúbətxʷ əlgʷəʔ. →
291 gʷəl → ləčádᶻ ťaq̓təxʷ.
292 cick̓ʷəxʷ əlgʷəʔ ləsxʷák̓ʷiləxʷ.
293 huy → ʔáhəxʷ əlgʷəʔ ʔal tiʔił. →

294 gʷəl → x̌əłəłəxʷ x̌əč tiʔəʔ caadił dxʷsxʷíʔxʷiʔxʷiʔ, ləgʷləgʷəb.
295 ł(u)asčál kʷi łushúys əlgʷəʔ. →
296 čad swátixʷtəd tiʔəʔ dəxʷʔátubs.

297 čádᶻiləxʷ əlgʷəʔ.
298 dił kʷi gʷəsʔás kʷi lə[ʔə]x̌íd.

299 Sure enough, around the point
a big sea-going canoe was coming.
300 A big canoe was coming from over there.
301 It belonged to [what] seemed to be a child who was paddling.
302 He was in the stern.
303 He was paddling.
304 He was coming.
305 He came from over there.
306 He rounded the point.
307 That one was coming.

308 There they were.
309 They hid in the logs.
310 There were logs with many branches, what is called driftwood.
311 The driftwoood was where they were hiding,
312 their canoe and all.

313 So, he came now.
314 And he stopped.
315 It was a little to the water side of them that he stopped.
316 He was a child.
317 It was a big canoe that he was paddling.
318 He was only a child.
319 And it was there that this one stopped.
320 He was sort of anchored himself, [or] however he did it.
321 He stopped there.
322 So,
it was there that that one was
the child is a little to the water side of them.

323 There he went [and] he dove.
324 He dove.
325 What is going to happen later on to the one who dove?

326 They just kept still.
327 "We will just keep quiet."
328 There that boy emerged.
329 This was in both hands: halibut [a deep sea-water fish],
so that was his catch!

299 təɬ diʔɬ kʷi sdᶻalqs ʔə tiʔiɬ hi·kʷ ʔəʔútx̌s ləʔə́ƛ̕.
300 hikʷ q̓iľbid tudiʔ ləʔə́ƛ̕. →
301 gʷəɬ x̌əɬ ti č̓áč̓as tiʔiɬ ləʔúluɬ.
302 ʔiɬʔil(l)áq.
303 ləʔúluɬ. →
304 ləʔə́ƛ̕.
305 tudiʔ ʔuʔə́ƛ̕. →
306 ʔudᶻálqs.
307 ʔə·ƛ̕ tiʔiɬ c(əd)iɬ.

308 ʔáhəxʷ əlgʷəʔ. →
309 ʔəsčádᶻil ʔal tiʔiɬ qʷɬqʷɬáyʔ.
310 x̌aƛ̕ log <ƛ̕ədəxʷəs...,> [s]tab tə ƛ̕udáʔa[təbs] dᶻək̓ʷáluʔ.
311 dᶻək̓ʷdᶻək̓ʷáluʔ tiʔiɬ səsčádᶻils əlgʷəʔ.
312 bək̓ʷ tsiʔəʔ q̓íľbids əlgʷəʔ.

313 hay, ʔəƛ̕áxʷ. →
314 gʷəl ləgʷəƛ̕əla·ḷd. →
315 ʔal tiʔiɬ čaʔkʷbíds əlgʷəʔ təsgʷəƛ̕əla·ḷd ʔə tiʔiɬ.
316 č̓áč̓as tiʔiɬ.
317 hikʷ q̓íľbid tiʔəʔ dəxʷuʔúluɬs.
318 tux̌ʷ bəč̓áč̓as.
319 ʔa gʷəl ʔáhəxʷ kʷi sgʷəƛ̕əlád ʔə tiʔəʔ cədiɬ.
320 x̌əɬ ti ʔubáʔscut ʔəsčál kʷədiʔ səshúys.
321 gʷəƛ̕əla·ḷd ʔa.
322 hay,
ʔa ʔuʔəyʔístəʔ tiʔəʔ cədiɬ →
ti č̓áč̓as ʔal ti čaʔkʷbids əlgʷəʔ.

323 diɬəxʷ kʷi sʔux̌ʷs sʔusilsəxʷ.
324 ʔúsil.
325 haw̓ ɬuʔəx̌íd ʔə tíľx̌i ti ʔal tiʔəʔ ʔuʔúsil.

326 x̌ʷuľəxʷ əlgʷəʔ ʔəsgʷəƛ̕əlád. →
327 "x̌ʷuľ čəɬ ɬəsʔiʔíyəqcut."
328 diɬ kʷi sƛ̕iq ʔə tiʔiɬ č̓áč̓as.
329 yəľyəláčiʔ ʔə tiʔəʔ cədiɬ sčútx̌, ə́w̓ə tiʔəʔ suxʷíʔxʷiʔs.

330 Then he put the halibut in the canoe.
331 He threw it [in].
332 He had taken two.
333 So, that is just what he was doing.

334 And then, that boy dove again.
335 He dove again.
336 He was fishing for halibut.
337 "He must be fishing below us."
338 [They wondered] how long he would disappear.

339 There he emerged again.
340 He had taken his catch again.
341 He put it up again.
342 There were [two] big halibut.
343 And he put them in the canoe again.
344 That one threw his catch [into the canoe].

345 They just looked at it.
346 They thought this.
347 "Oh, this is rare.
348 It must be that fellow's food."
349 By then they were starving.
350 They were hungry.
351 They were lost.
352 I wonder how much (of a) catch he has put in the canoe.

353 Then,
he went again.
354 He would always disappear for a long time.
355 He would disappear for a long time.

356 One spoke.
357 "What do you think about this?
358 We ought to get one of those halibut;
we could carry our canoe [down]."

359 And he emerged again.
360 [but] for a long time he disappeared.

330 gʷəl q̓ílid tiʔəʔ sčútx̌. →
331 xʷə́bəd. →
332 sáliʔ tiʔił ʔəskʷədád.
333 hay, x̌ʷul̓ ʔuʔisʔistáb. →

334 huy gʷəl bəʔúsil tiʔił c(əd)ił č̓áč̓as.
335 bəʔúsil.
336 ʔuxʷíʔxʷiʔ əw̓ə ʔə tiʔił sčutx̌. →
337 "xʷuʔələʔ ƛ̓ə[su]xʷíʔxʷiʔs tiʔəʔ čaʔkʷbíd čəł."
338 xʷuʔələʔ ʔəsʔəx̌íd kʷi sgʷəšəbáds. →

339 dił kʷi bəsƛ̓íqs.
340 bəkʷədád tiʔił sxʷíʔxʷiʔs. →
341 bəšə́qəd.
342 híkʷ(h)ikʷ sčutx̌.
343 gʷəl → bəq̓ilid əlgʷəʔ. →
344 xʷə́btəb ʔə tiʔəʔ cədił cədił tiʔəʔ sxʷíʔxʷiʔs.

345 x̌ʷul̓əxʷ əlgʷəʔ ʔə(s)šúuc.
346 [ʔəxʷ]cútəbəxʷ əlgʷəʔ ʔə tiʔəʔ. →
347 "ʔu· day̓əxʷ.
348 díłəxʷ dᶻəł ʔə tə gədú tiʔił sʔə́łəds."
349 tu[x̌ʷ] huy ʔəsyúbiləxʷ əlgʷəʔ. →
350 ʔəstətágʷəxʷəxʷ.
351 ʔəsx̌ʷíl̓əxʷ
352 xʷuʔ(ə)ləʔ k̓ʷid kʷədíʔ sxʷíʔxʷiʔs ʔuq̓ílid. →

353 hay,
bəʔúx̌ʷəxʷ. →
354 ƛ̓uháʔkʷ kʷi ƛ̓usgʷəšəbáds.
355 hágʷəxʷ kʷi ƛ̓usgʷəšəbáds. <k. . . ,>

356 cútəxʷ tiʔəʔ díičuʔ.
357 "dəxʷ čəxʷ ʔu kʷ(i) ad(d)əxʷcútəb.
358 dił ƛ̓ub čəł gʷəskʷə́d(d)xʷ kʷi dəčuʔ ʔə tiʔił sčutx̌
čła gʷəbələxʷácad tə q̓íl̓bid čəł." <gʷəl gʷə. . . ,>

359 gʷəl gʷəbəƛ̓íqiq.
360 haʔkʷ tə ƛ̓usgʷəšəbáds.

361 Then they prepared themselves like that.
362 They would lie in wait for him to dive.
363 They went.
364 And they arrive at the canoe.
365 And they took a halibut.
366 And they unloaded it.
367 They put it in their [own] canoe.
368 They went ashore again.
369 And they carried it [i.e., their hunting canoe] again.
370 And they hid.

371 They got in (under it).
372 They got in (under it).

373 There this child emerged.
374 He put his catch into the canoe.
375 Then he paused there.
376 Suddenly he got in the canoe.
377 He got in the canoe.
378 Yes, he looked at his catch.
379 No.

380 And then there they were with what they had stolen.
381 The one from there knew it,
the child [knew] they had stolen it,

382 Then the boy pointed.
383 Where were the ones who had stolen it?
384 He stood up in his canoe.
385 Then he pointed.
386 He pointed.
387 Yes, he was pointing.

388 Where will his arm stop, indeed?
389 There, it stopped.
390 Sure enough!

391 "The no-good [kid] knows about us.
392 His hand has stopped [and it's pointing] toward us.
393 This is something strange."

huy, húyucutəxʷ əlgʷəʔ ʔəsʔís[təʔ]. →
X̌áq̓ʷadəxʷ əlgʷəʔ tə [ʔa] səsʔúsils.
ʔux̌ʷ əlgʷəʔ. →
gʷəl ləłčís tiʔəʔ q̓il̓bid. →
gʷəl ləkʷədád tiʔəʔ <s...,> sčutx̌. →
gʷəl ləq̓ʷíbid əlgʷəʔ. →
q̓ílid əlgʷəʔ dxʷʔal tiʔəʔ q̓íl̓bids.
bələłálil. →
gʷəl bələxʷácad əlgʷəʔ.
gʷəl ləčádᶻil əlgʷəʔ.

dəgʷágʷil.
dəgʷágʷiləxʷ.

dił kʷi sX̌iq ʔə tiʔəʔ č̓áč̓as.
q̓ílid tiʔəʔ sxʷíʔxʷiʔs.
hay, gʷəX̌íX̌əlàd ʔa.
tíləbəxʷ <ʔuq̓ʷib...,> ʔuq̓ílagʷiləxʷ.
q̓ílagʷiləxʷ.
ʔi., šúuc tiʔəʔ sxʷíʔxʷiʔs, ʔi.
xʷiʔ. <hay gʷəl...,>

hay gʷəl ʔatxʷ əlgʷəʔ tiʔəʔ sqádaʔs.
háydubəxʷ ʔə tudiʔ <ʔu...,> ʔuqádadid əlgʷəʔ č̓áč̓as.

hay, → tč̓ádiʔəxʷ tiʔəʔ č̓áč̓as.
dxʷčad tiʔəʔ ʔuqádadid.
kíisəxʷ ʔal tiʔił q̓íl̓bids. →
huy, → tč̓ádiʔəxʷ.
tč̓ádiʔəxʷ. →
ʔi·, lətč̓ádiʔ.

čad kʷi łusgʷəX̌əlád ʔə tiʔəʔ čáləs(s), ʔi.
diʔł kʷi sgʷəX̌əláds. →
yúhuʔu.

"ʔuháydub čəł ʔə tə xʷiʔ ləháʔł.
gʷəX̌əlád tə čáləss dxʷʔal díbəł.
<huy...,> huy dúdkʷibəł."

394 And so then he went ashore.
395 He went ashore.
396 And he reached them.
397 And he took them.
398 He simply took the two of them.
399 That one simply took them.
400 And he took them by the arms.
401 And the child grabbed them by [their] necks.
402 And he took them to the canoe.
403 And he threw them on board.
404 He took their canoe.
405 And he went with it.
406 And
he just tied it [to his canoe].
407 This one tied it.
408 And then he put in the canoe what it was that they had stolen,
the halibut.

409 Then they became slaves.
410 Then they knew.
411 "He is something else ______.
412 We thought he was a child.
413 But he has great strength."
414 Then he took them.
415 He took them home to a place way over there.
416 They became slaves.

417 They did not know where they had been put ashore
by that cedar log.
418 They were unfamiliar with the land.
419 Then it was far, far away where they had been run off with.
420 They were very sorry now.
421 And they were very hungry too
from someone having managed to get them way over there.

394 hay, huy gʷə(l) ła·l̩lil.
395 ła·l̩lil →
396 gʷə(l) → łčísəb əlgʷəʔ. →
397 gʷəl → ləkʷə́d.
398 x̌ʷul' ʔukʷə́d tiʔəʔ caadił.
399 x̌ʷul' ʔukʷə́d tiʔił cədił. →
400 gʷəl <ləda. . .,> ləkʷəʷdkʷədláx̌aditəbəxʷ. →
401 gʷəl → ləx̌íbx̌ibapsəbtəb əlgʷəʔ ʔə tiʔəʔ č̓áč̓as. →
402 gʷəl
ʔúx̌ʷtub əlgʷəʔ dxʷʔal tiʔəʔ q̓il'bid. →
403 gʷəl → ləxʷə́btəb əlgʷəʔ dxʷʔal ʔəsq̓íl.
404 kʷədáxʷ tsiʔəʔ q̓il'bids əlgʷəʔ. →
405 gʷəl → ləʔúx̌ʷtub. →
406 gʷəl <lə. . .,>
x̌ʷúl'əxʷ ʔułíditəb.
407 łíditəb ʔə tiʔəʔ cədił.
408 huy gʷəl → q̓ílitəbəxʷ tiʔəʔ tusqádaʔs əlgʷəʔ sčutx̌.

409 hay, túdəqiləxʷ əlgʷəʔ.
410 háydxʷəxʷ əlgʷəʔ. →
411 "ʔəsdúkʷ əẁə tiʔəʔ <tiʔəʔ, tiʔəʔ, ʔucut ______>. →
412 ʔəxʷcútəbid čəł č̓áč̓as.
413 huy, dᶻəgʷáʔ qʷiq̓ʷ."
414 huy, ʔúx̌ʷtubəxʷ əlgʷəʔ. →
415 t̓uk̓ʷtubəxʷ əlgʷəʔ dxʷʔal kʷədiʔ diʔ[iʔ]. →
416 túdəqiləxʷ əlgʷəʔ.

417 xʷiʔ kʷi səs(h)áydxʷs əlgʷəʔ tiʔəʔ dəxʷƛ̓áliltubs əlgʷəʔ
ʔə tiʔił x̌páyʔac. <s. . .,>
418 sčáłaʔs əlgʷəʔ swátixʷtəd.
419 huy, lil, lil tiʔəʔ dəxʷsáxʷəbtubs əlgʷəʔ.
420 cick̓ʷəxʷ əlgʷəʔ ʔəsx̌ə́łəłəxʷ x̌əč. →
421 gʷəl b(ə)astágʷəxʷəxʷ əlgʷəʔ
dxʷʔa·l kʷi słčíldubs əlgʷəʔ dxʷʔal kʷədíʔ díʔiʔ. →

422 There were many dwellings [there].
423 The houses were a long sort of house, whatever they were;
it seems they were houses for those who dwelled [there].
424 There were a lot of people, it seems.
425 Then
those people told them [about themselves].

426 They must be what are called dwarfs
where they were brought.
427 The little people are dwarfs.
428 Then they are adults.
429 The dwarfs are a lot of little people.
430 That was where they were brought
by this one they thought was a child.
431 But he was adult.

432 He took that [catch].
433 And he took the catch, for the others, up from shore
434 They do not eat their food after cooking it.
435 They just eat it raw.
436 So dwarfs are different.

437 Then
there were great piles of dentalia in the house
on the end toward the water.
438 These dentalia are their possessions.
439 [They had gathered] those dentalia a long time ago.
440 What they would eat for their food was sort of like clams,
sort of like barnacles
441 But the dentalia were big, big and good,
their possessions in the first days long ago.
442 It was just the same way with us
in the past generations.

443 So
they [the seal hunters] were just desiring
this great quantity that was lying there.

422 qa· ʔəsłáłlil.
423 haac x̌əł ti ʔálʔal ʔu stab →
gʷəstábəs ʔálʔalʔal ʔə tiʔəʔ ʔəsłáłlil.
424 qa kʷədšəd ʔáciłtalbixʷ.
425 hay,
cút(t)əbəxʷ əlgʷəʔ ʔə tiʔił cədił ʔáciłtalbixʷ.

426 haw̓əʔ dił əw̓ə ti ƛ̕ucút(t)əb qʷiqʷqʷistáy̓bixʷ
tiʔəʔ dəxʷƛčíldubs.
427 qʷiqʷqʷistáy̓bixʷ mám̓ad ʔáciłtalbixʷ. →
428 tux̌ʷ (h)uy lúƛ̕luƛ̕.
429 mám̓ad ʔácʔaciłtalbixʷ tiʔił qʷiqʷqʷistáy̓bixʷ.
430 díłəxʷ dəxʷƛčíldubsəxʷ əlgʷəʔ <ʔə tiʔəʔ...,>
ʔə tiʔəʔ cədił č̓áč̓as kʷi x̌əčbids əlgʷəʔ. →
431 gʷa·ʔ → bəlúƛ̕.

432 kʷədátəb tiʔił. →
433 gʷəl čúbətub tiʔəʔ sxʷiʔxʷ(iʔ) ʔə tiʔił cáadił.
434 xʷiʔ gʷəsulák̓ʷəds əlgʷəʔ tiʔəʔ sʔáłəds ʔal kʷi ʔəsq̓ʷál.
435 x̌ʷul̓ əlgʷəʔ ləlák̓ʷəd x̌ic̓.
436 huy, ləlíʔ qʷiqʷqʷistáy̓bixʷ.

437 huy,
put ʔəspúkʷpukʷəb tiʔəʔ sʔu·l̩ləx̌ čəgʷádiʔ. →
438 tiʔəʔ ƛ̕usʔu·ləx̌ dił stábigʷs. → <ʔal...,>
439 ʔal kʷədiʔ tuhaʔkʷ tiʔił sʔúləx̌.
440 ƛ̕uʔəłbíd ʔə tiʔił c(əd)ił ƛ̕əsuʔáłəds əlgʷəʔ
ƛ̕ux̌əł ti <x̌əł ti...,> gʷəsʔáx̌ʷuʔ x̌əł ti c̓ubc̓ub. →
441 tux̌ʷ (h)uy hikʷ(h)ikʷ (h)aʔł
sʔúləx̌ stábigʷs ʔal tiʔił tudᶻíxʷ →
tusləx̌íl ʔal kʷədiʔ tuháʔkʷ. →
442 ƛ̕al̓ b(ə)asʔístəʔ ʔal díbəł
ʔáləxʷ tiʔəʔ tudxʷʔə́ƛ̕[əb].

443 hay,
x̌ʷul̓əxʷ əlgʷəʔ ʔəshíq̓ʷabid tiʔəʔ <ʔə...,> qa ʔəsqʷát.

444 Then this one spoke to them.
445 He had them seated.
446 I guess someone told that certain child.
447 He had the people seated there
where mats had been prepared for them.
448 They are there now.
449 There they were now seated.
450 They had become slaves.
451 "What are they going to do with us in the future?"
452 In fact, their canoe had just been put there.
453 It was also carried, together with the things [in it].
454 So, there they were.

455 They would not eat what was [served un-]cooked.
456 Their food was simply raw.

457 Then
I guess they were not inside the house for long.
458 And then
there was a noise from above.
459 There was a noise from above.

460 It seems that the ducks suddenly attacked these dwarfs.
461 There were all kinds of ducks, ducks from everyplace,
belonging to the saltwater,
those also belonging to the uplands too,
ducks belonging to the marshes.
462 Those ducks suddenly attacked them.
463 They suddenly attacked them.
464 Then this one hollered; it was a certain one.
465 Maybe it was Black Diver.

444 huy, cút(t)əbəxʷ əlgʷəʔ ʔə tiʔəʔ. →
445 ʔəsgʷáadiltxʷ tiʔił.
446 xʷuʔələʔ cút(t)əb tiʔił cədił čáčas. →
447 gʷáadiltxʷ tiʔił ʔáciłtalbixʷ ʔal tə ʔa ʔəsłágʷiltub əlgʷəʔ.
448 ʔáhəxʷ əlgʷəʔ ʔal tiʔił.
449 ʔáhəxʷ əlgʷəʔ ʔal tiʔił ʔəsgʷáadil. →
450 ʔəshúyiləxʷ stúdəq.
451 "łuʔəx̌í(d)tub čəł ʔə kʷi łutíl̓x̌i."
452 xʷəłúb x̌əł ti x̌ʷul̓ ʔuʔátəb tə q̓íl̓bids əlgʷəʔ. →
453 ƛ̓al̓ b(ə)uxʷácatəb čad
ʔəsq̓ʷuʔ ʔə tiʔəʔ stab.
454 hay, ʔáhəxʷ əlgʷəʔ.

455 xʷiʔ gʷəsuʔə́łəds əlgʷəʔ ʔə kʷi gʷasq̓ʷə́l. →
456 x̌ʷul̓ x̌ic̓ tiʔił suʔə́łəds əlgʷəʔ.

457 huy,
xʷúʔələʔ xʷiʔ ləháʔkʷ kʷi tushədʔíw̓s əlgʷəʔ. →
458 gʷəl (h)uy,
huy, gʷəcútadəxʷ tiʔił tul̓šə́q.
459 gʷəcútadəxʷ kʷədiʔ tul̓šə́q. →

460 gʷəháw̓əʔ ʔušídᶻtəbəxʷ tiʔəʔ caadił
qʷiqʷqʷistáy̓bixʷ ʔə tiʔəʔ buʔqʷ.
461 bálgʷas buʔqʷ
kʷi bəkʷ sčáds ʔə ti buʔqʷ
gʷəł x̌ʷəlč, <tiʔił bə...,>
tiʔił bəgʷəł ƛ̓aq̓t,
gʷəł spáłx̌ad buʔqʷ.
462 šídᶻəxʷ tiʔił buʔqʷ.
463 gʷəl šídᶻəxʷ.
464 huy, qʷíʔqʷiʔadəxʷ tsiʔacəc, tsiʔəʔ cədił. <xʷu...,>
465 ʔuq̓ʷuʔap xʷuʔ(ə)ləʔ.

466 They were there inside [the house].
467 Then they were told something.
468 They were sort of figuring it out.
469 "We will be suddenly attacked
by someone who will fight."
470 They [the dwarfs] are watching as
[the ducks] come after them.
471 They came in on them.
472 And then they spoke.

473 The ducks flew up abruptly.
474 Oh, they flew up abruptly.
475 And then
they threw [down] on these dwarfs these particular quills
that were [coming out from the] exchange of feathers
[i.e., from their molting].

476 Then and there they were beaten by the ducks,
all kinds of ducks.
477 They were being hit [with the quills].
478 Right away the dwarfs were dying.
479 They were being pierced by the things
being thrown down by those certain ones.
480 Right away the dwarfs were dying
from the quills of the feathers of the ducks.

481 Oh, they were lying all about.
482 And those who had made them into slaves were dying.

483 And then, [the ducks] flew up all at once.
484 They were clubbed by those certain people [the brothers].
485 They fought a few.
486 And they clubbed them with [their own] paddle.
487 One spoke [whispered to the other].
488 "[We] could just ______.
489 "You could club them [swinging] my paddle
among these good ducks."
490 Then they clubbed them with that paddle.

466 ʔáhəxʷ əlgʷəʔ ʔəshədʔíw̓. <huy.>
467 huy → yəcəbtúbəxʷ əlgʷəʔ. →
468 x̌ə́łəxʷ ti ʔəst̓úgʷud əlgʷəʔ. →
469 "łušídᶻtəb čəł ʔə kʷi łuyábuk̓ʷ."
470 ʔə(s)šúłəxʷ əlgʷəʔ ʔə tiʔił →
słčísəbsəxʷ. →
471 hədʔíw̓cəbəxʷ əlgʷəʔ. →
472 huy gʷəl, cut.

473 sásaq̓ʷəxʷ tiʔəʔ buʔqʷ. →
474 ʔu· sásaq̓ʷəxʷ. →
475 gʷəl (h)uy,
ʔíx̌ʷičtəbəxʷ tiʔəʔ qʷiqʷqʷistáy̓bixʷ ʔə tiʔəʔ diłił tiʔəʔ →
<ƛu x̌əł ti...,> →
ƛəsuc̓uqʷəbs
ƛəsuʔáy̓gʷasabacəb ʔə tiʔił st̓uʔq̓ʷ.

476 tiʔił diłiłəxʷ dəxʷəgʷəláltəbs ʔə tiʔəʔ <ʔə tiʔəʔ...,> buʔqʷ,→
bək̓ʷ bálgʷas buʔqʷ→
477 ləpúsutəb. →
478 tiləb ləʔátəbəd tiʔił qʷiqʷqʷistáy̓bixʷ.
479 ləcáq̓atəb ʔə tiʔił ləxʷə́btəb ʔə tiʔił cədił tiʔił.
480 tiləb ləʔátəbəd tiʔəʔ qʷiqʷqʷistáy̓bixʷ
ʔə tiʔił sc̓uqʷəb ʔə tiʔił st̓uʔq̓ʷ ʔə tiʔił buʔqʷ.

481 ʔu·, gʷəqʷátqʷatəd tiʔił. →
482 gʷəl šúbali tiʔił <tiʔił...,> cədił dəxʷəstúdəqils.

483 huy gʷəl, gʷəłtqʷádəxʷ. →
484 c̓áxʷatəbəxʷ ʔə tiʔił cədił ʔáciłtalbixʷ.
485 x̌áƛƛaƛisəxʷ tiʔəʔ k̓ʷídid. →
486 gʷəl → c̓áxʷadəxʷ əlgʷəʔ [ʔə] kʷi diłił x̌ʷubt.
487 cút(t)əb ʔə ti.
488 "tux̌ʷ kʷi gʷə ______.
489 "gʷəc̓áxʷadəxʷ čəxʷ ʔə kʷi tul' tiʔəʔ haʔł buʔqʷ
ʔə tiʔəʔ dx̌ʷubt"
490 huy, → c̓áxʷadəxʷ əlgʷəʔ → ʔə tiʔił x̌ʷubt.

491 And then he hollered.
492 The "ducks" are [all] laid out.
493 Then Black Diver hollered.
494 "Humans are the cause of your troubles, my brothers.
495 Humans are the cause of your troubles.
496 Raise your arms, my brothers.
497 Raise your arms, my brothers."
498 And then those ducks flew up all at once.

499 Many of them had fallen.
500 The [ones] that they had killed had fallen.
501 They [the hunters] will make [their] food [out of the ducks].

502 And then
they went after those dwarfs.
503 What is causing them to die?
504 Indeed it was just these that are new [feathers];
the quills of the feathers come
when [the ducks] molt.
505 That is how they killed these [dwarfs].
506 Then they [the hunters] pulled them out of the dwarfs.

507 Right away one revived.
508 Right away he sat up.
509 And they went to the others.
510 How many did they put their hands on?
511 They also sat up.
512 They also revived.
513 Then they found out about them.
514 "Oh, we had better do this to them."

491 huy gʷəl qʷíʔqʷiʔadəxʷ.
492 ʔuqʷqʷátiləxʷ tiʔił *ducks*.
493 huy → qʷíʔadəxʷ tsiʔəʔ cədił q̓ʷúʔap. <"ʔàciła...,">
494 "ʔàcilˇtalbixʷaládxʷ tə dəxʷtəš ʔáləp dʔálalš.
495 ʔàcilˇtalbixʷaládxʷ tə dəxʷtəš ʔáləp.
496 šəqláx̌adəb łi dʔálalš.
497 šəqláx̌adəb łi dʔálalš.
498 hay gʷəl bəgʷəłtqʷádəxʷ tiʔił cədił buʔqʷ.

499 qa· kʷədiʔ ʔuqʷátqʷat.
500 qʷátqʷat sx̌ʷəyálqs əlgʷəʔ.
501 šə́łəxʷs əlgʷəʔ łusʔə́łəd.

502 huy gʷəl
ʔúx̌ʷcəxʷ əlgʷəʔ tiʔəʔ caadił qʷiqʷqʷistáy̓bixʷ. →
503 stab <tiʔəʔ dəxʷ...,>
tiʔəʔ dəxʷuʔátəbəds əlgʷəʔ.
504 gʷəháw̓əʔ bədił tiʔəʔ
tux̌ʷ <ƛ̕udəxʷu...,>
ƛ̕ułáw̓t ƛ̕usʔə́ƛ̕ ʔə tiʔił ćuqʷəb <ʔə tə...,>
ʔə tə <stəb...,> sƛ̕uʔq̓ʷ
<ʔə...,> ʔáy̓waʔsabacəbəs tiʔił. →
505 tiʔił dił əw̓ə dəxʷgʷəláltəbs tiʔiʔəʔ.
506 huy, x̌əcədáxʷ əlgʷəʔ tul̓ʔal tiʔəʔ cədił qʷiqʷqʷistáy̓bixʷ.

507 tíləb ʔup̓álil tiʔəʔ dəčuʔ. →
508 tiləb ʔugʷədíl.
509 gʷəl bələʔúx̌ʷc əlgʷəʔ t[ə ʔa] ʔiłkʷə́lq. →
510 k̓ʷid kʷədiʔ səsʔáhačiʔs.
511 bələgʷədíl. →
512 bələp̓álil.
513 huy, háydxʷyidəxʷ əlgʷəʔ. →
514 "ʔu, ƛ̕ub čəł ʔuʔístəʔtxʷ."

515 Then the dwarfs revived.
516 There were their ducks.
517 They had clubbed them with that paddle.
518 They revived.

519 There were a lot of dwarfs reviving.
520 Then they [the dwarfs] were delighted by those [hunters].
521 They were delighted that they were there.
522 For then they knew.
523 They had been given life by these
whom they had made slaves.
524 Then they knew.
525 The ducks there were the ones who had attacked them.
526 This is what was causing them to die.
527 They revived.

528 And then they were all right.

529 Then these [dwarfs] were told.
530 "You folks should look after these people.
531 What are they going to do?"

532 They [the brothers] were asked.
533 "How will you folks prepare our food?"

534 "We prepare it that way.
535 There are these ducks.
536 That is why we slaughtered them."

537 "And how will you folks prepare it?"

538 They could sort of understand a little of what the dwarfs say,
I guess.
539 So they told them.
540 "We will build a fire for these [ducks]."

515 huy, → p̓áľp̓aliləxʷ tiʔəʔ qʷiqʷqʷistáy̓bixʷ.
516 ʔa tiʔəʔ <st...,> →
búʔqʷs əlgʷəʔ. →
517 tučáxʷad əlgʷəʔ ʔə tiʔił cədił x̌ʷubt.
518 p̓á·lil tiʔił cədił. →

519 qa· tiʔił [s]up̓álil ʔə tiʔił qʷiqʷqʷistáy̓bixʷ. →
520 huy, híiłbitəbəxʷ əlgʷəʔ ʔə tiʔəʔ caadił.
521 híiłəxʷ → əlgʷəʔ ʔal kʷədiʔ dəxʷʔáʔs. →
522 tux̌ʷ ʔəs(h)áydxʷ əlgʷəʔ. → <ʔu, ʔu, ʔu, ʔus...,>
523 ʔuhəlíʔdub əlgʷəʔ ʔə tiʔəʔ
sušəłs əlgʷəʔ stúdəq.
524 huy, ʔəs(h)áydxʷ əlgʷəʔ. →
525 buʔqʷ tiʔəʔ ʔudxʷtə́šs ʔa.
526 dił tsiʔəʔ ƛ̕ustáb tsiʔəʔ dəxʷəʔátəbəds əlgʷəʔ.
527 p̓álil əlgʷəʔ. →

528 gʷəl hay, ƛ̕úbil.

529 hay, tucút(t)əbəxʷ tiʔəʔ caadił.
530 "ƛ̕úbəxʷ čələp ʔušúucəxʷ tiʔəʔ ʔáciłtalbixʷ. →
531 ł(u)asčáləxʷ kʷi łushúys."

532 ƛ̕uwíliq̓ʷitəbəxʷ əlgʷəʔ. →
533 "ʔəsčál kʷi łushúyudləp tiʔəʔ sʔə́łəd čəł."

534 "ƛ̕uhúyud čəł ʔə tiʔił. →
535 ʔa tiʔəʔ buʔqʷ. →
536 dił dəxʷx̌ʷádᶻad čəł ti."

537 "gʷəl ʔəsčál kʷi łushuyudləp." →

538 <x̌əł tihəxʷ əlgʷəʔ łə...,>
x̌əł tihəxʷ xʷúʔələʔ <xʷiʔ ləxʷ...,> →
gʷələlíʔluud əlgʷəʔ →
kʷi gʷəsuʔídigʷat ʔə tiʔəʔ qʷiqʷqʷistáy̓bixʷ.
539 huy, cúucəxʷ əlgʷəʔ. →
540 "<ƛ̕u...,> łuhúdyid čəł tiʔacəc."

541 "Oh, you folks should build a fire for your game,
and you take it to the other side,
way over on the other side where you folks build a fire
and you folks cook it the way you customarily eat it.
542 You folks do it like that.
543 You folks should take it far away even though
it is not our way.
544 For we do not understand
this eating what has been cooked."

545 Then these [brothers] plucked these good ducks.
546 Then they plucked them,
plucked them.

547 They would take them.
548 And they made a fire for them.
549 And they made a fire for them where they were cooked.
550 Then they roasted the ducks.
551 They cooked them where they had made a fire.

552 They were good ducks that they chose for their food.
553 Then they will live [sustain themselves with this food]
on the far side.
554 On the far side [is where] they were spoken to.
555 And then they ate.
556 They ate the ducks.
557 That is how they were able to live.
558 The ducks were good.

559 These were the enemies of the dwarfs;
they used to battle for a long time.
560 They would be suddenly attacked.

561 One was speaking.
562 Then they sort of understood him.
563 And they were very glad for being helped to live,
by having the cause of their dying removed.

541 "ʔu· ƛub čələp ʔuhúdyid tiʔił sxʷíʔxʷiʔləp
čələpa ʔúx̌ʷtxʷ díʔax̌ad, →
ʔal túdiʔ díʔax̌ad kʷi shúdčupləp
čələpa q̓ʷəld ʔəsʔístəʔ ʔə kʷi ƛəsulə́k̓ʷədləp.
542 huyud łi ʔəsʔístəʔ.
543 ƛub čələp ʔuʔúx̌ʷtxʷ lil xʷəłúb xʷiʔ kʷədšəd.
544 huy čəł ƛ(u)asdᶻáƛbid <gʷə su...,>
gʷəsulək̓ʷəd čəł ʔal kʷi səsq̓ʷə́ls."

545 huy, x̌əctəbáxʷ ʔə tiʔəʔ caadił tiʔəʔ dił haʔł buʔqʷ. →
546 huy, x̌əcədáxʷ əlgʷəʔ,
x̌əc[əd].

547 ƛuʔúx̌ʷtxʷəxʷ əlgʷəʔ. →
548 gʷəl ʔuhúdyitəbəxʷ. →
549 gʷəl → húdyitəbəxʷ ʔal kʷədiʔ dəxʷq̓ʷəltəbs.
550 huy q̓ʷəlbáxʷ əlgʷəʔ ʔə tiʔəʔ buʔqʷ. →
551 q̓ʷəldáxʷ əlgʷəʔ ʔal tiʔəʔ dəxʷəshúdčups.

552 haʔł buʔqʷ tiʔəʔ ʔubísid əlgʷəʔ sʔə́łəds əlgʷəʔ.
553 huy → łuhəlíʔəxʷ əlgʷəʔ lílax̌ad.
554 lílax̌ad tiʔił scút(t)əbs əlgʷəʔ.
555 huy gʷəl tuʔəłədáxʷ əlgʷəʔ.
556 ʔəłədáxʷ əlgʷəʔ ʔə tiʔəʔ buʔqʷ. → <ʔə...,>
557 díłəxʷ tədəxʷhəlí(ʔ)s.
558 haʔł buʔqʷ.

559 dił šəbád ʔə tiʔəʔ qʷiqʷqʷistáy̓bixʷ,
ƛusʔiłux̌ílix̌s haʔkʷ tiʔiʔił.
560 ƛušídᶻ(t)əb əlgʷəʔ. →

561 cútcutəxʷ kʷədiʔ díičuʔ.
562 huy, x̌əł ti ʔəslúudəxʷ əlgʷəʔ.
563 gʷəl hikʷ ʔuhíił əlgʷəʔ ʔə tiʔəʔ shəlíʔdubs əlgʷəʔ →
ʔə tiʔił sxʷə́ctəbs tiʔił dəxʷuʔátəbəds əlgʷəʔ. →

564 They revived.
565 They conferred about it at length.
566 "You folks [the speaker's fellow dwarfs] should look after those people well.
567 They looked after us.
568 They helped us live."

569 Then they ate.
570 Then they were fine.
571 These men became strong.

572 And then
they gathered the dentalia.
573 And they gathered what was good [among] the dentalia.
574 It was new to those others.
575 Then that was their food—those dentalia.
576 There was a lot that they had gathered.
577 That is what they had made.
578 They just casually collected them.
579 Then those possessions were there; dentalia for us,
over there, they are what they are [used shells].

580 And then,
this one spoke,
as if he were *siʔáb* among them.
581 "I wonder how you folks [would] think about it
if you were to return these people.
582 You folks should return them.
583 "And
you folks might invite that one there,
the old man who journeys
along this way,
who goes there.

564 ʔup̓áľp̓alil.
565 hígʷəxʷ əlgʷəʔ ʔutátabədəxʷ. →
566 "ƛ̓úbəxʷ čələp ʔə(s)šúuc tiʔił ʔácʔaciłtalbixʷ ʔə kʷi haʔł.
567 ʔušúucbuł. →
568 ʔuhəlíʔdubuł."

569 hay, ʔəłədáxʷ əlgʷəʔ. →
570 huy, ƛ̓úbiləxʷ. →
571 qʷíq̓ʷqʷíq̓ʷiləxʷ tiʔəʔ caadił stúbubš.

ᚆᚅ

572 hay gʷəl ʔa,
q̓ʷúʔədəxʷ əlgʷəʔ tiʔəʔ sʔúləx̌. →
573 gʷəl → q̓ʷúʔədəxʷ əlgʷəʔ tə díłəxʷ haʔł ʔə kʷi tusʔúləx̌.
574 łáw̓tbid ʔə tiʔəʔ caadił. →
575 huy dił sʔə́łəds → əlgʷəʔ tiʔił sʔúləx̌.
576 qa· kʷ(i ʔ)uq̓ʷuʔəd → əlgʷəʔ. →
577 díłəxʷ sə(s)šə́łs əlgʷəʔ.
578 tux̌ʷ əlgʷəʔ p̓áƛ̓aƛ̓ <ʔəs ʔəshúytxʷ ʔə. . . ,> səsʔúləx̌s.
579 huy stábigʷs ʔal tiʔəʔ gʷəł díbəł tiʔił sʔúləx̌ →
ʔal tiʔəʔ gʷəł tiʔəʔ dəxʷʔáʔs əlgʷəʔ.

ᚆᚅ ᚆᚅ

580 huy gʷəl,
cút(t)əbəxʷ → ʔə tiʔəʔ cədił
x̌əł ti siʔiʔáb ʔal tiʔił cədił.
581 "xʷúʔələʔ ʔəsčáləxʷ kʷi x̌əčbídləp tiʔəʔ ʔáciłtalbixʷ →
gʷəʔàbáqədəxʷ łi.
582 ƛ̓úbəxʷ čələp gʷəʔábàqəd.
583 gʷəl
gʷəgʷíhidəxʷ čələp ti ʔal tiʔił
ti luƛ̓ ləʔíbəš <ƛ̓ələ. . . ,> →
liłʔáləxʷ tiʔəʔ t[ə ʔa] ƛ̓əsəʔúx̌ʷs.

584 "And you folks invite him.
585 And he is the one who could load these people.
586 And he could take them.
587 He knows where.
588 Because that is where the old whale drops in
sometimes."

589 The whale is truly coming.
590 Then they were told.
591 "You folks be ready and you [...].
592 You will be returned by that whale over there
who will be coming.
593 You folks will get on board in there and you folks will
be taken home.
594 Because that whale drops by there.
595 He goes by where you folks are from.
596 You folks should go home.
597 You people will arrive safely.

598 "You folks helped us survive what happened to us.
599 You take those dentalia that you have gathered.
600 You take it and you will load it.
601 You folks will have it all along with you.
602 [You] will go when that whale puts you on board.
603 We told the whale about you folks.
604 He will return you."

605 Then the whale came.
606 He was going along surfacing now and again.
607 Yes, and he arrived there.
608 And he floated.

609 Then
the dentalia were put inside,
however those dentalia were prepared [i.e., packaged].
610 And of the dentalia the bigger ones were good [i.e., best].
611 The dentalia were long.
612 They were good.
613 Then the possessions of those who were there were those dentalia.

614 And so then they were taken.
615 And they were put on board.

584 gʷəl gʷəgʷíhidəxʷ čələp. →
585 gʷəl diɬ →
gʷəq̓ílid tiʔəʔ ʔáciɬtalbixʷ. →
586 gʷəl gʷəʔúx̌ʷtxʷ.
587 ʔəs(h)áydxʷ dxʷčad. →
588 yəx̌i ƛ̕udxʷʔá kʷi ƛ̕əsubíbəč ti (ʔa)l →
tiʔəʔ luƛ̕ čxʷluʔ."

589 təɬáxʷ ləʔə́ƛ̕ tiʔəʔ čxʷluʔ. →
590 huy cút(t)əbəxʷ tiʔəʔ caadiɬ.
591 "ʔəsqʷíbəxʷ čələp čələpa <ɬu...,> [sentence unfinished]
592 ɬuʔábàqtəbəxʷ čələp dxʷʔal tiʔiɬ tudiʔ diʔiʔ čxʷluʔ ɬələʔə́ƛ̕.
593 ɬuq̓ílagʷiləxʷ čələp liɬʔá čələpa ɬut̓uk̓ʷtub. →
594 yəx̌i ƛ̕(u)ubíbəč dxʷʔa tiʔiɬ čxʷluʔ. →
595 ƛ̕ələbálx̌ʷ ʔal tiʔiɬ čad dəxʷʔáləp.
596 ƛ̕úbəxʷ čələp ɬut̓úk̓ʷəxʷ. →
597 ɬutəɬ[əɬ]áxʷ gʷəlápu ʔáciɬtalbixʷ.

598 "huy čələp ʔuhəlíʔdubuɬ ʔə tiʔəʔ shúy čəɬ.
599 ləskʷədád čələp tiʔiɬ sʔúləx̌ səsʔúləx̌ləp.
600 ləskʷədád čələp čələpa ɬuq̓ílid. →
601 bək̓ʷ čələp ɬulíɬʔátxʷ.
602 ɬuʔúx̌ʷ dxʷʔal kʷi sq̓ílitəbləp ʔə tiʔiɬ čxʷluʔ.
603 <ʔə...,> ʔəscúucəxʷ čəɬ tiʔiɬ čxʷluʔ dxʷʔal gʷəlápu. →
604 ɬuʔábàqtubuɬəd."

605 huy ʔəƛ̕áxʷ tiʔəʔ čxʷluʔ. →
606 ləƛ̕íƛ̕q.
607 ʔi· gʷə(l) ləɬčíl dxʷʔa. →
608 gʷəl ləp̓úsəb.

609 huy,
dəgʷátəbəxʷ tiʔəʔ sʔúləx̌
ʔal stab kʷi səshúytubs tiʔiɬ sʔúləx̌.
610 gʷəl háʔɬəxʷ ʔə kʷi sʔúləx̌ gʷəhíkʷ(h)ikʷ.
611 háachaac sʔúləx̌. →
612 haʔɬ.
613 huy stábigʷs <ʔal...,>
ʔal tiʔəʔ caadiɬ dəxʷʔáʔs əlgʷəʔ tiʔiɬ sʔúləx̌.

614 gʷəl (h)uy gʷəl,
kʷədátəbəxʷ əlgʷəʔ. →
615 gʷəl q̓ílitəbəxʷ əlgʷəʔ. →

616 And then
the people shook their hands.
617 "Everything will be there.
Your canoe,
618 it will go along [too].
619 Because this is a big whale.
620 It is big;
there is a lot [of room].
621 It is not a bit crowded where it is."

622 Then they were told.
623 This whale told these people [the hunters].
624 "I will not dive [i.e., sound].
625 I will dive a little.
626 But not long and I will emerge again.
627 And when I go, I will be careful
as I go with regard to you folks,
628 to keep from cutting off your breath as I take you.
629 Then this is what you folks will do.
630 You folks will know when I stop
that is where I will have brought you.
631 I know where you folks are from.
632 And it will be on the far side that I will let you folks go.
633 So you folks will disembark.
634 Everything will be there, your canoe will go
and you folks will arrive safely in good [shape]
to your family,
your relatives."

635 Their mother was very worried.
636 She and their grandmother were overcome with crying.
637 The old woman had cut her hair.
638 They mourned.

639 They would say
640 whenever a hair seal emerged.
641 And they would say [when] a porpoise [emerged],
642 "That is your game [which is] repeatedly surfacing, my son.
643 That is your game [which is] repeatedly surfacing, my son.
644 That is your game [which is] repeatedly surfacing."

616 gʷəl (h)uy
kʷədáči(ʔ)təbəxʷ əlgʷəʔ ʔə tiʔəʔ ʔáciłtalbixʷ.
617 "łubə́k̓ʷ tsiʔəʔ <ʔəs, tsiʔił. . . ,> q̓íl̓bidləp. →
618 łəliłʔátub.
619 yəx̌i hi·kʷ tiʔił čxʷluʔ.
620 hi·kʷ
qa·.
621 xʷiʔ kʷi gʷəstáb gʷəsəsč̓x̌ídᶻ ʔal tiʔił dəxʷʔás."
622 huy cút(t)əbəxʷ.
623 cút(t)əbəxʷ tiʔəʔ caadił ʔáciłtalbixʷ ʔə tiʔəʔ čxʷluʔ.
624 "xʷíʔəxʷ kʷi łədsəʔúsil.
625 łuʔúʔsil čəd. →
626 tux̌ʷ xʷiʔ lətíb čəda łəbələƛ̕íq.
627 gʷəl tux̌ʷ ʔáləxʷ kʷi łudsʔúx̌ʷəxʷ čəda x̌ʷúl̓əxʷ łələgʷəč̓ácut →
kʷi łədsəʔúx̌ʷ <dxʷʔal kʷi. . . ,> dxʷʔal gʷəlápu.
628 dxʷʔal kʷi gʷəsqk̓ʷáʔłləp ʔal kʷi gʷədsʔúx̌ʷtubułədəxʷ.
629 hay, díłəxʷ łushúyləp.
630 x̌ʷul̓ čələp ł(u)as(h)áydxʷ
ʔal kʷi łudsgʷəƛ̕əlád →
čad ʔal kʷi łudsłčísəbułəd. →
631 ʔəs(h)áydxʷ čəd ti dəxʷtul̓ʔál(l)əp.
632 gʷəl tux̌ʷ łulílax̌ad kʷi <łuds. . . ,> łudskʷáʔtubułəd.
633 hay čələp łuq̓ʷíb.
634 łubə́k̓ʷ tsiʔəʔ q̓íl̓bidləp łuʔúx̌ʷ,
čələpa łutə́łəł ʔə kʷi haʔł
dxʷʔal kʷi <tu. . . ,> tuʔíišədləp,
tuyəl̓yəlábləp."

635 pu·təxʷ tudúkʷucut tsiʔił tusk̓ʷúys əlgʷəʔ. →
636 təš sx̌a(hə)b ʔi tsiʔəʔ tukiáʔs əlgʷəʔ.
637 ʔəsłíč̓usəxʷ tsiʔił luƛ̕. →
638 ʔudᶻa·qad. →

639 ƛ̕ucú(t)cut
640 ʔəbíl̓əxʷ ləƛ̕íq kʷi sup̓qs.
641 gʷəl ləcú(t)cut tsiʔił cədił tiʔił qʷsyúʔ.
642 "dił tiʔəʔ adsxʷíʔxʷiʔ tə ləši·[dᶻ]šidᶻ dbədáʔ.
643 dił tiʔəʔ adsxʷíʔxʷiʔ tə ləši·[dᶻ]šidᶻ dbədáʔ.
644 dił tiʔəʔ adsxʷíʔxʷiʔ tə ləši·[dᶻšidᶻ]."

645 The old people felt bad.
646 And they would cry along the shore of the sea.

647 The weather in this land was good.
648 And this whale was taking them.

649 "That is your grandmother and your whatchamacallit talking."
650 That old lady really must have been crying.
651 I guess she was feeling bad.

652 Then they passed [where the women were mourning].
653 And then this whale let them go.
654 Suddenly they dropped on the shore.
655 There was their canoe.
656 It was good.
657 It was surprisingly taut.
658 It was good.
659 Then that was over.

660 This was the one that clubbed itself [with its fins].
661 [now I remember] This is what happened.
662 Something bad looked at them, a "young lady."
663 She was menstruating [for the first time].
664 Then that whale clubbed itself [with its fins].

665 And then their dentalia spilled.
666 It was there, into the sea, from where they were,
that was [where] their dentalia spilled.

667 And he [the whale] just let them go with their canoe.
668 And it had been loaded surprisingly well.
669 That, I recall, is the way they had been.
670 Then that is how they went.
671 They managed to get away.
672 But it happened.

645 x̌ə́łəłəxʷ x̌əč tiʔəʔ lúƛ̕luƛ̕. →
646 gʷəl ƛ̕(u)ux̌á(hə)bəxʷ algʷəʔ ʔílgʷił ʔə tiʔəʔ x̌ʷəlč.

647 ʔəsháʔləb tiʔəʔ swátixʷtəd.
648 gʷəl ləʔúx̌ʷtub algʷəʔ ʔə tiʔəʔ čxʷluʔ. → <dił ti...,> →

649 "dił tsiʔəʔ adkiáʔ ʔi tsiʔəʔ <ad...,> adstáb tsiʔəʔ ʔucú(t)cut."
650 dił ʔux̌á(hə)bəxʷ əw̓ə sixʷ tsiʔəʔ luƛ̕.
651 xʷuʔələʔ ƛ̕ux̌ə́łəłəxʷ x̌əč.

652 huy, bəlx̌ʷáxʷ.
653 gʷəl (h)uy kʷáʔtəbəxʷ algʷəʔ ʔə tiʔəʔ cədił čxʷluʔ.
654 tíləb t̕aq̓t kʷi sbəčs algʷəʔ.
655 ʔa tsiʔəʔ q̓il̕bids algʷəʔ.
656 haʔł.
657 tíləb ʔəscíkʷ.
658 haʔł.
659 hay, huy tiʔił.

660 di[ł] tu č̓áxʷacutəxʷ. →
661 k̓ʷəlíł tiʔił tushúys.
662 šúucəbəxʷ algʷəʔ ʔə tsiʔəʔ <saʔ s—> *young lady.* →
663 ʔəsdᶻúl.
664 huy → č̓áxʷacutəxʷ tiʔił čxʷluʔ. →

665 gʷəl (h)uy, → k̓ʷłáxʷ tiʔił tusʔúləx̌s algʷəʔ.
666 ʔal tə ʔa čaʔkʷbíd ʔə tiʔəʔ cədił <dəxʷ...,>
tədəxʷtul̕ʔás algʷəʔ. →
[ʔal tiʔił] kʷi sk̓ʷəł ʔə tiʔił tusʔúləx̌s algʷəʔ.

667 gʷəl tux̌ʷəxʷ algʷəʔ x̌ʷul̕əxʷ ʔukʷáʔtəb ʔə tiʔəʔ q̓íl̕bids algʷəʔ. →
668 gʷəl tíləb ləsq̓íl haʔł.
669 ʔəsʔístəʔ k̓ʷəlíł kʷi tushúys algʷəʔ.
670 hay dił tusʔúx̌ʷs. →
671 tuskʷáʔdubuts.
672 tux̌ʷ huy. →

673 Their dentalia were spilled.
674 There were only a few left of
lots of good dentalia that they had taken
which was the reason there were a lot of dentalia where they were.

675 Because
the dentalia spilled right there.
676 Things like that drifted up and lodged on the shore
where their dentalia are.

677 They spilled on account of this bad [menstruating] woman.
678 Someone scrutinized what was coming ashore there.

679 It was sea-traveling.
680 Then it clubbed itself.
681 This whale is sacred.
682 Because they did not know of the sea-travel from shore.
683 It was because it became wild that it clubbed itself.

684 And
suddenly those dentalia that they had loaded spilled.
685 Suddenly they came back out.
686 They had their canoe loaded again.
687 It just went on.
688 It did.
689 Then it sort of came out,
vomited by this one.

690 Then they went up inland.
691 They sea-journeyed some more.
692 Perhaps
this is when they arrived where they were from.

693 There they were.
694 And then there was a boy at a point way off over there.
695 There he was.

673 tuk̓ʷə́ł tiʔił tusʔúləx̌s əlgʷəʔ.
674 x̌ʷúlˀəxʷ tuk̓ʷík̓ʷəd kʷsi tələskʷə́d əlgʷəʔ ʔə tiʔił
haʔł sʔúləx̌ qa kʷi dəxʷdíłs tuqá kʷi tusʔúləx̌ ʔal tiʔił cədił →
dəxʷʔás əlgʷəʔ.

675 yə(x̌i) huy <tu...,>
tuk̓ʷə́ł ʔáha tiʔił c(əd)ił sʔúləx̌.
676 ƛ̕up̓ədíləxʷ kʷi (ʔə)sʔístəʔ dxʷʔal tiʔił dəxʷʔás əlgʷəʔ
təsəsʔúləx̌s əlgʷəʔ.

677 ʔuk̓ʷə́ł təš tsiʔəʔ saʔ słádəyʔ. → <ʔu...,>
678 ʔuk̓ʷáład tə ʔa ləłálil.

679 ləʔúluł.
680 huy, č̓áxʷacutəxʷ tiʔəʔ.
681 k̓ʷiʔát tiʔəʔ cədił čxʷlúʔ. →
682 yəx̌i huy <huy xʷiʔ lə...,>
xʷiʔ gʷəs(h)áy(dxʷ)s gʷəsəʔúlułs ʔal kʷədiʔ liłt̓áq̓t.
683 gʷəl tux̌ʷ tiʔəʔ tələ[d]xʷuk̓ʷəčácuts x̌ʷulˀ tiʔił dəxʷuč̓áxʷacuts. →

684 gʷəl
tíləb ʔuk̓ʷə́ł tiʔił c(əd)ił təsəsq̓íləbs ʔə tiʔił cədił sʔúləx̌.
685 tíləbəxʷ b(ə)uƛ̕íq tiʔəʔ caadił.
686 bələsq̓íltubəxʷ ʔə tiʔəʔ cədił q̓ílˀbids əlgʷəʔ.
687 x̌ʷulˀəxʷ bəʔúx̌ʷ. →
688 ʔutáb.
689 hay x̌əł ti → ʔuƛ̕íqitəb
ʔudᶻúxʷat(t)əb ʔə tiʔəʔ cədił.

690 hay, t̓áq̓təxʷ əlgʷəʔ. →
691 x̌ʷúlˀəxʷ əlgʷəʔ b(ə)uʔúluł.
692 gʷəháw̓əʔ
dił słčílsəxʷ əlgʷəʔ dxʷʔal tiʔił cədił tədəxʷʔás.

693 ʔáha(ə)xʷ əlgʷəʔ.
694 gʷəl (h)uy
ʔuʔihíʔstəʔ tiʔił č̓áčas ʔal kʷədiʔ ti čətqs díʔiʔ.
695 ʔa tə ʔa. →

696 And they were there.
697 They had come ashore.
698 And then
that boy came.

699 And this one said to the other,
700 "Couldn't this be our little younger brother who is there?"
701 When they saw their little younger brother,
702 and this [one] said,
703 "That was our little younger brother.
704 It would be nice for us to call him."
705 So they called this boy.
706 And he came close.

707 "We are [your] older brothers.
708 We were put ashore by the whale when we returned.
709 Our hands had been made to stick.
710 Someone had us stolen.

711 "And we have arrived.
712 You should go home and tell your relatives.
713 You have found us on this side.
714 We will not go home right away.
715 They should prepare the place
and [then] we will go home.
716 And they would come after us and we will be there.
717 We will be ready and we will go ashore.
718 Their relatives will gather and we will go ashore.
719 We will disembark."

720 This boy went.
721 And he told his relatives.
722 Right away they get mad at him.
723 "Oh, so! Are they not—those very ones—
your older brothers who have died?
724 And you are talking about them."

696 gʷəl ʔáhəxʷ əlgʷəʔ. <ʔəs. . . ,>
697 ʔəsłáliləxʷ əlgʷəʔ.
698 gʷəl (h)uy,
ʔəƛ̕áxʷ t[ə ʔa] č̓áč̓as.

699 gʷəl ləcút(t)əb ʔə tiʔacəc tiʔəʔ diʔəʔ.
700 "ləlíʔ ʔu sixʷ ʔə ti c(əd)ił tusúʔsúq̓ʷaʔ čəł tiʔəʔ ʔuʔihístəʔ."
701 ʔáləxʷ tiʔił tu(s)šúdxʷs əlgʷəʔ tiʔił tusúʔsuq̓ʷaʔs, →
702 gʷəl cút(t)əbəxʷ ʔə tiʔəʔ, <cút(t)əbəxʷ ʔə tiʔəʔ. . . ,>
703 "dił ti tusúʔsuq̓ʷaʔ čəł tiʔił.
704 haʔł čəł ługʷíhid."
705 huy, gʷihidəxʷ əlgʷəʔ tiʔəʔ č̓áč̓as. →
706 gʷəl č̓ítcutəxʷ.

707 "díbəł tiʔəʔ dəxʷsqátəd. → <ʔu. . . ,> →
708 ʔułálildub čəł ʔə ti čxʷlúʔ ʔal tiʔəʔ ʔuʔábaqtəb čəł.
709 ti tusƛ̕íq̓ači[ʔ]btub čəł. →
710 łuhúyutub čəł sqádaʔ.

711 gʷəl ʔułčíl čəł.
712 ƛ̕ub čəxʷ ʔut̕úk̕ʷ čxʷa yəcəb dxʷʔal tiʔił adʔíišəd. →
713 ʔuʔəy̓dúbuł čəxʷ ʔal tiʔəʔ ʔəƛ̕áƛ̕ad.
714 xʷiʔ kʷi stíləb čəł łut̕úk̕ʷ.
715 ƛ̕ub ʔuqʷíbid əlgʷəʔ kʷi dəxʷʔás
čła łut̕úk̕ʷəxʷ. <łu. . . ʔə. . . ,> →
716 gʷəl ł(u)ʔəƛ̕cbuł əlgʷəʔ čła łuʔá <čła łu. . . ,>.
717 yaw̓ čəł ł(u)asqʷíb čła łułálil.
718 ł(u)asq̓ʷúʔ tiʔił ʔíišəds əlgʷəʔ čła łułálil. → <łu. . . ,>
719 łuq̓ʷíb [čəł]."

720 ʔúx̌ʷəxʷ tiʔəʔ č̓áč̓as. →
721 gʷəl yəcəbáxʷ dxʷʔal tiʔił ʔíišəds. →
722 tíləbəxʷ ʔudúkʷtub.
723 "yaw̓ ʔu dił ʔu bədił tiʔił adsəxʷsqátəd tušúbali. →
724 gʷəl bələcuyácəbləp."

725 Then they beat the boy some more.
726 He got spanked.

727 And he cried.
728 He intently repeated.
729 "But those are my older brother(s), those over there."

730 They got mad at him again.
731 "Don't say any more.
732 Go on.
733 Get away."

734 He returned.
735 And he told his older brother[s].
736 "I just get beaten by my elders.
737 For this I got spanked.
738 And I was doubted."

739 "Then
you should take these things that will be given [to you],
blankets [and] whatever.
740 You will take this belonging of mine that I give you.
741 [I] am saying,
742 You will take it."

743 "Truly I found my older brother,
my two older brothers over there.
744 They want you folks to gather.
745 "Then you folks will go after them
and you folks will invite them.
746 And they will come up from shore to the house.
747 They will be prepared.
748 You folks gather your house planks.

725 huy, bəgʷəláltəbəxʷ tiʔəʔ č̓áč̓as. →
726 č̓áxʷaptəbəxʷ. →

727 gʷəl x̌á(hə)bəxʷ.
728 put bəyə́cəb. →
729 "huy dił ti dsqa tiʔił, tiʔił ʔal tudiʔ." →

730 bədúkʷtub.
731 "xʷíʔəxʷ sixʷ kʷi b(ə)adscú(t)/cut. →
732 híwiləxʷ →
733 lílcut."

734 tubəlkʷáxʷ. →
735 gʷəl bəyə́cəb dxʷʔal tiʔəʔ sqás.
736 "x̌ʷul̓ čəd ʔugʷəláltəb ʔə <ti. . . ,> ti dslúƛ̓luƛ̓. →
737 ʔə tiʔəʔ ʔuč̓áxʷaptəb čəd.
738 gʷəl dxʷsqʷácdub čəd." →

739 "gʷəl
ƛ̓úbəxʷ čəxʷ łələskʷədád tiʔacəc stab tiʔił łusʔábyitəbs →
sʔíc̓əb, ʔustáb.
740 łələskʷədád čəxʷ ti dił dsgʷaʔ dsʔábyicid. →
741 cútbicid [čəd].
742 łələskʷədád čəxʷ." →

743 "təł čəd ʔuʔəy̓dxʷ tiʔił dsqá,
dəxʷsqátəd [sə]sá[ʔ]liʔ ʔal túdiʔ.
744 x̌áƛ̓txʷ əlgʷəʔ kʷi səsq̓ʷúʔləpəxʷ.
745 hay čələp łuʔúx̌ʷcəxʷ →
čələpa ługʷí(h)idəxʷ.
746 gʷəl łučúbəhəxʷ əlgʷəʔ yaw̓ dxʷʔal ti ʔálʔal.
747 ƛ̓(u)asqʷíbəxʷ. →
748 q̓ʷúʔq̓ʷuʔəd tiʔəʔ sqʷłáyʔtxʷləp.

749 And it will be made long-sided.
750 That is why it was made like that."
751 The boy spoke.
752 He told them.

753 And then
they said,
754 "It is true, I guess, about this poor fellow
[i.e., what he has been saying].
755 You folks should not beat him any more.
756 You folks should look into this.
757 Do it quickly, you folks.
758 It is true, I guess, what he says."

759 Then these people collapsed it [took down their house partitions].
760 And
they gathered these,
their house planks,
nothing but [the finest] things,
cattail mats, what they use for their houses.
761 Then they made just one big house [out of it],
a big house for them to gather [in].

762 Then two elders went after them.
763 They arrived.

764 And then they were told.
765 "This is us.
766 But we want this: you folks should be prepared
and then we will tell how we were made unfortunate
and you folks became unfortunate [too].
767 You folks thought
768 we had died."

749 gʷəl łuháadᶻadiʔ kʷi ɬəsəshúys.
750 tiʔił <tədəxʷ. . . ,> tədəxʷhúysəxʷ ʔəsʔístəʔ." →
751 cútəxʷ tiʔəʔ č̓áč̓as.
752 yəcəbáxʷ. →

753 gʷəl (h)uy,
cút(t)əb. →
754 "təɬ xʷúʔələʔ ʔə tiʔəʔ sʔušəbábdxʷ. →
755 ƛ̕úbəxʷ čələp xʷiʔ ləbəgʷəláld.
756 ƛ̕ub → čələp ʔušúuc tiʔəʔ. →
757 húyucut ɬi ʔə kʷi ʔał. →
758 təɬ xʷúʔələʔ tiʔəʔ sucú(t)cuts."

759 huy, dᶻíx̌icutəxʷ tiʔəʔ ʔáciłtalbixʷ. →
760 gʷəl
q̓ʷúʔədəxʷ tiʔəʔ,
tiʔił ƛ̕uqʷɬáyʔtxʷs əlgʷəʔ
x̌ʷúl̓ul̓ ƛ̕ustab, <ƛ̕u. . . ,>
ƛ̕uk̓ʷat̓áq, stab tiʔił ƛ̕(u)uʔálʔalʔals əlgʷəʔ. →
761 huy, húyudəxʷ əlgʷəʔ [tiʔəʔ] x̌ʷul̓ dəč̓úʔ hikʷ,
hikʷ ʔálʔal dxʷʔal kʷi <ɬəsəs. . . ,>
ɬusq̓ʷúʔsəxʷ əlgʷəʔ.

762 huy ʔúx̌ʷcəbəxʷ tiʔił cədił ʔə tiʔəʔ səsáʔliʔ
tuslúƛ̕luƛ̕s.
763 ɬč̓ísəbəxʷ. →

764 gʷəl (h)uy cút(t)əbəxʷ. →
765 "díbəɬ tiʔəʔ. →
766 tux̌ʷ čəɬ
x̌áƛ̕txʷ kʷi sƛ̕úbləp ʔəsqʷíb č̓ɬa łułč̓íltxʷəxʷ
dxʷʔal kʷi tushúyutəb čəɬ sʔušəbábdxʷ
<č̓ɬa tu. . . ,> čələpa tuhúyəxʷ sʔušəbábdxʷ. →
767 [dxʷs]cútəbəxʷ čələp. →
768 ʔuʔátəbəd čəɬ."

769 Then they went.
770 Those people conducted them up from shore.
771 They gathered them.

772 And then they recounted
what happened to them,
about their hands having been made to stick,
about having been overpowered by this one,
that old man,
their brother-in-law.

773 Their sister was the wife of this canoe builder.
774 And this woman didn't give him any food, which was
why the old man got angry.
775 This is the way they recalled it [i.e., their adventure].

776 And their hands were made to stick.
777 It was carved for them.
778 And
this strange thing ran off with them.
779 This is what they recounted.

780 "We were simply put ashore far away where we were run off with
way over at the edge of the world
where the dwarfs are that is
where we were indeed taken.
781 When it got there,
782 then the land cleared.
783 Because there had been fog.
784 There was not anything that could be seen."

785 And they were simply arrived with.
786 And it cleared up.
787 This land became visible there where they found themselves.
788 "And we are far away.
789 Where?"

769 huy tuʔúx̌ʷəxʷ əlgʷəʔ. → <tu...,>
770 čúbətubəxʷ əlgʷəʔ tiʔił ʔáciłtalbixʷ. →
771 ʔuq̓ʷúʔtəbəxʷ əlgʷəʔ.

772 huy gʷəl tuyəcəbáxʷ əlgʷəʔ →
ʔə tiʔəʔ tushúyutəbs əlgʷəʔ →
ʔə tiʔił tusƛ̕íq̓ači(ʔ)yibtubs əlgʷəʔ
<tus...,> tusgʷəláltəbs əlgʷəʔ ʔə tiʔácəc,
ʔə tiʔił cədił tulúƛ̕,
<tu...,> tux̌áłtəds əlgʷəʔ.→

773 ʔalšs əlgʷəʔ tsiʔəʔ čəgʷás ʔə tiʔəʔ dxʷsp̓áyəq.
774 gʷəl xʷiʔ gʷəƛ̕usułíltəbs ʔə tsiʔəʔ słádəyʔ tiʔə
də(xʷ)x̌ícil ʔə tiʔił luƛ̕.
775 ʔəsʔístəʔ kʷi tədəxʷʔuʔlábs. →

776 gʷəl ƛ̕íq̓ači(ʔ)yibtubəxʷ əlgʷəʔ. →
777 p̓áyəq[yitəb]əxʷ → əlgʷəʔ. →
778 gʷəl
sáxʷəbtubəxʷ → əlgʷəʔ ʔə tiʔəʔ sdukʷ.
779 díłəxʷ syəcəbs əlgʷəʔ.

780 "x̌ʷúl̕əxʷ čəł ʔułálildub ʔal tiʔił li·l tiʔił tu(s)sáxʷəbtub čəł
ʔal túdiʔ sbəčáx̌ad ʔə tə swátixʷtəd
dəxʷʔá ʔə tiʔił qʷíqʷqʷistáy̓bixʷ →
tiʔił (s)łčíldub čəł əw̓ə.
781 słaʔs,
782 gʷəl tugʷáx̌ tə swátixʷtəd.
783 yəx̌i t(u)asqʷšáabəxʷ.
784 xʷ(iʔ)áxʷ gʷəstábəxʷ gʷə(s)šúdub."

785 gʷəl x̌ʷul̕ tułčíldub əlgʷəʔ. →
786 gʷəl tugʷáx̌. →
787 tuwəlíʔil tiʔəʔ swátixʷtəd
tiʔił tə tədəxʷʔəy̓cu[ts]. →
788 "gʷəl líləxʷ čəł. →
789 čádəxʷ." →

790 It seems that it was the Dwarf Land where they had arrived.
791 There they were now.
792 "We were there with the dwarfs.
793 Then these dwarfs were attacked suddenly by these ducks."
794 They fought for a long time.
795 These ducks simply warred on the dwarfs.
796 These ducks entered from the roof.
797 One said,
798 "From there come the ducks and we are slain here.
799 You folks just prepare yourselves where you are
and nothing [will] happen to you.'"

800 They were there simply wherever it was they had stepped
where they had hidden, [he] and his brother.
801 There they had stuffed themselves in.

802 Then the battle started.
803 Then
the ducks came in —
all kinds of ducks.
804 The first were different.
805 The first were different.
806 There was this kind
[and this] kind.
807 There was loon and
silver diver, and so on.
808 One, it fell. [i.e., one by one they came.]
809 This thing, that [one] hollered.
810 This one spoke.

811 When these people were all finished, they lay all about.
812 These [quills] had been thrown at them.
813 What was used for shooting the dwarfs?
814 Right away they died.
815 Right away they died.
816 Then they died.

790 gʷəháw̓əʔ qʷi[qʷ]qʷistáy̓bixʷ swátixʷtəd tiʔəʔ dəxʷƛ̓číls.
791 ʔáhəxʷ. →
792 "ʔa čəɬ ʔal tiʔiɬ qʷi[qʷ]qʷistáy̓bixʷ.
793 huy šidᶻtəbəxʷ → tiʔəʔ qʷi[qʷ]qʷistáy̓bixʷ ʔə tiʔəʔ buʔqʷ."
794 haʔkʷ ƛ̓(u)uyábuk̓ʷ. →
795 x̌ʷul̓ ƛ̓(u)ux̌ílix̌tub tiʔəʔ qʷi[qʷ]qʷistáy̓bixʷ ʔə tiʔəʔ buʔqʷ.
796 hədʔíw̓əxʷ tiʔəʔ buʔqʷ tul̓šqálatxʷ. →
797 cú(t)cut tiʔəʔ diič̓uʔ. →
798 'ƛ̓utúl̓[ʔa] <ta...> tə ƛ̓usʔə́ƛ̓ ʔə tiʔiɬ buʔqʷ
čɬa ƛ̓ušúbutəb ʔal ti.
799 x̌ʷul̓ čələp ʔəshúyucut čad kʷi dəxʷʔáləp →
čələpa <xʷiʔ lə gʷəl...,>
xʷiʔ ləʔəx̌í(d)tub.'"

800 ʔáhəxʷ əlgʷəʔ x̌ʷúl̓əxʷ ʔal kʷədiʔ čad kʷi səscàq̓šád(d)ubs
səsčádᶻils əlgʷəʔ ʔi tiʔəʔ ʔay̓əds.
801 ʔa tiʔəʔ səsƛ̓úq̓ʷagʷils əlgʷəʔ. →

802 huy ʔíləxʷ tiʔəʔ sx̌ílix̌. →
803 huy
hədʔíw̓əxʷ tiʔiɬ cədiɬ buʔqʷ
kʷi bálgʷas ʔə ti buʔqʷ. →
804 ləlíʔ kʷi dᶻixʷ. →
805 ləlíʔ kʷi dᶻixʷ.
806 tiʔəʔ ʔi stab,
ʔi stab.
807 swúqʷadiʔ ʔi <stəb ʔis ʔiq̓ʷ...,>
x̌ʷətís, ʔi stab. →
808 [də]č̓áxʷ sbə́č.
809 tiʔácəc stab tsi tsiʔiɬ tusqʷíʔqʷiʔadəxʷ.
810 cútəxʷ t[s]iʔəʔ cədiɬ. →

811 ʔal tiʔiɬ sbək̓ʷíləxʷ ʔə tiʔəʔ ʔáciɬtalbixʷ ʔuqʷqʷátiləxʷ.
812 ləxʷə́btəb [ʔə] tiʔəʔ. →
813 stab tiʔəʔ dəxʷut̓úc̓utəbs tiʔəʔ qʷi[qʷ]qʷistáy̓bixʷ. →
814 tíləb ləʔátəbəd. →
815 tíləb ləʔátəbəd. →
816 huy šúbalihəxʷ.

817 They [the brothers?] were alone now.
818 [But the ducks] are making [duck] noises where they are.
819 Then they said,
820 "We should club these ducks."
821 It was good food that they were expertly battling.
822 "What can we use to club all these things,
these ducks that are good?"
823 Then they clubbed them with a paddle.
824 Because they had their paddles.
825 They clubbed them all over so they would have a lot of food.
826 Then they left them alone.

827 Then someone went.
828 Black Diver called out.
829 "Raise your arms, my brothers.
830 Humans are the cause of your troubles."
831 With a roar those ducks took to flight abruptly.
832 Again they went.
833 Again they flew up abruptly.
834 And then they went out.

835 There were only these that were lying about there
and others.
836 They gathered what would be their food.
837 He told them.
838 "Our food will be gathered.
839 Indeed we will fix it.
840 We will prepare it for them and we'll do it, pluck it."
841 They placed them there.

842 "Then
what is it that is causing these dwarfs to die?
843 What?"
844 Then they went.
845 And they examined these.

846 It seems that it is this one [which is] kind of like the thing which
was thrown.
847 And it pierced their bodies.

817 dáy̓ay̓əxʷ əlgʷəʔ. →
818 ləʔíʔilil ʔal tiʔəʔ dəxʷʔás. →
819 huy cútəxʷ.
820 "ƛ̕úbəxʷ čəł ʔuč̓áxʷalikʷ ʔə tiʔəʔ buʔqʷ."
821 haʔł sʔə́łəd tiʔəʔ ʔudᶻəgʷáʔil əw̓ə ƛ̕əsiłux̌ílix̌.
822 "(s)tábəxʷ kʷi <gʷəd...,>
gʷədəxʷč̓áxʷalikʷ čəł ʔə tiʔəʔ bək̓ʷ stab, →
tiʔəʔ haʔł ʔə tə buʔqʷ."
823 huy č̓áxʷalikʷəxʷ əlgʷəʔ ʔə tiʔəʔ x̌ʷubt. →
824 yəx̌i ʔa tiʔił x̌ʷubts əlgʷəʔ.
825 č̓áxʷdupədəxʷ əlgʷəʔ tiʔił <ʔə...,> stáb kʷi gʷəsqás →
kʷi gʷəsʔə́łəds əlgʷəʔ.
826 hay, kʷáʔəd əlgʷəʔ. →

827 huy ʔúx̌ʷəxʷ ti.
828 qʷíʔadəxʷ tsiʔácəc <stəb...,> q̓ʷuʔap.
<"šəq ʔə ʔə...,"> →
829 "šəqlax̌adəb łi dʔálalš.
830 ʔàciłtalbixʷaládxʷ tə dəxʷtəš(s) ʔaləp."
831 ʔu· tugʷətxʷádəxʷəs tiʔił buʔqʷ.
832 bəʔúx̌ʷəxʷ. →
833 bəsásaq̓ʷəxʷ.
834 huy, gʷəl šáadᶻal.

835 dáy̓ay̓əxʷ tiʔəʔ ʔəsqʷátqʷat tiʔəʔ ʔa ʔi cáadił.
836 q̓ʷuʔəd əlgʷəʔ tiʔəʔ <s...,> łusʔə́łəds əlgʷəʔ. →
837 cúuc.
838 "ł(u)asq̓ʷúʔ tiʔəʔ sʔə́łəd čəł. →
839 day̓ čəł łutábad.
840 łuhúdyid [čəł] čła łutáb, x̌ácəd."
841 ʔáʔədəxʷ əlgʷəʔ. →

842 "huy,
stab kʷi dəxʷušúbali ʔə tiʔácəc qʷí[qʷ]qʷistáy̓bixʷ. →
843 stab." →
844 huy, ʔúx̌ʷəxʷ əlgʷəʔ. →
845 gʷəl k̓ʷáładəxʷ əlgʷəʔ tiʔəʔ caadił.

846 gʷəháw̓əʔ dił tsiʔəʔ cədił x̌əł ti stab tsiʔił x̌ʷul̓ ƛ̕ələxʷábtəb. →
847 gʷəl ləc̓áq̓abac tsiʔił.

848 The feathers coming in would be new.
849 And those that were there come back out sort of like quills.
850 It was said.
851 This is what does them in, so it seems.

852 They removed them.
853 They removed what they had been shot with.
854 Right away this dwarf sat up.
855 He revived.

856 Then they went to them.
857 And
it seems that they should try to revive them.
858 So they gathered them.
859 They gathered them.
860 And they removed these bad things they had been shot with.
861 And they revived.

862 They removed them.
863 They removed them.
864 They removed them.

865 They [the bodies of the dwarfs] were just kind of pierced
[i.e., the quills did not penetrate deeply].
866 But they [the dwarfs] died anyway.
867 Then they revived them.

868 Then they were delighted, these folks.
869 Wonderful!

870 "These people whom we have taken have given us life.
871 Oh, you folks should think about it.
872 How will [we handle this]?

848 ƛ̕ułáẇt ƛ̕əsuʔə́ƛ̕ ʔə kʷ(i) st̓uʔq̇ʷ.
849 gʷəl ʔa huʔxʷ tsiʔił cədił dəxʷuƛ̕íqs x̌əł ti ƛ̕usċúqʷəb. →
850 ƛ̕ucút(t)əb.
851 dił dəxʷutə́šs ʔátub háẇəʔ.

852 ləxʷəcədáxʷ əlgʷəʔ. →
853 ləxʷəcədáxʷ əlgʷəʔ tiʔił dəxʷut̓ú[č]t̓uċtubs.
854 tíləbəxʷ b(ə)ugʷədíl tiʔəʔ cədił qʷi[qʷ]qʷistáẏbixʷ.
855 ləṗálil. →

856 huy ʔúx̌ʷcəxʷ əlgʷəʔ tiʔił. →
857 gʷəl
<dəxʷ. . . ,> x̌əł ti ƛ̕ub łuṗálildxʷ əlgʷəʔ.
858 huy bəq̇ʷúʔədəxʷ.
859 q̇ʷúʔədəxʷ. →
860 gʷəl líldəxʷ tiʔił c(əd)ił saʔ dəxʷut̓úċs. →
861 gʷəl ṗál̓ṗaliləxʷ əlgʷəʔ. →

862 ləx̌ə́cəd əlgʷəʔ. →
863 ləx̌ə́cəd.
864 ləx̌ə́cəd. →

865 x̌ʷul̓ x̌əł ti ƛ̕(u)asċítqs. →
866 gʷəl b(ə)asyúbiləxʷ.
867 hay, ṗálildxʷ əlgʷəʔ. →

868 huy híiłəxʷ əlgʷəʔ tiʔəʔ caadił. →
869 yu·.

870 "ʔuhəlíʔtəb čəł ʔə tiʔəʔ ʔáciłtalbixʷ
təsəskʷədáb čəł.
871 ʔu·, ƛ̕úbəxʷ čələp ʔuptídgʷəsbid. →
872 ʔəsčál kʷi łushúys.

873 It is because of them that we are alive,
that we get up in spite of those who [tried to] annihilate us."

874 And then someone said.
875 "What are you folks doing with these fallen ducks?"
876 Because they were people to them,
to these who are dwarfs.
877 They were people.
878 And they scorned those ducks with whom they had battled.

879 "Oh, that will be our food.
880 These ducks are our good food."

881 "You folks should take them somewhere and leave them.
882 You folks will just build a fire for them.
883 On the other side you folks will cook them.
884 [Tape inaudible here.]

885 "We would have them roasted.
886 We would cook them on that fire.

887 "So you folks will do that."

888 Then the [dwarf] people spoke.
889 "We are delighted about you folks.
890 You folks will indeed be returned
whenever we call for the whale.
891 There is a whale that travels around here.
892 He will arrive where you are from.

893 "You young people have given us life.
894 You are how we are alive,
how we revived.
895 So you folks have given us life by your being here.

873 cáadił tiʔəʔ dəxʷ(h)əlíʔ čəł, →
dəxʷgʷáadil čəł ʔə ti ʔal tiʔəʔ ʔux̌ʷádᶻatubuł."

874 huy gʷəl cut. →
875 "<ʔədəxʷ. . . ,>
dəxʷʔəx̌í[d]txʷləp tiʔəʔ ʔəsqʷát buʔqʷ."
876 [yə]x̌i huy ʔácʔàciłtalbixʷ ʔal caadił,
tiʔəʔ cáadił ʔə qʷi[qʷ]qʷistáy̓bixʷ.
877 ʔácʔàciłtalbixʷ →
878 gʷəl ʔəsdᶻílid əlgʷəʔ tiʔił buʔqʷ sʔiłux̌ílix̌s.

879 "ʔu·, łusʔə́łəd čəł tiʔił. →
880 haʔł sʔə́łəd čəł tiʔəʔ buʔqʷ."

881 "ƛ̕ub čələp ʔuʔúx̌ʷtxʷ dxʷčad čələpa ʔatxʷ.
882 day̓ čələp łuhúdyid. →
883 díʔax̌ad čələp łuq̓ʷə́ld. →
884 ʔəstab ______ləp." →

885 "ƛ̕(u)asq̓ʷə́lbəd čəł.
886 ƛ̕uq̓ʷə́·ld čəł ʔal tiʔił hud."

887 "huy łuhúyucut čələp ʔəsʔístəʔ."

888 huy <t. . . ,> cút(t)əbəxʷ ʔə tiʔəʔ ʔáciłtalbixʷ.
889 "híiłbid čəł ti gʷəlápu.
890 day̓ čələp łuʔábàqtəb ʔal kʷi pə(d)táb ʔal kʷi <łus. . . ,>
gʷəgʷíhid čəł ti čxʷlúʔ.
891 "ʔa ti čxʷlúʔ <ƛ̕u. . . ,>
ƛ̕udᶻə́k̓ʷdᶻək̓ʷ ʔal tiʔəʔ. →
892 "ƛ̕(u)ułíłčil dxʷʔal kʷi cədił <dəxʷtul̓. . . ,> ad(d)əxʷtul̓ʔá.

893 "dəgʷí sqáqagʷəł ʔuhəlíʔdubuł.
894 dəgʷí· → gʷəl dəxʷ(h)əlíʔ čəł, →
dəxʷp̓ál̓p̓alil čəł. →
895 "huy čələp ʔuhəlíʔdubułəxʷ ʔə tiʔəʔ sdiʔáʔləp. →

896 "No.
897 We simply used to be opened [i.e., invaded] by those ducks.
898 They would shoot us.
899 We died right away.
900 We died right away.
901 No one survived.
902 Then they would slaughter us.
903 They would suddenly attack us.
904 When we would fight, it did us no good."

905 Then
they were happy for them there.
906 Then they truly went to the other side.

907 And his companion built a fire.
908 They plucked these ducks that had been brought down.
909 Then they roasted them.
910 Because they were starving.
911 They were hungry.

912 The dwarfs did not eat what was cooked.
913 The things they ate were just raw.
914 They did not eat those [cooked?] salmon,
those "fish,"
their food, or anything.
915 No.
916 Every[thing] was just sort of —
just raw.
917 That was why they died.
918 They didn't help themselves [to the hunters' food].

919 Then they built a fire.
920 They roasted.
921 And they ate.
922 Their breath[ing] sort of became stronger.

896 "xʷí·ʔ.
897 x̌ʷul̓ čəł ƛ̓ələʔəxʷsʔə́q̓ʷdub <ʔə tiʔəʔ bu...,>
ʔə tiʔił buʔqʷ.
898 ƛ̓ut̓úc̓utubuł. →
899 tíləb čəł ləʔátəbəd. →
900 tíləb čəł ləʔátəbəd. →
901 xʷiʔ kʷi gʷat gʷəhəlíʔ.
902 huy ƛ̓ux̌ʷádᶻatubuł əlgʷəʔ.
903 ƛ̓ušídᶻ(t)ubuł əlgʷəʔ.
904 ƛ̓ux̌ílix̌əli tux̌ʷ xʷiʔ kʷi stab dəxʷháʔł čəł."

905 hay
ǰúʔilbitəbəxʷ əlgʷəʔ ʔal tiʔił.
906 huy t(ə)łáxʷ əlgʷəʔ ʔúx̌ʷəxʷ dxʷdíʔax̌ad. →

907 gʷəl húdčupəxʷ ti ʔáy̓əds.
908 x̌əctəbáxʷ tiʔəʔ buʔqʷ təsəsc̓qʷíb. →
909 huy q̓ʷəlbáxʷ əlgʷəʔ. →
910 yəx̌i ʔəsyəyúbiləxʷ əlgʷəʔ. →
911 ʔəstətágʷəxʷəxʷ.

912 xʷiʔ gʷəsuʔə́łəd ʔə tə qʷi[qʷ]qʷistáy̓bixʷ <ʔə kʷəs...,>
ʔə kʷ(i ʔ)əsq̓ʷə́l. →
913 x̌ʷul̓ x̌ic̓ təsulə́k̓ʷəds əlgʷəʔ tiʔəʔ stab.
914 xʷiʔ → gʷəslə́k̓ʷəds əlgʷəʔ tiʔił bəsʔuládxʷ,
tiʔił stab *fish*,
tiʔił stab ƛ̓əsuʔə́łəds əlgʷəʔ gʷəstáb. →
915 xʷí·ʔ. →
916 bək̓ʷ x̌ʷul̓ x̌əł ti
x̌ʷul̓ x̌ic̓.
917 dił haw̓əʔ dəxʷušúbalihəxʷ ʔə tiʔəʔ cáadił.
918 xʷiʔ gʷəbəsuwáw̓əxʷs əlgʷəʔ.

919 huy, tuhúdčupəxʷ əlgʷəʔ. →
920 q̓ʷəlbáxʷ. →
921 gʷəl tuʔəłədáxʷ əlgʷəʔ. →
922 x̌əł ti tuqʷiq̓ʷáʔłdəłil.

923 Finally they talked to them.
924 They gathered these strange things that were in piles which were called dentalia.
925 Belongings—these they gathered in order to be taken [home with them].
926 That is how they [came to be] put ashore at those [people of their own village].

927a This is what they told their relatives had happened to them.

927b They were run off with because of their sister.
928 [Her] bad mind had done [caused] it.
929 Her husband had injured his brothers-in-law.

930 This is the way it was when this woman became bad.
931 She was taken, that one was their sister,
932 and something happened to her.
933 That was the end.

934 I do not know what happened [to her],
935 how she was killed.

936 Now that is the end of this story.

923 hay dᶻahák̓ʷuʔəxʷ əlgʷəʔ
tátabtubəxʷ ʔə tiʔiʔíɬ.
924 ʔúləx̌əxʷ əlgʷəʔ ʔə tiʔəʔ cədiɬ sdúkʷdukʷ ʔəspúkʷpukʷəb →
tiʔiɬ c(əd)iɬ ʔucú(t)cut(t)əb sʔúləx̌.
925 stábigʷs—díɬəxʷ tuq̓ʷúʔədəxʷ əlgʷəʔ dxʷʔal kʷi ɬusʔúx̌ʷtubs.
926 tiʔiɬ tədəxʷƛ̓álildubs əlgʷəʔ dxʷʔal tiʔiɬ cáadiɬ.

927a díɬəxʷ syə́cəbtxʷs tiʔəʔ ʔíišəds əlgʷəʔ
tiʔiɬ ʔálalustubs əlgʷəʔ

927b tu(s)sáxʷəbtubs liɬʔálʔal <tsiʔəʔ...,> tsiʔácəc
ʔalšs əlgʷəʔ. →
928 tuhúydxʷ tiʔiɬ saʔ x̌əč. <tu...,> →
929 tugʷəláltəb ʔə tiʔəʔ sƛ̌ístxʷs tiʔəʔ x̌ə́ɬx̌əɬtəds.

930 ʔəsʔístəʔ tiʔiɬ tədəxʷsáʔil ʔə tsiʔəʔ sɬádəyʔ.
931 tukʷədátəbəxʷ tsiʔiɬ,
tsiʔiɬ cədiɬ ʔalšs əlgʷəʔ. →
932 gʷəl tuʔəx̌í(d)tubəxʷ díɬəxʷ. →
933 tu(s)šác̓əxʷ.

934 xʷ(iʔ)áxʷ gʷədsəs(h)áydxʷ tuʔəx̌í(d)tub. →
935 ʔə(s)čál kʷi dəxʷgʷəláltəbs.

936 hay, diɬ šac̓ ʔə tə c(əd)iɬ syəyəhúb.

# NOTES TO TEXT 7

1 *sgʷəlub.* It should be noted that there were no pheasants in Puget Sound country during precontact times. In other versions of this story, the canoe maker is a human being, sometimes named "Canoemaker," or a shaman who is good at carving.

6 *sčistxʷs.* Mrs. Lamont misspeaks: *ʔalšs* is the word she wants.

17 Mrs. Lamont's rising, extended delivery of *ƛ̕ulčil* indicates that the brothers arrive often.

34–35 Narrator's aside. In "*bibədbədaʔ*" Mrs. Lamont uses the reduplicating pattern designating "litter," rather than "young human children"—an example of that interplay between the human and animal traits of her characters in which she seems to delight (see, e.g., text 2).

46 In addition to the fact that the ashes would absorb grease, there may be at work here a literary tradition of using ashes for concealment. In Harry Moses's story "Daylight" (Hilbert 1980:107–109), when Mink is stealing the daylight, he covers himself with ashes.

82 Is this sentence an author's aside, or is it the comment of an onlooker who sees the wife piling her plate too high? Although Mrs. Lamont does not give the line any special intonation, it conveys the impression of irony or sarcasm.

234 *gʷətəsgʷás.* Mrs. Lamont misspeaks on the tape recording, saying "*gʷəcəsgʷaʔ əš.*" The seal hunters' harpoon was about 15 feet long, with a detachable barbed head, to which a line was attached. After the animal was struck, the shaft fell away; and the only link between animal and hunter was the line, one end of which was attached to the harpoon point now embedded in the seal, and the other end of which lay coiled in the canoe, playing out through the hands of the harpooner. As she speaks, Mrs. Lamont is trying to remember the technical term for this line.

235 After the seal is struck, it may sound. Usually, the dive is not very deep, but the reaction of this seal is extreme.

259–260 Fog is an indication that something powerful is happening. The fact that this region usually has good weather suggests that the seal hunters will survive and perhaps even prosper because of this adventure.

267 Five is the pattern number in Southern Lushootseed literature, as opposed to four in the northern tradition.

276 For a people whose chief mode of travel was by canoe on a swift and treacherous river, and one of whose chief means of getting food was by setting nets, snags—parts of tree trunks with limbs or roots attached—were a danger both physical and economic. (The daughter of Lushootseed literature's best-known villainess, Basket Ogress, is named Tree Roots.)

357 *dəxʷ čəxʷ ʔu*: To Vi Hilbert, the construction indicates that the seal hunters are speaking in a confidential, not-to-be-overheard, manner.

385–389 The halibut hunter extends his arm, and it moves like a compass needle until it points directly at the seal hunters.

406 The dwarf tied the seal hunters' canoe to his own.

409ff The seal hunters have not been made slaves by being captured in a slave-raiding expedition: thus, their position is not that of true slaves.

Perhaps it is better to understand their predicament as (in Vi Hilbert's words) "having been made unfortunate by their capture." They are an oddity in the dwarfs' village and have no family resources there to help them make a place for themselves. Note the dwarfs' kindly treatment of the young men despite their position as captives.

411 Mrs. Lamont says something that has been transcribed "*tiʔəʔ. . . tiʔəʔ. . .*"; but for all practical purposes, the tape recording is unintelligible here.

423 *haac ʔalʔal* seems to be a loan translation from English, as Lushootseed people in precontact times did not refer to their dwellings as "longhouses."

426 *qʷiqʷqʷistaỷbixʷ*, also heard on the tape recording as "*qʷiqʷqʷisaybixʷ*," has been glossed by elders variously as "dwarf," "Eskimo," and "strange little people with great powers."

437ff. In the dwarf world, things are backward compared to the way they are in the Lushootseed world. In the recent past, some tribes conceptualized the land of the dead as a land where everything was just as it is here, but upside-down and backward (Lane 1953:172). Perhaps Mrs. Lamont's presentation of the land of the dwarfs owes something to this concept of the land of the dead.

478–480 The line division obscures the parallelism between 478–479 and 480.

482 *cədiɬ dəxʷəstudəqils*: the dwarfs.

484 *tiʔiɬ cədiɬ ʔaciɬtalbixʷ*: the seal hunters.

488–489 Mrs. Lamont delivers these lines in a whisper, and they are hard to understand. Like line 357, they contain unusual features indicating that the seal hunter is speaking confidentially.

493 *huy*. Mrs. Lamont seems to say "*ƛuy*" on the tape recording, but "*huy*" is the word she wants.

494 *-alaʔdxʷ*. We have no explanation for the presence of this suffix.

501 *ʔəlgʷəʔ*: the seal hunters.

541ff *diʔax̌ad*. The hunters are requested to take the ducks away to the other side of the village because the dwarfs find the hunters' eating habits repulsive.

579 Mrs. Lamont seems to be pointing out that the dwarfs have dentalia handy in their world, while in the human world it is hard to find.

583 It is not known exactly what kind of whale *č̓xʷəluʔ* is; the statements about the old person's usually traveling a certain route (583, 594) may refer to a migration route. Though large whales do come into Puget Sound, only the smaller killer whale or blackfish has been recorded as a spirit power for the Skagit.

610 The large dentalia were the best ones for trading.

632 Just as the seal hunters had to go to the far side (*lilax̌ad*) of the dwarfs' village to indulge a desire for cooked ducks unacceptable to the dwarfs, so the whale now brings them not directly to their own village, but to the far side (*lilax̌ad*), because they still must make the transition back into human society.

637 "At the death of parents, husband, wife, child, brother or sister, both men and women cut their hair twice. Half was cut four or five days after the death occurred, and four or five days later the remainder was cut to mourning length, just below the ears" (Haeberlin and Gunther 1930:54).

647 The reference to good weather means that the seal hunters will have a successful trip (cf. line 260).

678 The unstated subject of this sentence is the young lady.

685 *bəuɬiq* is "*muƛiqc*" (an old-fashioned pronunciation) on the tape recording.

714–715 Although nothing is said directly, the audience knows that the house has to be ceremonially prepared for the young men's return, so that they can sing the spirit powers that they have earned from their ordeal (cf. text 5, lines 177–196).

720ff. When the traveler returns, there is often a scene in which he is not recognized (see text 5, lines 145–176 and text 6, lines 131–160) or his messenger is not believed. (The scene at the end of text 6, in which the woman—perhaps herself a spirit power—cannot recognize the human traveler, even with the aid of a spyglass, is a playful variant on this theme.)

The speed of Mrs. Lamont's delivery here may indicate that the passage is a standardized, obligatory trope.

723 In Lushootseed custom, the recently deceased are never talked about (see text 1b, note to line 22).

726 The mention of spanking is probably an anachronism. Even though talking about the recently deceased is a serious offense, the Lushootseed seldom corrected their children by hitting them.

748 *sqʷɬayʔtxʷ*. Vi Hilbert thinks that "*sqʷəɬay*" may refer to partitions woven of cattails or cedar bark. (*sqəlikʷ* is the word for blanket; *sqʷəɬay* may be related.)

In the longhouse, partitions divided sleeping platforms into sections for each nuclear family's use. When a large gathering was planned, the partitions were removed to convert the house into one large hall.

753ff. This change of heart by the people may rely somewhat on the "youngest/smartest" literary convention (see text 6, note to line 349).

781 *sła?s*. This is "*sła??*" on the tape recording, but Mrs. Lamont probably meant "*sła?s*," which is what the gloss reflects.

# BIBLIOGRAPHY


Adamson, Thelma

1934 *Folktales of the Coast Salish.* Memoirs of the American Folklore Society, vol. 27. New York.

Allen, Frank

1961 "Seal Hunter and Canoe Maker." *Research Studies* 29(3): 106–114.

Alter, Robert

1981 *The Art of Biblical Narrative.* New York: Basic Books.

Amoss, Pamela T.

1978 *Coast Salish Spirit Dancing: The Survival of an Ancestral Religion.* Seattle: University of Washington Press.

Ballard, Arthur C.

1927 "Some Tales of the Southern Puget Sound Salish." University of Washington Publications in Anthropology 2(3):57–81. Seattle.

1929 "Mythology of Southern Puget Sound." University of Washington Publications in Anthropology 3(2):31–150. Seattle.

Barnett, Homer

1955 *The Coast Salish of British Columbia.* Eugene: University of Oregon Press.

Bates, Dawn, Thomas M. Hess, and Vi Hilbert

1993 *Lushootseed Dictionary.* Seattle: University of Washington Press.

Beck, Horace

1958 "The Acculturation of Old World Tales by the American Indians." *Midwest Folklore* 8:205–216.

Benjamin, Walter

1968 *Illuminations.* New York: Schocken Books.

Berlin, Adele

1985 *The Dynamics of Biblical Parallelism.* Bloomington: Indiana University Press.

Bierwert, Crisca

1979 "The Sockeye Wife and Other Stories: An Analysis of the Interrelationships of Food, Luxury and Sexual Liaisons among the Halkomelem Salish." Unpublished ms.

1982 *Sahoyaleekw: Weaver's Art.* Seattle: Thomas Burke Memorial Washington State Museum.

1986 "Tracery in the Mistlines: Semeiotic Readings of Sto:lo Culture." Ph.D. dissertation, University of Washington.

1991 "The Figure of Speech Is Amatory." *Studies in American Indian Literatures*, ser. 2, 3(1):40–79.

1993 "'Poetic Fancy': A Glimpse at the Translative Commentary of Martin J. Sampson." In *New Voices in Native American Literary Criticism*, edited by Arnold Krupat, 529–542. Washington, D.C.: Smithsonian Institution Press.

Boas, Franz

1930 *Religion of the Kwakiutl Indians.* Columbia University Contributions to Anthropology, vol. 10. New York.

1966 *Kwakiutl Ethnography.* Edited by Helen Codere. Chicago: University of Chicago Press.

Bright, William

1984 *American Indian Linguistics and Literature.* Berlin: Mouton.

Carlson, Barry F., and Thomas M. Hess

1978 "Canoe Names in the Northwest, an Areal Study." *Northwest Anthropological Research Notes* 12(1):17–24.

Cary, Carl

1977 "The Story of the Big Box." *Alcheringa* 3(1):91–95

Charlie, Domanic

1966 "Creation of the Squamish People: The *s'CHUNK People of Gibson's Landing." In *Squamish Legends*, by Chief August Jack Khahtsahlano and Domanic Charlie, edited by Oliver Wells, [12–13, Sardis, B.C.]: Charles Chamberlain and Frank T. Coan.

Collins, June M.

1949 "John Fornsby: The Personal Document of a Coast Salish Indian." In Marian Smith, ed., 1949, 287–341.

1974 *Valley of the Spirits: The Upper Skagit Indians of Western Washington.* American Ethnological Society Monographs, vol. 56. Seattle: University of Washington Press.

Darnell, Regna

1974 "Correlates of Cree Narrative Performance." In *Explorations in the Ethnology of Speaking*, edited by Richard Bauman and Joel Sherzer, 315–336. Cambridge: Cambridge University Press.

Dauenhauer, Nora Marks, and Richard Dauenhauer

1987 *Haa Shuka', Our Ancestors: Tlingit Oral Narratives.* Classics of Tlingit Oral Literature, vol. 1. Seattle: University of Washington Press.

1990 *Haa Tuwun aagu Yis, for Healing Our Spirit: Tlingit Oratory.* Seattle: University of Washington Press.

Duff, Wilson

1952 "The Upper Stalo Indians: An Introductory Ethnography." M.A. thesis, University of Washington.

Dundes, Alan
1964 *The Morphology of American Indian Folktales.* Folklore Fellows Communications, no. 195. Helsinki: Suomalainen tiedeakatemia.

Dundes, Alan, ed.
1984 *Sacred Narrative: Readings in the Theory of Myth.* Berkeley: University of California Press.

Dunn, John
1988 "Aesthetic Properties of a Coast Tsimshian Text Fragment." *Working Papers of the 23rd International Conference on Salish and Neighboring Languages.* Newberry Library Center for the History of the American Indian. Occasional Papers Series, 78–89.

Eels, Myron
1985 *The Indians of Puget Sound: The Notebooks of Myron Eels.* Edited by George B. Castile. Seattle: University of Washington Press.

Elmendorf, W. W.
1960 *The Structure of Twana Culture.* Washington State University Research Studies Monographic Supplement 2. Pullman: Washington State University.
1961 "Skokomish and Other Coast Salish Tales." *Research Studies* 29 (1):1–37, (2):84–117, (3):119–150. Pullman, Washington.
1993 *Twana Narratives: Narrative Historical Accounts of a Coast Salish Culture.* Seattle: University of Washington Press; Vancouver: University of British Columbia Press.

Evers, Larry
n.d. "Iisaw: Hopi Coyote Stories, with Helen Sekaquaptewa." In *Words and Place: Native Literature from the American Southwest* (videotape). New York: Clearwater Publishing.

Evers, Larry, and Felipe Molina
1987 *Yaqui Deer Songs/Maso Bwikam: A Native American Poetry.* Suntracks, vol. 14. Tucson: University of Arizona Press.

Gaster, Theodor H.
1954 "Myth and Story." *Numen* 1:184–212; reprinted in Dundes, ed., 1984, 110–136.

Gustafson, Paula
1980 *Salish Weaving.* Seattle: University of Washington Press.

Haeberlin, Hermann
1924 "Mythology of Puget Sound." *Journal of American Folklore* 37(4):371–438.

Haeberlin, Hermann, and Erna Gunther
1930 *The Indians of Puget Sound.* University of Washington Publications in Anthropology 4(1), rpt. 1973. Seattle.

Herzog, George
1949 "Salish Music." In Marian Smith, ed., 1949, 93–109.

Hess, Thomas M.
1966 "Snohomish Chameleon Morphology." *International Journal of American Linguistics* 32:350–356.
1973 "Agent in a Coast Salish Language." *International Journal of American Linguistics* 39:89–94.
1977 "Lushootseed Dialects." *Anthropological Linguistics* 19(9): 403–419.
1979a "A Comparison of Marine and Riverine Orientation Vocabulary in Two Coast Salish Languages." *Anthropological Linguistics* 21(8):363–378.
1979b "Central Coast Salish Words for Deer: Their Wavelike Distribution." *International Journal of American Linguistics* 45:5–16.
1995 *Lushootseed Reader with Introductory Grammar: Vol. 1, Four Stories from Edward Sam.* University of Montana Occasional Papers in Linguistics, 11. Missoula.

Hilbert, Vi
1980 *Huboo: Lushootseed Literature in English.* Seattle: The Author.
1984 *Storytelling at Upper Skagit* (videotape). Seattle: Lushootseed Research, Inc.
1985 *Haboo: Native Literatures of the Puget Sound Region.* Seattle: University of Washington Press.

Hilbert, Vi, and Thomas M. Hess
1978 "Lushootseed: How Daylight Was Stolen." *International Journal of American Linguistics Native American Text Series* 2:4–32.

Hymes, Dell
1981 *"In Vain I Tried to Tell You:" Essays in Native American Ethnopoetics.* Philadelphia: University of Pennsylvania Press.
1985 "Language, Memory and Selective Performance: Cultee's 'Salmon's Myth' as Twice Told to Boas." *Journal of American Folklore* 98:391–434.

Hymes, Virginia
1987 "Warm Springs Sahaptin Narrative Analysis." In Sherzer and Woodbury, eds., 1987, 62–102.

Jacobs, Melville

1945 *Kalapuya Texts.* University of Washington Publications in Anthropology, vol. 11. Seattle.

1958 "Clackamas Chinook Texts: Part I." *International Journal of American Linguistics* 24(2):1–293.

1959a *The Content and Style of an Oral Literature: Clackamas Chinook Myths and Tales.* Chicago: University of Chicago Press; Viking Fund Publication in Anthropology, no. 26. New York: Wenner-Gren Foundation for Anthropological Research.

1959b "Review of Propp, *Morphology of the Folktale.*" *Journal of American Folklore* 72:195–196

1966 "A Look Ahead in Oral Literature Research." *Journal of American Folklore* 79:413–427.

Jakobson, Roman, and Stephen Rudy

1987 "Yeats's 'Sorrow of Love' through the Years." In *Language in Literature*, edited by Krystyna Pomorska and Stephen Rudy, 216–249. Cambridge: Harvard University Press.

Jenness, Diamond

1955 *The Faith of a Coast Salish Indian.* Anthropology in British Columbia Memoir, no. 3. Victoria: British Columbia Provincial Museum.

Jilek, Wolfgang

1982 *Indian Healing: Shamanic Ceremonialism in the Pacific Northwest Today.* Surrey, B.C.: Hancock House.

Kew, J. E. Michael

1970 *Coast Salish Ceremonial Life: Status and Identity in a Modern Village.* Ph.D. dissertation, University of Washington.

Kew, J. E. Michael, and Della Kew

1981 " 'People Need Friends, It Makes Their Minds Strong': A Coast Salish Curing Rite." In *The World Is As Sharp As a Knife: An Anthology in Honour of Wilson Duff*, edited by Donald N. Abbott, 29–35. Victoria: British Columbia Provincial Museum.

Kinkade, M. Dale

1987 "Bluejay and His Sister." In Swann and Krupat, eds., 1987, 255–296.

Kroeber, Karl

1978 "Poem, Dream, and the Consuming of Culture." *Georgia Review* 32(2):266–280.

1979 "Deconstructionist Criticism and American Indian Literature." *Boundary 2* 7(3):73–92.

Kroeber, Karl, ed.
1981 *Traditional American Indian Literatures: Texts and Interpretations.* Lincoln: University of Nebraska Press.

Krupat, Arnold, ed.
1993 *New Voices in Native American Literary Criticism.* Washington, D.C.: Smithsonian Institution Press.

Lamont, Martha
forthcoming "Crow, with Her Seagull Slaves, Looks for a Husband." Translated and transcribed by T. C. S. Langen, edited by Barre Toelken and Larry Evers. *Oral Tradition*, special issue.

Lane, Barbara S.
1953 "A Comparative and Analytic Study of Some Aspects of Northwest Coast Religion." Ph.D. dissertation, University of Washington.

Langen, T. C. S.
1989a "Estoy-eh-muut and the Morphologists." *Studies in American Indian Literatures*, ser. 2, 1(1):1–12.
1989b "The Organization of Thought in Puget Salish (Lushootseed) Narrative: Martha Lamont's 'Mink and Changer.'" *Multi-Ethnic Literatures of the United States* 16(1):77–94.
1990 "How Long Does 'Mythification' Take?" Proceedings of the 25th International Conference on Salishan and Neighboring Languages. Vancouver, B.C., 15–18 August 225–232.
forthcoming "Nostalgia and Ambiguity in Martha Lamont's 'Crow and Her Seagull Slaves.'" In *Memory and Cultural Politics: New Approaches to Ethnic American Literature*, edited by Amritjit Singh. Boston: Northeastern University Press.

Lévi-Strauss, Claude
1973 "Structure and Form: Reflections on a Work by Vladimir Propp." In *Structural Anthropology*, vol. 2, translated by Monique Layton, 115–145. Reprint, New York: Basic Books, 1976.

Liberman, Anatoly
1984 "Introduction: Vladimir Jakovlevich Propp." In *Theory and History of Folklore*, edited by Anatoly Liberman, translated by Adriana Y. Martin et al., ix–lxxxi. Theory and History of Literature, vol. 5. Minneapolis: University of Minnesota Press.

Marr, Carolyn J.
1979 "A History of Salish Weaving: The Effects of Culture Change on a Textile Tradition." M.A. thesis, University of Denver.

Martin, Wallace
1986 *Recent Theories of Narrative*. Ithaca: Cornell University Press.

Mattina, Anthony
1985 *The Golden Woman. The Colville Narrative of Peter J. Seymour*. Tucson: University of Arizona Press.
1987 "Native American Indian Mythography." In Swann and Krupat, eds., 1987, 129–148.

Maud, Ralph
1982 *A Guide to B.C. Indian Myth and Legend*. Vancouver, B.C.: Talonbooks.

Miller, Jay
1985 "Salish Kinship: Why Decedence?" Proceedings of The 20th International Conference on Salishan and Neighboring Languages. Vancouver, B. C., 15-17 August, pp. 213-222.
1988 *Shamanic Odyssey: The Lushootseed Salish Journey to the Land of the Dead*. Menlo Park, Calif.: Ballena Press.

Moses, Marya, and T. C. S. Langen
forthcoming "*x̌ənimúliča?* at Home: Reading Martha Lamont's Crow Story at Tulalip Today." Edited by Barre Toelken and Larry Evers *Oral Tradition*, special issue.

Palmer, Katherine Van Winkle
1925 *Honne, The Spirit of the Chehalis*. Geneva, N.Y.: Humphrey.

Parsons, Elsie Clews
1918 "Pueblo-Indian Folk-Tales, Probably of Spanish Provenience." *Journal of American Folklore* 31:216–55

Propp, Vladimir
1968 *Morphology of the Folktale*. Translated by Laurence Scott, Publications of the American Folklore Society, Bibliographic and Special Series, vol. 9. Indiana University Research Center in Anthropology, Folklore, and Linguistics, Publication 10. Rev. ed., Austin: University of Texas Press.

1984 "Historical Roots of the Wondertale: Premises" and "Historical Roots of the Wondertale: The Wondertale as a Whole." Translated by Maxine L. Bronstein and Lee Haring. In *Theory and History of Folklore*, edited by Anatoly Liberman, translated by Adriana Y. Martin et al., 101–115; 116–123. Theory and History of Literature, vol. 5. Minneapolis: University of Minnesota Press.

Ramsey, Jarold

1976 "Simon Fraser's Canoe; or, Capsizing into Myth." *Sound Heritage* 5(3):9–13; revised and reprinted in Ramsey 1983, 121–132.

1977 "The Bible in Western Indian Mythology." *Journal of American Folklore* 90:442–454; revised and reprinted in Ramsey 1983, 166–180.

1983 *Reading the Fire: Essays in the Traditional Literatures of the Far West.* Lincoln: University of Nebraska Press.

Ransom, Jay Ellis

1945 "Notes on Duwamish Phonology and Morphology." *International Journal of American Linguistics* 11(4):204–210.

Sampson, Chief Martin J.

1972 *Indians of Skagit County.* Skagit County Historical Series, 2. Mount Vernon, Wash.: Skagit County Historical Society.

Shelton, Ruth

1988 *Memories of Ruth Shelton: Draft Copy.* Transcribed and translated by Vi Hilbert. Seattle: Lushootseed Research.

Sherzer, Joel, and Anthony C. Woodbury, eds.

1987 *Native American Discourse: Poetics and Rhetoric.* Studies in Oral and Literate Culture, vol 13. Cambridge: Cambridge University Press.

Silko, Leslie Marmon

1981 *Storyteller.* New York: Seaver.

Smith, Marian

1940 *The Puyallup-Nisqually.* Columbia University Contributions to Anthropology, vol. 32. New York: Columbia University Press.

Smith, Marian, ed.

1949 *Indians of the Urban Northwest.* Columbia University Contributions to Anthropology, vol. 36. New York: Columbia University Press.

Snyder, Sally

1964 "Skagit Society and Its Existential Basis: An Ethnofolkloristic Reconstruction." Ph.D. dissertation, University of Washington.

Snyder, Warren A.

1968a *Southern Puget Sound Salish: Phonology and Morphology.* Sacramento Anthropological Society Papers 8. Sacramento, Calif.

1968b *Southern Puget Sound Salish: Texts, Place Names and Dictionary.* Sacramento Anthropological Society Papers 9. Sacramento, Calif.

Suttles, Wayne

1951 "Economic Life of the Coast Salish Indians of Haro and Rosario Straits." Ph.D. dissertation, University of Washington.

1952 "Notes on Coast Salish Sea-Mammal Hunting." *Anthropology in British Columbia* 3:10–20; reprinted in Suttles 1987a, 233–247.

1958 "Private Knowledge, Morality and Social Classes among the Coast Salish." *American Anthropologist* 60(3):497–507; reprinted in Suttles 1987a, 3–14.

1960 "Affinal Ties, Subsistence, and Prestige among the Coast Salish." *American Anthropologist* 62(2):296–305; reprinted in Suttles 1987a, 15–25.

1987a *Coast Salish Essays.* Vancouver: Talonbooks; Seattle: University of Washington Press.

1987b "Four Anthropological-Linguistic Notes and Queries." Proceedings of the 22nd International Conference on Salishan and Neighboring Languages, Victoria, B.C. 13–15 August, 185–192.

Suttles, Wayne, ed.

1990 *Northwest Coast.* Vol. 7 of *Handbook of North American Indians,* edited by William C. Sturtevant. Washington, D.C.: Smithsonian Institution.

Swann, Brian, ed.

1983 *Smoothing the Ground: Essays on Native American Oral Literature.* Berkeley: University of California Press.

1992 *On the Translation of Native American Literatures.* Washington, D.C.: Smithsonian Institution Press.

Swann, Brian, and Arnold Krupat, eds.

1987 *Recovering the Word: Essays on Native American Literature.* Berkeley: University of California Press.

Tedlock, Dennis

1972 *Finding the Center: Narrative Poetry of the Zuni Indians.* Lincoln: University of Nebraska Press.

1983 *The Spoken Word and the Work of Interpretation.* Philadelphia: University of Pennsylvania Press.

Teit, James
1916 "European Tales from the Upper Thompson Indians." *Journal of American Folklore* 29:301–310.
Thalmann, William G.
1984 *Conventions of Form and Thought in Early Greek Epic Poetry*. Baltimore: Johns Hopkins University Press.
Thompson, Stith
1919 *European Tales among the North American Indians*. Colorado College Publications, no. 2., Colorado Springs.
Thompson, Stith, ed.
1968 *Tales of the North American Indians*. Bloomington: Indiana University Press.
Tweddell, Colin E.
1950 "The Snoqualmie-Duwamish Dialects of Puget Sound Coast Salish." University of Washington Publications in Anthropology 12:1–78. Seattle.
Van Eijk, J. P., and Thomas M. Hess
1986 "Noun and Verb in Salish." *Lingua* 69:319–331.
Wagner, Louis A.
1968 "Preface to the Second Edition." In *Morphology of the Folktale*. Translated by Laurence Scott, ix–x. Publications of the American Folklore Society, Bibliographic and Special Series, vol. 9. Indiana University Research Center in Anthropology, Folklore, and Linguistics, Publication 10. Rev. ed., Austin: University of Texas Press.
Waterman, Thomas T.
1973 *Notes on the Ethnology of the Indians of Puget Sound*. Museum of the American Indian, Heye Foundation. Notes and Monographs, Miscellaneous Series 59. New York.
Waterman, Thomas T., and Geraldine Coffin
1920 "Types of Canoes on Puget Sound." Museum of the American Indian, Heye Foundation. Notes and Monographs, Miscellaneous Series 9. New York.
Wiget, Andrew
1987 "Telling the Tale: A Performance Analysis of a Hopi Coyote Story." In Swann and Krupat, eds., 1987, 297–336.
Woodbury, Anthony C.
1987 "Rhetorical Structure in a Central Alaskan Yupik Eskimo Traditional Narrative." In Sherzer and Woodbury, eds., 1987, 176–239.

# INDEX

In *Studies in the Anthropology of North American Indians*

*The Semantics of Time: Aspectual Categorization in Koyukon Athabaskan*
By Melissa Axelrod

*Lushootseed Texts: An Introduction to Puget Salish Narrative Aesthetics*
Edited by Crisca Bierwert

*People of The Dalles: The Indians of Wascopam Mission*
By Robert Boyd

*From the Sands to the Mountain: Change and Persistence in a Southern Paiute Community*
By Pamela A. Bunte and Robert J. Franklin

*A Grammar of Comanche*
By Jean Ormsbee Charney

*Northern Haida Songs*
By John Enrico and Wendy Bross Stuart

*Prophecy and Power among the Dogrib Indians*
By June Helm

*The Canadian Sioux*
By James H. Howard

*Comanche Political History: An Ethnohistorical Perspective, 1706–1875*
By Thomas W. Kavanagh

*Koasati Dictionary*
By Geoffrey D. Kimball with the assistance of Bel Abbey, Martha John, and Ruth Poncho

*Koasati Grammar*
By Geoffrey D. Kimball with the assistance of Bel Abbey, Nora Abbey, Martha John, Ed John, and Ruth Poncho

*The Medicine Men: Oglala Sioux Ceremony and Healing*
By Thomas H. Lewis

*Wolverine Myths and Visions: Dene Traditions from Northern Alberta*
Edited by Patrick Moore and Angela Wheelock

*Ceremonies of the Pawnee*
By James R. Murie
Edited by Douglas R. Parks

*Archaeology and Ethnohistory of the Omaha Indians: The Big Village Site*
By John M. O'Shea and John Ludwickson

*Traditional Narratives of the Arikara Indians* (4 vols.)
By Douglas R. Parks

www.ingramcontent.com/pod-product-compliance
Lightning Source LLC
Chambersburg PA
CBHW020926310726
48980CB00005B/401

*9780803212626*